Praise for

ANN CHAMBERLIN

"Chamberlin, a prolific writer of historical fiction and fantasy novels, succeeds brilliantly... Immersive, well-researched, and deeply evocative."
—*Kirkus Reviews*, about *The Linden's Red Plague*

"Enraptures and delights, drawing the reader into an imagined world of fifth-century Europe infused with the magic of old ways and old gods. Like all of Chamberlin's work, this book comes very highly recommended."
—Susan McDuffie, Historical Novels Review/Editors' Choice, about *Twilight of the Gods*

"*The Merlin of St. Gilles' Well* is wonderful! . . . It's the best book I've read in months and months; a terrific premise, and so beautifully imagined and described, I can only gnash my teeth in envy . . . Every word is literally magic—evoking another world, an older time—and the echoes of the Old Ways that live on in us, unseen."
—*Diana Gabaldon*, author of the Outlander series, review of Ann Chamberlin's *The Merlin of St. Gilles' Well*

Also by
ANN CHAMBERLIN

HISTORICAL NOVELS

The Valkyries Trilogy
Choosers of the Slain
The Linden's Red Plague
Twilight of the Gods

The Sword and the Well Trilogy
The Woman at the Well
The Sword of God
The Sword and the Well

The Joan of Arc Tapestries
The Merlin of St. Gilles' Well
The Merlin of the Oakwood
Das Erbe der Ermiten (available only in German)
Gloria: The Merlin and the Saint

The Reign of the Favored Women Trilogy
Sofia
The Sultan's Daughter
The Reign of the Favored Women

Leaving Eden
Snakesleeper (originally titled *Tamar*)
The Virgin and the Tower

MYSTERY

The Book of Wizzy

NONFICTION

A History of Women's Seclusion in the Middle East: The Veil in the Looking Glass
Clogs and Shawls: Mormons, Moorlands, and the Search for Zion

SCRATCH-AND-SNIFF PICTURE BOOKS

The Fair Maid and the Pirates
The Witch's Cottage

LA BELLE ÉPOQUE & THE TERRIBLE YEAR

—

ANN CHAMBERLIN

Epigraph Books
Rhinebeck, New York

La Belle Époque & The Terrible Year: A Novel © 2024 by Ann Chamberlin

All rights reserved. No part of this book may be used or reproduced in any manner without the consent of the author except for in critical articles or reviews. Contact the publisher for information.

Paperback ISBN 978-1-960090-86-7
Hardcover ISBN 978-1-960090-87-4
eBook ISBN 978-1-960090-88-1

Book and cover design by Colin Rolfe

Epigraph Books
22 East Market Street, Suite 304
Rhinebeck, NY 12572
(845) 876-4861
epigraphpublishing.com

For Mel

LA BELLE ÉPOQUE

THE NIGHT BEFORE, Madame Toussaint the concierge was just finishing the day's final mop of the blue-flowered tile floor of the vestibule when the skies let loose with hail.

She looked up the full flight of darkened stairs through all seven stories—seven floors of other sounds: the children on the second floor, the piano on the third, a man and woman arguing on the fifth—to the roof on which the sound hammered.

Guilt. That's what the memory brought. The memory of her departed husband saying, "We will never live under that man's roof on the Rue Férou."

Paris had soaked under lifeless clouds for a week—hence the thrice-a-day moppings to combat mud and umbrella dribbles that made their way clear up to the fifth floor, not to mention the depredations of the plasterers renovating the fourth for new tenants.

Madame Toussaint had installed an umbrella stand and encouraged tenants to use it. If they did, they wouldn't have to run back however many flights if they forgot. And she promised to keep an eye on those with ivory handles. Few took advantage. In fact—she stole a glance in that direction now—only the Widow Flôte's somber black one was there now. They had to drag their *parapluies* and the dripping water all the way up . . .

Mopping the floor in such weather always made the old wound in Madame Toussaint's back ache. She had expected her visitor might appear anytime during that wet week. But once the hail began, she stopped her work mid-swipe. Quickly she watered the already-soaked geraniums in the courtyard with the contents of the bucket, then sluiced the pavement of dancing white pellets with the rest and wrung out the mop.

She had time only to open her narrow kitchen window to let in the cat, towel the poor spike-haired creature dry, and set a quarter of one of the sausages on the chipped dish for him before adding the meat to the cassoulet set on the back of her fire. She pulled the pot of water to the center of the heat. She thought, as she often did, of her meagre flames rising through all seven floors of the building, heating every other tenant with her poor gatherings of wood from the local cabinet maker and broken crates from the vegetable monger, while the tenants' refuse of every kind flowed the other way down onto her . . .

And then he was there. The ring of the bell from his hand sounded like no one else, at least very different from Monsieur Arnaud, whom she had heard use his keys not two minutes earlier, just as the dish went down on the flagstone for the cat.

Her visitor was soaked to the skin and trembling like the last of the leaves on the sycamores in the Jardin de Luxembourg. It was probably just the cold and damp. But hail could sound like raining bullets. She knew that, only too well. It might have been the hail.

Checking behind her to see that Monsieur Arnaud from the fifth floor had already reached the first-floor landing and couldn't see, she let in the half-drowned man.

Just as Madame Toussaint pushed her visitor out of the drafty lobby and into the warmth of her room, Monsieur Arnaud's top hat and regal mustachios reappeared around the upper balustrade. "Madame?" Was the hesitation in his dandyish voice because he'd seen something?

"*Oui*, Monsieur?" She pulled the door to her room almost closed behind her and clung to it as if it were contraband.

Another half-a-beat of quizzical hesitation. "I am expecting an important delivery from the haberdasher's tomorrow morning. I hope you will receive and hold it for my return."

"Of course, Monsieur. As always."

"As always" meant he would not tip her much for the service, two sous at most if they were already loose in the pocket of his striped trousers. But she would do it anyway.

As always. Of course, Monsieur.

Monsieur Arnaud gave his umbrella a snap, then tucked it under his arm. He took off his hat and shook the hail off its brim down onto her newly mopped floor with a few damp petals of the forced paper-white narcissi in his fading boutonniere. Along with these went the ash from his cigar. Then Monsieur Arnaud continued his trudge—a little worse for the absinthe, she suspected—up the flights to his apartment.

In the square meter of the kitchen alcove, her visitor stood on the flagstones, trembling in a puddle of his own making. The smell of him . . .

"Good God." Madame Toussaint tried to stifle the exclamation but could not.

It wasn't the smell. The visitor was brandishing her kitchen knife, directed straight at her heart.

"Put the knife down," she whispered.

He didn't obey, but turned the blade from her to himself. She muffled a scream with her hand, just waiting to see the spurt of blood as he cut the jugular in his thin throat. They were so close, it would splash on her, hot and sticky.

Then she saw his left hand come away with a clump of his own matted grey hair. He'd cut it—not his own throat—as the play of shadows had deceived her into thinking. He tossed the clump into the fire.

"You—you remembered." Gratitude swelled almost to tears. The last time he'd brought lice with him, and she hadn't been able to stifle a complaint. In fact, she thought she could see nits now, there in the firelight—bits of hail that weren't melting. Choking smoke filled the kitchen, the whole apartment.

"But let's get you out of those wet clothes first." It took courage. She touched his right hand, the mud on it gritty. She felt the knuckles clench defensively, then relax. He gave up the knife.

She noted he hadn't said a word yet. She didn't really expect a "*Bonsoir, chérie,*" not after all these years, but still . . . She told herself his teeth were chattering too much to separate them for words.

The square meter of kitchen alcove didn't offer space for the both of them. She reached around to feed the fire, saw the last glowing filaments of hair, then ushered the visitor back into the main room. His wet clothes clung to him like a second skin; she helped him out of them.

"Let's burn this sweater, shall we? I've knit you a new one." Those spare hours sat in her fingers like tight cable stitches. "I'll show you. Do you like this green? Madame gave me a good price on it. But let's hold off on burning the old one now. It's so wet, it'll smother the fire."

When he stood naked, she washed him like a child with the newly warmed water, the hands so creased with dirt that even soaking wouldn't help. She saw the powder-burn scars, and the ache settled in her heart. If he would only let her clip his nails.

He seemed thinner, even, than last time, although of course not as thin as when they'd been living on the rats he could capture. Maybe he still ate rats, saving their little sharp-toothed skulls like the hunting trophies of a grand seigneur. And what he fished from the Seine with a bent hat pin for a hook. And pigeons trapped beneath the metal girders of the Gare de Montparnasse. And what he begged.

The scars. The genitalia, shrunken with cold.

"Now let's do the hair." She did not pick up the knife again, but shoved it even further out of reach. She pulled scissors from her mending basket.

He liked his hair long. Not that it gave him strength, like Samson, but because it covered outward signs of his greatest weakness that time could not erase, wicked scars that could not grow hair. That he did not fight her off, but only flinched as lock after lock came away, was hopeful. Almost endearing.

The smell of burning hair, then beard, stifled the room—stifled her brain with memories and their horror. She uncovered new grey, new wrinkles. She soldiered on, clipping as close to the skin as she could. The lice she found and squeezed blood from between fingernails were not the worst things she uncovered. She uncovered the scars. Those on the body did not bother her so much as those on the head, those that had changed her visitor forever.

She threw her duvet around the still-trembling shoulders and sat him in her only chair. She filled her one bowl with cassoulet and put it in his left hand, a spoon in the other. She did not pour wine. The cat watched it all with one eye and much annoyance from his place beside the stove.

She filled the kitchen with clothes hung to dry; the pants she even gave a scrub in the kettle of reheated water with strokes of strong lye soap. She discovered a dozen places in want of her needle, if only he'd stay long enough to let her.

She found he still held bowl and spoon and cooling cassoulet as if he had forgotten what to do with them. So she spoon-fed him like a child, mopping bean bits out of the inept stubble she'd left on his chin. She herself ate the burned-on leftovers.

Later, she crept in beside him on the bed she'd built to fit the cramped space—narrow like that of a novice in a convent—and held him until the trembling stopped, and he slept. Their feet just fitted together into the triangular cubbyhole formed under the stairs that rose to the apartments overhead.

She heard a woman's quick step and sobbing on the stairs. The painter Mahler—crass German longing to be Parisian, his studio with the large north-facing windows on the left half of the fifth—his wheedling voice pursued the female stranger. Another model he couldn't pay who had given him all and would have nothing to eat tonight but eternal fame.

Madame Toussaint listened for, but did not hear, Mahler turn his spleen next on the paterfamilias of the second floor, although that was also traditional. Lieutenant-colonel Herlemont, a high-ranking cavalry officer, and the painter could not pass one another on the stairs without exchanging heated words. In recent months this was usually about the Dreyfus affair, which had all Paris at one another's throats.

At this late hour, she heard nothing at all from Herlemont, who was, in fact, a man of sober habits, inflicting them on his young and numerous family as well. Nor did she hear from the building's two single female tenants: the widow Flôte and Madame Pépin.

The widow Flôte rarely left her rooms on the fourth, right-hand side—and then only between ten in the morning and four in the afternoon. She often had visitors at night, however, mainly wealthy widows like herself. They held séances. Madame Toussaint had been invited, since the story was that she, too, was a widow.

"I have no one dead I wish to talk to," she had replied. Certainly not at the price Madame Flôte charged. And the medium's powers did not seem to extend to the living who had no wish to speak.

Madame Pépin, fifth-floor-left, on the other hand, was better known as Mademoiselle Coco Toes-in-the-Air. A discrete liaison with a married man named Pépin allowed her to accept a respectable life and an apartment in a building such as this on the Rue Férou in the sixth arrondissement. If, however, she left the building after five in the evening, she rarely returned before noon the next day, especially if Monsieur Pépin had not been heard or seen for over a week. Toes-in-the-Air was her stage name at the Moulin Rouge, reference of course to her expertise at the can-can in split-crotch pantalets, as well as to more horizontal employment in the same sector.

The late-evening appearance of any of these tenants was not to be expected.

Later, Madame Toussaint heard the Cailloux, madame and monsieur, come home talking with animation about the spectacle they had just seen. Names dropped like the persistent rain: "Ravel, Puccini, Debussy" and the "divine Bernhardt." Their only, treasured son, they hastened to remind each other in the same breath, had entered the conservatoire at twelve and visited infrequently. The mud from their shoes would be mixed with horse droppings. You could hardly avoid it while seeking a vacant cab in the dark when the Opéra let out.

And sometime later, after her visitor's trembling that shook the whole bed had stopped and she, too, had slept a little, Madame Toussaint awoke to what at first she took to be the sound of mice in the joists overhead. She berated herself for having fed the cat too much sausage so he would not hunt. The animal, she saw, sat in the chair now—empty but for four pairs of stockings and other indistinguishable articles of clothing—and returned her stare with glowing eyes. Still, had it been the mice, he would at least have been looking towards the sound. What had awakened her must be human, and did not interest him for an instant.

Directly overhead was Monsieur d'Ermenville's bedroom with its windows opening onto the rear court. People called him a count, Monsieur le Comte. Madame Toussaint would not. Monsieur First-Floor snored. This after-midnight sound was not snoring, which she usually slept through. She heard the sound again: a scuffle, a muffled cry over her head. She tried not to let it bother her.

Monsieur and Madame d'Ermenville, the so-called Comte and the Comtesse, had the highest standing of any tenants in the fashionable building. They owned the edifice, hence their occupation of the first floor with its short flight of stairs, its high ceilings, and its lavish flower-filled balconies just at avenue tree level. They also claimed three of the *chambres* under the tiny dormers on the sixth floor for their *bonnes*, their "good" female servants: the cook, the housemaid, and Madame d'Ermenville's personal maid and nurse.

Madame d'Ermenville, as everyone knew, was an invalid and had never borne children. And her husband was entitled to the sexual favors of his choice of the *bonnes*. Sometimes he visited them on the sixth floor, but that risked being seen on the stairs. The *bonnes* were up and down the stairs going about their duties at all hours of the day and night, so although everyone suspected and even knew what was going on, everyone could pretend they didn't. Madame Toussaint decided it was probably the housemaid, the youngest, Jeanne-Marie, in the room overhead with him right now.

Madame Toussaint shifted her arm grown numb under her visitor and pretended not to hear yet another bedroom scuffle. Couldn't the elite always do what they wanted?

Her visitor seemed disquieted by the same sounds. He moaned in his sleep. She pulled him tighter, her face into his neck. He smelled better now, almost like his old self when she had first known him: male and strong. Her fingers touched the thick, raised scars.

In the dark, she could hear that the rain and hail had stopped. That didn't halt the usual drip of moisture down the inside wall and onto the corner of her bed. She shifted away from it, heard the creaking of window frame as the fire died and cold came in, and refused to let even that disrupt the animal comfort of that bed.

The next time she awoke, it was to hear Lieutenant-colonel Herlemont on the stair over her feet. Whether he was actually required to be to his duties at such an early hour or whether he did it for his constitution and martial discipline was a matter of conjecture. Madame Toussaint wondered that the man did not rattle his sword down the banister every morning like a boy with a stick along a wrought-iron fence—and that he didn't take the opportunity to show off his spurs as well. What effect would that have on her stairs and their red-carpet runner? She hated to think. Even though these descents were not de rigueur, his boots and the martial march were.

This morning, a certain catch in his step on the third riser made her wonder if his old war wound might be bothering him due to the weather.

His children, the oldest five, anyway, followed an hour later—clattering, running, arguing their way to school—the boys at the École Militaire almost from the time they could toddle. The girls at home had a string of governesses to teach them everything from philosophy to English. But one of these firm-minded women, who lived in a *chambre de bonne* on the sixth floor, saw to it that the girls marched around the Jardin de Luxembourg for exercise every morning, come rain or shine.

Between the two bursts, Madame Toussaint's visitor had vanished without her even knowing it. He couldn't stand a roof over his head for long, not since . . .

What could she do? She couldn't hold him longer than he wanted. He could grow violent.

But he was the only one in the world who still could call her by her given name. Nathalie. She would like to be Nathalie again, just for an hour. A quarter of an hour.

Nathalie and Paul. Once Paris had conjured by their joined names.

He hadn't said it this time; he hadn't spoken at all.

Madame Toussaint saw that he had dressed in what must have been still-damp clothes, switching only his old, unraveling and mud-caked cardigan for the new one she had knit and left for him on the chair.

The workmen for the fourth floor let themselves in just after the bells of Saint-Germain-des-Prés rang eight in the morning, not a moment earlier. Closer, Saint-Sulpice followed. The men climbed the stair, wine bottles ringing in lunch sacks, toolboxes taking gouges out of the plaster wall, no doubt with an eye to future employment.

The Herlemont girls returned, panting and chattering, their cheeks filling the vestibule with glowing red health. The nanny and a baby or two would claim the pram in the corner shortly for their own morning airing. Madame Toussaint really should get up to attend to the Opéra horse manure, await Monsieur Arnaud's delivery from the haberdasher's, and wheel out the dustbins. She could not be this self-indulgent and keep her job . . .

A crash and scream on the floor above brought Madame Toussaint fully awake at last. She could reach her doorknob from her bed, and when she threw open her door, the d'Ermenville's housemaid Jeanne-Marie fairly tumbled down the stairs and into the concierge loge. The cat shot for safety behind the stove. Jeanne-Marie could say nothing but gasp for the breath to scream again and point to the stair from the chair Madame Toussaint ushered her to.

She had wanted to keep the spirit of her visitor in it just a while longer . . .

Leaving the poor girl there, Madame Toussaint pulled on her cap and a skirt over her chemise without petticoat or drawers, and rushed up the stairs. She was just buttoning her bodice—misbuttoning it, she saw—when she reached the half-open d'Ermenville door. She hadn't put her corset on underneath; buttoning her bodice was impossible without a corset, so she gave up.

"*Bonjour?*" she called to no answer.

A well of silence led her tentatively to the ruins of a breakfast tray just at the door to Monsieur's bedroom. Madame took only one step over a puddle of water, soggy croissant, teapot shards, and even a hothouse rose thrown from its slender vase before stopping in her tracks and covering her mouth to restrain her own scream.

Monsieur d'Ermenville wore a half-open smoking jacket and pajama trousers. The silk had once been green, but it was hard to tell that now. The man's belly was a cavern of red, his clothing black with blood. The intestines bore a horrible resemblance to the sausages a butcher's shop might string across the green hooks over his front door. Madame Toussaint didn't have to go nearer to check for a pulse. No man could still be alive after such an attack. And she had no stomach for it. *Just like sausages on hooks over the butcher's next to the mutton carcass with its staring eyes . . .*

The shocked white face over the ruined torso, though slumped against the wall where violence seemed to have thrown him beneath the window, shocked her to an echoing silence. That face had too much of the visitor she'd entertained in the dark hours.

Back in the apartment's hallway, a breath or two revived the concierge. Madame Toussaint had seen much in her life, not enough to make her inured but enough to make her know that a leap to action was the best way for her to deal with incomprehensible horror. She went next door to Madame's room, where she found the aristocratic woman cowering in bed, clinging to the arms of her lady's maid, Mademoiselle Sylvie.

"Is Madame all right? Are you?"

Receiving positive but mute replies to both questions, Madame Toussaint told them not to move, not to go into the room next door. "I'm going for help."

In the kitchen, she found the cook, Mademoiselle Joséphine, almost deaf, who had heard nothing and had settled down to her very large bowl of very sweet morning coffee with her swollen feet propped on the fender. By signs, Madame Toussaint tried to tell the older woman to stay put too; she seemed glad enough to do so.

No one else was in the apartment. Knowing her night-time visitor would have helped himself to her own bottle of cheap wine as he left—there was no place to hide anything in her small room—Madame Toussaint took a bottle from Monsieur d'Ermenville's sideboard in the salon on her way out.

A curious memory of the heat of anger burned through her, a feeling of dangerous power, her hand around the neck of that bottle. She suppressed it. Today it was, after all, only cognac.

On the landing, she heard Monsieur Cailloux's first pupil of the day pounding away at scales on the piano. That alone seemed as it should be.

Back in her own room, Madame Toussaint poured Jeanne-Marie a barely rinsed glass of le Comte's cognac and told her to drink it. About two fingers swirled in the bottom of the decanter. Madame Toussaint poured herself a glass.

The edge started to wear off Jeanne-Marie's horror. She had milk-white skin in the best of times, set off by striking red hair and freckles. The girl sat back in the chair onto—Madame Toussaint had to notice—the filthy sweater her visitor had left behind. Madame Toussaint edged Jeanne-Marie off the garment, scooped it up and tossed it into the stove where it began to smolder on the almost-dead fire. She threw off her cap and bodice until she could adjust them properly.

"Drink that up, and I'll tell you what has to be done." Madame Toussaint closed the stove door and came around to sit on the bed, knee-to-knee with the maid. She ignored the feeling that her late-night visitor's warmth must still be in the crumpled sheet, on its end that curled up to cover the pillow.

The young gendarme to whom Madame Toussaint sometimes gave a cup of tea on cold days—his beat would bring him down Rue Férou any minute now. The lad's nightstick hardly seemed equal to the task, but that would have to happen.

But first—back to the maid, who sat in numb shock. The girl—who couldn't be twenty yet, half Madame Toussaint's age—wore her little white cap askew, and spilled tea and croissant down her white apron. Madame Toussaint took the hand without the glass in hers. The girl tried to look up bravely, but then her eyes opened wide in renewed horror and she drew back.

Were the lice already in evidence, despite her care? Madame Toussaint rubbed at her hair that had the girl's rivetted attention. It suddenly itched inexplicably. The concierge's fingers came away a dusty brown. Jeanne-Marie dropped her eyes to Madame Toussaint's shoulder and screamed again, spilling her drink. Madame Toussaint looked at her own shoulder, looked behind her to the head of the bed and also withdrew in horror. What she had taken to be merely the usual ooze of dampness down the wall's stone ran, in the watery light of morning, blood red. Monsieur had bled out just over her head.

In truth, did not the refuse of the world flow down onto her? Fighting nausea, growling with horror, Madame Toussaint ladled water from the kettle with which she'd washed her visitor and scrubbed down to the roots. Her teeth chattering, she tore the crumpled sheet off the bed and used it to scrub at the wall. In her wild imagination, it was the visitor's blood. In any case, stray remnants of his presence vanished.

She tried to burn the sheet, but the sweater still took up most of the fire box, the smoldering stench of damp burning wool only just becoming unpleasant. Instead, she had to stick the crumpled sheet into the cold kettle of water. Her chemise followed. She doubted she could ever wear it again. She scrubbed at her own skin rougher than she'd scrubbed at the visitor's, as if she'd chafe down to blood. Better her own blood than . . .

Finding her other chemise still damp from laundering, she threw it on anyway, and a shawl to stop the chattering of her teeth. Finally, panting with the effort and the emotion, Madame Toussaint sat down next to the silent housemaid again and poured two more shots, the initial one her own.

Jeanne-Marie spoke her first words since her discovery. A whisper. Her Breton accent as lonely as a rocky seashore in a winter storm. "You don't know how many times I wished to murder him myself. Feeling that soft belly with my nails as he lay on me."

"I know, *chérie*," Madame Toussaint told her. "I've felt the same."

They finished off the bottle. The rich know how to buy their liquor. It was very good cognac and went down like a sigh.

· II ·
THE TERRIBLE YEAR
—

Vivid scenes from Nathalie's past overcame her when she drank too much, even when in company, if the maid Jeanne-Marie could count as company. That's why Nathalie avoided it; no more than *un verre* with dinner. The quality she could afford did not encourage more indulgence, in any case.

This time, the golden glow of the cognac replicated the light of those first autumn days of the siege of 1870, more than twenty-five years before. The Prussians had soundly beaten the armies of the Second French Empire near the fortress of Sedan on the Belgian border. The Prussians had captured that coward, the self-proclaimed Emperor Napoleon III, and sent him to prison in Schloß Wilhelmshöhe. His own soldiers had booed the carriage that carried him away and thrown stones at it.

Napoleon III had clumsily tried to be his departed uncle and namesake, but succeeded only in the tyrannical portion of the first Corsican's character. Duly elected because of the name, Napoleon III had overthrown the elected government and proclaimed himself emperor when he learned that the constitution would not allow him a second term. Then he had started the war with their sleeping-bear neighbor to divert attention from discontent at home. The citizens of Paris, their ranks swelled by defeated soldiers, might almost have embraced Bismarck for ridding them of their own war-mongering tyrant.

But of course, the Prussians, once roused, pressed their advantage. They annexed the border provinces of Alsace and Lorraine—Lorraine, the birthplace of France's great heroine, Joan of Arc. By the end of that September, they had formed a tightening cordon around the French capital itself.

Autumn was golden. The time of harvest, as ever, was a time of plenty. What shortages had begun to creep into the city could be joked away by the defiant Parisians.

"You should return to your family in the country," more than one friend encouraged Nathalie. "Now, while the siege is still porous." Some even gave her leads as to empty supply wagons heading north that she could hitch a ride on once the trains stopped running.

And many would be the hungry nights in the months to come that Nathalie—no one called her anything but Nathalie in those happy, youthful days—would dream of her parents and their hereditary farm just on the rail route out of St. Lazare, between Giverny and Rouen. The spotted Norman cows. The golden glow of their rich butter would have helped as the flour in the baguettes grew coarser and coarser, turned to sawdust, and then vanished altogether.

Over their needlework in the tailor's shop where they worked, she and her friends discussed the rumors that spread as the noose tightened. "Do you think things will get as bad as they say things have been in the past?"

At least the rumor that ground human bones were going into the bakers' ovens as they had during the siege of 1590, during the wars of religion, never seemed to be true. "Surely the modern world has nothing like that sort of fanatical religion to drive people to do the most sacrilegious things," Nathalie had said as she shivered with the rest of them at the thought. Or did it?

Her parents had written, begging her to give up this foolish, now life-threatening, choice to seek her fortune in the big city and come home. "You know, Monsieur Charbonneau's wife has died in childbirth. With four little ones, he will remarry quickly, and the farm is just next door. This is the life God means for you, dearest."

Even her taciturn brother, who would inherit the farm, had penned a few words to the same effect. If she would not be a farmer's wife, the sister of a farmer was another option. Ironically, it was Gaston's message that had confirmed her in her choice. She would rather die than eat one more supper by firelight across from that growling, unhappy, unsociable man, her older brother, who never entertained a thought beyond his cows.

When other farmers sent flocks of cows and sheep to the capital, Gaston refused. Other farmers' dwindling herds pastured now in the Bois de Boulogne—where Nathalie and her friends liked to stroll on a Sunday—cropping the grass down to the roots. And citizens had chopped down a tree or two over the bovine heads for fuel. Gaston's patriotism stopped at the willow-lattice fence at the end of his own fields.

No, Nathalie had made the choice to stay with her fellow citizens that fall. The sense of community, hope, and good will were addictive. What one arrogant emperor had failed to do, the Commune of Paris could succeed in.

Her last twinge of doubt about her choice was that she was a helpless female when brawny, grim-faced, male soldiers were needed. Only an extra mouth to feed? It came heavily the day the director in the tailor's shop let her go. Of course, high-class gentlemen were not buying new opera capes with the siege on. No more red satin linings she had so enjoyed sewing, at least for a while. That was certain. High-class gentlemen had abandoned the city for their country estates at the first sign of the Prussian eagle fluttering over Saint-Denis.

So Nathalie and two of her best friends, also let go, found themselves midmorning on the steep pavement outside the tailor's shop. Work-a-day crinoline swinging into crinoline and the narrow brims of still-summery beribboned straw hats marked the boundaries of their tight friendship.

The young women joked about what would have been a major setback in regular days—the loss of a job. What meant the daily grind when a siege was beginning, and the streets of Paris streamed with soldiers?

But the young women were serious too. "Our rent's due," Bernadette worried.

Still, they were young. The day was warm and golden, and all around them was Paris, the City of Light. Their fellow citizens, brave, stalwart, determined . . .

• • •

"Ah, we were young," the concierge sighed aloud as she poured another round of cognac for the housemaid. "Young and innocent."

• • •

A young man in a blue uniform that had seen heavy wear at Sedan shared the pavement with them. He was out of place in the Faubourg-Montmartre, a neighborhood devoted to the needle trades—out of place in normal times. But these were not normal times.

"*Citoyennes.*" The soldier accosted them.

Nathalie stepped aside so there was space for him within the circle of their skirts. For one moment, their eyes met—his brown, intense, and alive with a purpose that made her look quickly away.

"*Citoyennes*," he repeated that title that flushed his face with the fervor of the eight-decades-old revolution—the word the *Marseillaise* evoked to follow the cry, "To arms!" Only he said it in the feminine. "You are needlewomen?"

Louise giggled at him. She couldn't resist a man in uniform, even though Nathalie had to question the wisdom of any who had blindly followed the deposed emperor.

"*Enfin*, we were until a quarter of an hour ago." Everything was "*enfin*" with Louise—"finally"—as if all conclusions were obvious.

"France has need of your needles," the soldier said. "Can you come to the train station at the Porte d'Orléans? We can find you food and a roof over your heads."

"For how long?" Bernadette asked. She was the shyest.

Under the effect of those eyes, Nathalie still hadn't said anything.

"A few weeks at least."

"*Enfin*, you brave soldiers will see that the Prussians don't stay for more than a few weeks, won't you?"

Louise's attempt at flirtation was lost. The soldier had no reply but "Vive la France!" Other unemployed needlewomen had just appeared on the pavement above them, and he hurried to give them the same message.

"Should we go?" Nathalie asked her friends, finding her voice at last.

"Of course we should go," insisted Louise. "And the sooner the better, or those women from Stendahl's shop will get the jobs."

"The train station?" Bernadette repeated the soldier's directions. "Do you suppose they mean to put us on a train and send us to work some place outside Paris?"

Bernadette was hopeful. She did not want to endure the siege. "You cannot say anything too harsh about your brother, Nathalie, that would keep me from living under his roof in Normandy to escape this," she had said on more than one occasion. "I would marry him."

"I will not let you ruin your life with him," Nathalie had always replied and had refused to make the connection for her friend. Now, for a moment, she wasn't so sure that both of them should not have left the city long ago.

"*Enfin*, I suppose they mean us to sew officers' uniforms," Louise decided. "I call first choice on any zouave to walk through the rail-station door."

Every *quartier* was mounting its own militia to come to Paris's defense alongside the regular army. Uniforms, the fancier the better, were all the rage. Although it was not unheard of for the watch on the earthen works to be set in tartan or sheepskin, that was also where much of the satin that had formerly gone to opera capes was going now: This brigade demanded red sashes; the infantry, yellow- striped tunics; the chasseurs, green feathers; the local brigade, bright blue shirts. The embroidered à *l'orient* jackets, plumed hats, and billowing trousers of the zouaves in red and blue were the pinnacle of style.

Nathalie tried to focus on the decision before them and to separate it from the effect of the young soldier's brown eyes. Tying a red sash across that chest would be an invitation for a Prussian bullet more than for the ladies' attention.

"Red satin bandages aren't practical, if they want us to roll them," she suggested. "And wouldn't the resources and our time be better spent elsewhere than on flashy uniforms if real battle is going to erupt in the streets around us?"

"*Enfin*, if morale remains high, burnished with new uniforms, such an unthinkable thing will not happen," Louise insisted.

The idea of going to Porte d'Orléans prevailed. "Although I suggest we leave our crinolines behind," Nathalie said finally.

"*Enfin*, more practicality, Nathalie?"

"This is war, Louise. Skirts are likely to catch fire. How much more so with crinolines?"

"All my skirts will drag on the ground if I don't have that support. Aren't you more likely to trip over your hem and injure yourself that way than to catch on fire?"

"Promise me you'll at least think about it," Nathalie said as they parted.

Then each girl ran to her lodgings to stuff a bundle with a few clothes and sewing equipment for the venture. Louise and Bernadette shared a room near the recently built Sainte-Trinité. Nathalie's path lay northward, towards Butte Montmartre.

She found she had to pick her way through a crowd as she approached Place Saint-Pierre, and rather than turning off left towards her lodging, she couldn't resist drawing a little closer to see what the interest might be. If it were dangerous in this time of siege, people would be running the other way.

Following the multitude, she turned onto Rue des Acacias. Then, through the space between two of the decrepit buildings on the right-hand side, the sky was suddenly filled with something unlike anything she'd ever seen before. She stopped dead in her tracks, her mouth open in wonder. Caught in a net of ropes, a blue and yellow cloud the size of a two-story home floated above the crowded square. Painted on its side were the words "Le Neptune." It swung and rose lazily, tethered to the ground, higher than the butte itself—the hill where a few disreputable bars clung. Wild shrubbery's leaves beginning to turn golden on that height formed the apparition's backdrop. Colorful banners fluttered from its great round sides, and a cart-sized basket swung between it and the ground.

"What is it?" she couldn't help asking the man who stepped on her toe as he, too, craned for a view. A carter by the looks of him, short and brawny.

"A hot-air balloon, of course," was his reply.

Nathalie had heard of such things. Scientists were supposed to have risen in such contraptions to make their discoveries, but mostly balloons were only for show, part of dare-devil exhibitions. Fifty or so years ago, Madame Sophie Blanchard had plunged to her death when the balloon she had floated in burst into flames from the fireworks accompanying her assent from the Tivoli Gardens.

"Ah, the Parisians," Nathalie commented. "They will have exhibitions even with the Prussians pressed at our gates."

"This is not a frivolous exhibition for your entertainment when you should be at work, young lady." The man took pride in showing off his knowledge. "Monsieur Nadar, bouncing so high there in that little basket, is attempting to show us that balloons may have uses in times of war. There was some reconnaissance use at Sedan."

Nathalie squinted her eyes again and thought she could see a tiny figure so far above them holding a spyglass to his eye. "Brilliant," she admitted, her heart soaring with hope for her citizens' chances in the upcoming fight. "He must be able to see everything a hawk sees before he drops from the sky on his prey." She wouldn't be surprised if, from that height, Monsieur Nadar could spy on her family's farm as far away as Giverny, which took three hours to reach by train.

The man at her elbow shrugged noncommittally. "So far, a few glints of metal through the trees, the fresh dirt of new earthworks and dust clouds on the roads are all Monsieur Nadar has reported in the notes he drops to the ground. He will have to produce a little more than that to make this stunt worth such great expense."

Nathalie struggled against the lure of the sight and pulled away as soon as she could. She had to meet her friends. But when would she ever see something like that again? At Porte d'Orléans while bent over her needle all day on some vain soldier's gold-fringed sash? She gave a full report to Louise and Bernadette when they met up—she the late one. Somehow, she lacked words to impress her friends with what she had seen that had delayed her.

"*Enfin*, it will be all your fault if that red-haired girl from Stendahl's gets the zouave first," Louise dismissed.

"We gave Madame notice," Bernadette said of their lodging situation.

For her part, Nathalie had offered her landlady half of next month's rent to keep the place for her, another reason she was late. Madame Beaumont had declined. "We're under siege, *chérie*. Who am I going to get to take your place in such times, when people are leaving town in droves? Keep your things there, and I'll manage."

"I could crowd you, my friends, into my room in desperate times," she promised them.

They had met in front of their favorite chocolatier on the Rue Faubourg-Montmartre. The shop was closed on account of the situation, so they couldn't celebrate their new adventure and their last pay envelope with a frilly paper-surrounded chocolate nougat each.

Undaunted by this depravation, and Nathalie equally undaunted by the disappointing reception for her news about the balloon, the three set off across town. They crossed the Boulevard Montmartre where the city walls had once stood, no longer useful against the new and more deadly weapons the Prussians had. Parisian militias marched down the broad, straight street now.

"*Enfin*, the boulevards have replaced a jumble of houses and alleys to give a clear view," Louise commented.

"I wonder if that was the government's purpose when they made the replacement," Nathalie mused.

"Surely not," said Bernadette. "They would not prepare so for the enemy's arrival."

"Bite your tongue." Louise was so certain she didn't need to preface it by her announcement of a conclusion. "The enemy will never get here. Our brave men will protect us."

Nathalie spoke her thoughts. "Not for the enemy. I wonder if the government didn't build such streets so they could keep an eye on us." And fire on us, should we choose to revolt. That second thought was so horrific that she couldn't say it aloud.

The girls passed cafés where men leapt to tabletops to harangue patrons with what they thought should happen next, the latest ill-founded rumors, tales of German spies in their midst. One man gave scientific proof that if all resources were pooled to form a massive sledgehammer, one blow could wipe out an enemy battalion, but he had no idea how such a thing could be wielded. Another suggested a gun that would play Wagner to entice the Prussians to draw close—and then mow them down.

Cavalry horses stood tied to every tree beside the Palais Royal that had not been chopped down for firewood. The half-completed new Opéra had been turned into a military depot. Within the Tuileries, two bands of men who had come together to practice maneuvers had instead come to blows over the politics of the failed empire and of Sedan. The brawl threatened to spread to the courtyard of the Louvre.

Here and there they passed through a noxious miasma of smell from some unidentified heap. "The street cleaners were all Germans," Louise said, holding a handkerchief to her nose, "and now they've left us with this."

Nathalie and her friends followed the Seine to cross at the Pont Neuf, Paris's oldest bridge, paying their respects to the great old lady, Notre Dame. The booths and tents that seemed like skirts around her stone base were doing a brisk business selling rosaries and amulets, but the crippled beggars were more numerous than ever.

Most of the river's boats bobbed idly at their docks, except for those of a few desolate fishermen who were not catching much. The pleasure boats, the *bateaux-mouches,* that had been the delight of the Exhibition three years previously had been pressed into war service. Big guns and refugees from Sedan weighed down their decks now. No *bouquinistes* lined the quays with their books and prints. Who could read when history was happening right before their eyes?

The Latin Quarter was strangely empty of the young scholars from all over Europe the young women might have flirted with under other circumstances. They skirted the Jardin du Luxembourg, Nathalie imagining along with the others that she might someday find true love and live in one of the fashionable new haussmannian buildings in the neighborhood. The gardens led to the long, tree-lined lane of the Observatory—more horses, more soldiers cooking on the smoky fires of new-felled trees. The cemetery of Montparnasse created not too long ago from farmland outside the city—Nathalie hated to think how soon it might be filled with new corpses.

Eight kilometers in all, with the ground rising now up from the Seine to the buttes on the left bank. And all the while they sang the anthem, named for a woman and banned under the emperor as too revolutionary, but embellished with their own words:

To needles, *citoyennes,*
Form your battalions,
March, march,
So impure blood
Flows in the furrows of our fields.

The most blood the girls imagined on that golden autumn day while their city was still mostly intact was the tiny red bead of a prick from their own needles.

...

In the meantime, on that wintery day more than twenty-five years later, the d'Ermenville's cook, Madame Joséphine, finished her coffee, thought she should wash up before starting a warming stew for luncheon, and went to see why that lazy Bretonne Jeanne-Marie hadn't returned with the Comte's breakfast tray.

Madame Joséphine returned much more quickly than she had exited the safety of her kitchen. She locked the door, then screamed bloody murder out into the street from her window with its frame of potting herbs.

And so, the authorities arrived at the fashionable apartment building on Rue Férou.

LA BELLE ÉPOQUE

"MADAME. MADAME LA Concierge. Are you there? Are you all right?"

Madame Toussaint recognized the voice and accent of the young gendarme. She'd often had him in for tea as he made his morning rounds; gendarmes patrolled in pairs at night, alone during daylight hours.

"Of course, this is part of my job, Madame," he'd always said with his sly little smile as he'd warmed his hands by her fire. "Get to know the *riveraines*. Hear the gossip."

Now, the panic in his voice told her that he had, indeed, discovered the body. His worst fear was that the murderer had run through the whole building, killing indiscriminately. On his watch.

On her watch. Madame Toussaint left her huddle with Jeanne-Marie and rose off the bed to answer the door. "*Oui*, Monsieur. Please, a moment. I am fine." The wobble of her legs through the two short steps told her she lied. She clung to the door frame after she pulled it open.

Although he had the uniform for it, the young man had to stretch to fill the title Monsieur. He was no older than Nathalie herself had been at the start of the siege. He wore the merest pencil sketch of a moustache and heavily pomaded hair that tended to give out in the damp, now revealed as he politely held his kepi in his hand. With such devices, he tried to gain the confident appearance of his colleagues.

Still, with neither tongue nor face could he hide the fact that he was a Creole from the Caribbean, at least a quarter the descendant of black slaves. Although not legitimate—he'd confessed this to her too—his education had been seen to by his French father, who had also seen that he could immigrate from the islands for better opportunities. His name was Théophile; Madame Toussaint was not certain whether this was a given or a family name. Maybe as a bastard with his background, they didn't make the distinction.

As she stood in the doorway, Madame Toussaint had to smile at the red lining to his calf-length blue cape wrapped against the weather, perhaps against his vulnerability. "I once sewed such capes for gentlemen to wear to the opera," she had told him, making conversation over their tea. The idea had delighted him, that he, with his background, might someday go to the opera.

The sight Madame Toussaint presented to him today did not please him so well. "Madame?"

Her bodice was still awry, but at least at some point, Jeanne-Marie had helped Madame Toussaint into her skirt and corset over the damp chemise.

Had they heard heavy boots racing up the stairs over their heads? Madame Toussaint couldn't remember.

Worse was the bottle in her hand. It was empty. "I would offer you some," she tried to make light of it, "but it seems that Jeanne-Marie and I have finished it off."

"Such . . . such a fine label, Madame," the gendarme stammered.

"Indeed. But you mustn't think I can afford such luxuries. It is—was—Monsieur d'Ermenville's."

If possible, Théophile grew paler and hugged the cape closer. Did it distress him so that she refused to give the dead man his preferred title? "Madame," he said. "I regret to inform you that Monsieur le Comte is—"

"*Oui, oui*, Monsieur. Jeanne-Marie and I know. 'Le Comte' has been murdered. Jeanne-Marie, poor girl, discovered him."

Théophile's eyes grew wide. "Madame . . . Mesdames," he added Jeanne-Marie to the address, "You will have to come with me." Then he made the attempt not to make it sound so much like an arrest. "My commander will want to interview you. He wants to interview everyone in the building," he added as an afterthought, deflecting whatever suspicions had flashed in his brain.

Madame Toussaint took a step back. The alcohol! Slowly, slowly, appearances were beginning to dawn on her. "Monsieur le Commissaire is already here?"

"Yes. And there is no space for him . . . for him to interview you in your loge."

She, the concierge in charge of the building's front door, had failed to mark the man's arrival. That wasn't good.

The young gendarme ushered them up the stairs, back again to the first floor. Madame Toussaint fought the cognac to gain the realization that her knowledge would be pivotal to discovering the murderer. He—she assumed he was a *he*, given the physical brutality of the deed—had to have been in the building last night. And, under normal circumstances, she would have a tally in the back of her mind of who had entered and who had not. So how had the gendarme, his superior—and, now as they prepared to reenter the apartment, she saw at least three other crime-solving officials—arrived without her knowledge? Even as cognac-fogged as her brain was, Madame Toussaint tried to work it out.

The cook, in hysterics, had cried out the window. Théophile had responded, either because he was actually in the street or because someone—a shopkeeper, perhaps the florist, throwing open her shutters—had just seen the blue-caped figure go around the corner and had sent the shop girl after him.

And dutiful Théophile, with aspirations of advancement, had come on the run. Théophile had a key to the building. Madame Toussaint knew he did, as he had for many of the posher domiciles, just in case.

Another possible scenario was that someone from the murdered man's apartment had come down to let the first policeman in with little noise, so that neither Madame Toussaint nor the maid had noticed their tread on the stairs practically over their heads.

Who could that be? It wouldn't be Jeanne-Marie; she was in shock in the concierge's loge. It wouldn't be the cook, who was in a panic in the bastion of her kitchen. Besides, the cook's feet were always swollen. It wouldn't be Madame d'Ermenville, who was an invalid. It wouldn't be "le Comte", who was dead. That left only Madame's personal maid, Sylvie.

Very well. Mademoiselle Sylvie, whom Madame Toussaint had left clinging to her mistress with orders not to move, had moved. Had moved rather unhysterically, it seemed. A good quality in a lady's maid who had to constantly indulge Madame's hysterics. Mademoiselle Sylvie (slipper-footed, Madame Toussaint imagined) had come down, let the gendarme in—and then, no doubt while the young man guarded the body or looked for clues, had followed his orders to run to the prefecture for reinforcements equal to the seriousness of the crime.

And, yes, then over her head had come all these tramping boots, the spur Madame Toussaint had needed to finally start setting her clothes to rights to face the day. By the time she reached the first-floor landing and the d'Ermenvilles' doorway under Théophile's watch, Madame Toussaint had decided that was the only way the events could have happened. This helped to overcome the annoyance she felt at herself for the miscalculation of remedying with fine cognac the shock and the flood of memories red with horror that had swamped her brain up until that point.

Théophile held open the door to the salon for her and Jeanne-Marie in a very gentlemanly fashion. Madame Toussaint had already been in the room once that morning; the cognac had come from that well-stocked sideboard. The room was lighter now. Gaslight flickered within the cut-glass mantels flanking the fireplace and in the pair of chandeliers overhead. A fire performed a *danse macabre* in the grate. The heavy winter drapes had been pulled back onto the grey drizzle of the street outside.

Only now did Madame Toussaint wonder what details of the scene she might have missed in the shadows of her first visit, in her concern for Jeanne-Marie. Madame Toussaint felt a chill as she realized that the murderer himself might have been lurking in the shadows of this room.

He wasn't here now. At least, no one was lurking suspiciously.

On the other—the courtyard, bedroom—side of the apartment where the body still was, gendarmes were conducting their investigation. They filled the intervening hallway with a smell and flashes as if photography, to Madame Toussaint's mind, were a lightning storm. To escape this, Madame d'Ermenville had been bundled out of bed, into her wheelchair, and then into the salon, where she sat, a tiny figure under a yellowed lace cap, cocooned in duvets and bolsters. Madame Toussaint felt a twinge of sadness for the woman, that she who could afford anything should be so limited in her choices. And now she was a widow.

Tall, big-boned, hook-nosed Mademoiselle Sylvie sat beside her, mending linen pillowcases. The way the light fell in the drawing room, it struck Madame Toussaint just how old the lady's maid must be. Those etched wrinkles would have precluded the title "Mademoiselle" in most other women, married or not.

The oddest thing about that scene were Mademoiselle's stitches. How the woman could have retained her position with such sloppy needlework, all knots and tangled thread, had long been a query in the back of Madame Toussaint's mind. Often the maid brought mending down to the concierge's loge—on the sly, the concierge thought—to have her do the work for a few sous.

And the cook lay prostrate on the chaise longue. "She—the cook—was able to testify that she found her good butcher knife out of place this morning, although not much else," Théophile managed to murmur in Madame Toussaint's ear as he pushed her forward. "Clean, but out of place."

So that was the murder weapon. From the d'Ermenville's own kitchen...

The police commissaire, a Monsieur Roule-Armagnac, was resplendent in silver braid. Madame Toussaint found something familiar about him, and since he was seldom seen outside the prefecture where he lived free of charge with a wife and children, it couldn't be from his saunters around the neighborhood preceded by that silver-handled cane. People—the man with a noisy neighbor, the wife with a husband who'd started drinking again—went to him as they might once have gone to a priest. Gendarmes brought the malefactor in and, without benefit of judge or jury, justice was served, usually in the form of a good talking-to. No head-of-school's dim bureau ever held such terror for its constituents.

And yet, for the murder of one of the quartier's most illustrious lights, here the commissaire was, come in state, bound to find the guilty party in short order. Commissaire Roule-Armagnac had chosen to command perched on a Louis XV chair, probably owned by the king himself. Madame Toussaint's distinct impression upon his first entry, that she knew the man, fled. She quickly gave up on trying to remember from what past this acquaintance was, more concerned that the chair was not a happy choice for a man of his bulk. He did not seem wary that the furniture might break under him. His beefy jaws grew even more out of control with tawny, gray-turning sideburns. He clenched a monocle in front of his left eye and smoked very large, very potent cigars with no consideration for the invalid in the room.

He did not introduce himself to the new arrivals to the drawing room. Either he didn't have time or thought the world knew him. He also didn't rise at the arrival of ladies—certainly not of their class—but demanded of Madame Toussaint the moment she walked into the room, "And you are—?"

Madame Toussaint bobbed a little curtsey. His tone seemed to demand it. "Nathalie Toussaint."

"Married?"

She looked toward Madame d'Ermenville, who seemed to be dozing. Nonetheless, she let the woman's presence affect her answer. "Widow."

"You are the one who found the victim?"

"No, I'm the concierge."

"As concierge, you should be able to help us find the culprit."

"You may be sure I will do all I can." She thought he might start by taking notes, but he seemed to trust his memory; no notebook was in evidence.

"You should know all the comings and goings in a building. That is part of a concierge's duties."

"Monsieur le Commissaire is correct. At the moment, given what evidence I have of last night's comings and goings, it seems to me the culprit must be someone who lives here."

Even though she had started by telling him he was correct in the politest terms, he seemed to take umbrage at her voicing an opinion. Or perhaps she had just used too many words.

"It is difficult to believe." He studied his cigar. "A building of such standing."

"It is only my opinion. At this point."

"You're telling me there were no strangers in the building last night?"

All the warmth of the bed had washed from her. She could say with perfect calm, "None."

"You're willing to swear to it?"

"*Oui*, Monsieur le Commissaire."

"You keep a watch on the front door, but is there another door? A back door?"

"The door to the courtyard, yes, where the trash bins are kept." This thought eroded Madame Toussaint's confidence in what she'd just sworn to. She swayed a little, and it was not the cognac.

"And that door is always unlocked?"

"So the tenants can dispose of their waste, of course." Waste that dripped down on her, into the yard just outside her window, growing rancid on the sweltering days of summer, as always.

"Unfortunately, our quartier is prosperous." The commissaire studied the glowing tip of his cigar. "Madame la Comtesse and her maid will soon be able to tell us if anything is missing, but such neighborhoods attract burglars. And, it seems, murderers."

"The stone wall in the yard is three meters high at least, Monsieur le Commissaire."

"Abutting on—?"

"Two neighboring yards from similar buildings. I know those concierges."

"Working as a cabal, perhaps."

"The wall is topped by broken glass, Monsieur le Commissaire. We would never visit each other that way, although sometimes we greet one another without being able to see. It is absurd. Women of a certain age wouldn't go that way, over the wall. Nor would many a criminal, I dare say." Again, she'd said too many words, but once kicked into gear with the problem at hand, this was how her mind was running.

"Criminals are very cunning. And physically fit."

"*Oui*, Monsieur le Commissaire." Madame Toussaint hated to admit it, but the commissaire might know her building better than she did. At least, it couldn't hurt to let him think so, perched as he was on his chair without moving like a silver-braided king. And so now she could curb her tongue.

"Théophile?"

The young gendarme stepped forward. "Monsieur le Commissaire?"

"Go down and investigate the courtyard. Scuffs showing someone might have climbed the wall. Bits of torn fabric on the glass. You know the drill."

"*Oui*, Monsieur le Commissaire." The young man moved to leave.

"And Théophile."

"Monsieur le Commissaire?"

"Check the concierge's loge as well. Take Clémence with you."

"*Oui*, Monsieur le Commissaire."

"It may not be necessary to disturb the rest of the tenants at all."

"*Oui*, Monsieur le Commissaire."

Théophile saluted and left. Madame Toussaint felt herself sway again.

"You are the concierge, you say?" The commissaire's snap brought her quickly back on solid ground.

"*Oui*, Monsieur le Commissaire." He didn't want her help? Very well. She would give it only grudgingly.

· IV ·
THE TERRIBLE YEAR
—

Paris in the fall of 1870; the Prussian siege closed in. The needlewomen of the Gare d'Orléans formed their battalions at tables—trestles made of rough boards and old doors laid across sawhorses—stretching the whole length of the former railway sidings. The women, over a hundred of them, sat side-by-side on stools, rickety chairs, and bug-eaten logs, facing each other and the fabric.

Some of the needlewomen had been *filles de joie* pressed into service off the boulevards; the Gare is where Nathalie first met the woman, a mere girl then, who in the 1890s called herself Coco Toes-in-the-Air. But with so many siege-idle soldiers descended upon Paris, such women were not many at the trestles.

A Madame Godard supervised the seamstresses. And, of course, there was Paul, foremost in Nathalie's memory.

The fabric, bolts of bright silk, was unfurled on the trestles. The rapid thuds echoed under the high-girdered roof. "Just like the steam engines used to," Paul said.

Every bolt that had been donated—sometimes, the rumors ran, unwillingly from the fashionable needle trade quarter at the foot of Montmartre—went into the patchwork: the long, striped sacks. For Nathalie and her friends were not sewing soldiers' uniforms as Louise had imagined, but balloons. Balloons such as the one that had taken Nathalie's breath away that morning against the Butte of Montmartre. Hot-air balloons were now the only way France's capital could communicate with the rest of the country, the country that was going to have to coordinate in order to save Paris.

Young ladies of fashion were, in normal times, the most common purchasers of silks to take to their dressmakers—ten meters snatched, twenty to be twisted up for the bustle. Therefore, most of the balloons the seamstress battalions formed were in pastels: mauve, pink, pale green, lemon yellow. Designers christened the colors noteworthy names which the seamstresses recited to one another as they worked: seashell, lavender, blush, seafoam, orchid. Peach, pomegranate, burgundy—names of food and drink—were particularly favored as intonations recited by siege-hungry tongues.

Watered silk lay side by side with brocaded patterns next to shimmering charmeuse, next to crêpe de Chine. These striped with the demoiselles' mourning mothers' more somber blacks, greys, and purples. The wise understood there was plenty to mourn since the start of Napoleon III's little war. Night was drawing in earlier and earlier. So was the cold.

"*Enfin*, how I would have loved to wear this." Louise stopped sewing a moment to hold the rich fabric up to her cheek, then dropped it down across her shoulders to the annoyance of the women sewing beside her who had the tissue pulled away from their fingers. "Off the shoulder. With ruffles and a bunch of violets at the bosom." She had seen Paul coming and wanted to say the word "bosom" in his hearing, even if all that was revealed now were two shabby shawls on her shoulders. "Does not this color suit me by candlelight?"

"Such was the vision of the grand balls that unspeakable emperor used to throw at the Tuileries," Paul replied. He was helping other men bring lanterns to the women.

"Did you attend one of those balls, Monsieur?" Her neighbors reclaimed lengths of fabric, but Louise's needle remained pointed heavenward in hands clasped with rapture.

"Yes, Citoyenne, I did."

"So you danced to Strauss himself?"

"Few wanted to dance, only stand and listen enraptured at the waltz as the master himself conducted it. If it isn't unpatriotic to mention a Prussian musician."

"And, *enfin*, did you escort a young lady? Who was she? Would we have heard her name?"

"It no longer matters. Her father long ago forbade me ever to see her again. Careful fathers tend to do so."

"Ah, a dangerous man." Louise gave Nathalie's shin a kick before launching into a reverie. "*Enfin*, I hear there were crabs this big around on beds of ice, all you could eat. And the oysters with lemon—and pyramids of Napoleon pastries with cream and mille-feuille as light and buttery—"

"Don't speak of food," several of the women groaned. A thin barley gruel had been served the night before and again, cold, this morning, with neither salt nor cream.

"I went to the Tuileries." Paul spoke in passing and would not pause long, even for a revealed bosom or the memory of oysters. "Back in the days when the French were governed by bourgeois spectacle. But let's give them a new, more practical spectacle, shall we? Something for the benefit of all society."

Needles were refingered and plied with more diligence after that. Flushed with patriotism and urgency, Nathalie was inspired to incite her coworkers too. "Small stitches, sisters, close and tight. Remember that the lives of our brave aviators depend on you."

"*Enfin*, that's the way to flirt with Citoyen Paul, is it?" Louise rubbed her exhausted eyes and studied her seam. "I see he set the light so it's best for you, Citoyenne Nathalie. A man's bed would be so much warmer than the floor we sleep on in the corner of the deserted station."

Nathalie dismissed her friend's notions with a shake of her head.

But the silk only lasted so long. After that, the women had to make do with percaline calico, which, when treated with a mixture of linseed oil and lead monoxide taken from the ceramics trade, had almost the same properties. Sailors, used to tarring their ships, mixed and applied the varnish that, in the closed space, made even those far from the operation lightheaded.

The dresses most of them had come in while the weather was still pleasant were calico, hardly heavy enough for winter. By the time the weather turned, most of them had lost the attractive curves they'd been proud of, and were glad to fit their woolens, glossy with wear, over the summer weight. Not everyone had this luxury.

Needles could not be too thick; that punctured the fabric too much. Thinner needles snapped with annoying frequency, raising rumors that the Prussians, who were the source of most steel in France, had sabotaged the project even before hostilities began. Militia forays to raid Montmartre shops for more silk were also constantly engaged to find more papers of needles.

Thimbles, too, were a necessary commodity in short supply. Some the women had brought with them were very nice indeed: rings of silver, ceramic ones circled with tiny painted flowers. Nathalie was grateful for the tortoise-shell thimble her mother had given her when she left for Paris; it had been her grandmother's. Nathalie kept it carefully and thought often of how it fit so well because the shape of hands was hereditary in her family. She remembered little of her grandmother, but she remembered the hands—before arthritis twisted them out of recognition and beyond sewing—while bathing her, holding her close in front of the fire in the evening. Nostalgia stabbed as a needle would her middle finger without the tiny guard when she saw that she had grown into her grandmother's hands as well as into the heirloom thimble.

Nothing like a siege to bring on nostalgia to be fought down with every breath, another weapon of the enemy. So Nathalie forced herself to remember her mother saying over sudsy water, "All I wanted in a daughter was that her hands be small enough to scrub the milk jugs yet strong enough to press the udders to the very last drop."

Scissors could be shared—except by the lefthanded, who'd been segregated down at one end of the trestles with their own pair. Scissors, but not needles and not thimbles. The young men about—Louise flirted with them all—would offer to replace broken or misplaced thimbles, gallantly whittling scraps of wood or roughly sewing leather pieces together into a thick, plain cap.

"It's just an excuse to hold a young lady's hand," Paul said, "for measure."

And when Louise misplaced her third thimble, he said, "Now, she does that on purpose." Nathalie knew that was true.

Paul said other things worth hearing. "The men weaving the giant cargo baskets over there, they are supervised by Old Henri. He is blind and made the finest baskets all his life, selling them door to door. No one in Paris is buying baskets these days. Old ones have to be mended to last through the siege; some are being boiled into bouillon. But we still need his skills. We need the skills of every Frenchman."

At the other end of the station, these baskets were suspended from the girders of the ceiling to train future pilots, since once his guy-line was loosed, the pilot lost all control of where he was going, except that he was out of Paris. A continuing supply of new pilots was needed. "Sailors seem to make the best pilots. They are adept at the use of ropes and don't get seasick," Citoyen Paul explained.

"*Enfin*, a trim sailor's shirt would be fine to sink my needle into," Louise commented. "Something that would fit him like a second skin, and not get caught up in the rigging. And those expensive buttons."

Rope makers—also mostly "sailors and fishermen with no place to sail to," Paul said—formed the nets to ensnare the balloon sacks.

The times when Paris, "the City of Light," first heard gunfire were surreal. People, including all from the train station, hurried in a festival mood to the heights. They found their way to the windmills of Montsouris that had fallen strangely silent since there wasn't grain to grind. Or they went further east to Butte des Cailles. Children and telescopes and skimpy picnics in tow, the citizens debated whether the deep booms might be the Prussian Krupp's great gun, which had won the prize at the Parisian Exhibition three years earlier for the largest gun ever. Were all those puffs of smoke the rapid-fire *mitrailleuse*, based on the American Gatling's invention that had been so tardy in arrival, but which must surely now save the day?

Then had come the surreal silences when the populace stood and watched the defeated zouaves struggle back into town. "Deserters! Cowards!" some cried on the street.

"*Enfin*, they will need comfort, a boost in morale," Louise suggested, but quietly.

People seemed to only know how to cheer and elate. Even Louise fell into the common confused silence as wounded horses pulled ambulances toward the hospitals at Val de Grace and Les Invalides. And all the theatres pressed into service to house the casualties.

Followed by the hearses, the same poor horses in the traces.

The cry "another sortie! This time to the east" no longer raised an eyebrow. The Gare d'Orléans became Nathalie's only reality.

As the days grew colder, sometimes in the morning the silk would be stiff with frozen dew. Or careless seams would have popped. Then Paul would enlist needlewomen to restitch with numb hands. He seemed to like to choose Nathalie: "You are not afraid to leave the warmth of your bed. It must be all that getting up to milk the cows." But cow teats were warm.

Other holes required glue and paper—sometimes old newsprint of the badly spelled gazettes from Versailles the Prussians printed and allowed to be smuggled in to demoralize the population. But truly, it was amazing just how airtight the creations could be.

"They are like beached whales," Paul said about the half-filled envelopes that lay at the other end of the Gare d'Orléans, panting, waiting.

When a man went inside that tent-like space—large enough to house two families—in order to coax the air into the very cul-de-sac, Paul said, "That's our Jonah, in the fish's belly."

Filling the balloons with gas could plunge the whole city into darkness as it took all the gaslight fuel. "Besides, it is extremely dangerous," Paul said.

"Paul says, Paul says, Paul says . . ." Louise complained, pulling her stitches so tight the fabric puckered. Hunger made her ill-tempered. Hunger and rejection. "*Enfin*, all we hear around this place is what Citoyen Paul says."

"Well, he is the commander here," Bernadette suggested. "We would all do well to heed him."

"*Enfin*, Nathalie is the one who ought to pay him more heed," Louise said.

"Oh, Louise, stop," Nathalie begged, finishing off a length of thread. "Pass the spool, please."

That particular day, in their particular stretch of the trestles, it was orange thread—"Pumpkin," the label called it--on turquoise.

"What food is turquoise?" Bernadette wanted to know.

"The mold in Roquefort," Nathalie supplied quickly.

"Who would wear a gown with such stitching?" Louise's words were now more like a sigh than the scorn of the modish woman of fashion. "Like a circus clown. *Enfin*, it sets my teeth on edge. If my teeth didn't really want a nice *chop à point* between them."

"Pass the scissors, please."

"*Enfin*, why else does Citoyen Paul stop so often by this spot in all the long trestle length? Bernadette, my dear, it's not for you or for me."

"To keep you sewing instead of chatting, Louise, my dear." Nathalie pulled her threads straight and, with a lick of her fingers, knotted the ends.

"Because you're always losing your thimble," Bernadette said, flexing her fingers to rid them of the cramp, of the cold.

"*Enfin*, I can't help it if I lose things. And Paul is never the one who volunteers to make me a new one. I bet he would if Nathalie lost hers."

Nathalie felt herself flushing, though Louise was clearly talking nonsense. "So you may be certain I take care not to lose mine. Citoyen Paul has no time for such foolishness, and neither have I."

Paul was the young soldier who had first accosted them on the pavement outside the tailor's shop door the day they were laid off. Nathalie had recognized him at once, the moment their eyes met again. He was ubiquitous in the Gare d'Orléans, still in his plain blue, Sedan-worn uniform—in desperate want of a needlewoman to mend knees and elbows, even the seat. And, after a month, it looked like you could take in a good five centimeters at each side.

He refused all mending offers, using a similar formula to what Nathalie had used. "There are more important things to sew right now."

He had asked them to call him Citoyen, that title from the Revolution. Then one morning, across the echoing train station, the girls heard a man say, "*Oui, mon colonel.*" He was saluting and addressing Paul.

The next time Paul strode past their station on the trestles, Louise called out, "Monsieur le Colonel."

He stopped and scowled. "I thought I told you to call me Citoyen. Or Comrade. Comrade will do."

"Oh, yes. Excuse me. But are you truly a colonel? I think I could make you stripes from this gold silk we had to cut to taper the balloon to its narrow neck. Five stripes, right there on your shoulder. It will only go to patches otherwise, which seems such a shame."

"Do not waste your time on stripes for me, Citoyenne. Balloons. The balloons need your needle, not me."

"Or Nathalie. *Enfin*, Nathalie would do it for you. Nathalie would love to do it."

Nathalie kicked her friend's shin under the trestle.

"But why," Louise persisted, "if you truly are a colonel, will you not wear the insignia you're entitled to?"

Paul didn't answer them then. That came later. That day was clear and fine.

On fine days, with a lot of heaving and hoing, the final product was carried out into the open, where fires using hoarded fuel would be stoked—a coveted, warm job—and slowly, slowly begin to billow and fill the balloons.

Nathalie and her friends kept sewing, waiting, listening intently to the bustle around them. "That pine burned much too fast. We're almost out of fuel."

"The locomotive's coal pile is gone as well."

"Follow me." That voice Nathalie recognized as Paul without even looking up. "We'll gather up the stray pieces of coal in sacks, from between the rails, one by one. And no, don't tell me that's women's work."

Enfin, as Louise would say, pulled up by nothing but silk and air, the basket would right itself, and Paul would announce, "Time to load. Come, Citoyennes. Put up your needles. You deserve to take glory in your work, too."

So they stepped outside to the switching yard, blinking in the cold, bright sunlight. It was always bright when a flight was going to be attempted. Even Nathalie, who had seen the previous balloon below Montmartre, gasped aloud when her gaze was drawn up and up and up to all the colors of the debutantes glowing not by candlelight but in broad daylight. The balloon reached as high as the girders of the station, higher, drifting on its tether and casting its shifting shadow against the glass panes as shortly it would, if all went well, against the clouds over free France.

It was beautiful. Who would think that little stitches could make something so beautiful, so powerful? Something, in the end, so potentially freeing.

V
LA BELLE ÉPOQUE

IN THE SALON of the d'Ermenville's first-floor apartment, Madame Toussaint was beginning to lose the assurance she'd had that the police commissaire's pomposity was a sign of his incompetence. The memories the man evoked in her from twenty years before roiled with mindless hate, violence, vengeance. Were these still the man's basic characteristics if you scratched the present respectable surface?

She had been thinking that if she were in charge, she would interview all the women in this room separately to make sure they didn't corroborate stories. And being allowed to sit down would be nice. But, she told herself, it was not her place to say. Half of the things she'd just said to the commissaire's popping monocle were not her place to say.

"You are not the one who found him," the man said.

"No, Monsieur le Commissaire."

Madame Toussaint reached behind her for Jeanne-Marie's elbow and drew the girl forward. "This young lady did." First of all, the stories must corroborate.

"And you are—?" The commissaire scowled and lit another cigar.

Jeanne-Marie whispered her name. Madame Toussaint, who had never heard the family name before, only heard that it was one of those Breton names ending in the throaty *c'h*.

"Speak up. I didn't hear you." The monocle was adjusted like the eyepiece of a microscope.

Jeanne-Marie struggled like a fish on a hook, as if the commissaire were the murderer, holding the same bloody knife to her throat.

"She's our maid of all work," Mademoiselle Sylvie said over her needle, trying to be of help in two ways at once.

I did such work, Madame Toussaint considered telling the woman. When I was young. It would be a way to break the ice, which had never been easy before. And perhaps offer some helpful hints as to how to make a neater darn.

But a lady's maid was far superior to the common concierge, and Mademoiselle Sylvie would never let anyone forget it. Perhaps a time would come over the next hours to make this advance. Madame Toussaint determined to look for it. And in the process, learn what she could of the crime.

Commissaire Roule-Armagnac looked Jeanne-Marie up and down again and expressed his assessment aloud. "Spinster." He did not say "virgin," which is what she looked like: a virgin martyr cringing in the nave of a church. It went without saying that because she was a maid, a *bonne*, young and comely, she would be obliged to service someone, in this case the dead Monsieur d'Ermenville. And since the secularizing revolution in France, no angel was going to come down to save her.

"About what time did you make this discovery?" Monsieur le Commissaire pursued. Again, Jeanne-Marie couldn't get the words out. "Don't you speak French?" was his next, harsher question.

"*Oui*, Monsieur." Instead of the emphasizing *si*, which a native speaker would have done. Madame Toussaint flinched for the girl.

"What time was it when you discovered the body?" The pauses between his words, the broad gestures with his cigar—including some to the belly to evoke the horrible sight in the master bedroom—indicated that he wasn't going to believe her. Or at least, he thought her, like all maids, a simpleton.

Jeanne-Marie looked around desperately for aid. Every morning, she woke when someone pounded on the door to her room. That's when her morning began, not by the clock. She dressed hastily in uniform in her fireless, lightless chamber. When had the cook sent her into the master's chamber with the tray and to stoke the fire? Monsieur le Comte, as the girl called him, usually liked his breakfast early for one of his class, at eight-thirty, but Jeanne-Marie no doubt depended on the cook to shove the tray in her hands.

Jeanne-Marie, in fact, glanced at the cook. The older woman had a compress over her eyes, still prone on the chaise longue, and was snoring gently, as those who had received a shock might do. She would be no help. Besides, she was too deaf to be following the discourse.

D'Ermenville might even demand that his maid perform other services in his bed of a morning, Madame Toussaint thought. That potential must have made Jeanne-Marie jumpy every time she gingerly balanced the tray to tap on that door with its flowery, white-painted molding.

Madame Toussaint stepped to Jeanne-Marie's side. Having calculated from when she had heard Saint-Germain's bells ring—assuming those were on schedule—and how much time she might have dozed, the concierge could say, "I heard the crash at eight-thirty this morning, Monsieur le Commissaire."

She could venture no guess as to when she'd heard the cry in the night, however.

"And you are—?"

"The concierge, Monsieur le Commissaire." If his pride kept him from taking notes and this repetition was the result, the investigation was not going to go smoothly.

The commissaire shifted his monocle—another vanity, *non?*—to view her better. Perhaps it was the courage of the bottle, but Madame Toussaint stood her ground and met him eye to eye.

"And what crash would that be?" he asked.

Now, Madame Toussaint looked away and down. She hoped that didn't make her appear guilty, but even with three shots of cognac in her, she couldn't look back up. She'd finally seen it. If you took away the whiskers, twenty years, and twenty kilos from that face and frame . . .

"The crash, Madame?"

"When Jeanne-Marie dropped the breakfast tray. Directly over my head." The cook wouldn't have heard it. "Madame d'Ermenville and Mademoiselle Sylvie must have heard it, too, in the next room." Neither of these women confirmed or denied the assertion, and the commissaire did not press them. "Down in the concierge's loge, Monsieur," Madame Toussaint added. "That's where I heard it." The lameness of the remark caused her to blush—if that wasn't more the effect of the cognac.

Not all the commissaire's distraction she was struggling against was his own fault. A young gendarme—she decided it must be Clémence, a plump, pink-faced boy—had entered, saluted, and announced, "The courtyard is clean, Monsieur." Madame Toussaint took that statement as praise. She was the one, after all, who scrubbed it once a day. And there had been rain.

"And there is glass on the top of the wall." Clémence looked mournfully at his hand, which was bleeding. He'd attempted to scale the wall himself, no doubt collapsing in the lids of her dustbins as he stood on them. "Not even the best cat burglar could manage it."

So convinced had Madame Toussaint been by her first determination—the perpetrator must be a tenant in the building—that until now she hadn't given that rear means of entry full consideration. A determined cat burglar could throw a blanket over the glass. Or wear a pair of heavy-duty leather blacksmith's gloves, perhaps. If the two other concierges spoke for the security of their entryways, however, Madame Toussaint would once again reject this means of entry.

But then there was the flower shop. The door from the flower shop was another entry into the building's main floor lobby. The commissaire should be told of that . . .

Commissaire Roule-Armagnac gave a sound of disgust that included spitting out a stray bit of tobacco from the cigar. Now did not seem to be the time to interfere in the man's investigation. Beside her, Jeanne-Marie flinched again, and it was probably not all at the sight of the young man's blood. She was responsible for the cleanliness of the Turkish carpet which the spittle had just hit.

"Take that hand off to the coroner, Monsieur Clémence." The commissaire growled with disgust and a toss of the head towards the door. "He can have a look at it when he's finished with the body."

"*Oui*, Monsieur," the boy was only too glad to say. He saluted with both hands, one cradled in the other.

"A moment yet." Commissaire Roule-Armagnac stopped him.

"*Oui*, Monsieur le Commissaire?"

"Was there a breakfast tray?"

"*Oui*, Monsieur. In pieces in the doorway. A croissant. A rose. A broken teapot."

"Thank you, Monsieur Clémence. That will do."

Madame Toussaint silently thanked the young man for corroborating that simple part her story as he exited.

The commissaire turned back to the women before him. "And did you see anything untoward? Besides the body, I mean. Young lady—the maid with the unpronounceable surname. I'm talking to you."

"No, Monsieur."

"Hear anything? Any stranger in the apartment? Or are you, like Madame *la cuisiniere* over there, deaf as well?"

Jeanne-Marie shook her head. Even monocled, the commissaire did not catch the gesture. Madame Toussaint moved closer to the girl and took her hand, helping her to say the "No, Monsieur," required.

Madame Toussaint bent close to the white ruffled cap and whispered, "Were you with him last night, *chérie*? Did he make you . . .?" She hadn't bothered to ask over cognac in the loge, but now it seemed important.

The girl shook her head vehemently and looked prepared to faint. "Not last night, no. Thank God." So that wasn't the cry Madame Toussaint had heard in the night.

Or perhaps the lady's maid? Did Monsieur d'Ermenville like variation? Surely not Mademoiselle Sylvie. She and her mistress seemed to have only one mind between them, and it did not include servicing the master.

The commissaire leapt out of his chair as if he had heard the first ominous crack of delicately carved wood. "Mesdames. You conspire together?"

Before she could answer this accusation, Madame Toussaint realized the commissaire had more to say. In his hand he held his pocket watch that had been chained across his belly, as solid as the lower arc of the Eiffel Tower. "It is now half past ten. Why has it taken you all this time to come forward with the news?"

Good question. The man posed it, his jowly, whiskered face only centimeters from Jeanne-Marie's. Madame Toussaint found it was quite close enough to her own, and she took a dizzy step backwards. At the same time, the commissaire reeled on his own feet. How he could smell it over the cloud of cigar smoke that followed him everywhere, but he could. "Liquor? Do I smell liquor on your breath—both of you? At this hour of the morning? When you have duties?" The corpulent face flushed with fury. Neither Madame Toussaint nor Jeanne-Marie managed a word.

Monsieur le Commissaire reeled back all the way to the side table beside the chair he had taken which, besides holding an anemic ceramic shepherdess, still held the cognac bottle Théophile had set down. The monocle scowled, squinted, nearly snapped in two, at the label. "This? This is what you've been drinking? And polished the bottle off?"

"There were hardly two fingers in it." Only after she said it did Madame Toussaint realize how besottedly stupid her words must sound. Fortunately, she was quite certain that, in his anger, the commissaire failed to hear her.

"Cognac? And this brand? Where did servants such as you get such a fine label?"

"I took it," Madame Toussaint confessed by pointing at Monsieur d'Ermenville's heavy sideboard of potions. You couldn't even see where the cognac had been.

"Stole it. A thief for a concierge."

Now Madame Toussaint found her own ire rising against all her better judgment to say as little as possible. "Monsieur le Commissaire," she said. "I beg you to understand that mademoiselle had had a horrible shock. She needed a drink, and I had none in my loge. When I came up and saw— well, what she had seen—I did not think Monsieur d'Ermenville, may he rest in peace, would begrudge her just that much."

"You do not accord him the title of Comte?"

Madame Toussaint refused to answer. "After all this young woman, a stranger to this town, has endured these months in this household."

"I beg your pardon." This indignation came from behind her, from Mademoiselle Sylvie.

Madame Toussaint whipped around to counter this and saw that the lady's maid had risen to her feet, to her full dignified height, setting aside her stitchery.

Before any more words could fly, the young gendarme Théophile entered the room. "Monsieur le Commissaire, you must come and see what I have found. In the concierge's loge." He stole a glance at Madame Toussaint, and she knew all her lies—years of lies, in fact—were about to circle around to bite her.

"Well, what is it?" The empty cognac bottle still swung in the commissaire's hand. He did not seem to relish the thought of going down another flight of stairs and then up again as the panting Théophile had just done. "Monsieur, speak up."

"In a kettle of cold water in the kitchen, Monsieur. A sheet. And a lady's chemise. Bloody, Monsieur, and set to soak."

Silence crushed the living room for a full minute. No one even began to shuffle or murmur until Saint-Sulpice ringing eleven broke the spell.

"The depravity." Commissaire Roule-Armagnac's words were the first. "The depravity," he repeated with more fervor, "of the French working classes. To murder their betters for a bottle of Cognac de Grande Champagne. Gendarme, send for the black Maria. Take them both away at once."

Madame Toussaint could almost hear the loud metallic slide of the guillotine directly over her head. *Thunk...*

· VI ·
THE TERRIBLE YEAR
—

In the switching yard, when the workers of Gare d'Orléans could tear their gaze away from the majestic floating whale, everyone watched the minnow of a windsock.

"Too stiff a breeze," someone called.

"I don't like the look of that dark cloud suddenly risen in the west," grumbled somebody else.

"It is winter, after all. Why do they never hold sieges in summer?"

All science's recent developments in meteorology were of little use. A barometer and compass were the only instruments loaded on the balloon for each flight.

"Shall we unload them for another day? Such equipment is too precious to waste."

"Fifteen more minutes. Let's give it fifteen minutes."

Otherwise, the aviators were flying blind. The telegraph cut by the Prussians meant, among all the other messages that didn't get through, word of storms blowing in off the Atlantic didn't reach Paris either.

The windsock fluttered and sighed; the audience sighed with it. Would the mission be aborted again today? Tomorrow it was bound to storm. No visibility. All that wasted fuel! Men, including Citoyen Paul, stood around closer to the balloon to make the final decision. Douse the fire now and wait for another day?

Sometimes Citoyen Paul would find Natalie out of the waiting crowd and ask, "You grew up on a farm, learned how to watch the weather signs. We in the city have lost the skill. What do you say?"

"I noticed the red sky last night," Nathalie replied. "My father and brother would go out and plant winter wheat on such a day." A field of tiny green shoots of winter wheat seemed like such a luxury. A balloon would fly over such a place, catch a precious glimpse. A balloon might even land in such a field.

"There! Do you not see that shift in the clouds? This flight will get to Amiens, sure."

Balloons went one direction only—out.

"They are impossible to steer," Paul said. "Only drift along on wind currents. Tossing out ballast is the only way to make them go higher—if necessary, if desperate. Some of the silk you sew sails tragically into the waters of the Channel. All on board perish."

Weather cocks spun.

"This time, this passenger knows enough about the process to start a balloon factory in Chartres or Dreux. There must be sources of silk with the dressmakers of Rouen. In Bordeaux."

Wind shook dead leaves off the trees.

"But it's one thing to aim for the whole rest of the world when you have no rudder, no tacking mechanism. Quite another to come this way, to try to hit Paris over the Prussian bayonets. Like aiming for one feather on one bird in a whole flock." A suddenly startled flock of pigeons swirled away over the station girders, as if to prove the point. The hunters in the group didn't try their luck this time, but like the rest, studied how blue-grey wings caught the thermals.

"Sometimes mystified peasants run out with pitchforks to kill the monstrous, fanciful-colored beasts that land, panting hot air in their fields," Paul said. "The pilots are grateful merely to be alive and to eat carrots fresh dug from those fields. We have broken legs on rough landings. We have reports of such happenings. Worse."

Just so long as it was up and over the Prussians and their sharpshooters. With the help of Paul's descriptions, Nathalie's mind's eye created scenes of Prussian bayonets stabbing the silk. The next step in her dire imagination included what would happen if the flight failed: stabbing that silk with a pretty debutante's body inside when the Prussians breached Paris.

In any case, the pilots never came back. "It's a one-way ticket," Paul said, "out of Paris." In Paris, things could only get worse; that went without saying.

The lighter-than-air contrivances Nathalie and her friends created carried mail from the besieged citizens of the capital to friends and relatives on the outside. Sometimes sacks of twenty-five thousand messages went at once, mostly cramped on the single-thickness *cartes postales* the authorities had devised for lightness: "air mail."

Nathalie herself wrote such a card to her family in Normandy, hoping the postman wherever the balloon landed, whether south or east or west, would see that eventually the message went north. She never heard back. Such messages were more for morale.

Other cards bearing discouraging messages in German to drop upon the enemy were also printed by the ream. The awe-inspiring balloons floating just beyond rifle range were offered as testimony of French superiority. Nathalie's favorite card read: "Crazy people, shall we always throttle each other for the pleasure and pride of kings?" in German. She thought it could do with a French translation in case it fell on the other side.

One, or at most two, passengers could accompany the pilot. These were without exception men wounded in the sorties out to the Prussian lines, evacuated to find better care beyond the straitened and crowded circumstances of Paris.

Louise questioned, "*Enfin*, when will you demand your turn to go up in the balloon, Citoyen?"

Citoyen Paul answered with a question of his own. "You see the gold braid on those cowards?" He gave a dismissive gesture. "That's why I don't want any such trappings. That's the old, oppressive army."

When Louise said, "But they have been wounded for France," Paul replied, "And how much of that is syphilis? The glorious spectacle hides the corrupted interior."

"*Enfin*, what's that supposed to mean?" Louise wanted to know, but got no answer.

"And the pilots? No, let them have that sort of glory. Let me suffer the same as my men. Die the same as they.

"All we can hope is that the pilots have the wherewithal to remember the secret military plans they carry in their heads to coordinate the French army in the countryside. Such plans must not fall into enemy hands. Is that man strong enough to not divulge the plans if the balloon blows into

Prussian lines or gets shot down?" He didn't say the word "torture," but everyone thought it.

And then they stopped thinking it as if it were only a word on paper set to a candle. There was a sudden scurry among the men at the base of the balloon. A woosh came out of the firebox. "*Lâchez tout*!" the aviator in his basket cried, thin reeds only lying between his feet and the open air. "Cast off!"

Sailors in uniform cast off the lines. The balloon leaped, swung. Towards the station roof? No! The basket missed the girders by a meter, then swept giddily away. In a cheer, the audience let out the breath they didn't know they'd been holding. Hats and kerchiefs waved.

The deep basso profundo of Prussian artillery followed the visual puffs of smoke. More breath holding. The bright circus colors shrank to no bigger than a hand, than a centime. The whole Gare watched until the balloon disappeared completely against the lowering sun, then they hurried back to work. The spectacle gave their menial tasks more meaning.

Citoyen Paul, Nathalie discovered, was still at her side. He moved away when she met his eye, blinking with the black spots staring at the clear western sky had given her. "Let's hope for Tours with that one," Paul said.

. . .

Day bled into day like dyes might do into one another.

Eventually, Citoyen Paul gave five reasons why he did not want colonel stripes, one each of the next five times he passed the seamstresses at their trestles.

First: "Don't think I'm like those generals at Sedan who crept through camp in their dirty uniforms after the defeat, afraid to show themselves to the men. I have nothing to be ashamed of, except that I led good men to follow that cowardly *roué*. That man abusing the name Napoleon destroyed the Republic that common men created. All the while, I should have been following those men."

Second: "That was in the former imperial army. A true army of democratic citizens needs complete reform, and there's not much place for colonels in it."

Third: "At Sedan I saw that the Prussian sharp shooters aim for those men dripping the most gold braid like chicken entrails over their shoulders. Gold or red sashes, any of these things, make you a target, and when you are gone, your column is instantly thrown into a deadly chaos."

The next time: "Because I have seen that my men—the poor, hard-working men of France—die more miserably than those of us with rank do. I would rather die with my men; else, how can I ask them to follow me?" Perhaps this contradicted what he'd said before. He was coming closer to his conclusion, and Nathalie secretly loved clues to how his mind worked.

Finally: "The army, my dear *citoyennes*, is such a top-down organization. How can it function for the good of all if some—usually the most impractical—give orders, and those who could not flee into exile in luxury in England even if they wanted to—if they simply obey blindly? Vive la France."

Which did he believe? Maybe all five at once. Or maybe his thought was evolving under the siege's pressure, and he did Nathalie and her friends the honor of trying out each new wrinkle.

Then they overheard another of the men calling him "Colonel Toussaint."

"But didn't Napoleon I give the Toussaints the honorific name d'Ermenvilles?" Louise asked in wonder, her usual carefree banter again subdued. "And the title comte to go along with it? Not just colonel? Comte, *enfin*?"

"The Assembly did away with all such titles," Nathalie assured her friends. "Years ago."

"But that would explain how he's a colonel and so young," Bernadette observed, "something that gave you doubt before."

"*Enfin*," Nathalie used Louise's own word back at her. "He cannot possibly be interested in me."

Louise seemed to agree. She did not tease Citoyen Paul for being a comte. Who would dare?

Nathalie dared. "Are you, in fact, a secret comte, Citoyen?"

She watched carefully as his stride skipped a beat. "Nonsense, Citoyenne. France has no aristocracy. You think of monarchist England. Or of our oppressive Prussian enemies."

The next time Citoyen Paul passed, his cold-cloud breath appeared like he blew more smoke, which convinced Nathalie somewhere there must be fire. He said, "Didn't we take the guillotine to every aristocratic throat from the king on down in 1789?"

"Perhaps your family escaped across the Channel," she pressed.

Another skip in his beat.

As he passed once more, she asked, "Or are you from the new peerage Napoleon I couldn't create an empire without, handing out lands and titles?"

"Land and titles which were only supposed to last until the death of the man so rewarded," he retorted.

"Well, are you?"

No answer.

To her friends, as his ramrod straight back went by, Nathalie pointed out, "You see how he avoids the subject?"

When next he came by, he said. "France has totally outlawed any peerage, one of the sops the Assembly used to try to put down the Revolution of 1848."

"You, Citoyen, must have been alive in forty-eight. Old enough to have been of the peerage before it was abolished."

"Abolished. Forever. Along with pretending to give us universal suffrage."

"Did they not give Frenchmen universal suffrage? You don't have to own land now to vote."

"They forgot the Frenchwomen," he said. Nathalie had never had such an idea enter her head before.

She had to think about that, and to her silence and whatever must have crossed her expression, Citoyen Paul said, "You see, Citoyenne. Revolution did not happen just in eighty-nine, or thirty-one, or forty-eight. It must happen every generation or so, to keep the politicians honest and to wipe out any sort of new peerage under any other name men may try to install—such as capitalism, the law of the marketplace. In fact, I have read in the writings of the American advocate of their constitution, Thomas Jefferson: 'The end of democracy and the defeat of the American Revolution will occur when government falls into the hands of lending institutions and moneyed incorporations.' He also wrote what I just said, 'Every generation needs a new revolution.'"

"The Americans have managed longer than we have."

"The Americans just came out of that bloody Civil War. What is that if not a revolution, although they have given it another name? The Americans also have that huge continent into which to force the dissatisfied who would otherwise become revolutionaries. They turn their guns on the native population and give the name 'revolt' to the mowed-down savages. You just wait and see what happens there, the steam unreleased, once they reach the Pacific, gold-rich California, and every mine has been claimed, every rail scheme bankrupted, every dollar minted, every native acre developed.

"But forgive me, Citoyenne. America is not my problem. The defense of France is. France, where we reached the cliffs of the western sea in Roman times, where the last of the counties and dukedoms were handed out and put in hereditary hands centuries ago. Equality must be forged from what we have."

He turned to the station as a whole, because many had dropped their work to listen. "Citoyennes, citoyens, do not stop to argue politics. Pick up your needles, your basket rushes. Man the barricades France gives you today."

When Nathalie and her friends were left to discuss these words on their own, Louise said, "*Enfin*, there are still comtes in Paris, for all your Citoyen Paul says."

"For pity's sake, Louise. He is not my anything."

"Who did we sell half our opera capes to when you and I still worked in the shop on Montmartre? Monsieur le Comte this, Monsieur le Comte that. *Enfin*, I am quite sure Monsieur le Comte d'Ermenville was one of them."

"I think I remember him too," Bernadette piped up.

"Citoyen Paul is correct." Nathalie held her needle in a tight grip and held her ground, the citoyen's ground. "France outlawed the peerage in 1848. Those counts we served were Russians, Prussians, banished from their own countries."

"Yes, where would you land up if you were an exiled count but in Paris? Even if you were exiled from England. Or Ermenville? You know very well that if you walked into a bank with the *d'* in front of your name, they wouldn't treat you like they treat the rest of us. *Enfin*, you'd be shown into the inner room with its cigar smoke and its plush chairs. And the answer would always be, '*Oui*, Monsieur le Comte,' there beyond the hearing of us the proletariat."

And Nathalie knew her friend Louise was right, too, though she couldn't imagine it of this Paul who wouldn't even wear a colonel's stripes.

• • •

The weather changed, the picnics ended. Distant gunfire urged every thud of bolts of cloth along the trestles, every snip of the scissors, every stitch. Bernadette admitted quietly that she would like to leave by balloon, even if the very thought of flying so high made her want to faint.

Some passengers did go up with the understanding that they would fly back. These were the pigeons. Homing pigeon fanciers kept cotes on the roof of many a building in Paris. The practice of taking birds out of town and timing their return home had been a competitive sport. The sport seemed fated to die out as provisions grew scarcer and pigeons found their way into meat pies.

But now the feathered creatures proved more useful to keep alive than many another citizen. Carried out of the city in cages strapped to balloon baskets, they would instinctively fly back to their homes from Tours or Orléans or Bordeaux or any place in broader France that could send important intelligence, although very little of it ever proved hopeful. The Prussians captured Versailles, then Orléans, then beyond.

"If only the birds could carry food," Nathalie mused to Citoyen Paul late one afternoon. The lowering sun slanted in through glass panes in the Gare roof, many of them broken now, encouraging other, less clever species of pigeon to enter and seek shelter and loose their droppings on the workers, their bedding, and the strips of silk below.

Citoyen Paul stopped longer than was his custom in order to tell a story. "The story of a princess of ancient times: Given in marriage to the pharaoh of Egypt and forced to leave her native Syria. Always, she pined for the sweet cherries of her childhood until her husband devised a way to have a cherry attached under each wing of a homing pigeon and thus, once a year, carry the fruit to her ruby lips."

Nathalie stared at him, wondering that a man driven by such ideology could also recite poetry. He made her long for the cherries of her childhood, warm off the tree, eaten by the handful while she stood barefoot in the orchard and spat the pits away.

"Any cherry trees inside Paris have been chopped down for firewood before they can ever bloom again." The man who had woven the spell half a minute ago could just as easily break it again. "Our birds only carry messages for the higher-ups banded to their legs. They have invented a way, using cameras, to reduce the size of the messages so much more information can be included on one strip.

"You are from the country, are you not?" Paul went on to ask her.

"*Oui*, Monsieur. I mean to say, 'Citoyen'."

"Then you are the one I need. Come with me, please."

Wondering, she stuck her needle in the seam where she was and followed him across the railroad siding. Here, pigeons chuckled and cooed in their cages.

"We need someone to care for the birds until their flights take off. To go and fetch them from their owners—things like that. They can't be too different from chickens. You've dealt with chickens before?"

"*Oui*, Citoyen. We have a dovecote on our farm as well."

"Good. It will not be full-time work. Your needle will still get plenty of exercise. Just when we have birds to fly, then I'll need you."

"I understand." So that was how she earned the further envy of her seamstress sisters.

Nathalie liked the birds, as she had liked them at home. Even the smell of their guano was nostalgic, and the drift of stray feathers in the air around them. Her secret favorite was the tough old cock with a brown head and a missing toe from some earlier battle. His native cote was in the sixth arrondissement. She named him Malin, "cunning." He was brutal to his hens, so they were always glad to see him go on another mission. No other cock would challenge him. And he was hard to handle. He responded to none of the calming positions. Nathalie found she had to disregard pecks that drew blood, wild wing flapping that blew dust in her eyes and whipped her face when she held him. There was no thimble for handling a pigeon, and no gloves.

"It's fine. I don't really want gloves," she told Paul when he promised to try to find her some. "He is so warm. I can feel the quick, brave heart beating there. And I think it calms him a little, the contact."

Despite his wild ways, Malin always came back, flying through the smoke and barrage of the Prussian artillery and the falcons they had imported from Germany as a countermeasure. Malin always came back.

Citoyen Paul seemed proud of her work, although he never said so. She, for her part, tried not to bring too many "Paul saids" when she returned to her stool beside the trestles. Why should she incite jealousy when she didn't think there was anything to be jealous of?

And then came the day, at the end of October, when Paul asked something more of her. Something braver. "*Enfin*, much more intimate too." Louise said when Nathalie told her. "If there's food involved, I hope you'll remember your friends and bring some back to us."

VII
LA BELLE ÉPOQUE

La Santé Prison stood on the site of what had first been a coal market, then a hospital built by Anne of Austria. Later it had taken over the role of the infamous Couvent des Madelonnettes in the third arrondissement. Les Madelonnettes had begun life as a convent where female sinners who wanted to reform could retire from the world. That specialized holy order had evolved to include the sisters of St. Lazare in grey habits and black face veils held against their will, often mistresses turned in by disgruntled wives and mothers. After the Revolution, the prison had transformed again to hold such malefactors as the Marquis de Sade, the revolutionary Jean-François Varlet, the full monarchist cast of a Théâtre Français production taken into custody at the curtain call on a September evening in 1793, and the fictional Jean Valjean.

How very appropriate, Madame Toussaint told herself over a hundred years later. But whether it was because she was a revolutionary, a discarded mistress, or an actress—others would have to decide. She did not share such thoughts with her cellmate; they would only depress the girl further.

It was hard enough for Madame Toussaint to focus where she knew her thoughts really ought to be: thinking over each of the tenants of the building on Rue Férou and everything she knew about them for leads as to who must have committed the horrific crime, the murder of Monsieur d'Ermenville.

"Top to bottom now, Jeanne-Marie," she said more than once, trying to be systematic. "What about the artist, Monsieur Mahler? Fifth floor, right. A German. Who can trust them? What do you know about him?"

"Madame, one time on the stair he tried to— Well, he wanted me to come and pose for him."

"You watch that, my girl." Madame Toussaint remembered hearing Monsieur Mahler's last model in tears on the stairs in the lobby the night before. "The man is a tyrant. And he very rarely has the money for rent, let alone to pay his models." Not to mention that "artist's model" was often the same thing as "whore." "Money is a great motive for murder, and more than once your master threatened to evict him."

"Monsieur Mahler said he liked how the light fell on my cheeks—" Jeanne-Marie burst into tears. "How foolish I am. How naïve. I wish I were home. I miss Bretagne."

Madame Toussaint had to drop her puzzling to console the girl, and then didn't dare continue, fearing to evoke more misery. Madame Toussaint, who hadn't thought of the parody in ages and who hadn't prayed in even longer, found herself reciting the irreligious political verses not addressed to the Mother of God but to the emblem of revolutionary spirit:

Hail Marianne, full of strength. The people are with thee. Blessed be the Republic . . .

Holy Virgin Marianne, liberty of the captive . . .

The cell in La Santé Prison was larger than the concierge's loge on Rue Férou. The ceilings were higher, which must be a blessing in summer. Now, in January of 1895, the prison's modern heating brought through pipes kept the place warmer and shielded from damp—better than all of Madame Toussaint's costly efforts at home. More winter-grey light came through a high arched window as well.

True, the food was dismal. Madame thought with longing of the remains of her cassoulet at the edge of her dead fire at home. She and the maid Jeanne-Marie, unlike many of the other inmates, had no one on the outside to cook for them, to carry favorite dishes across town in tightly clamped metal tins. They had to make do with the thin broth and coarse bread the prison provided—and charged for, on a running account. But unlike on Rue Férou, there was never the temptation not to eat because it was too much trouble to cook for one person alone. Or to be forced to it because Monsieur d'Ermenville had liked to enter the lobby to homey smells, even before he reached the efforts of his own cook on the first floor.

Indeed, except for the food, and were it not for her concern for the maid Jeanne-Marie incarcerated with her, and for the grim fact of the guillotine at the end, Madame Toussaint decided she could live out the rest of her days here. It seemed so appropriate. Here, where many of the comrades she'd known over twenty-five years ago—the lucky ones—had ended up.

The food, the water—and the fact that what you ate and drank had to go somewhere, and that somewhere was the bucket in the corner. Even with a lid, her own smell sharp among all the other smells in this place shamed her. It smelled of herself, her own mortality.

Of course, it had only been a matter of hours since the black Maria had deposited them in the prison yard. Nevertheless, it was with something of dismay that Madame Toussaint heard the clang of the metal door being unlocked, then groaning as it was thrown open again. The vision of the prison's stern matron flanked by three guards, instead of the fashionable guests Madame Toussaint might open to on Rue Férou, increased her alarm.

"Come out. You're free," the matron barked, but grudgingly.

Jeanne-Marie's confusion clearly turned to terror. Madame Toussaint had stepped back to allow the completely innocent and thoroughly traumatized girl to exit first. Because the girl hesitated, the guards had to lunge in and pull her out by the arms.

"Madame," Jeanne-Marie cried over her shoulder. "What can it mean?"

"It means you're innocent, of course." Madame Toussaint tried to explain when the guards and the matron wouldn't. As she had been trying to explain throughout all the past hours. "Mademoiselle Sylvie knows you were safe in your room under the roof all night long. Your horror at this morning's discovery was unfeigned. They cannot keep you."

Making no such claims of her own innocence, Madame Toussaint followed without assistance, only to be stopped roughly when she made the turn left to follow Jeanne-Marie across the deck.

"No, not you," the matron barked again, and now the guards dropped Jeanne-Marie and strong-armed the cell's other occupant, Madame

Toussaint, instead. So Madame Toussaint understood that the orders had not been in the plural, only the formal singular, for Jeanne-Marie alone.

Madame Toussaint felt more concern for the young housemaid than she did for herself. What could freedom possibly mean for the girl, her job in jeopardy, no possible references? Who would hire a woman straight from La Santé? Or even give her a roof over her head?

"Courage, *ma petite*," Madame Toussaint tried to say, only to get a sharp shove from the matron.

"You go that way, with them," the matron added words to her actions, then turned to the left and the outside with Jeanne-Marie between her and one of the guards. The other guards stood silent to the right, the way deeper into the bowels of the prison.

"Madame," Jeanne-Marie cried, like a lamb baaing for its mother.

"Never fear, *ma chérie*." Madame Toussaint risked another shove to call over her shoulder. "Take your freedom. You are innocent, and the world knows it." She only hoped that was true. And that innocence didn't mean a bigger chance of becoming prey.

Madame Toussaint's march between her two guards deeper into the prison echoed over the heavy metal railings, up and down all three floors of metal doors and empty, peeling walls. It was colder in the atrium. Also, assaulting her ears, came reverberations that defied pinpointing the source: bodiless screams of the insane, the profanities of those at odds with the system—and when were the two not the two sides of the same coin? Also, a strong undertow, the hiss-hiss-hiss of one word, followed their march steps: "Concierge. La concierge. It's her. It's the concierge."

For what was more an object of horror? Only the single more notorious inmate of La Santé Prison on that day: defrocked Captain Alfred Dreyfus—Jew, Alsatian, found guilty of selling military secrets to the Prussians—had committed worse treachery, if the newspapers everyone followed were to be believed. The army was meant to keep the nation safe, just as the security of a private building was entrusted to the hands of the concierge. Both stood accused of violating the deepest of trusts upon which all society was based. Cheap whores and pickpockets, thieves and swindlers, brawlers, even the common murderer—these counted themselves upstanding citizens in comparison, and put a venom in their hisses that could kill.

"Concierge."

Dreyfus got an isolation cell. Perhaps days in such close quarters with people who hated and feared her so much even before her trial would, after all, become intolerable for Madame Toussaint. A quick pitch over the railing here would be preferable . . .

But now the guards had brought her down the clattering metal staircase and installed her alone in a room with only two chairs facing each other across a flimsy table, no window at all. Ominously, the echoing screams and hisses that rang through the rest of the prison were strangled here. No whipping rod stood in the corner; no manacles wept their corrosion down the wall. Nonetheless, the ghost of rust seemed to linger under new plaster, reminding her of what these walls could do, what they had done, and what they could hide. She remembered the feel of Paul's scars under her hands after she'd cut his hair the night before. And she rubbed her hands hard, as if that could rid them of the feel.

She didn't have long to stew with these thoughts. A moment later, the guards reopened the door to admit a different uniform. It was the young gendarme Théophile. "Good evening, Madame," he greeted her.

"Monsieur."

"Please, be seated."

Madame Toussaint hesitated to do so, still staring at the rusty ghosts on the wall.

"You've been here before, in La Santé." He set a tray down on the table between them. Unidentifiable mounds rested under a grey cloth. They might be food. They had the smell, not of warm juices, but of a meal that had burned. Almost like when rats got roasted, fur and all. This, too, would have to be endured. She shrugged and looked away.

"We found the records."

She shrugged.

"You should have told us that you'd been here before."

She shrugged again, then said, "It was a long time ago. Before you came to Paris. Probably even before you were born. Paris was a very different place." Only then could she sit; exhaustion had overcome her.

"Tell me again how you explain the blood on your sheets and chemise in the water in your kitchen. It interests me that you didn't claim at first that it was a woman's—excuse me, Madame."

"I appreciate your delicacy, Monsieur. I would have said it if it were the truth, but it isn't. It is no longer that way with me as it is with younger women."

"And it's not the young maid, er, what's her name?"

"Jeanne-Marie. No, she has never slept in my room."

"So your explanation is—?"

"As I told you and the commissaire before, Jeanne-Marie noticed that I had blood on my face. The room where Monsieur d'Ermenville died is right over the concierge's loge. Sometimes when it rains, the walls run with damp, but this time—" Madame Toussaint shuddered, even at this third telling. "The wall ran with blood onto my bed and the chemise I was wearing."

Théophile grunted; her story had not changed.

"I'm sure if you go and check, you'll still detect some blood on that wall. I was not in a state of mind to clean as well as I would have liked."

Théophile removed a notebook and pencil from his pocket and began to take notes, unlike his commander. "We have let the young maid go."

"For which I thank you. It is impossible that she has anything to do with this horrific crime except to be the unfortunate one to discover the body."

"And yet, you say nothing of your own guilt or innocence, Madame."

Madame Toussaint realized he spoke the truth. This fact, along with not mentioning her previous incarceration, would not look good in the eyes of the law. Of this he made a note.

"I am innocent, Monsieur." Because the words sounded false, even to her own ears, she added, "I assure you," which only served to exaggerate the impression.

Impatience flicked across the young man's face. "I am inclined to believe you, Madame. The woman who so kindly invited me in for tea on bitter cold days seems incapable of such a deed, in my mind."

"Thank you for your trust, Monsieur."

"But I have to tell you, Commissaire Roule-Armagnac, my commander, is of a completely different mind. He almost wouldn't let me come to this questioning, since he thinks I am blinded in this case. It must be that I am but a novice in these matters. But new evidence has come to light that makes me tend to disagree with him. I uncovered it myself."

"Monsieur?"

"My commander was all prepared to declare our investigations at an end, that we had the culprits in custody—meaning you, Madame, and the Mademoiselle—when a gentleman took objection to this."

"A gentleman? What gentleman would that be?" A tenant? Someone else? A stranger?

"I'm not at liberty to tell you, Madame. Suffice it to say that, seeing us packing up and preparing to leave the crime scene, this gentleman exclaimed, 'What's this? Is the questioning to end here?'

"'We did not think to bother the rest of the building unnecessarily,' my commander told him."

Madame Toussaint recognized the commissaire's voice at once on his subordinate's tongue, which made her certain he was doing a good job of mimicking the unidentified gentleman, too. Who was it? She would have to know him.

"'Didn't the women you have taken declare their innocence?'" Théophile mimicked that man again. Who was it?

"'In fact, they didn't,' said my commander. 'At least not fervently enough for my liking.'

"'But—but I have important information,' Monsieur insisted. 'Pertinent to the case.'

"'Do you, Monsieur?'

"'Indeed, I do.'

"'Very well, Monsieur.' I could tell my commander's patience was wearing thin. 'And what might that be?'

"'There was a man in this building last night.'

"'Indeed, Monsieur?'

"'A stranger. A man of bad reputation. You should make an effort to discover who he was.' Monsieur seemed to be choosing his words with the utmost care."

Again, Madame Toussaint tried to imagine who the informant could be.

"'Indeed, Monsieur?'" Théophile continued his tale in the commissaire's unmistakable voice.

"'A man who could be quite capable of such a violent deed.'" The unnamed witness. "'A man rejected by all civil society.'

"'Yes?'

"'A clochard, in fact.'

"'A clochard, Monsieur?'"

The word came from *cloche*, meaning "a bell," and referred to people who lived within hearing of a church's bells so they could come quickly when charity was dispensed. They were the homeless, living under bridges and in doorways. They were always numerous—as scripture said, "the poor are always with you"—nameless, feared, blamed for every crime.

They were her visitor. They were, in a single name, Paul.

Madame Toussaint closed her eyes in defeat. Paul had, then, been seen. Despite all her care.

"Do you have anything to say about this, Madame?" Théophile asked. "You know nothing of such a man?"

"Nothing," she heard herself say.

"Truly? As concierge—must I remind you? —it is your responsibility to know everyone who enters the building, to discover their business, and to refuse them entry if they can give no good accounting of themselves."

Her mind exploded like an ant hill her brother had kicked over one hot summer's day. "Cows step in these," Gaston had muttered. "They can break their legs." But all Madame Toussaint had seen were the roiling ants, the workers scurrying in twenty directions, each carrying a precious white egg in its mandibles.

Then, as now, Madame Toussaint felt only the need for flight and for protection. "Who told you this?"

"That's not important, Madame. What's important is that we have this information you neglected to tell us."

No. She could not betray Paul. "I know nothing of such a man."

"I was convinced that must be the case, too, and I told my commander so. But then he told me to investigate your stove." Théophile pushed the tray he'd brought with him into the room across the table toward her and removed the cover.

She had not expected much of prison fare, but this took her back to the worst days of the siege.

"Recognize these things? Half burned. A man's old sweater, although truth be told I remember just this item on your needles as you and I sat drinking tea and you knitting. But a man's sweater, not yours. Enough remains to tell this by its size and design."

He looked at her hard. Madame Toussaint said nothing. "And here?"

He stirred a second pile of almost-ash with the tip of his pencil. "Not a sweater. Hair. Human hair."

What did they think she'd done? Cut Monsieur d'Ermenville's hair off and burned it for some madwoman's reason after she'd brutally stabbed him to death? No, of course not. Anyone could tell this was not the murder victim's hair—this long and unkept. Could they tell if the two heads were related?

"Not le Comte's hair," Théophile confirmed. "And not your hair, either, Madame. More grey. Filthy. Madame, it can hardly go better for you if you are covering for the murderer, if you gave him access to the building, than if you wielded the knife yourself."

"He had a right to be there." She whispered, but managed to meet Théophile's gaze steadily. "Ask Monsieur d'Ermenville—" Only after she'd said it did she realize that the horror of one discovery had overwhelmed the other.

"Monsieur le Comte is dead, Madame."

"Yes, yes, of course. May he rest in peace." That was said defensively. She didn't really wish it, much less believe it.

"This man? This stranger, this clochard? Who is he? Where is he? Help us find him, Madame, and it may go easier for you."

Madame Toussaint wanted the guillotine right then. She wouldn't have to speak if they cut her throat. "He had a right to be there," she repeated.

"If so, why can you not tell me his name?"

"It's just that Monsieur d'Ermenville doesn't—didn't—like the rest of the tenants to know."

"And why is that? I'm sure you can see our difficulty, without le Comte alive to confirm this assertion."

"Because—because Monsieur is correct. He is a clochard."

"And why would Monsieur le Comte want a clochard haunting his residence?"

Madame Toussaint couldn't answer.

"So where does this stranger usually live?"

"Monsieur, I have told you. He is a clochard. I cannot tell where he lives. A different bed every night. Under this bridge, at the end of that alley."

"Why are you so protective of him, Madame?"

Indeed. Why?

"Surely he has his favorite haunts," the young gendarme pressed. "You know them. You can tell us. We will hunt for him."

The image of police hunting Paul like a wild animal threatened to make her mad. She knew what Paul's reaction to the experience would be. "Monsieur, I cannot find him even when I want to. And if you corner him, I assure you, it will not go as you plan. He is not a well man, Monsieur."

"We could bring him in. To an asylum."

The very notion made Madame Toussaint give a little cry of despair. "An asylum? That would kill him." Just like being even one night within these prison walls would, with their ancient echoes.

"His name, Madame?"

"He didn't kill Monsieur d'Ermenville. I swear to you." Somebody did. Somebody in the building. Somebody she knew.

"Let the law be the judge of that."

The truth was, Madame Toussaint suddenly saw, that Paul could have committed the crime, yes. God knew, he had motive, all he had endured. Opportunity? She had been sleeping. She had not awakened when he left. She was quite certain that Paul had been in her arms when she heard the scuffle and cry over their heads. But maybe she'd dreamed it. Maybe the death had occurred at a different time, and those sounds had been something else.

And she, even she, could never be sure, quite sure, that Paul's temper would hold. She remembered the knife in his hand last night and what her first fear had been.

"He didn't do it. He couldn't." She swallowed. "He was in my loge all night."

"Your loge, Madame? It is a very small room." Clearly, Théophile was remembering the exercise of fitting his own limbs and a teapot into that space. And he also seemed to remember, with a glance to the new-plastered walls, that under the law, torture was still possible to extract confessions.

"In my bed, Monsieur."

Théophile considered this, no doubt with a young man's standards of what you let into your bed and what you did not. "In your bed, Madame?" He did not find her statement credible and made a note, probably to that effect.

After a moment's thought, he said. "Yes. That's where the bloody sheets and chemise may have come from. This clochard brought them down to you to cover his crime."

"No, Monsieur. I explained to you. The running damp down the wall."

The young man cleared his throat. He clearly didn't believe her. He tried again to form a statement, returning to a previous train of thought. "In your loge. Then this . . . this stranger might be able to clear your name, as Monsieur who saw him come in hoped. But what is this stranger's name?"

Madame Toussaint sat silent.

"Madame?"

What was the use in holding to the pretense anymore?

"Paul Toussaint. I am not a widow as they—as is often convenient to give out, although the man I married might as well have died. Paul Toussaint," she repeated. "He was also once a prisoner within these walls. You can find his records, too. It will say, 'torture.'"

And the final admission, "He is my husband."

· VII ·
THE TERRIBLE YEAR
—

"Metz has fallen. The city of Metz has fallen."

Rain had begun to drum on the roof of Gare d'Orléans, sometimes through it where panes had broken and not been replaced. The crushing rumor running down the line of needlewomen was spoken in tones the patter almost drowned out. Too horrible. Too unthinkable.

First Strasbourg, the besieged citizens reduced to eating their famous delicacy, *foie gras*, straight, by the can-full for two weeks. Too rich and indigestible—like straight butter, they discovered—in any but the tenderest morsels *avec ses toasts*.

Now Metz.

"Who told you so?" Nathalie wanted to know of the woman seated beside her who whispered the dread news close to her shoulder. The path of this disaster from the town to her ear was convoluted but seemed to originate with an ambulance driver, somebody's second cousin, stationed near the Prussian lines. The Parisians, it seemed, were meant to be kept in the dark.

And three days before, northern lights had filled the sky over the besieged city with blood red. "The Prussians intend to smoke us out," the rumor had run.

"I can't believe it," Nathalie reacted to the Metz rumor. "I don't want to believe it." But the longer it settled in her brain, embroidered by the murmurs around her, the greater the probability became. She finished two more needles full of thread in the halo of the early morning lamp and then decided it was time to feed the pigeons. She would learn something better than rumor at the source of the best outside messages.

"Is it true?"

Citoyen Paul had been discussing something with a group of men at this side of the railway tracks around which grew the weeds the pigeons found most delectable. She bent to tear up a few handfuls so as not to interrupt the men. Had the trains been running, grinding over the first shoot that attempted life, what would she have found to feed the birds?

Paul left the group and came over when he saw her. Something heavy in his step told her the rumor was true.

"Yes. General Bazaine ran out of food on the twentieth, and the Army of the Rhine lived on the flesh of their horses at the rate of a thousand a day until now. The nearly two hundred thousand troops we hoped would break through their own siege and come to relieve us in Paris have now joined many of my men from Sedan in prisoner-of-war camps in Germany."

He let that sink in while she watched the quick snatch-snatch flash of white wattles on grey through the reeds of the pigeon cage and listened to the hushed coo-coo that greeted her. She could not meet the pain in his face, nor expose her own. Nonetheless, she could tell he felt the weight of that captivity as if he were in those dismal barracks and tents with the men himself, "his" men.

"But I didn't see that we got any message that might have brought such news," she offered, grasping at straws.

"No." As it turned out, the reported route—through ambulance driver overhearing the Prussian celebrations and a second cousin—was pretty accurate.

"The other news." Citoyen Paul took a breath to ease the blow of his words. "President Thiers returned to Paris late last night."

"To confirm the surrender?"

"Yes, and to announce that his own mission has failed as well."

President Marie Joseph Louis Adolphe Thiers. Nathalie wondered if Citoyen Paul bore the burden of a similar aristocratic ramble of names. If he was, in truth, a comte—in a world where such things still existed—or even a lesser scion of the d'Ermenville family, she supposed he must. When you planned to produce very few heirs so the fortune wouldn't get dissipated, you had to honor as many creators of that fortune as you could, all at one go. And saints. But "Paul" was good enough for Citoyen Paul.

Thiers was president of the Republic, so named in the scramble of necessity after the emperor's abdication. Maybe Paul's father knew him personally. Maybe Paul did himself.

In the desperate attempt to find aid in the war against the Prussians, Thiers had traveled to London, then St. Petersburg and finally Vienna, courting all the Prussians' traditional enemies. In his seventies, the old man had hardly been up to the task. Notoriously, he had fallen asleep while Prime Minister Gladstone was orating.

"He failed. Britain, Russia, and Austria have turned their backs on us," Citoyen Paul said. "None will send help."

"And Thiers has returned to Paris? He could not have crossed the siege lines without the Prussians' knowledge and permission."

"Of course. You see the situation clearly. He means to negotiate a surrender with Bismarck as soon as possible." Citoyen Paul underlined the dire nature of the case.

"Never." Nathalie heard herself say. It was as if she'd been asked to unpick every single stitch she'd made all day, every day, over the past two months.

"Some of us," Citoyen Paul nodded in the direction of the group of men he'd been with while she'd been plucking weeds, "have decided to join with other citizens in a protest march on the government at l'Hôtel de Ville today."

Rain pattered on the roof over their heads. "Would you care to join us?" he asked.

"Could I—?"

He understood her hesitation. "Of course. Many of us believe it is criminal that women do not have the vote. Weren't they the backbone of the Revolution? And in forty-eight? Elections would go very differently if they did. Men alone gave us this traitor Thiers. It'd be much better for society as a whole—and not just for the male bankers and industrialists—if women had their say."

Nathalie nodded as if these thoughts had been in her mind for years. In truth, they'd only sat like a vague fog at the edge of her being, unable to find words, even in the secrecy of her mind. Without someone else to offer the idea, it was like a dirty image respectable women would not utter. Hearing someone else speak them flushed her with instant conviction.

"Can I invite my friends to come? If we're going to surrender, we won't need any more balloons stitched, will we?"

"But we're not going to surrender, are we?"

"No. Never." She heard herself say it again. "And less so for everyone who stands with you. With us. If we cannot vote, at least we can march."

"We're going to take over the government of old Thiers and make him listen to the voice of the people. All the people."

"We are." Nathalie's voice echoed off the damp ceiling louder than her mother would have approved.

When she went to them, however, her friends exchanged glances and then stared at her as if she'd grown a second head. "It's just a protest against the idea of surrender. A *manif*." Nathalie used the shortened, familiar form of the word as if such actions were pet members of the family—as they almost were.

"Revolution," Nathalie heard someone say. She looked hard but couldn't see who it had been. The word did give her a frisson of fear.

But Citoyen Paul was waiting for her across the Gare, so she found courage she'd never known before to respond to the insinuation. "Revolution? Of course. Isn't the Republic built on revolution? And we have to maintain it that way. You cannot think, after all our hard work, that Prussian occupation would be a good thing? Those barbarians marching through our City of Light? The fall of Metz will be child's play compared to it. And much more on our doorstep." Nathalie heard herself sounding like someone haranguing the crowd from his soap box, and that was not how she wanted to interact with her friends. They stared at her as if she were, indeed, a stranger.

Louise, a true friend, sought to say, "*Enfin*, I'd sleep with a Prussian officer for an entrecôte de boeuf right now—not horse, thank you—shedding its bloody juices on my plate as I cut into it."

"Oh, Louise, you would not," remonstrated more than one.

"You, Louise? An officer? You'd take the flea-infested orderly."

"You don't think you'd be the one cooked bloody, *à point*, if you slept with such a Hun?"

"All of you, stop talking of food." This was Coco, throwing her spool of thread down in exasperation.

When that plea silenced them, the seamstresses stared at the roof and decided they'd rather sew on a day like this, even if no more balloons were needed. "I'm too hungry to march," whimpered Bernadette.

"If you get hungry enough, isn't that when you march?" Nathalie pressed on. "Isn't that what true Frenchwomen did when Marie Antoinette told us to eat brioche?"

"That Prussian Marie Antoinette." At least this brought forth a flicker of *liberté, égalité, fraternité.*

"I think she was an Austrian, not a Prussian."

"Same thing. At this point—same thing."

Louise, a little pang of jealousy in her tone, switched the subject and spoke of "intimacy."

"It's not like that between me and Citoyen Paul," Nathalie insisted. "This is only political."

"Only political. Just stepping out with a man of that class is revolutionary. *Enfin*, when is *l'amour* not political?" was the girl's parting shot.

Nathalie alone left with the men to begin the march to the Right Bank. Citoyen Paul had the only umbrella, and he shared it with her since she still had nothing but her summer straw hat.

They had to walk very close together.

• • •

Much had changed since Nathalie's carefree walk across Paris in the other direction with her friends six weeks before.

Before the new haussmannian houses, the concierges, who should have been cleaning the first floor, were not in their loges but spreading the news from tongue to tongue: the fall of Metz. The uncertain future of Paris. The treachery of Thiers.

The concierges watched the growing numbers of their fellow working-class citizens heading northward with something between wariness and eagerness. They stood at the doorways halfway between the starving lower order and the bourgeoisie and didn't always know where their devotion should stand. It didn't help that many of them were immigrants, often from Switzerland.

Just beside the half-built Saint-Pierre-de-Montrouge church—looking bleak and naked with damp seeping down its unfinished tower—the marchers from Porte d'Orléans found their way blocked. Materials from the construction site as well as all sorts of rubbish from the neighborhood that couldn't be burned or hauled out of the city formed a barrier higher than the umbrella.

"In case the Prussians leave their lines and fight their way into the city," Citoyen Paul explained.

The gravity of his tone played the whole scenario out in her mind: how she and her fellow seamstresses—whom she was already missing—would receive the alarm. They would confirm its truth, "said the ambulance driver, who knows my cousin." They would abandon their needles, hurry up the avenue d'Orléans from the station and seek refuge behind this jumbled wall. Nathalie estimated that she, Citoyen Paul, and the other marchers had been afoot already a quarter of an hour or more. Would the Prussians even give them that much time before the house-to-house fighting started?

And Louise's bloody steak on the plate. No female would be safe.

Put this way, against guns as big as the Krupp, the jumbled pile didn't seem much fortification at all. Maybe President Thiers had a point—

No. Never.

The men of the balloon factory at Gare d'Orléans negotiated with the barricade's guardians, hardly more than boys, which added another concerning wrinkle to the invasion scenario. After approval, for which they had to thank Colonel Paul and his way with jittery soldiers, they were shown the best way up and over. The removal of heavy beams helped, but the running sludge beneath did not. They slipped and slid, and their shoes grew heavy with mud. Nathalie recognized the cab and broken wheel of a fine carriage, a chair with the caning given out, and shutters with chipping paint all dangerously seeded with nails, points upwards. Citoyen Paul took her hand, and she lifted her skirts to step up and over.

"Good men," Citoyen Paul told them, and the lads beamed with pride in the light of his praise. "I see no one has to teach you how to pry up the cobbles for defensive missiles."

The mountains of these cubical stones, just hand size, added to the defender side of the barricade. But they also added to Nathalie's realization of just how insignificant the attempt at fortification was. Boys with stones against the Krupp?

"Our fathers and older brothers left for l'Hôtel de Ville earlier," the boys told him.

Their mothers, many of whom had been standing in that line before the greengrocer's since before dawn, saw Nathalie in the march. They decided to end their fruitless wait. Half of them could replace their sons on the barricade, so the boys could go and prove themselves men too. And the other half of the women also joined the march.

"Where do you think you're going?" Citoyen Paul grabbed Nathalie's arm.

"L'Hôtel de Ville, of course," she replied. "I thought I'd walk with the women. There are a number of umbrellas to share among them."

"And I hoped you would stay with me. I was enjoying our conversation."

Nathalie thought back to before they had arrived at the barricade. He had been talking, mostly. He had obviously given votes for women, that notion she'd never imagined, a lot of thought. "Used to be only men with property could vote in France. Now we have universal male suffrage. It's just the next, obvious, step. Women such as yourself have to work, same as men. Deal with the unfair economical system at even more disadvantage. They bear the children and are often left without other help. Surely, for the future of France—"

She had enjoyed the talk, yes. It had invigorated her for this long, cold, wet walk. In fact, it warmed her, almost made her dizzy. She stayed under his umbrella. And so, she was at his side when they faced their next barrier.

・・・

A man moved out from under an overhang where he'd taken shelter and stepped in front of them. Citoyen Paul stopped so abruptly that one of the umbrella tines caught Nathalie on the side of her straw hat.

"Hello, Paul," the man said with a lopsided grin.

Even though the man sharing his umbrella with her urged people to call him Citoyen Paul, the gentlemen in the world who would call him by the single familiar syllable could not possibly fill the fingers of one hand.

And then there was Paul's reply, a single unelaborated name. "Eugène."

"I thought I'd run into you here."

"I did send a message, inviting you to join our march. I'm delighted you've decided—"

"So I did know what route to find you on this morning."

"You won't join us?" Citoyen Paul didn't seem at all surprised.

The man called Eugène hardly gave that the value of the shake of his head. "We should, however, sit down and have a talk, Paul."

"Unlike others, I do not want to abandon my fellow *citoyens* in their hour of need. Eugène."

Nathalie felt the stranger's uncomfortable, appraising glance on her. He said, "Oh, is that what you call her? Fellow *citoyenne?*"

"Excuse me." Nathalie left the shelter of the umbrella in an attempt to go after the other women, fast disappearing down the empty road in the direction of the Jardin de Luxembourg. More cobbles that could be torn up.

Citoyen Paul's hand at Nathalie's waist was suddenly insistent. Was he concerned about her safety in the face of this man? Or about his own? "You should stay," he told her, more the commanding male to her than she'd ever noticed before. "I want you to hear this. You'll learn something."

Eugène grinned. "You'd do well to listen and learn, too, Brother. When you think anyone can teach you anything. But first we should get out of this beastly weather. Not many cafes are open under the present circumstances, but I did scout out La 'Tite Chope, just here. You'll find their luncheon menu—" he searched for the word and found "—diverting."

"First—Citoyenne Nathalie Langlois, I would like to present my brother, Eugène Toussaint."

Although she was clearly lower class, Citoyen Paul had named her first as if she were a lady. A flicker of annoyance registered in Eugène's eyes, so clearly this was a political statement and no slight social slip.

And he was named Toussaint, as Louise had discerned, with all its noble baggage. His brother. How many family names did they share between them? Now that she understood the relationship, she could see the strong resemblance. The men might be looking in a mirror, although one glass—the chipped one—reflected a scruffy, insignia-less military man; and the other—the mirror in a heavy gold frame—reflected the top hat and warm, elegant cape that might have been made in Nathalie's old workshop, worn over a frock coat.

If not for the hat, Eugène was shorter and darker, but otherwise the resemblance was clear.

And the smile—that wry, almost wicked, smile. Monsieur Toussaint tipped rainwater off the brim of his top hat as if he'd turned on a faucet. "Mademoiselle, *enchanté*," he said, again pointedly ignoring the faux pas of introductions.

And that was the first time she'd met the man who would be murdered in the room over her head in 1895.

IX
LA BELLE ÉPOQUE

MADAME TOUSSAINT STRAIGHTENED her dress and bonnet that did not seem the worse for a few hours in La Santé Prison. Thus prepared, she faced the cold darkness of freedom outside the sepia rubble of the massive walls.

"Madame. Madame la Concierge!"

Madame Toussaint flinched as she stepped out into the dark street alone and the heavy metal prison door clanged shut on the unnatural central heating behind her. Someone was calling her, jeering her, cursing her. Someone—not just in the prison; the whole city of Paris, it seemed—thought her guilty. Rumors of her crime hissed before her, even though she'd spent no more than four hours in the cell.

As she adjusted to being outside the cocoon of the prison's echoes, however, another instant allowed her to pinpoint the sound and see that it came from under the dripping awning of the café across the street. À la Bonne Santé—"to good health," like a toast—offered welcoming light and warmth in the damp darkness. The place was named after the prison, which came after the hospital that stood in the same place in the eighteenth century. Famously, the families of just-released prisoners waited here for their loved ones and then, after embraces, sat them down and gave them their first taste of freedom, clinking glasses and wishing "good health."

A figure had been sitting huddled in the corner of the outdoor seating most out of the wind. The shape stood up now and, clumsy with cold, rushed towards her.

"Jeanne-Marie." Madame Toussaint took the girl in her prison-warm arms. Jeanne-Marie was trembling. "Whatever are you doing out here?"

"W . . . waiting for you."

"But *chérie*, they released you hours ago. Why aren't you home, warm in your bed?"

"I went home. I mean, I went to Rue Férou. They were very hesitant to let me in."

"Who's 'they'?" Madame Toussaint asked, although she already had her suspicions.

"Mademoiselle Sylvie, who said she spoke for Madame la Comtesse, although I didn't see the mistress at all. Who could blame her, having just lost her husband in such a horrible way?" Jeanne-Marie began to cry—not for the first time in the last twenty-four hours.

"Come." Madame Toussaint took the girl's arm and pushed her out of the rain and towards the café door. "Let's go inside, have some more tea, maybe a bowl of soup—I remember their onion soup is quite lovely, or it was many years ago—and you can tell me all about it."

Jeanne-Marie held back. "But Madame. How will I pay for it? I just spent my last sou on this tea."

Madame Toussaint glanced over her shoulder. "Never mind. I'll take care of it. And why, for heaven's sake, were you sitting outside?"

"I didn't want to miss you when you came out. If I got too warm, I feared I might fall asleep. Today has made me very, very tired."

"So has it made us all. But *chérie*, you could have no idea that they would let me free. And so soon. You, no question of your innocence. Me? They'd like to keep me until I rot."

"Madame. But why? I know you did nothing wrong."

Madame Toussaint gave the naïve girl a gentle squeeze as she placed the order for another pot of tea and two bowls of soup.

So much that happened in Paris happened in the cafés, but for some reason the weather, her emotions, the death of Monsieur d'Ermenville— they all made her remember that one specific time when she'd first met the murdered man. That café with its siege-starvation menu. With Paul.

The maître d' looked at them askance. He must have heard Jeanne-Marie call Madame Toussaint to her. The "Crime of the Concierge" must be all over the evening papers, hanging on their bamboo rods in the corner for the patrons to peruse. He who had hosted many a liberated felon before now baulked at this one. Nevertheless, he bowed over the napkin folded on his arm, a little worse for the day's wear, and soldiered on.

"Tell me your story first, *chérie*," Madame Toussaint urged. "And then, perhaps, we can get around to mine."

Jeanne-Marie, through fits and starts and sobs and two cups of tea, told how she had hurried back to the sixth arrondissement the moment she had been liberated. "But Mademoiselle Sylvie didn't seem at all glad to see me," she said.

"She wouldn't, would she?"

"'Very well, if you must, come in,' she said."

Taking my job as concierge, Madame Toussaint noted silently.

"I could come in, Mademoiselle Sylvie said, but only if I set to work right away cleaning up . . . cleaning up . . . the bedroom."

"Ah." Madame Toussaint understood by the girl's pale look what there was to clean up in the grand apartment on the first floor.

"Madame, I fainted," the girl admitted with cast-down eyes.

"And who could blame you?" Madame Toussaint took the girl's cold hand in her own and didn't let go until it could wrap around the bowl of soup with its lovely fringe of melted cheese.

The soup was as good as Madame Toussaint remembered it; better, perhaps, because of its taste of freedom and how hungry she was. She tapped on the crust of bread and melted cheese that stuck to her spoon and reached the rich broth and onions below.

"As soon as I came to, Mademoiselle Sylvie called me a drunkard and a thief. I was told I mustn't take up space on the chaise longue anymore. If I couldn't do the work that was asked of me"—including servicing the master, Madame Toussaint thought bitterly—"then I must go. With no reference, only time to get my things."

The things, which did not include the maid's uniform which she would have to buy new at her next position, sat in a bundle, a very small bundle, at the girl's feet.

"Madame." The girl brushed away a tear to keep it from falling into her soup. "I don't know where to go, what to do, all alone in the city. If you hadn't come . . ."

"Yes, what would you have done if they hadn't let me out?" The girl would have to learn to take care of herself, not just follow orders every waking minute, and that would mean starting by thinking this one through.

"Stay here, of course, as I did."

"And when they closed, if they hadn't released me?"

Jeanne-Marie's eyes widened with the horror of it. "I don't know."

"You have no money?" That news made Madame Toussaint hesitate to eat the next spoonful of soup.

The girl shook her head. "I spent the last on the pot of tea you discovered me with, as I said. I had to pay for the uniform. I get . . . got . . . charged room and board. I had saved a little last week and, feeling flush, bought this bonnet. I see now how stupid that was. Most of it I need to send to my parents in Bretagne."

Madame Toussaint nodded her understanding.

"I don't know what to do. I don't have the money to buy a ticket home to Bretagne. What shall I do? Become a homeless clocharde?"

Until this point, they had been keeping their voices hushed enough not to be overheard. The panic in the young woman's "clocharde" spread beyond the circle of their single table. Madame Toussaint might have quieted her by suggesting that sometimes that was the only option. For some people. But she was too interested in the reaction of one of the café's few other patrons that evening to say anything before the girl went on.

"There's the Seine," the young woman said with determined desperation.

"Oh, not that, *chérie*." Too many young women in the impossible circumstances of service—pregnant by their masters, let go through no fault of their own with no reference—too many ended up water-logged, dead in the Seine. "We'll think of something. Together."

"Your loge? The concierge's loge? Is there room for me there?" Jeanne-Marie's tone revealed her hesitation. The idea didn't really appeal to her. Under that roof again? Clearly, she remembered how narrow the space was. She remembered the courtyard wall running with blood.

"I would be happy to make space for you, *chérie*," Madame Toussaint assured her companion, "but if they won't let you in, they're hardly likely to let me return, are they? Not without some serious negotiating. And I don't even get to return for my own little bundle and the few francs I have saved."

"I don't understand why not, Madame. You? How long have you held that job faithfully?"

"Twenty years. More. Which may be part of the problem. I know too much."

"Madame?"

Madame Toussaint changed her tack. "Am I not a worse thief and drunkard than you? They think I let the murderer in."

"Surely not knowingly, Madame. The police let you go as well."

"*Ma petite*, they let me go because they hope I'll lead them to—"

The girl looked all around them. "You're being followed?"

"Hush. Don't give us away. But it was part of the conditions under which I was released so suddenly."

"To whom?" The girl leaned over the narrow table as part of the effort to lower her tone. "To whom do they hope you'll lead them?"

"To someone they suspect more than me."

"Who, Madame? The murderer?"

"No. Just someone—"

"Well, if it will help clear your name, why don't you—?"

"*Chérie*, it's not as easy as that."

"You don't know where he is?"

Madame Toussaint poured herself the last of the tea to cover the fact that she wasn't replying right away. She sipped, even though there was no more than a sip left, before replying. "Someone—some *gentleman*—among the tenants in the building gave the police some information that—"

"That set you free? A blessing on them, I say." Something about a Breton accent made the efficacy of such a blessing seem much more likely.

"Well, I wish he had not."

"Who was it?"

"The police wouldn't tell me. But I have my suspicions."

"Who? No. Let me guess. Let us review all the male tenants of the building."

"This is not the murderer, mind," Madame Toussaint cautioned the younger woman. "Just a list of those who were in the position to see—what I would have preferred to keep secret."

"Understood. That artist on the fifth floor who's asked me to pose for him. I've never liked him. Besides, who has time to sit about not moving for hours on end?"

"You might have time now, now that you've lost your position."

"He makes my flesh creep."

"Well, yes. He is a Prussian trying to paint with the light hand of our impressionists, which seems to be heritably impossible. And far too many nudes." Madame Toussaint remembered the argument and the crying young woman on the stairs. "But I think I know what occupied his mind yesterday evening."

"Another nude?"

"I don't think the person who snitched was he."

"It wouldn't be Lieutenant-colonel Herlemont, would it?"

"No doubt he was safe at home in the bosom of his family."

"Monsieur Cailloux, the piano teacher?"

"That is a possibility. I heard him and Madame Cailloux, however, come in from the Opéra much later than when—when our tattler could have seen the suspicious stranger's entrance."

"Monsieur Cailloux." Jeanne-Marie repeated the name with consideration, but was finding the idea more difficult to swallow.

"We're just thinking about who could have seen the stranger enter now, remember? Not the murderer himself."

"Of course."

"Monsieur Cailloux was teaching the piano to his usual student quite early this morning, completely as if nothing out of the ordinary had happened at all. If it was him, the actual murderer, we'll have to discover a motive. It doesn't seem likely."

"Then who?"

Madame Toussaint remembered the hail, the cigar ash, the petals from the boutonniere, detritus she'd had no time to clean up from the lobby this whole day. "I think it was Monsieur Arnaud."

"Monsieur Arnaud?" the young housemaid repeated. "I cannot believe any ill of him."

"He is a man much taken by outward appearances. But no, I do not think he meant ill. He just had an interest in the truth. Unfortunately for me, it doubles the likelihood that I will not be welcomed the next time I go to Rue Férou."

"But I waited on him often when he came to visit Madame la Comtesse. He was always considerate of me, a poor housemaid, which many were not."

"He visits Monsieur d'Ermenville?"

Madame Toussaint was somewhat taken aback. How could such an acquaintance be news to her, the concierge? But then, once the tenants and their guests had passed the first landing—unless she happened to be on her daily sweep of the stairs, top to bottom—how was she to know what went on between floors?

"No . . ." Jeanne-Marie hesitated mid-thought.

"Jeanne-Marie, tell me more. Monsieur Arnaud visits Monsieur d'Ermenville?"

"Well, I suppose Monsieur le Comte, may he rest in peace, must also have received Monsieur Arnaud. But no. I can't really remember that happening."

"Not Monsieur d'Ermenville?"

"His visits were always much anticipated. By Madame la Comtesse, by Madame Joséphine the cook. And by Mademoiselle Sylvie too. He is everyone's favorite, like my uncle Luc at home . . ."

Madame Toussaint considered the almost comatose "comtesse" she had seen just that morning taking in the news of her husband's death. "Even Madame d'Ermenville, you say? But she isn't well."

"A visit from Monsieur Arnaud is always certain to see her come out of her room, dressed in her most elegant gowns. She has nothing of fashion, nothing that does not require a crinoline, that's how dated she is. And she must have lost ten kilos since her curves filled them out properly. But still, anyone can tell how elegant the gowns were. And her jewelry! You cannot imagine."

In fact, Madame Toussaint could imagine. She had seen Madame d'Ermenville in full array on any number of occasions but not for ten years or more. It was remarkable, but Jeanne-Marie had no reason to lie about such a thing. The girl hadn't a modicum of guile about her. She was still too young in the ways of the world.

"No." The guilelessness sprang to the fore once more. "I cannot believe any ill of Monsieur Arnaud."

"Of course not," Madame Toussaint agreed. "He spoke the complete truth to the gendarmes. I would only be happier were that truth not quite so . . . so inconvenient for me."

"And for this they're having you tailed?" The girl's voice regained some of its youthfulness, the excitement of being the hunter instead of the hunted. You would think she'd had enough of that for one day. Youth.

"I know it. Don't turn to look now, but the man in the top hat who entered just shortly after us, who sits now nursing a glass of Merlot. He is dressed as a civilian but has gendarme written all over him. When we get up, he'll pay his tab and follow right behind."

"Are you going to try to shake him?"

"Do keep your voice down, *chérie*," Madame Toussaint cautioned.

"Oh, of course." Jeanne-Marie flushed at her mistake.

"I now have a plan where we must go. For tonight."

"Where?"

"It will be just the sort of place our tracker will expect us to bed down. But first—" Mustering as much dignity as she could, Madame Toussaint rose from the table and crossed to the gendarme in the top hat, whom she caught just as he was downing the end of his Merlot in a gulp.

"Excuse me, Monsieur," she addressed him.

"Yes, yes, Madame?" he sputtered.

"I must prevail upon your gallantry tonight."

"Yes?"

"My companion and I do not have a sou between us, and if you do not pay for us, the maître d' will be obliged to call on you to arrest us and take us straight back across the street. And you wouldn't want that, would you?"

"I think I would—"

"No, you wouldn't," she assured him. "If we are rearrested, we cannot lead you to the man you're interested in. You will have failed in your job." The gendarme shifted uncomfortably in his disguise. He let that idea sink in and then decided he had no choice.

"The omnibus fare to Montmartre for the both of us," Madame Toussaint said when she knew she had him. "And leave the waiter a nice *pourboire* so he can finish off that bottle of Merlot you had him open."

Madame Toussaint gathered her things. "Come, Jeanne-Marie. We've a long way to go. If we get a good start, we may well shake him while he counts out his coins."

· X ·
THE TERRIBLE YEAR
—

> Siege Bread
>
> ❊
>
> Horse Soup
>
> ❊
>
> Salad of Fresh Dandelion
> from le Jardin du Luxembourg
> with its Vinaigrette
>
> ❊
>
> Dog Cutlets–aux Petits Pois
> Ragout of Cat–à la Parisienne
> Donkey–à la sauce Soubise
> Fricassee of Rats and Mice–
> à la Chinoise
> Fillet of Mule–à la Portugaise
> Roast Ostrich–à l'Allemagne

THE BLACKBOARD WITH the luncheon menu for La 'Tite Chope that Monday, All Saints' Eve of 1870, stood propped up in the window.

"That Soubise will be heavy on the onions, and most of them sprouted, you may be sure," Eugène Toussaint commented, hanging up his cape and hat on the hook, indicating a long stay.

"I wonder how you tell mule from donkey," he mused. "I mean, on the palette, not on the hoof."

"I wonder that our host dares to offer anything named for the Germans on a day like today." His brother Paul finally joined in the commentary as they might have done with every meal they'd eaten together since childhood. And they are allowing me to hear this. Nathalie felt the honor.

"Wouldn't it be more patriotic to call it 'à l'Alsacienne'?" Paul continued.

"Well, we may lay everything on this menu to the presence of the Prussian Germans, no?" his brother replied. This gallows humor was everywhere in the siege. "Whether or not there is sauerkraut, whether or not beer is used to cover what might be off."

"And the frites. Don't forget the frites. Frites with everything—until we run out of potatoes."

"At the Gare d'Orléans last night, we had what was billed as fish and chips à l'Anglaise. They were well-used deep-fat fried potatoes cut in the usual strips beside potatoes cut the size of cod filets, dipped in water batter, also deep-fat fried."

"Where did they get ostrich during a siege?" Nathalie asked, remembering last night's meal, which had been her most recent, but looking forward to this next one.

"Ah, a woman interested in provenance and terroir. Very chic." Nathalie felt Eugène's sharp bite. Directed at her, it felt no less painful than when he took jabs at Paul.

"As who is not when you can stand in line all day and still not be sure where your next meal is coming from?" She thought Citoyen Paul might be trying to defend her from his brother's sharpness. Did they call that siege gallantry?

"The ostrich—that must come from the zoo," Eugène told her. "They had a nesting pair before, which women were always after for the feathers for their hats. They intend to kill the elephant early next week, and I mean to get a large steak, no matter the cost."

Nathalie could not suppress a groan of horror. At the same time, how often had she and her friends exclaimed to one another over their needles, "I'm so hungry, I could eat an elephant"?

"It's much better than letting the animals starve to death, isn't it, Mademoiselle? When all the fodder has gone to the army's horses."

She had to agree that was probably true. She looked at Paul and knew the workshop at the Gare d'Orléans would not be standing in line for such pricey foodstuffs.

The host came, napkin over his arm, and had no shortage of wine to pair with anything their choice might be, even in the midst of the siege. "Besides, it keeps you warm." First, he demanded that each of them speak ("Can't have Prussian spies in here"), then left them to start pouring the best Eugène insisted on buying.

Around them, chairs were piled on tables, having been brought in as the weather changed and for ease of mopping the floor. This left room for only two tables, but nobody else was in the establishment, perhaps hadn't been for a week. The handwritten menu on the chalkboard seemed by the smudges to be at least that old.

"I hope you're paying for this, brother," Citoyen Paul said. "When they don't show the prices, they may be flexible. And if you have to ask, you can't afford it."

"Yes, you inherited the title." Eugène's bitterness was palpable.

Nathalie looked at Citoyen Paul. Is this what he wanted her to learn? Not only was he a colonel. Louise was right. He was a comte. Le Comte d'Ermenville—if there still was such a thing—had shared his umbrella with her this morning.

Only, "There is no such thing as the Count d'Ermenville in France anymore," Citoyen Paul reminded them all.

"The rest of us have to work for a living," Eugène added, ignoring what his brother had just said.

"Getting huge loans from the banks on that anachronistic title—on my name—gouging architects and contractors to knock down slums, investing in these new haussmannian buildings and then sending someone else to strong-arm astronomical rents out of hapless tenants," his brother countered. "I don't call that exactly working for a living."

"It'll pay for your lunch. Buying an officer's commission in a losing army when you could have just been a comte and sat around all day on the country estate away from all of this—that will not."

They considered the ostrich, but then the host came out and rubbed that line of the menu out with his sleeve. "Too old," he said. "It gave us all the runs last night. We fed it to the dog. Who is now the fresh cutlets. They're very lean, those cutlets." As if that were a recommendation, in lean times.

Nathalie followed the Toussaint brothers' lead—she had been advised to do that should she ever share a table with her betters. They ordered the soup. Horse meat? That hadn't been uncommon in Paris before the siege, *chevalin* butchers displaying brightly painted carvings that might have come off carousels over their doors. The Army of the Rhine had just survived ten days on it. Dead horses used to be a common enough sight in the streets until the carters came. Nathalie wondered if this beast had pulled an ambulance or a hearse until moments before sinking to his knees in the traces. Snails, frog's legs, cracking open the bones for the rich marrow roasted with fleur de sel, these were other starvation rations.

The soup was warm, rich with garlic and turnips, and the bread was somewhat better than they knew at the workshop. Waves of chill had begun to possess Nathalie's whole body, sitting in wet clothes in the café; the stove stoked to warm the soup was the only heat source.

"Can we get back around to the topic of the rents on my apartments?" Eugène Toussaint asked after they'd ordered a second bowl each.

"If we must." The bread in Citoyen Paul's hands crumbled instead of breaking as bread usually does. It was of such a texture, siege bread.

"As you must know, the government has passed certain outlandish laws—"

"In case you haven't noticed, we are under siege." Citoyen Paul bit the words then bit the bread. "Certain measures are the only way to insure fairness."

"How is it fair that I may not oust a tenant who refuses to pay?"

"Really, Eugène. People are starving. Winter is coming on. They must have a roof over their heads."

"Until Prussian shells come to blow all our work away. Paul, I don't care how much your heart bleeds. May I just beg you not to use your influence, which is not meagre—admit it, Comte or not-Comte—to keep old Thiers from negotiating a surrender. A surrender, please. So life can get back to normal."

"How will it be normal with Prussians marching down the Champs-Élysées?"

"Don't thwart old man Thiers as he tries to get us the best deal we can. I don't need to tell you that the other building owners in my street and I spend most of our time trying to gauge trajectories from the Prussian lines to our particular houses. And we place bets."

"I'd like to ask, how is it normal if you and your banker pals go back to eating up the living of hard-working men and women, siege or no siege?"

"So now we come down to it, don't we? Mademoiselle, this man you've hooked up with—I hate to break it to you, but he's a communist. Unapologetic. The communist comte. How's that for an oxymoron? Red as blood. Red as horse meat."

"That is the hardest thing about the siege: men like me forced to be cooped up in Paris with men like my brother," Paul grumbled. "The Prussians could just leave us alone to kill each other."

Eugène took another swig of wine and chuckled amicably at the threat.

Paul turned to Nathalie now too, as if she were Blind Justice, to weigh the scales between them. "Citoyenne Nathalie, if you had heard Comrade Karl Marx speak at the First International in Geneva where working men from Italy, England, and France came together to stand against the exploitation of their labor, you would—"

"Now who is speaking of making alliances with Germans? Karl Marx, indeed. And a Jew to boot."

"Who should know more about oppression than a Jew?"

"Who should know more about international cabal? A Jew who married a woman of the nobility and so brought her to ruin. Just mentioning that as a warning, since there is a comte at our table." He looked hard at Nathalie. "And a gullible young lady."

Nathalie did think a trip to Geneva must be beyond most working people she knew. But then, it was good that they had comtes who could make the trip for them.

"When you and bankers make deals across national boundaries, so must the working people." Paul's best defense was hard ideology. "Labor unions must grow and evolve. If the working people—and the grunt soldiers—do not shake hands with their fellows across national borders, do not form one great union, their jobs will simply move in the hands of the capitalists from one country to the next. Thiers' hand in Bismarck's as they stand for the photographer does not bode well for the small artisan."

"Speaking of the small artisan, that's another emergency law the sooner ended the better. You cannot keep things in a pawn shop during the day? I own a pawn shop over in the tenth arrondissement, Mademoiselle."

Citoyen Paul replied, "Most of the things in that window of yours are tools small artisans have had to hawk to put food on their tables during the siege. They need the tools during the day to undertake what labor they can. Citoyenne Nathalie, your family are farmers."

It was as if the Mademoiselle and the citoyenne were trying to tear her apart. As if horse flesh were not enough, they had to have hers.

Citoyen Paul went on. "The Revolution in 1789 gave the land farmers work into their hands, taking it from the unjust feudal lords. Taking the means of production—his saw, his awl, his hammer—from the laborer in the city is a modern sort of feudalism." Nathalie thought possessively of her own small, all-important tools: her grandmother's thimble, her needle.

Citoyen Paul's focus riveted back onto his brother as if he had been a sharpshooter in the army. "Not to mention taking the house over his head and charging for that, so the next generation of feudal serfs grows up also enslaved. Another revolution is called for. The bourgeoisie have lost the moral capacity to rule. They have forgotten liberty, equality, fraternity."

She should say something. She should speak to this uneasy fraternity so unlike that evoked by the revolutionary slogan. Maybe that's why the term came last, because it was so difficult to achieve. They both wanted her to say something. She'd never been with men who wanted her to speak before. Usually, a man wanted her only to be. And look pretty. And prepare his meal and darn his socks as well.

One of these men before her even wanted her to vote. She had nothing to say. But she also noticed that Eugène Toussaint's wife was not invited to something so unladylike as this meeting. Eugène Toussaint must certainly think Citoyenne Nathalie Langlois a hellion.

A third bowl of soup each was called for, but Nathalie found she couldn't take more than the first two very hot sips. Her stomach must have shrunk over the past months. She offered the bowl to Citoyen Paul, who continued to urge her with spoonfuls like a picky child, but who also soon polished it off on his own.

The host had new-crop apples for dessert, no cheese. "They're nice," he agreed. "But this'll be the last crop. The apple-wood's in the stove, heating the soup."

"Thanks for lunch, Eugène," Citoyen Paul said as he opened the umbrella under the café's overhang once more.

"I haven't changed your pig-headed mind, have I?" his brother said with a sigh. "Nor yours, young lady? He will lead you down a primrose path, that one will. Don't tell me I never warned you."

"Come, Citoyenne. We're late to l'Hôtel de Ville. A quick walk will keep you warm."

City Hall wasn't only where the protests would be. Nobody thought to mention what was perhaps just a slip of the tongue. And probably only Nathalie's mind went that way. Since the first Revolution, it was where marriages were required to be performed as well.

XI
LA BELLE ÉPOQUE

AFTER MIDNIGHT ON a weeknight, the audience at the Moulin Rouge—like their final drinks—was only a dribble at the bottom of the hall. The tobacco smoke, however, might have collected from the day the cabaret first opened five years previous. From where Madame Toussaint and Jeanne-Marie sat just under the rafters at the top of the hall, it seemed the spotlights cut it like a dense almond cake.

A shiver from outside's cold night air touched Madame Toussaint even in the overheated room. The siege of 1870 had been the world's first use of electric search lights, playing on the notion that technology might save the canny inventors from Prussian shells. In the end, twenty-five years later, this is what the technology went for, and it hardly seemed like salvation.

A rough and ribald slither of cat gut violin strings announced the number—Offenbach's rowdy gallop. Then the brass and percussion took up the tune at full voice, fast and heavy on the rhythm, including bells.

The girls bloomed out of a froth of petticoats in patriotic blue, white, and red—then up went the skirts and the many legs bent, swung, kicked—bent, swung, and kicked—as though with the single controlling mind of a centipede. Black silk stockings gartered to midthigh left a good hand's width of bare flesh before the brief pantalets began.

French tricolor flags twirled overhead. The rosettes the dancers wore on perky liberty caps and on their otherwise flimsily covered breasts were exact copies of the emblems Madame Toussaint remembered creating from the bureaucratic red tape in l'Hôtel de Ville on that wet and crazy night she was married. Marianne, the goddess of reason and liberty, spirit of the Revolution, reduced to a dance hall.

Parallel rows of perfectly timed cartwheels opened a path for Coco Toes-in-the-Air to come down center stage. Madame Toussaint hardly recognized the woman who lived as a sober tenant on the fifth floor of the building on the Rue Férou, much less the girl she'd met sewing balloons on the trestle tables twenty-five years before. Blood-red lips, a post-coital glow on her cheeks. But there was no doubt who she was: "Co" had been painted on the bottom of each of her high-buttoned boots. Her kicks reached above the heads of her chorus, and every kick proclaimed her name: *Co-co-co-co-co.*

The chorus followed her up into the audience. None of Paris's great luminaries were there to admire them, not on a weekday night: neither the diminutive form of Toulouse-Lautrec nor Degas, stale from his young ballet dancers. And the celebrated La Goulue, who spun like a star on the skating rink when she danced, did not take over the stage that night. Spectators who claimed artistic interest had left before Jeanne-Marie and Madame Toussaint arrived, after the infamous Cleopatra number. That racy exhibition had caused a scandal when it first claimed the stage. Now, people said, night after night, the girls struggled not to look completely bored, which bored the audience, even when the famous Egyptian queen entered wearing nothing but the snake. Her ladies wore high headdresses and glittering beads—and below that, nothing at all. Feeling protective of the young housemaid from the countryside, Madame Toussaint was glad they'd missed that low-brow version of l'Opéra's *Aida*.

But some of the patrons—those who held their liquor better than those now slumped over electric green pools of spilled absinthe—got up on unsteady feet to dance along with *le cancan*. These men wore full evening dress and top hats, tight trousers and tight pointed shoes, many with the angular visages of addicts. Their clumsy, awkward movements cut a sharp contrast to the women's open flamboyance and precision. If the men were to tear off their coattails and starched collars, and untuck their shirts, Madame Toussaint imagined Jeanne-Marie's reaction beside her would be whatever the Breton version of "*mère de dieu*" might be.

From the midst of skirts flung over heads came flirtatious taunts, impossible to say from which pair of legs. The taunts increased when, besides kicking and twirling, the women had to hold an adventurous drunk upright. One man managed to set his top hat suggestively on Coco's toe, where she spun it through seven measures. Another man prodded skirts with his cane.

Having worked their way back onto the stage once more, the dancers fell like dominoes into the splits in the grand finale, then the lights went dead with a hiss. The illusion snapped. The world of absinthe headaches and a shortage of cash to pay *l'addition* returned.

Madame Toussaint kept a close eye on their police tail. Far from his usual beat, he had been stopped at the stage door when Madame Toussaint's message to the fifth-floor tenant had given them free entry. The man sat rigidly uncomfortable now—having had to pay full price at the *caisse* for the final number alone—drinking another Merlot, his scowl on them. Again, when the stage lights went down, two very large bouncers denied him entry backstage. His protest that he was police carried no weight with them, less than had he simply been an admirer. That was the last Madame Toussaint saw or heard of him that night.

Backstage, the young dancers who had managed to get further engagement for that night hurried off to meet their johns at the stage door and to haul them on staggering feet back to whatever room they rented by the half hour. Those who had failed jostled in front of the mirrors to wipe off makeup and yawn "*tant pis*" at each other.

Coco settled her toes back on the ground, transformed herself back into Madame Pépin from the fifth floor, and welcomed Madame Toussaint and Jeanne-Marie to the greasy, floral, sickly-perfumed space backstage.

"Did you like the show?" The performer anxious for praise lingered in the somber, tight-laced, black bodice and small, hen-feathered hat. A half-veil's netting that concealed her eyes had replaced the flamboyant blue, white, and red ostrich plumes.

Jeanne-Marie gushed to the level Coco craved. "Madame, you were wonderful."

Coco gave the young woman the once over. "Pretty enough," was her appraisal. "But unless you've been turning cartwheels for pleasure since you were three—*Non?*"

Jeanne-Marie shook her head sadly. "*Maman* did not think it was ladylike."

Coco laughed out loud and lit a cigarette. "Well, *maman* was right, *chérie*. It's not. Ladylike."

Madame Toussaint broke in to explain their situation—murder, prison, eviction, police tail and all. "Can you help us? Just for tonight?"

Coco was instantly back as Madame Pépin, the cigarette extinguished. She didn't, however, immediately address that night's pressing needs. Jeanne-Marie's future was still uppermost on her mind. "Don't be too downcast. In this line of work, you've still got to turn tricks after hours to make a living."

She used the phrase "*gagner la vie,*" that strange expression that meant "win life," literally. As if, Madame Toussaint thought, victory—life—could only go to a very few. The desire, the acceptance not to compete put you among the vast majority: losers. In Madame Toussaint's view, Jeanne-Marie had had the same need to perform duties for Monsieur d'Ermenville outside the supposedly respectable job of maid—and no extra compensation. A flush on the girl's face indicated that she felt the same way.

"The only secure move is to get a *régulier,*" Madame Pépin observed, "who'll set you up on the fifth floor of a building on the Rue Férou. And then he's likely—as mine did—to up and have a stroke around Christmastime."

"Oh, Madame," Madame Toussaint exclaimed, giving Coco the respectability their present relationship invited. "Is that what happened to Monsieur Pépin? I knew I hadn't seen him in a while. He used to bring the rent to my loge himself, when he came to visit you, Madame. This month's came by courier. I wondered why."

"Well, now you know. And one day soon you'll take to calling me Coco again. He cannot make it up to the fifth floor in any case."

"Will he recover?"

"Who can say? The doctors do not give it much hope. Some month soon, you won't even see a courier for fifth-floor-left. Which is why it is good for a woman to always keep her toe in the business." Madame Pépin gently stroked the high-buttoned boots left carefully on the shelf over the makeup table, now with its surrounding bulbs turned off. You couldn't see the painted "Co-co" now, but everyone knew it was there.

"A girl should never let herself get too comfortable, no matter whose mistress she becomes," Madame Pépin went on.

Madame Toussaint, considering her present situation, knew that was good advice, but sometimes you couldn't do anything about it.

"When the rent doesn't come," Madame Pépin said, "the real Madame Pépin and the bevy of daughters she needs to marry respectably will turn me out. Probably the young ladies will move into the apartment one by one like clockwork as they start out married life."

Madame Toussaint made calculations as to how this would change her life as concierge. She would miss her friend, certainly. Only someone who'd been at the Gare d'Orléans knew what that had been like. But of course, it wasn't altogether a given that the loge would be hers to return to when this was over.

"That's why I keep my room here in the boarding house on Montmartre," Coco continued, "although, yes, I let it out to friends by the half hour. Now, with these dreadful happenings in the Rue Férou, I won't go back to that room where most of my nice things are. Not for a day or two, that's certain."

Madame Toussaint thought of the room she'd left in this same neighborhood twenty-five years ago. The landlady had promised to keep it. Madame Toussaint doubted that even the building was still standing.

"When that day comes," Madame Pépin concluded without futile tears, "you'll see me take up a place sitting in the public space of one of those seamstress shops like where we used to work, Nathalie, before . . . before the Terrible Year."

Madame Toussaint had to embrace her old friend, just for saying the long-dead name, Nathalie. "You mean you'll go back to seamstress?"

"Not at all. Most of those shops do only the simplest alterations and repairs now, if anything. All just cover. They're all fronts to keep the girls from police scrutiny."

Madame Toussaint spared a thought for the police tail to whom she and Jeanne-Marie had given the slip.

Madame Pépin went on. "Men tell their friends. You go in and the woman behind the desk—at my age, that would be me—brings out her book and keeps the ledger. 'Taking in seams, two francs.' That might be the girl named Rayon d'Or at two o'clock. 'Adding a gusset': Mademoiselle Ripe Cheese at nine. I cannot compete at the other exercise that happens behind the counter in what used to be workshops. Not anymore."

"But Coco, dear." The old name came back like a sweet to Madame Toussaint's tongue. "I saw you kick over your head not twenty minutes ago. You're very fit."

"Yes. No doubt I'll be able to kick my toes in the air when I'm ninety. It's the rest of the body that hasn't held up quite so well. I could never appear in the Cleopatra number, for example. That naked scrutiny? The old girls simply must have a corset these days, spangle it as you wish." Madame Pépin smoothed the somber black bombazine now cinching her already tiny waist before it ballooned into the derrière bustle and flat-fronted skirt. Then she sighed. Madame Toussaint joined her, remembering the glory days when neither really needed a corset. When they both thought their needles worked to save France.

"But look," Madame Pépin said. "Our reminiscences have put the little one to sleep."

It was true. Jeanne-Marie had fallen asleep curled up on a worn love seat.

"The poor thing." Madame Toussaint found a cape and threw it over the girl. "Waking up to the dead Comte this morning, dealing with the police, time in le Prison de La Santé . . ."

"They took you there? Truly?"

Madame Toussaint nodded, suddenly as weary as Jeanne-Marie.

"Well, you do look a little worse for wear yourself, my dear. And the little thing has fallen asleep just where I was going to suggest she do so. You see?" Madame Pépin gestured to the cramped space around them. "This is all I can offer. It does have the advantage of being the warmest room in the building once the spotlights dim."

"I must thank you again, Coco."

"Not at all. Dancers crash here all the time when they're hiding out, escaping abusive *réguliers*. When they've been evicted. When they've received a bill of bad health from the police inspection, and a womb veil—*une cape cervicale*—won't cover it, so they're out of work for a while. Any number of reasons. The management doesn't mind if the stay is limited. They'll mind even less if you take a needle to some of those costumes in that basket over there. A torn flounce on the skirt—that can be deadly if a boot heel gets caught in it.

"I know we have a lot more to talk about. But not tonight. Meet you tomorrow at the café across the square. All the girls go there for breakfast—great omelets—but no earlier than noon."

Madame Pépin bade them goodnight. Madame Toussaint loosened her corset for comfort and found her bed on a chaise longue canopied by a row of can-can skirts. One of the dancers had claimed the spot earlier to cold-pack a twisted ankle, and there was a damp patch.

Madame Toussaint had more pressing things to worry about than a little dampness. Concern about Paul and the chances that he would be found and accused of the murder with no proof of innocence took precedence. Secondarily, she was concerned about who had committed the crime; she played various possible scenarios over in her mind. She was also concerned about where she would live now, if none of the options she had come up with played out favorably. What would she do? She had not planned her options to life on the Rue Férou as well as Coco had.

Exhausted as she was, she might still have slept through them all had she not found feathers tickling her nose in the dark. She assumed they were strays from the feather boas, for what act she could only imagine. She had seen a full chorus line of them—pink—against the far wall. The persistent tickling made her get up, fumble for the light cord and investigate, however.

In a terrarium just at the foot of her bed resided what she at first took to be a leather handbag or pair of high boots. She couldn't stifle a little cry when she realized it was Cleopatra's boa constrictor, as thick around as Madame Toussaint's own thigh, slithering against the glass and prodding the air with his tongue. Cleopatra, she had heard, carried him in the famous number, laying the thick body over her shoulder to plant kisses on the lance-point head. The tail she curled strategically between her legs so she could execute that move—squat in heels, flash knees apart and together—without complete exposure.

The serpent had just finished a meal of a live pullet. Hence the stray feathers blowing across the chaise longue, and Madame Toussaint's disturbed sleep. As she dreamed about homing pigeons in Prussian meat pies . . .

· XII ·
THE TERRIBLE YEAR
—

THE CLOSER THE marchers got to l'Hôtel de Ville of Paris under siege, the more citizens in trousers with Revolutionary red stripes they saw putting up their shutters. As they walked, Nathalie found her tongue loosened by the soup, the wine, and the conversation she'd heard between the brothers. She discovered Citoyen Paul more on her side, the support of her trust in him more solid than ever. His vision was a ray of hope out of the darkness of the siege.

"And what of education in your vision?" she asked, thinking of her own in the little country school: Sister Filomena with her slashing ruler. And the priest. From the time she first came with her hair in pigtails, a girl was told in hushed whispers to avoid his office alone at any cost.

No wonder, she thought, I left school early and decided to seek my fortune with my needle in Paris. Tales of the depths to which a woman can fall here, where she's anonymous, seemed pale in comparison. Even though I enjoyed books. And numbers.

"For girls as well as boys, that goes without saying," he replied. "And the Church should get out of education. How can we form a true secular state if the catechism is more important than physics for young minds?" Again, he put words to her thoughts exactly.

"And what about the raising of children?" she asked. "I have seen them begging on the streets—in their mothers' arms, as toddlers."

"The National Guard," by which he meant an organization including all the little volunteer militias that had sprung up in the various quartiers in

Paris, "has passed measures to see that a soldier's wife receives half his pay. This includes those with children born out of wedlock."

"Out of wedlock?"

"It's a beginning. What good does it do society to lose a single mind or pair of hands because of what parents have done or failed to do?"

Over the Pont d'Arcole, l'Hôtel de Ville came into view now: four long ranks of large windows drawn with Renaissance precision along one side of a large square. This square had once been a strand for unloading goods from the river to the city, then gave its name to strikers. And it was an execution square.

The rain began to fall heavier. Although it was still midafternoon, most of the light came from the building and hardly at all from the crowd's torches that were difficult to keep burning in the wet. The walls surrounding the glowing windows—that Paris stone, *calcaire lutécien*, encrusted with wood soot—seemed no longer daunting and judgmental, but as ethereal as mist over the hardness of her shadowed, angry, chanting citizens.

Again, the very façade made Nathalie think of marriage.

Absurd. Much more important things were afoot here.

Still, she knew she had to ask quickly. "And what of marriage, Citoyen Paul? What is your vision for marriage?"

"If society provides for the children, what is the institution but a means for a man to treat a woman as the capitalist uses the worker in his factory, to make profit off her unpaid labor? The wage that by capital's unwritten laws can never equal a half of what the capitalist will get for the product. In the kitchen, in the laundry, in the bedroom. His unpaid nurse when he is ill, his—"

Again, her deepest feelings found spoken word. "Yes, yes. But—"

Her next question never took breath.

"It's Citoyen Paul." Someone saw them under the umbrella as they reached the first torchlight and called out the news.

"Citoyen Paul, at last!" called another.

Drums and trumpets stormed a fanfare. The chants carried them forward like waves, each group—workers of the same métier, neighborhood, club—had their own hymn, voicing what was most important to them.

"Vive la France."

"Liberty, equality, fraternity."

"Vive la République."

"Death to the Prussian lapdogs."

A row of soldiers saluted, their muskets butt up, the traditional sign that they were siding with the mob. "Send this man forward. To the steps."

Citoyen Paul grabbed her hand; his had been only centimeters from hers ever since La 'Tite Chope. He pulled her along with him as the crowd hustled him to its head.

"They've taken the building." News ushered them along with the chants.

"Unopposed."

"The Commune holds l'Hôtel de Ville."

"Welcome, Citoyen Paul."

"Only we're the Commune now. New terms for old the bourgeoisie have coopted. Welcome, Communard."

They even had a nod for Nathalie. "Communarde."

And Nathalie found herself among the men with names she'd only ever heard of or seen as political cartoons in the papers during the last spate of anarchist and communist trials: Blanqui, Mayor Clémenceau of Montmartre, Félix Pyat. Gustave Flourens, son of an enemy of the theories of Darwin and the pioneer of anesthesia, brought his own more radical theories of who were the fittest and destined to survive. He prepared to defend them with a magnificent Turkish scimitar.

・・・

A thorough search of l'Hôtel de Ville found no trace of President Thiers or any of his government. "We've found a secret escape passage in the cellars," one man announced to Paul and Nathalie, still hand in hand.

"It leads to National Army barracks manned by Bretons," said another.

"We can't hope to take a barracks," said a third.

"The good news is that the Bretons haven't come the other way."

"The bad news is that Thiers is halfway to Versailles and the arms of Bismarck by now," Paul muttered in deep disappointment.

The question of what to do next, even now that they held the empty hull of l'Hôtel de Ville, stymied the communards. Nathalie followed Paul around, disconcertingly aimless, from room to lavishly appointed room.

A few stray clerks and officers of the provisional government were held prisoner in a side chamber, but clearly, they were as much victims as any of the protesting citizens and would be freed before the night was over.

Félix Pyat—sixty years old with a romantic mane and beard, radical journalist and dramatist—made the council table his stage by kicking aside the inkwells. He expounded on the need to form a Committee of Public Safety to anyone who would listen, tearing up the green baize of the tabletop with the spurs he had taken from a theatre's costume shop for part of tonight's militant garb. Communards found government officials' stashes of liquor and didn't leave them alone.

Each room of l'Hôtel de Ville harbored its own government, complete with its orators, its bureaucrats, its sycophants, its workers. Each roomed faction had men ready to act as messengers to the crowd below and sitting in the windowsills with their legs dangling outside. This room demanded papers with a blue stamp for entry, this one black. Some had already reached the constitutional level of fisticuffs.

"A siege within a siege. Let them exercise their voices, their imaginations," Citoyen Paul told her, burning with his own idealism. "The best ideas on the tongues of the best men will find their way to the top." Although any sort of dialogue must be difficult with participants constantly drumming the rolling snare beat of the rappel that sent chills of the Revolution's Terror down Nathalie's spine; others blew on trumpets.

Old Louis Auguste Blanqui was not recognized in his grey beard, because the last time he had led a protest was while brunette. Unruly elements mistook the man's reverend demeanor for one of the vanished bureaucrats and roughed him up. He had to be rescued from the corner where he'd passed out.

The kitchen had been raided first of all and was now picked bare by hungry Parisians.

A plan of Paris with its new, broad boulevards cutting though old neighborhoods and the homes of the poor had been torn to pieces in a fury and left to filter down a staircase. The lingering smell of pipes and cigars, expected in rooms where men made deals all day, contended with the newly arrived aroma of wet dogs only partially washed by the rain.

And then Nathalie peeked around a door and, Paul in tow, found the records room, its inkwells, its quills and sloped writing desks. Some of the more literate revolutionaries were already there.

A list of those in arrears of taxes? Well, how else were they to heat the room if not by throwing that in the grate? A list of those under surveillance for unpatriotic thought and activity? Cross out your own name and put in Thiers' instead.

Paul chuckled at the antics of his fellows but then, always practical, found a clean sheet of paper and began, with the advice of others at his elbow, to form a list of those who should stand for the new government to replace the cowards who had fled.

"The usual offenders," he suggested.

Pyat, Louis Blanc. Victor Hugo's name went down—the author who'd just returned to Paris in time for the siege, having spent most of the emperor's rule in exile in the Channel Islands. *Les Misérables, The Hunchback of Notre Dame*, radical works when you read them closely. Henri de Rochefort, another revolutionary with aristocratic ties, just released from prison by the mob, pale and emaciated from his sojourn there but invigorated by the first taste of freedom. Some trial lists were thrown out of windows into the crowd waiting in the rain—stovepipe hats like a smoking factory of democracy, domed with umbrellas—waiting in the rain. Cheers or boos gave an idea of the possibility of success of this slate or that.

Then Paul Toussaint's name went down.

Nathalie shivered as Paul's steady hand swung up to form the final t. He offered his own name on the altar. A ghost of premonition passed close behind her. Easy as it was to form such a theoretical list, it would be just as easy for another hand to exchange this list for the most wanted.

Bundles of records in a full wall of cubby holes were tied together with red tape. "The proverbial red tape," its discoverer sang. "Let's cut it now."

Another man got hold of some of the flying ribbon and looped it into a cockade on his left breast. "There," he said. "Don't members of the Assembly wear such ribbons? So the proletariat, if they ever get within twenty meters of them, may fall on their knees before them and beg for justice? Now I am one of the Assembly. I demand justice."

Another got into the game. "Yes, and I have always wondered why we bother with these representatives who are backed by big money, who say one thing when they seek your vote and quite another when they get in the chamber with their cronies."

"One man, one vote. On everything in the Commune."

"Vive la France!"

"Vive la Commune!"

Nathalie set to work with scissors to cut lengths. Soon all the men in the records room were wearing ribbon, and the idea was spreading throughout the building beyond and into the street. Any red fabric, anything to pin it with, that's all it took. You, too, could be—should be—an assemblyman.

Paul helped her fasten an extra-long length like a corsage on her own lapel using the pin from her straw hat. When she looked at him, he said, "You work, you fight. You vote." The words made her tingle like a lover's sweet nothings. But that telltale list of prominent communards with Paul's name on it. Sweet nothings did not obliterate that truth.

Later they found the great leather-bound book nearly half as tall as Nathalie herself that held the marriage records. "Here. Let me at that," said one man whistling through a rotted tooth. "I'd like to cross my name out, ever since that woman of mine ran off with that damned artillery sergeant. And who can afford a divorce?" The quill tip snagged; ink splattered viciously, satisfyingly.

Then Paul got control of the book. He flipped back to the next open line. He dipped a pen and signed his name in the spot for the groom. Then he redipped and thrust the quill in Nathalie's direction. She hesitated.

"Go on," Paul urged with a gentle smile. "On the line for the bride. You can write your own name, can't you?" The feather seemed to fly to her hand, lighter than air.

"Now, who's to tell us whether we can marry or not?" he persisted. "My brother Eugène? The Church? A corrupt, treacherous bureaucracy?" Those eyes. She couldn't resist the fire in those eyes. She signed. And dated, November 1, 1870. Since it was already after midnight. All Saints' Day. Toussaint.

Witnesses waving pilfered wine bottles lined up to sign their names too, and then toasted. "Long life to the first couple of the Commune, Nathalie and Paul."

"Vive la Commune."

"Vive le Comte and la Comtesse."

"Vive Madame Toussaint."

"Vive la Commune."

Paul had signed both, the list of communards and the marriage. Were they both jokes? Would either have any lasting impact at all? Pilfered champagne bubbles filled Nathalie's nose and made her sneeze. And when Paul bent to kiss her, she shivered violently.

XIII
LA BELLE ÉPOQUE

"By daylight, I see that Montmartre is much changed since I was last here," Madame Toussaint told Madame Pépin when she and Jeanne-Marie arrived at the café across the square around noon.

"You mean when the whores used to ride around the neighborhood to their appointments on donkeys?" Madame Pépin, still in her sober black, rose from a cramped corner table where she'd saved the last two empty chairs in the establishment and bussed both of them on each cheek.

"I would, in fact, have it no other way." To Jeanne-Marie's questioning look, Madame Toussaint added the palliative, "It would bring back too many sorry memories."

"Is that your *flic*?" When they had settled, Madame Pépin nodded through the fogged front window toward the figure of a man in a faded blue workman or artist's smock leaning against the stone wall opposite.

"He followed us from the stage door to here," Madame Toussaint confirmed. "He must be the replacement for the fellow in evening tails from last night."

"I wonder how many illegal advances that gendarme in tails had to fend off last night." Madame Pépin chuckled. "This one tried to follow you in, took one look around and left in terror," she added.

She'd been right the previous evening: every patron this midday was female and associated with the trade in some way or another. Woman after woman came up to give Coco an update. This one's menses had finally come: "Thank God, with the potion you recommended I'm not with child after all. Even though it means I can't be in the Cleopatra number tonight."

This one was back from a restful visit to her sister in the country, "ready for work."

And this one. "No doubt about it. I've got the clap." She got it, she swore, from Monsieur So-and-so, "who ought to be put on a list." And what remedies were there for *that*?

Madame Pépin had also been right about the omelets. Madame Toussaint ordered the mushroom, herb, and cheese; it was lovely with a croissant, apricot preserves, and a large bowl of café au lait adding more steam to the window along with the breath of all the chatting women. The omelet was just perfect, crisp on the outside and runny inside.

Through the steam streamed the first sun in a week from a sky cold and clear. A sharp wind creaked the faux sails on the Moulin Rouge across the square. And on the window display counter, a black cat—a nod to the competing cabaret, *Le Chat Noir*—sunned lazily and undisturbed in the midst of a tray of gingerbread wafers, iced and garnished with curls of candied citron. The horrors of the day before—even the policeman outside standing about like a day laborer waiting to be hired where usually women for another sort of hire stood—vanished, and all seemed right with the world. Amazing what a little liquid in the middle of an omelet could do.

Madame Pépin ordered another croissant. "It's hard to keep the curves necessary in my line of work when you dance like I do every evening. Nobody wants to remember the siege and boney women when they come to the Moulin Rouge to forget."

This was all interrupted when a young woman, a hennaed redhead, pushed her way through the crowded chairs and tables with a copy of *Le Petit Parisien* in hand. She spread the newspaper's front page across the three empty omelet plates. To Madame Toussaint's horror, she saw an etching of her own face staring back at her. She looked old, crabby, evil. *Crime de la Concierge*! blared the headline. Madame Toussaint could read no more because it was upside down, or more likely because of the thudding red she saw before her eyes instead.

The convivial chatter of the café changed. Suddenly the questions were: "Has she escaped?" the redhead asked. "Has the dangerous criminal escaped?" The article must say nothing about Madame Toussaint's release from La Santé.

"Coco, what do you mean bringing her here?"

"Harboring a murderess?"

"Will she set fire to us in our beds?"

"Stab us all with butcher knives like she did Monsieur le Comte?"

Madame Pépin began by trying to calm the irrational fears, but they only grew. "Come, girls." She gathered her reticule, fur-lined tippet, gloves, and the hat with the veil. "Let's enjoy the sunshine while we may."

The three women left with Madame Pépin's parting shot to the crowd at large, "Ladies, I promise I will tell you all when I can. In the meantime, I assure you Madame Toussaint is innocent. And I beg you to consider: Who of you have not taken the blame for a man's misdeeds at one time or another in your life?" So the prostitute turned into the mouthpiece of the philosophy once employed biblically to save one of her own sisterhood from stoning.

The three women walked, blinking, out into the sunshine and the brisk wind. The man in the blue workman's shirt fell into step behind them. They took care to stay far enough ahead and to speak the more sensitive things when a passing cart or church bells or hawkers' cries must keep him from overhearing.

"Tell me all," Madame Pépin urged, once again the old friend from before. Madame Toussaint did, with added details from the housemaid. "So, no clue as to who really did it?" Coco asked at the end.

Madame Toussaint shook her head. "I still think it must be a tenant, although I do mean to recheck the center courtyard myself if—when I can get access to the building again."

Madame Pépin patted her reticule. "I have a key," she assured her two companions.

"And the florist's shop, Madame," Jeanne-Marie added. "Don't forget the door from the florist's shop."

Madame Toussaint stopped in her tracks. "Jeanne-Marie, you're right."

"Ah, so that's what that fourth door into the lobby is," Coco said. "I never thought about it before but just walked right past."

"Before the courtyard, I'm checking with Madame Auguste the florist."

"Come along." Coco caught Madame Toussaint by the elbow and urged her to keep walking. "Monsieur le Flic behind us nearly tread on your heels, Nathalie. Now he's dived into that alcove."

Coco saw an opening in the traffic and forged her way across both directions of Boulevard de Clichy and the tree-lined promenade between them with quick, strong steps, urging her companions to follow.

Those trees were only twenty years old, their progenitors having fueled desperate fires during the siege. And after.

Then the three women turned to watch as a horseless carriage puttered by, also taking advantage of the break in the weather. The driver joy-pumped the horn at them even though they'd made it safely across. "The creation of Monsieur Daimler," Coco divined.

"Another German." Cocooned day and night in the concierge loge, Madame Toussaint could not tell one automobile from another. "There will be mass casualties in the streets if this keeps up," she suggested. It struck her that the contraptions—that startled horses, spewed choking smoke instead of honest manure, and didn't like to give place to everyday pedestrian citizens—were a political statement. A statement that might have the same effect as the siege followed by the Commune with the same winners: those who could afford it. But, as with her other political beliefs, she stifled the thought now.

"They propose a race of such vehicles come summer," Coco said. "From Paris to Bordeaux."

"Like they race horses." The prospect excited Jeanne-Marie. "Monsieur le Comte just purchased a horseless carriage himself. Excuse me, may he rest in peace. But I've seen it, a beautiful Peugeot with the chrome lion trademark."

Madame Toussaint doubted she'd use the adjective, *beautiful*. "I have never seen it, or heard it, parked outside the building on Rue Férou."

"That's because Madame la Comtesse says it will give her the migraine. She refuses to ride in it and insists he keep it in a stable around by the police station, closer to Saint-Sulpice." Another point for the side that thought the invention would prove a menace to mankind.

"I don't know that I can be any help with sleuthing Monsieur le Comte's murder." Having reached the other side of the boulevard in one piece, Coco helped circle the subject back to the mystery at hand. Because they had accomplished the crossing without the blue workman's smock following them, it seemed a good time to speak without allegory, if only briefly. Madame Toussaint had to be grateful for the subtlety of her old friend.

"I wasn't even on the Left Bank when it happened," Coco continued.

"There are many who can testify to that fact. My legs, at least, were on prominent display."

"Coco, dear, you've already been more help than I can ever repay," Madame Toussaint said, and Jeanne-Marie echoed the gratitude.

"I take it you don't put much faith in the police," Coco said.

"They've given me no reason to," Madame Toussaint replied. "From the commissaire, definitely not. He has it in for me, for the whole working class." She didn't mention how she thought she had recognized the man from that time so long ago. "The young gendarme, he's not so prejudiced, but I'm not sure he can make his voice of reason heard over Roule-Armagnac's bravado."

"They will not exonerate you."

"Not unless they get Paul to take my place. Paul. It's Paul in the most trouble now."

The three turned back to make certain the tail was not too close yet. He had paused to read the paper at a kiosk, a paper livid with justification for his day's work.

"I must warn Paul," Madame Toussaint went on, "but I don't dare while I'm being followed."

"Let me think about that problem for a moment. I may be able to help out there."

"Besides, I'm not all that sure where to look for him."

"Paul? Who's Paul?" Jeanne-Marie asked.

Madame Toussaint exchanged a glance with Coco who, with a shrug, took that as permission to give her version of the matter. "You'll never imagine how jealous all of us needlewomen were when this one—" She jerked her thumb at Madame Toussaint. "Came up with him on her arm."

"Only at first I wasn't on his arm." Madame Toussaint wanted that to be clear.

"No. She was in his bed."

"Your lover?" Jeanne-Marie asked, wide-eyed with wonder, trying hard to hide any shock she might be feeling, even though she herself had been servicing a man of upper class.

"My husband, actually."

"He's alive? How?"

"It's a long story. He's the one Monsieur le Flic hopes I'll lead them to. I won't."

Jeanne-Marie pressed for the romance.

"Suffice it to say, *chérie*," Madame Toussaint told her, "one day—one late night, actually—we came out of l'Hôtel de Ville having written our names in the ledger, and I was already deathly ill with a fever."

"Everybody was hungry and cold," Coco recollected. "It made us very vulnerable. Cholera."

"Many died."

Coco agreed. "They were dying at the Gare, too. You remember our friend Louise?"

"Of course. So lively, so in love with the whole world."

"She was among the first—"

"And I always regret I wasn't with her. At the end."

"Never mind, Nathalie. You were sick yourself. And I was there for her."

"Thank you." They walked together in silence for a while, not seeing the shops they passed.

Then Madame Toussaint went on. "Anyway, Paul and I set off from l'Hôtel de Ville across the river in the rain, trying to make it back to the Gare d'Orléans, but the omnibuses weren't running, of course. We had only made it as far as the sixth arrondissement. I was dizzy, staggering. I couldn't walk. He was practically carrying me. I collapsed on a bench in the Luxembourg Gardens. Beside the dead fountain.

"'Just leave me here,' I begged, thinking I was about to die, wet and cold and alone."

"'On our wedding night?' he said. 'Kill me first.'"

"Now, isn't that romantic?" Coco asked, only half joking. "Who would have expected it of him, the way he was all business around the balloons?"

"He seemed to struggle with the thought for a while, or maybe that was just my perception through the delirium, before he said, 'Come. I know where we can find shelter.'"

"He practically carried me—"

"To Rue Férou?" Jeanne-Marie had been listening with rapt attention and now she had to hasten the revelation. "That's so close to the Luxembourg. To the building where we live? Or lived? Before yesterday morning?"

"The same," Madame Toussaint said. "Where all three of us live. The first time I was under that roof; I've hardly left a day since."

"Go on," the young woman begged.

"I remember lying on the chaise longue—the same one the cook claimed yesterday morning during her fainting fit, in the same room—while a great deal of discussion went on out in the hall. What did I care? I was warm. At least I ought to have been warm, for somehow they had a roaring fire where the rest of us had been skimping for two months. Nonetheless, wave after wave of chill was sweeping over me.

"In the end, I heard a man whose voice I thought I recognized and had heard just recently, shout, 'A fever? You ask me to bring cholera into my house? With my family?'

"Paul's voice was more of a murmur, consoling, begging.

"Then the other said, 'Well, our housemaid did just die. You can put her in that room.'

"Paul hoisted me up in his arms and carried me all the way up to the sixth floor." Madame Toussaint turned to speak to Jeanne-Marie, whose cheeks were flushed with the cold and the exercise. "Your *chambre de bonne*, in fact, *chérie*."

"I had no idea anyone had died there." Jeanne-Marie's reply was small and scared. No doubt she was rejoicing that she had been denied that room the previous day.

"It was a very long time ago, *chérie*. Before you were born."

"And ten redecoratings ago," Coco added to the comforting.

"They almost had another one die there, that long, cold November." Madame Toussaint found herself laughing instead of sinking into dismay at the memory. "I remember saying to Paul, 'Why do you take such good care of me? Didn't you tell me it was the woman's job to nurse the man? And for no pay?'

"He said, 'That was before I learned that we come to love those we care for, not the other way around.'

"I couldn't believe it. He loved my weakness as well as my strength. The vomit, the flux—

"I also remember, one day, the owner of the building coming upstairs—"

"The owner of the building?" Jeanne-Marie asked. "That would be Monsieur le Comte?"

"Monsieur d'Ermenville, yes. He came and argued with Paul. Again, they raised their voices out in the hall. I heard clearly that it was time for me to be going. I tried to get up; I should comply. I'd tell them I was ready.

"'You were *what?*' I heard the owner, Eugène d'Ermenville say. And 'You did what at l'Hôtel de Ville? Among that rabble? Your name is on paper? They can trace you here?'

"Clearly this wasn't my place. They wanted me gone. But I was too weak, and the words made me weaker. I sank back into Paul's chair and had to listen.

"'Eugène, I'll have you know I've married this woman.' Paul's dear voice.

"'You *what?*' The owner's voice reached a screech of fury.

"'If you doubt me, go look at the ledger in l'Hôtel de Ville. On the eve of Toussaint.'

"The owner was silent for a while, stewing in fury. Then he seemed to laugh it off. 'Well, I won't tell anybody about this shame you've brought on us. Not if you won't.'"

"So that was Monsieur le Comte?" Jeanne-Marie demanded again, impatiently. "The owner? He told me he built the place."

"Others built the place. Workmen whose poorer houses he'd acquisitioned, turned into skimpy wages . . ." Madame Toussaint began, thoughts she usually kept to herself spoken out loud to these women she was feeling so comfortable with. The girl was young; she wasn't listening.

"I know his name is—was—Eugène. He asked me to call him that. When we were alone." Had Jeanne-Marie had some feeling for the man they'd both last seen as a carcass ready to be hung from the butcher's hooks? To cover her blush, the girl quickly added, "It is a name few would call him. Only a family member. Or a—"

"Or a childhood friend. Yes. They were childhood friends." Madame Toussaint exchanged a glance with Coco, her own childhood friend, begging her not to betray more. Madame Toussaint was not prepared for the innocent girl to know that the two men were brothers. Wouldn't that just bring Paul more into the presumption of guilt? She herself, thinking objectively, had to admit it looked that way, and who knew what direction the girl's imagination, given too little information or too much, might go?

Coco caught the clue. She was always good at that. "You should have seen us over our needles at the Gare. First of all, Citoyen Paul comes back late the next morning after those events at l'Hôtel de Ville. Alone. Then he quickly leaves again. Then he starts being gone more than he's with us.

Eating better. He starts missing launches. Launches, even. The balloon works go to hell without him, this group squabbling with that. That group letting the standards of their work drop. Nothing seemed fair anymore. The men began to lord it over us women. And to demand favors for food. Citoyen Paul's brief visits were not enough to stop it."

Again, Jeanne-Marie wasn't listening. "But Madame Toussaint, that is so romantic."

"Yes," Coco said, confirming with another glance that Madame Toussaint wanted continued cover. "And romance and revolution do not mix. You love one or the other, not both."

"Revolution, Madame?"

Madame Toussaint came to a sudden halt. Half of what she said next was to sharpen the curve away from the topic of the building and its occupants, half because it struck her so forcibly. "This is the place. This is the very shop where I sewed gentlemen's capes. This is the very pavement, so steep. Only the cobbles got torn up and must have been replaced. The place where I first saw him, and he said, 'Vive la France.' Different ownership."

"As I told you, a front now. For *les filles de joie*." Since they had stopped, Coco took another look behind them. She must have seen the man in the blue workman's smock because she hurried them along and shifted the subject further still. "So it was one of the male tenants who told the police about Paul's visit the night before last?"

"The young gendarme let me know that much."

"But you can speak up for your husband's innocence—right, Madame?" Jeanne-Marie insisted.

Could she? Madame Toussaint worried that perhaps her own desires were coloring her memories of sleep in that bed a night ago, the sounds she had heard and when.

"Of course," she assured the girl. "In the same way, I don't want to jump to accusations with whoever saw Paul arrive—and not leave again. Again, I don't mean to say whichever man it was had anything to do with the crime," Madame Toussaint warned. "Only that he saw what I wish he had not."

"Of course," Coco agreed. "But let's run through them all and consider who it might be."

"Madame Toussaint and I already did so," Jeanne-Marie offered.

"Couldn't hurt to do it again," said Madame Toussaint. "Perhaps I've missed something. Like I missed the florist's door."

They did so, but only briefly. Madame Toussaint quickly reached the same conclusion she had before. "It was Monsieur Arnaud. I'm sure of it. I saw him. He shed cigar ash on the lobby floor. I'm sure, with neither Jeanne-Marie nor I to clean it up, the ash is there still.

"And—" A new thought struck her. "Jeanne-Marie, tell me again what you told me yesterday."

"About—?"

"About Madame d'Ermenville."

"La Comtesse?"

"Yes, and Monsieur Arnaud."

Jeanne-Marie recited the information. Madame Toussaint repeated it with emphasis. "Madame d'Ermenville, who is such an invalid, has been receiving Monsieur Arnaud many an evening in her salon in full courtly attire."

Madame Toussaint also suddenly remembered that Monsieur Arnaud had told her to expect a delivery from his haberdashers yesterday. His announcement of this was what had allowed him to see Paul. *Tant pis.* She hadn't been on the Rue Férou to fulfill that duty yesterday. Somebody else must have done that duty and taken the delivery. Who?

"All the time our young *bonne* Jeanne-Marie has been in service there, these soirées have been going on." Madame Toussaint brought her thoughts back to the current conversation. "What does that mean?"

Jeanne-Marie enjoyed her usefulness, adding to it. "And, Mesdames, I've thought about it. There's more. I've never seen it myself, but Madame Herlemont, the lieutenant-colonel's wife. Her governess has the *chambre de bonne* just down the hall from mine. One evening recently, she stopped me as we passed one another going back and forth to the toilet.

"'That Madame Sylvie is not in her room again tonight,' she whispered, the smell of her facial cream stinging my eyes as she bent to my ear.

"'Well,' I told her. 'It often happens that Madame la Comtesse is not well at night, and Mademoiselle Sylvie must sit up with her.' I had to stifle saying out loud, 'Thank the Good Lord it isn't me. Le Comte and his demands are quite enough.'

"And the governess winked and said, 'That's what they tell you, eh?'

"'Why shouldn't it be true?' I had to ask.

"'Because I just saw Mademoiselle sneaking into Monsieur Arnaud's room. That's why. On my way past the third floor. My next week's salary says she stays there all night.' Another whiff of facial cream as she swished off down the hall."

"I wonder what Lieutenant-colonel and Madame Herlemont would say to learn their sober governess is a betting woman," Coco mused. "Or that she uses facial cream. I thought such women were supposed to have pickle faces."

Madame Toussaint, for her part, couldn't believe her ears. "Monsieur Arnaud and Mademoiselle Sylvie? An item? Incredible. You'd think she, a simple lady's maid, wouldn't have enough cachet for him."

Jeanne-Marie must have liked the reaction she was getting; she finished her story. "As far as I can tell—although we'd had to keep the fires going all day, and I was exhausted—the governess was right. Mademoiselle Sylvie did not sleep in her room that night. Or the next."

"Incredible," Madame Toussaint said again. She didn't know as much about her building as she thought she did.

"I don't believe a word of it, either." Coco's voice had a lot of cabaret in it.

"You know Monsieur Arnaud, of course, Coco," Madame Toussaint said.

"Of course. Meet him going up and down the stairs where he never fails to tip his hat. 'Bonjour, Madame.' 'Bonsoir, Madame.'" Coco set the imaginary top hat she'd been pretending to doff firmly over her own chicken feathers now. "He does not tip his hat, however, when I see him elsewhere."

"Such as where?" Madame Toussaint couldn't keep the surprise from her question.

"Such as when I pass him on this street." They were back on the Boulevard de Clichy, this time at the far east end where it bent into Rochechouart.

"So Monsieur Arnaud enjoys a bit of the wild life. There's hardly a man in Paris, we might say, married or unmarried, who does not visit the sporting ladies at one time or another."

"Oh, no," Coco said, laughing at the great joke. "These are not the ladies at this end of the boulevard. Boys. Monsieur Arnaud likes the boys."

XIV
LA BELLE ÉPOQUE

Montmartre had changed so much since the day she'd first met Paul on the steep pavement. Madame Toussaint noticed it at every turn. The windmills now only churned out cabaret. Rabbit hutches continued to shelter under a few eaves; cocks crowed a challenge to passing pedestrians. But only the narrowest alleys were still unpaved—today, running mud with all that rain and sewage down the center. Sometimes a glimpse of two or three trees of the ancient orchards remained between the older, smaller houses and the time-worn fences fashioned of rough tree limbs. The vineyards that since Roman times had produced wine the equal of Argenteuil were now represented only by single specimens that struggled up towards the light and fruited only at the level of the second floor.

As far back as memory and records held, the thatched-roof Couvent des Dames, the namesake of the steeply slanting square called Des Abbesses, had been notorious for the easy virtue of their sisterhood. The Revolution had secularized the rite and only the names of religion remained, leaving little luxury for reforming prayer or cleansing confession on the side.

"Isn't it pleasant to walk around in this little bit of sunshine between storms?" Jeanne-Marie exulted, swinging her arms happily as if the death of Monsieur d'Ermenville had lifted a heavy burden from her pretty, young neck.

"You will be wanting to return to the building on Rue Férou, won't you?" Coco said.

"As soon as I can," Madame Toussaint replied. "I've got to find out everything I can about who might have committed this crime before the trail grows cold and there is no one to blame but Paul. I don't want too many of the tenants to know I'm there before I start snooping around, however. If they know, the guilty parties will be on their guard. I also hope—before I get stuck in one corner of one building—to make an attempt to find Paul. But to do that, I will have to lose the gendarme on my tail."

Coco glanced over her shoulder. The man was still with them. "That, I think, would be better done under cover of darkness."

Madame Toussaint agreed.

"Not me," Jeanne-Marie assured them with a little skip down the street. "I never want to return to that dismal house on Rue Férou."

"She will," Coco said. "When she gets hungry enough, and it starts to rain with no roof over her head. She'll miss her job then."

"Oh, Madame. Please don't think me ungrateful. Indeed, I don't know what Madame la Concierge and I would do without you."

"We can't expect Madame Pépin to give us room and board for much longer." Madame Toussaint expressed her own gratitude. "We've got to find you another job, Mademoiselle."

"Preferably not in my profession," Coco said, "although I'll say it again, I do think you'd do well. With that pretty face and youthful innocence. Neither of which, I fear, would last long."

"We're only taking that as a last resort, Coco dear," Madame Toussaint promised. "My need to return remains more pressing, however. The little money I've saved is there. My job—I think I might still have one."

"They arrested us both," Jeanne-Marie reminded them. "They will still want you in the concierge's loge?"

"There are reasons, *chérie*. Reasons that date back many years that you don't need to know. But first and foremost, I need to get back there to clear Paul's name."

Madame Toussaint stopped with her two friends before the window of a makeup shop to look at cosmetic kits with their cut-glass bottles nestled into green velvet, their tweezers, scissors, combs, and brushes with mother-of-pearl or ivory handles. Ground pearl facial powder, spermaceti cream, crushed lapis lazuli for the eyelids held pride of place.

Coco began giving Jeanne-Marie tips for her round face and "rustic complexion," even though there was no way the girl could afford any of the suggestions.

Madame Toussaint couldn't go into raptures of diversion over such things as the others could, so she continued to talk, whether or not her companions were listening.

"I would like to attempt to contact Paul, but I can't do that with a policeman on my tail," she repeated. "And if some sleight of hand . . ." She lowered her voice even though their shadow was completely bored with face paint and lingered at a distance out of earshot. No doubt there was more than frivolous purpose in Coco's choice of halting spot. "If some magic is going to make this possible, it is best done not in broad daylight."

"We're best not to go back to the café, either, not with your picture all over the front page of the papers," Coco said between the words "cinnabar" and "antimony."

"Yes, I am content to continue to walk around enjoying the sun, sitting on a bench when our feet get tired," Madame Toussaint said, pretending to take an interest in sweet almond oil. "But it makes me so anxious, to feel it's hours before I can do anything. I hope you both will help me think things through as we walk."

"Yes?" Coco flicked between conversations as she'd flick the hem of a cancan skirt. "You know, you may not be as hopeless during this time as all that. I am not the only one from the building seen walking these streets."

"You already mentioned Monsieur Arnaud. But can we assume he won't come on his sordid mission while it's daylight?"

"Yes, but also at least one of the men working in the apartment below me in Rue Férou."

Madame Toussaint had always imagined such workers to be good, hard-working family men. But who knew? Perhaps they already had too many young mouths to feed and had to spend hard-earned money preventing others. "But will they not also come during the evening hours, after work?"

"The one I'm thinking of comes during the day. I think he is working on a project in the neighborhood."

"Which one? Where?"

"I can't say which one. Many new buildings are going up in this corner of Paris, like everywhere, in the haussmannian fashion. I can't even remember exactly which street I've seen him in. But if we keep our eyes open and our feet moving, we just might find him."

"He won't have been in our building the night of the murder if he's a laborer."

"No, but he might know something."

Madame Toussaint tried to press their small party forward, anxious for this meeting.

"It won't do any good to look too purposeful." Coco glanced again behind them, indicating the tail. She turned back to the window and said to the youngest member of their trio, "Red beet juice, *chérie*, for the cheeks. For those of us not flush with funds. And lemon or orange juice in the eyes to make them shine if you have no belladonna. Afterwards, you can eat the leftovers. Not the belladonna, of course."

"The brutality of the attack." Madame Toussaint stayed on track. "Who could hate Monsieur d'Ermenville enough to do such a thing?"

"Nathalie, my dear. You have to ask? *You* have reasons."

Madame Toussaint had to confess that that was true. "Paul has reasons." She said the name even more innocent than hers—she hoped.

"Exactly why the gendarmerie wants to find him."

"I have reasons too," Jeanne-Marie piped up. "How many times did I imagine . . . ?"

"The little one has a point," Coco said, turning her back on the display in her interest. "Who was the previous housemaid, whose duties this one took up?"

"I knew her well," Madame Toussaint said. "It hasn't been that long, after all. Anaïs, from the Midi."

"All the duties? The bedroom, too?"

"Yes."

"Did she leave in the family way with no knowledge of how to fix the problem and no reference? That would be cause enough."

"She left the household to marry. A cobbler's apprentice, so she did well enough for herself, not to be in service the rest of her life."

"Like Mademoiselle Sylvie," Jeanne-Marie inserted into the conversation. "In service. For the rest of her life." The thought sobered the young face. "I think she is bitter about it."

"She is certainly bitter about something," Coco commented.

"Anaïs could probably have pretended to be a virgin on her wedding night," Madame Toussaint said, "which skills you should get Madame Coco here to teach you, *chérie*."

"Now, that's interesting." Coco, who had set off again leading their ramble, stopped to adjust her tippet in the reflection of the next store window. This vitrine was full of feathers and hats. Madame Toussaint saw nothing interesting behind the glass. But then, she didn't really care for hats. Not since the straw bonnet she'd worn through the whole Terrible Year. Today—just something simple to make her presentable on the street. The *flic* remained down at the last street corner, idly smoking.

"Faux virgin skills?" she asked.

"Well, yes, those too. But think. Madame la Comtesse has no children. And who more than a comte wants heirs?"

"'La Comtesse', as you call her, is bedridden. Or, at least I thought she was. Until I heard about Monsieur Arnaud's soirées with her."

Guilt consumed Jeanne-Marie for her thoughtless purchase with her last wage of the bonnet she wore now. Coco said it didn't suit her round, peasant face, "but exaggerates the cheeks. Although a bunch of faux cherries, just there, might salvage it." But when would the girl get another wage? Focused on this window of possibilities, she neither confirmed nor denied her previous testimony.

"But she wasn't always. Bedridden, I mean." Coco kept her half of both conversations going like a nanny pushing two toddlers in two separate park swings.

"True. Or, at least I thought she was. Until I heard about Monsieur Arnaud's soirées with her." That detail kept coming up. Madame Toussaint gave Jeanne-Marie a look of gratitude for that previous information—with no return glimpse.

"Madame la Comtesse has no children," Coco went on, spelling it out. "Anaïs had no children by her master."

"Now she does. By the cobbler. Two, and another on the way."

"You see? Infertility not her fault. And the little one here with us is not pregnant."

"Thank heavens."

"You didn't take any precautions?"

Jeanne-Marie flushed deeply without benefit of beet juice and mournfully shook her head.

"Well, next time you'll be more careful, won't you?" Coco urged. "Because this first time, you were just lucky. I'm willing to bet that man is—was—firing blanks."

Madame Toussaint nodded slowly, realization dawning. "Yes. That is interesting. Poor Madame d'Ermenville. That would make you take to your bed, wouldn't it? If the whole world blames you for not producing an heir, and there's nothing you can do about it. And you don't have to get up every morning to sweep the hall. That'd be enough to make you take a lover, wouldn't it?"

"Monsieur Arnaud is not her lover," Jeanne-Marie insisted. "I'm quite sure of that."

"So am I," Coco agreed. "I know which end of the street the boys are."

"And I can't think of anyone I ever let in who seemed to fit that bill." Madame Toussaint the concierge knew what she knew.

"Anyone from outside the building, that is."

"Not Monsieur Pépin?" Madame Toussaint had to ask.

If Coco struggled with jealousy, she didn't show it. She already shared the man with a wife and three daughters, after all. "Not since Christmas and his stroke, at any rate." She was definite. "And certainly not two nights ago."

"Someone with reasons to hate him. Reasons to hate him—" Madame Toussaint pondered as they moved on to the next window. Shoes. Everything a prostitute would need in one street. Everything except the client to fund the purchases.

"I, however, refuse to believe that even with experience in the farmyard at butchering time, you would be capable of what was done to that man," Madame Toussaint assured the girl. "You would have done a neater job of it, for starters. And I will never believe that scream I heard yesterday morning was the result of guile, a cover-up."

"I would think that, with the places his greed and heartlessness reached their tentacles, half the city of Paris has cause to hate him," Coco mused.

"The poorer half," Madame Toussaint agreed.

"And the not-so-poor. Bankers. Displaced slum dwellers."

"What displaced slum dweller could ever live in the Rue Férou? Life goes downhill from the displaced slum. For everyone. Everyone but me, the concierge. For whom it remained about the same."

"Granted. And me, too, of course. On the fifth floor."

"Sorry. You were saying? Bankers?"

"Ruined bankers. Competitive developers. Stiffed construction workers. Anything ring a bell?" Coco also pointed out a pair of black boots that laced up midcalf. "You can lace them tight as skin. And there are plenty of men who find nothing so seductive as white ruffles to the knee and boots to midcalf. A shapely calf. Let me have a look at yours, *chérie*. Yes, very nice."

"They would take some breaking in, however. Those boots." Madame Toussaint warned.

"Must you always be a spoilsport, Nathalie?"

"Yes, when I've got an unsolved murder on my hands."

"And a *flic* who just looked this way."

Madame Toussaint was glad for the reminder that they were being followed. "I don't see where the musician Monsieur Cailloux fits in this litany of suspects."

"You could ask him when you get there. 'Any deals gone sour, Monsieur? Outside the Opéra?'"

"I could do that," Madame Toussaint agreed.

"Then how about the lieutenant-colonel? On the second floor? Don't they train them in butchery in military school?"

"I did meet him. Once. Before. During the Terrible Year. I remembered the name, not the face. I remembered the blinking eyes, too. He fought under Paul as a young subaltern. Owed Paul his life, actually. From the last, desperate sortie of the siege. I can tell you the story." With a look back at the *flic*. "Later."

"Interesting. Yes, there might be something there. A man out for revenge because his troop lost the war to real estate."

"Only the lieutenant-colonel was still recovering from his injuries when the enemy switched from the Prussians to the French Army—the French Army at Versailles, where the Prussians were welcomed," Madame Toussaint remembered. "During that same time, Paul's devotion turned from the Army to the Commune's National Guard. Overnight, it seemed. As if by magic."

"And why should the lieutenant-colonel take murderous revenge now? If that's what it was. After all these years, we've sort of fallen into stupor of what passes for normal life."

Jeanne-Marie stopped posing her calves, to the distraction of the police tail, to ask, "I don't understand, Mesdames. The Army? The National Guard? What's the difference? Weren't they both protecting the French people?"

"Yes. Until Thiers and the Duke of Magenta capitulated to the Prussians," Madame Toussaint explained. "Until those traitors begged to be allowed to restore what they called '*la République,*' which could just as easily change back into another Empire under the first Napoleon IV to come along. The rest of us—the National Guard, every able-bodied man in Paris as well as female regiments—we formed during the siege for defense. This was after most of the Army had been captured and taken to German camps at Sedan and Metz. We supported the Commune, a more equitable system, a voice for all, which the French Army—at Versailles—" Surging on a wave of passion, she suddenly found she couldn't say the word.

"Crushed," Coco prompted, but quietly, taking Madame Toussaint's arm. "Crushed is the word you're looking for."

"My uncle Yann was in the French Army," Jeanne-Marie piped up, jealous perhaps of the turn from shoes to something between the other two women she clearly didn't share. "During the seventies."

"Breton?" Coco deduced. "Of course. Thiers and the duke had to scramble to get recruits from all the hinterlands. Some of them couldn't even speak French yet."

"Like Uncle Yann."

"Bring them here without training, without communal ties, without the ability to converse, to discover the humanity—"

"Uncle Yann was never the same, they said, after what he'd seen and done. He was the last of our family to come to Paris. Before me. Afterwards—afterwards, he killed himself." She made the sign of the cross.

"I am so sorry, *chérie.*"

"It's all right. I never really knew him. And they did have to bury him outside the churchyard, so we never talked about him during the pardons and so on."

"Tragedy upon tragedy. We none of us were the same. Many of us wanted to die."

Madame Toussaint finally found her voice again. "Perhaps you have suffered ill treatment in Paris because of where you're from," she said. "If so, I'm sorry. I, too, came from a farm in the countryside. But perhaps because of your uncle you have an inkling about why."

"Yes," Coco said. "And now we have a feeling for the sort of man who might want revenge on Monsieur le Comte. Someone who got crushed in that switch of loyalties."

"Someone like Paul," Madame Toussaint had to confess.

"It is not Paul," Coco insisted. "You will have to pull up your courage and face the French Army once again, Nathalie Toussaint. You will have to go interview the lieutenant-colonel, fearsome as he has become through advancement in the Army. As soon as you can get back to Rue Férou."

Madame Toussaint promised she would. "But not 'til I lose this tail. And can warn Paul."

XV
LA BELLE ÉPOQUE

"B*on*."

What had Coco just declared "good"? Their conclusion that Lieutenant-colonel Herlemont should be interviewed? Or was it the pair of pink satin heels with beadwork flowers in the shoemaker's shop window?

In either case, she was ready to move on. "Now what about construction workers?"

"With access to the building at Rue Férou? I can't think—"

"Perhaps you can't think, but I can. There I am, trying to sleep 'til a civilized hour—say, ten. And they start hammering on the ceiling."

"Of course. The renovators in fourth-floor-left."

"Precisely."

"I do like that idea. Nothing to do with Paul. But none of them were in the building two nights ago."

"Perhaps not, but they do have eyes and ears, don't they? Not only that, but residents tend to ignore their existence, even though, or perhaps because, they're making enough noise to wake the dead. They send debris down shoots to the bins below, passing people's windows. They have to go up to the roof to fix chimneys and vents. What don't they do? I bet they know the building as well as you do."

Madame Toussaint had to admit that was probably true, even though the renovators had only been working a couple of months.

The next window they passed was a photographer's.

"We should leave this one to Monsieur le Flic," she advised.

Flyspecks dimmed the women's view into a display of sets of black-and-white postcards arrayed in fans. The top card of each fan suggested even more exotic delights below, but they indicated: first, a gentleman gallantly handing a lady an item of lacy clothing of which she really was in need. Then an artist and his model, the easel set very strategically; the slip of a camisole from too energetic activity—riding; a cancan dancer—it might even have been Coco herself although the shoes didn't say so. And finally, the ever-popular bubble bath.

"Nonsense," Coco scoffed. "There's ever so much a young lady can learn from such a display."

Madame Toussaint turned her back on the window. "Yes. When it's time to scrub the panes."

Coco discussed poses with her young protégée. Over them, Madame Toussaint said, as if talking to herself, "So the renovators. I'll interview them too. When I get back to Rue Férou."

"Perhaps not." Coco interrupted the one conversation to join the other. "As I said, I think I have seen one of them—I think he may be the foreman—in this neighborhood."

Jeanne-Marie was practicing "the allure of the leg" under her skirts to the further enticement of the gendarme.

"Monsieur Hervé? In this neighborhood?"

"The man in his thirties? Balding? A dirty blue cap? Such a lean and hungry look?"

"Sounds like him. But murder? I cannot imagine it."

"Neither, frankly, can I. And I've had to imagine a lot of unlikely things in my life. I don't think he comes to this quartier for the high-life. I've never seen him at nighttime. Only during the day. I think he comes professionally. As I've said, I think he has a construction job. I think, in fact, he may be working up on the Mont. These hours waiting for nightfall may not be a complete waste after all."

All three women turned uphill, the direction Coco indicated.

The reaction Madame Toussaint had been trying to suppress throughout their stroll suddenly jumped out of nowhere and grabbed her, sending her heart racing. It was as if she had a fear of heights without being on a height, but she knew it wasn't that at all.

It is only because the name of the butte means *hill of the martyrs*, she tried to tell herself. It was called that before you ever came to live here fresh from the farm. Such calming advice didn't help.

"We could go up and see. Peek among the scaffolding until they shoo us off. Or one of us gets hit on the head by a falling beam."

"I—I'd rather not."

Coco gave Madame Toussaint and her hesitation an appraising look.

"I could stay here while you two go up," she offered.

"Yes, let's," Jeanne-Marie begged.

"We could go up to Rue des Rosiers," Coco suggested. "You can almost look down on the site from there. I hate to break up the crime-solving three musketeers before we have to."

The Rue des Rosiers was a memory of death Madame Toussaint didn't want to have laid bare before her. "Please. Let's not." The Street of the Rosebushes—no doubt there had been such bushes once, but with the intervening history, past events associated with the name were like a heap of roses trying to hide a coffin and the smell of putrefaction inside but not quite succeeding.

"What is the matter with the Street of the Rosebushes?" Jeanne-Marie asked. "It sounds delightful. I will go."

"Ah." Coco understood. "Well, you won't find it marked by that name these days. They have changed the name to Rue Chevalier-de-la-Barre. There's a boring mouthful—matches the street in its new incarnation. Trying to cover up the past."

"Although I like who they've renamed it for," said Madame Toussaint. "He's not just another chevalier—knight. If you know the history. Although yes, another martyr."

"What past? What history?" Jeanne-Marie begged. "Tell me."

"They've renamed the street since I was here." Madame Toussaint shrugged, noncommittal. "The Chevalier-de-la-Barre was a man who failed to cross himself as a church procession passed by and so was burned to death with Voltaire's *Philosophical Dictionary* nailed to his chest. Before the Revolution. A very long time ago, even for me."

"They're planning to make a statue of Monsieur le Chevalier to stand at the entry to the new basilica they're building," Coco added.

"That's something, I suppose. To commemorate—" Madame Toussaint stopped herself from saying more about shifting values and allegiances. How much of one revolutionary could you put on another at the doorstep of a church?

She also stopped them from continuing on that physical path. "But no, let's go another way. Until the statue stands, if it ever stands, there is the cover up of a more recent past."

Speaking of the recent past, the debris of the night's revels—broken bottles, broken *capôtes anglaises* like spent slugs, cigarette butts, vomit, pissoirs clogged or simply missed—no longer had rag-pickers and goats tended by bare-footed girls to tidy it up as once upon a time.

But then, children continued to chase each other across the rubbish and the square, up gas lampposts and down stairs where the grade was too steep for a paved slope. And some of them knew Madame Coco Pépin. They ran up to greet her. Their mothers were indebted to her; she was something of a grandmother figure.

"Why aren't you in school?" she chided.

Sometimes, apparently, she had sweets for them. "Not today, lads. Sorry." And to the next group. "In school? Or at least helping your mother out by selling matches to gentlemen for their pipes?"

"You, Madame Coco?" they sang back. "You don't know that gentlemen don't start coming to this neighborhood until after two, at the earliest?" No gentlemen except for the man in the faded workman's shirt from whom these boys kept a safe distance. Then they grinned sheepishly and ran off again.

"Your pockets are only saved from being picked because I'm here." Coco chuckled, almost proudly, as she told her friends this detail.

So life, like the remnants of vineyards, struggled on towards the sun. Were these boys put to the service of Monsieur Arnaud at night? As their sisters might already be following their mothers to the brothels?

"Our child, had he lived . . ." Madame Toussaint began aloud, then stopped herself. Only after she'd spoken the words, lulled by the unusual camaraderie to speak of subjects she usually kept carefully sequestered, did she taste how they burned her tongue.

Her child wouldn't have been the age of those *gamins*. He'd be closer in age to Jeanne-Marie. And probably suffering a male version of the same fate. If the police didn't find reason enough to blame the child, grown, for the murder of his uncle as they blamed Paul.

So Madame Toussaint didn't wish life to be other than it was and refused to continue when Coco said: "Your son? Nathalie, *chérie*. I never knew. Poor child." Did Coco mean the baby or Madame Toussaint herself?

And Jeanne-Marie pleaded, "Please, Madame, tell more, if it does not grieve you too much."

It did. Still. It hurt too much. Fortunately, Coco was leading their feet as well as the conversation. Away from the crowded, potentially hostile café. Leading the tailing gendarme off the scent. She took a quick, diverting turn that set their minds on the struggle to climb a very steep hill.

When she paused to catch her breath, Madame Toussaint looked up and stopped in her tracks. Ghostly white walls shimmered on Montmartre's summit, walls that hadn't been there the last time she'd seen the butte, so it seemed they had suddenly appeared by some evil spell, although if she counted the actual years, it had been over twenty. Was it a phantom, barely caged in scaffolding?

Since the younger woman was the closer, she grabbed Jeanne-Marie's arm.

"What is it, Madame?" the girl asked.

"Tell me what you see on the stairs going up to the summit."

"Stairs. The stairs, like the new construction, are white stone. There is a young couple—lovers, I suppose—sitting close together, enjoying the brief sun."

"They are not covered in lengths of white silk? As if from a balloon factory?"

Jeanne-Marie laughed nervously. "No, Madame."

"Good," Madame Toussaint said. "I don't see them either."

But she did. Each length was as long as a coffin, and screened onto each piece of fabric lay the image of a person, arms crossed over his chest, scruffy head at a ghastly angle. These were not the figures of long-ago martyrs in classical garb from the back corners of a church. These were working men and women in the rough, dirty clothes they'd died in those twenty-odd years before. Indeed, more than a few of them seemed to be the image of Paul—the steps, even the lovers, visible behind them.

She closed her eyes, and when she opened them, she knew she had just imagined these lengths of silk, but that didn't make them any less horrifying. "I can't do it." She gasped for air and longed for the safe stifle of the concierge's loge. "I can't go up there."

"Understood." Coco took Madame Toussaint's other arm and turned the party around. Jeanne-Marie seemed unclear about what was happening but sensed enough not to ask for an explanation. They hadn't come down off the mountain more than half a block—Nathalie was just regaining control of her breath—when they came face to face with a man in a workman's smock.

"*Ça y est*," Coco muttered. "Right into the arms of your *flic*."

Madame Toussaint had collected herself enough that she could smile at the confusion. "Not at all, Coco dear. Don't you recognize him? This is Monsieur Hervé."

"Ah, yes. The workman from our building. I told you I'd seen him around this neck of the woods."

"I recognize him too," Jeanne-Marie piped up. "I've met him on the stairs. Monsieur Hervé—"

She got neither explanation nor greeting out. The sound of a sharp policeman's whistle cut at them from across the street. Before they could discern its source, a second man in a smock had shot across the street and grabbed the first towards whom they had purposefully begun to step. The two men struggled. They swore.

"Leave upright citizens in peace, you damned *flic*." Coco, the cabaret dancer-cum-madame, rushed forward and started hitting the one who had been tailing them with her reticule.

Shopkeepers and their patrons poured out of their doors. Carters jumped down from their footboards. Street sweepers swung up their brooms. Soon the whole road was shouting. The other two gendarmes in their regular uniforms—capes and billy clubs flying—who had joined the fray from around the corner were outnumbered by the roused citizenry of Paris.

Now it was Jeanne-Marie's turn to clutch Madame Toussaint's arm in terror. "Madame, what is happening?"

"They think Monsieur Hervé is my husband Paul, the clochard companion of the murderous concierge the all-points bulletin is on the lookout for. They saw us gesture to him and jumped to their conclusions. They think I've led them to him at last, when I have not."

Madame Toussaint yelled into the tussle from the sidelines. "This is not Paul Toussaint. That's not my husband." She must have said it twenty times before the chaos subsided enough for her to hear her own voice. Nonetheless, she had to confess that a workman covered in dust and paint with a careless week's growth of stubble might be confused for someone who slept on the street.

"Monsieur Hervé is foreman of the crew doing renovations to the apartment on the fourth-floor-left." She tried again to make her voice heard above the row as she was pushed to one side.

Citizens revolting on the slopes of Montmartre. The memories threatened to overwhelm her. She tried to protect Jeanne-Marie, who—full of sudden indignation and youthful fury—was also shoving her way to the midst of the *mêlée*. Her attempt at protection was no use.

Two other dust-covered workmen, more forceful, could add, "Furthermore, he's come to work with us on the basilica this afternoon. We just finished lunch with him at the *bouillon* three doors down."—A *bouillon* being a workman's establishment that always had economical bowls of something hot on order, its walls lined with little drawers where a regular could keep his own napkin, cutlery, and bottle of wine if he so cared.

These men were regulars, as was half the crowd. That half could testify, "We've been working on the basilica since the beginning. Almost twenty years." Against such evidence, the gendarmes finally backed down. They didn't even take Monsieur Hervé in for questioning but made their apologies and stood "as you were."

"We need to get back to the site. Our pay will be docked." The workmen began to disperse in the direction of the butte's height.

"I need a drink," Coco said, turning to the empty *bouillon*. She took Madame Toussaint's arm once more. "Please join me."

Only Jeanne-Marie did the unexpected. "Mesdames," she said. "May I join you later? I can appreciate you want to avoid the climb."

Not for the reason she thinks, Madame Toussaint mused. That we are old and decrepit? Can't Coco still kick higher than her own head?

"But there's nothing I'd like more than to see the view from the height," Jeanne-Marie explained.

"I'll be happy to show Mademoiselle around the summit." Monsieur Hervé was straightening his police-ruffled attire. "And bring her back safely. There's not too much I need to attend to among the works. Just a consultation for the substrate of a mosaic."

"Of course." Madame Toussaint agreed there would be nothing better for the girl than to escape the company of two middle-aged ladies whose every thought was on death. "Montmartre is the highest point in Paris. The whole city lies at your feet. Enjoy the view, my dear."

There is no reason why the younger generation should be haunted by the same ghosts as we are, Madame Toussaint told herself. And perhaps it will help clear the child's mind of the vileness she is beginning to accumulate.

XVI
LA BELLE ÉPOQUE

A MERE HOUR and a half later, Monsieur Hervé proved as good as his word. He delivered Jeanne-Marie safe and sound but flushed with the exercise to join Madame Toussaint and Coco at their table in the almost-empty *bouillon*.

The policeman following them had taken his lunch at the same establishment. He now went to use that masculine landmark, the pissoir across the street. It resembled a colossus-sized cast-iron phallus. The *flic* could still keep an eye on the restaurant door by peering around the edifice's wall. The outhouse in the rear courtyard used by the women offered no such perspective.

Jeanne-Marie was ebullient. The older people allowed her to glory about all she had seen: "L'Arc de Triomphe, the Louvre. Notre Dame and the Île de la Cité. The Panthéon and Les Invalides with their proud domes. Saint Germain des Près. Saint-Sulpice. I think I could even see our building, at least the area, just this side of the green patch that is the Luxembourg Gardens. It's all visible from the top of the butte, laid out at your feet like a carpet. And of course, far off to the right, Monsieur Eiffel's tower."

"Monsieur Eiffel's grand prick," Coco muttered under her breath, her mind no doubt still on the pissoir as well, and called for more drinks all round.

"Ah, gracious Madame—" Monsieur Hervé, on Coco's tab, indulged in a cognac.

The yellow liquid in afternoon sunlight brought all sorts of images back to Madame Toussaint, not least her own pouring of the same beverage for Jeanne-Marie with the image of Monsieur d'Ermenville's corpse so fresh in her mind. She suppressed the thoughts to listen.

Monsieur Hervé went on. "Do I understand that you, too, are not enamored of the tallest manmade structure in the world? These six heavy years it's been standing? You are in good company. Is France never to be free of the depredations of the Germans? Our late lamented man of letters, Guy de Maupassant, took lunch in its first-floor café every day—so I understand—because that is the one place in Paris where it is not visible. At least, because it is made of soulless metal, I was never called to work on its construction."

Madame Toussaint, still nursing her first glass of rich red Malbec, was fully conscious that the grape was reputed to have been discovered by a peasant in the Hungarian portion of the Austrian empire. Again, German.

She found herself gaining an awareness of this working man's intelligence. Letting him and his crew in and out of the building over the past two months or so of construction—silently cursing the dust that wafted out of the fourth-floor apartment, the dings on her walls from the heavy tools, the plaster they tread in on their boots—had prejudiced her before, had made her think the barbarism of workmen was just one more assault she had to endure.

She was beginning to appreciate that he was a true craftsman, a person of taste and educated opinion even though he worked with his hands. Probably the work with his hands gave him a unique perception. Those who considered themselves his masters—who read building plans with their heads in the air and gave orders to their draftsmen evoked by dreams or an absinthe haze—could never equal that.

She had to ask, even before they got around to d'Ermenville's murder, "So what do you think of this project, Monsieur?" She lifted her head in the direction of the height of Montmartre from whence he and Jeanne-Marie had just descended. "We cannot blame that on an assault of Prussia."

"Can we not? Wasn't it during the cold, dark, hungry days of the siege that the archbishop of Paris decreed our sufferings were caused by our sins?" In a sudden burst of anger, he had said the word *siege*, a word most people kept to themselves as the shadow of Sacré Coeur grew. He looked from one woman to the next in desperation. Madame Toussaint met his gaze steadily. She was a concierge. And a survivor. He need fear neither her reaction nor her lack of discretion.

"Please continue, Monsieur," she said. And her two companions must have said the same thing with their faces, although she didn't want to turn her gaze from his to see.

With a breath, he did so. "We all needed to fall on our knees, the archbishop said, before the sacred heart of Jesus, and repent."

"That makes the edifice on the butte another assault of Frenchmen on Frenchmen, does it not?" Coco added her opinion.

Monsieur Hervé managed a smile in her direction. As he turned to her friend, Madame Toussaint saw his wounds taken in the recent fray with the gendarmes: a cut on one cheek cursorily dabbed at, a black eye blooming slowly into full color. Frenchmen on Frenchmen assault, the least Paul could expect if he was captured, innocent though he may be. And he would not have the stamina to shake it off as this man did.

"Monsieur, you've taken injury," she said.

Monsieur Hervé touched his cheek. He was not unconscious of the meanings here: Layer upon layer, people went through day by day without excavating, kicking over all traces. He gave a little smile that must have hurt, because he flinched.

"May I?" Madame Toussaint dipped her napkin in her wine and washed the cut.

He flinched more but then nodded with gratitude.

"Please, Monsieur. Continue with your tale."

Monsieur Hervé held up his cognac glass, pressing the cave-cool liquid to his eye. "At first the archbishop thought the half-finished Opéra would be the best site. Turn that temple dedicated to extravagance, indecency, and bad taste into something more holy. Then—well, then . . . I beg your apologies, Mesdames. It isn't polite, I know, to mention . . ."

"My friend and I are quite aware of the existence, once upon a time, of the Commune of Paris. And how it conquered this height." With another flash of phantom silk coffins flowing down Montmartre's steep steps before her eyes, Madame Toussaint nodded but could not bring herself to look in that direction.

"But I do not know," Jeanne-Marie exclaimed.

"It is best that way." The concierge reflexively monitored what came and went, even when not at the door of her building.

Monsieur Hervé mimicked Madame Toussaint's nod as if he had suddenly found safe haven. "They took the archbishop hostage, as you may know, as had happened in the Revolution. Then they shot him in retaliation for communards dead."

Madame Toussaint flinched as that long-ago shot rang in her own head.

Here Monsieur Hervé skipped over what he knew came between the death of the archbishop, reducing it to: "The prelate's name got added to the long list of martyrs associated with Montmartre beginning fifteen hundred years ago in Merovingian times if we believe the Church's legends. Others—others who died in the same more recent conflict did not receive the same honors."

Monsieur Hervé struggled to keep a historian's distance. "At first the army wanted to build a fort here, to command all of Paris, to keep the restive citizens in check. But then the Church moved against the secularization and the Rights of Man, which they believed were at the root of the Terrible Year. They appropriated the lands with the government's cooperation."

"There have been attempts to stop the project since it was begun, haven't there, Monsieur?" Madame Toussaint asked as he seemed to falter.

"Since 1873, yes. At one point the government, to their credit, actually showed great support for tearing down the already-standing foundations and building instead a monument to the goals of the Revolution: liberty, fraternity, equality. They would have included a statue to rival the great Lady Liberty we gifted to the United States and sent to stand in their harbor. But different forces won out. The dome is nearing completion. I don't suppose it will be taken down now. We are all obliged to confess our sins and worship, as did Marie Antoinette at Sacré Coeur, the sacred heart of Jesus." Monsieur Hervé struggled with tears in his eyes and his throat.

"I think, Monsieur, you are remembering the Commune that came in between," Madame Toussaint said.

He looked from her to Coco, then they all three looked at Jeanne-Marie. There were things people didn't bring up in mixed company, with strangers. With the young.

"It's all right, Monsieur. Madame and I also remember," Coco told him in much the same words as earlier. Sometimes when men visit a prostitute, all they want is someone to listen. Listen to what they cannot tell their wives or children.

Monsieur Hervé ordered another cognac. "I was ten." His words came slowly. "I suppose you could say the first job I had, learning the construction trade, was to help build the barricades. Gathering the rough materials from anywhere. I was so proud, standing at the top between my father and my mother. And then—and then the fighting started. Then the army overran us."

"The Prussians, you mean," Jeanne-Marie asked for clarification. "After the siege?"

"After the siege. But they were Frenchmen." Madame Toussaint tried to break it gently.

"After the Prussians had moved on," Coco concurred.

Monsieur Hervé took another drink to conjure up the past. "'Run, son, run,' my father yelled to me, ramming his final Minié ball home in his rifle. I didn't want to be a coward. I didn't want to run. I didn't want to leave my family. But I did."

His hands were a workman's hands, calloused, with broken and dirty nails. Madame Toussaint considered them good hands. "Later, when I heard no more shots, I slunk back, following along from doorway to alley, tripping over destruction. Bodies of our comrades." The struggle overcame him. He took a drink to firm his nerve. "I go to the cemetery—Père Lachaise, named for another cleric who gets more attention than he deserves. Now, on Toussaint, All Saints' Day, I go. When others are decorating the graves. And again in May. Ivy's growing now, up over the wall. But on that day, I watched. From behind a tombstone.

"They lined them up against the cemetery wall. So many, so crowded, they were three deep. My father stepped to the front, trying to protect them, my mother and my baby brother in her arms. Regular muskets didn't fire fast enough. They had to use those automatic *mitrailleuse*. In half a minute, my father couldn't protect them anymore. He dropped. They dropped on top of him. Others on top of them. And I was alone in the world. At ten."

He finished off his drink in one gulp. "They plan a massive mosaic for the dome of Sacré Coeur. That's what they needed me to consult about today. The fact is, I was born right around here, two streets over. The butte is riddled with caves and tunnels. People have dug here for centuries. Plaster of Paris, you know. The builders needed me from the beginning, all the work they had to do to shore up the summit for the new edifice. Filling in those holes. I knew every cavity. I hid in them during that week, the week of blood. 'Nits grow into lice,' they said.

"I lived in them, in the caves. After. That was certainly the end of school for me; I had to work every day of my life. And now they've sealed them all up. Hiding places are pretty hard to find in Paris these days."

Madame Toussaint thought briefly of Paul. He couldn't hide forever.

"I didn't want to be part of this building of Sacré Coeur," Monsieur Hervé continued. "The martyrs celebrated here are not my martyrs, not the real martyrs of the place. My martyrs ought to have this gilding, these icons of memory, suffering, and death. It's where we made our last stand. And in my mind, every nail I hammer, every whitewashing bit of plaster I lay on—it is—*it is for them.*"

Monsieur Hervé took another swing and continued. "They plan a mosaic, the basilica's designers: Jesus opening his chest to reveal his heart, burning with passion, suffused with blood, surrounded by thorns." Because he said "Jesus" and not "Our Lord" indicated that he was not a believer, never could be. "They make out that it's Jesus who suffers, not the men and women of Paris. That hole in the chest—it's too much like the hole they drilled into my father—"

They ordered another drink all round, Monsieur Hervé a third cognac. Jeanne-Marie warmed up with a Bretonne's native cider. Madame Toussaint decided she was ready for another Malbec.

"And yet, Monsieur, you come and help them to build this place." The fluttering martyrs screened on silk waved in front of her eyes once more.

Monsieur Hervé shrugged. "A man—a boy—gets hungry. His hands have only a certain set of skills. His education. Usually, I prefer to do renovation. Other buildings."

"Which brings me to my next question." Madame Toussaint hoped it wasn't disrespectful to be moving on like this. She hoped he would welcome other topics. "The building on Rue Férou."

"Yes, Madame. Where you are the concierge."

"Where you and your crew are presently doing renovations on the fourth floor."

"I should say I'm not crazy to be doing work in a modern haussmannian building either. But, as I said, a man gets hungry. And then he tries to replace the family he lost, and they—his wife and his children named for his parents—get hungry as well."

"I understand, Monsieur. We have all done such."

"We know how these edifices were built. Not so blatantly on the bodies of the poor as the basilica. But poor families were thrown out of what are now fashionable neighborhoods without recompense, all with slippery financing on the part of the developers. And they didn't always pay their workmen what they were owed."

"Monsieur d'Ermenville, whom some call le Comte, the owner of our building, for example."

A wary look crept into his eyes. "For example, yes."

"You do know Monsieur d'Ermenville was murdered the night before last?"

"I do."

"Did the police approach you about the matter? Ask questions? Of you? Of your men?"

"Not much. None of us was in the building at night, when the crime seems to have occurred, of course. Every man's family will vouch for that."

"You know all of your men well? None of them would have a reason to want Monsieur dead?"

"No. No more than the reason I have, and have just divulged to you. The police seem to be quite certain they know who the culprit is, begging your pardon, Madame."

Madame Toussaint acknowledged his unspoken but clearly expressed concern for her and her husband with a nod. "You do have a key to the premises?"

"Yes, Madame. You must be aware that's how we let ourselves in every morning."

"The future tenants gave it to you?"

"Actually, it was Monsieur le Comte—er, d'Ermenville. I've done a lot of work for him over the years. He often does me the favor of passing my name on to friends and acquaintances who need work done. He, unlike others, always pays—paid on time.

"The crew is laying the parquet today and tomorrow, so they didn't need me. That's why I took the chance to cross town to Montmartre to see to this job."

He put down his empty glass but went on without the soothing liquid. "I have to say, most of my crew on Rue Férou was pretty nervous to come to work today, thinking there's a murderer on the loose with access to the building.

"And the new tenants we're working for, I've heard from them too. Via telegraph. They spend winters in Monte Carlo. Her family owns a villa. They've read the Parisian papers. They're reconsidering their move. I'm not sure they will follow through with the lease. I'm not sure I would want to sleep under the same roof as such a horrific crime. And then, what if they decide not to pay me? It won't be the first time I've been stiffed, but never for such a reason."

"I know exactly what you mean," Coco said. "About men not paying after the job's been done. Or even half done."

"And now, Mesdames, Mademoiselle, I really must be on my way. Three cognacs before quitting time? The day may be a total loss."

"Thank you, Monsieur Hervé, for your time."

They all bade him good-bye, Madame Toussaint wondering which murder was more pressing to resolve. That of two nights ago? Or that of the family Hervé and the thousands who had died with them, festering for decades?

Monsieur Hervé, while he might have reasons and opportunity to murder d'Ermenville, just underlined the similar reasons Paul Toussaint had. And Madame Toussaint could only sympathize with both of them.

· XVII ·
THE TERRIBLE YEAR

—

NATHALIE AWOKE AND stretched in the narrow housemaid's bed, new life springing into each limb. Sunlight streamed through the single, slanted, dormer window. It was November, yes, almost the last day. She'd been at death's door for a month. The little room under the eaves had no fireplace, but it was at the top of the building, so the heat rose from the six lower floors. And none of the refuse.

Oh, yes, she ached, in a new, wonderful sort of way, at her very core. But the fever that had burned her, clean and new, was gone. Her head was clear. Above all, she was hungry. Hungry for Paul, hungry for life. A croissant and coffee wouldn't go amiss, either.

While she'd slept, Paul had left her side in that cramped bed. She thought she remembered him saying something as he went, something that lay with her like the ceramic eggs they used to put in the hens' nests to encourage laying. Hard and cold, his words and worry had seemed so out of place in the nest of her contentment, of her new-hatched health that made her feel immortal.

Paul saying, "Coal-gas, necessary for the balloons, is almost gone. There are no lights in the City of Lights at night. Not a single pigeon has made it through in eight days."

Paul's look of tender concern. "I'm afraid, *chérie*, even your favorite Malin has not had cunning enough this time. There is no way we can coordinate with the free French forces amassing under General Ducrot beyond the Prussian lines. The last word we had was that he had decided to come across to the southeast of the city, so we've spent the past days moving men and *matériel* across Paris from where we thought would be the best point, from the west. Can the Prussians have failed to see these movements? They will outmaneuver us. Can we trust our lives and the lives we hold dear to no more information than we had eight days ago?"

Had she just dreamed such crushing words? They seemed too hard, too real, too cruel, to be anything but a recurrence of her delirium. He also repeated sentiments that he'd said often over the past month, things she knew he believed to the depths of his soul. "While official France and Germany are rushing into a fratricidal war for the conceit of moribund monarchies, the workmen of France and Germany send each other messages of peace and good will."

What she did remember clearly had happened the night before: how she had watched for him from the window, then run down to meet him halfway up, on the fourth-floor landing with a warm embrace. "See how well I am, thanks to your devoted care," she demanded as they turned to climb back up to the room. "Don't you think I could go back to the Gare tomorrow?"

A look of concern and fear crossed his face. "I'm glad you're doing so well—"

"Thanks to you," she repeated, trying to cheer him.

"I'm glad I could be of help. But I would rather you hold off on making that move for a while."

"On Thursday, then? Friday?"

"Let us see what tomorrow brings."

Why could she not cheer him? "I am strong enough to walk to the Gare d'Orléans. See, I made it back to the top of the stairs. You didn't need to carry me this time. And once I've made it there, how tired can I get, just sitting and sewing? I could sew here, but it wouldn't be as useful without the whole row of us working along our full lengths of the balloons. And I want to do my part for the defense of Paris. Why won't you let me do my part?"

"One more day," he repeated. "But if you are so well—" He caught her in his arms after closing the door. "How about we make our marriage complete?"

And that was the first time he made love to her, after a month of cold compresses, gentle caresses, holding hands, holding the chamber pot. How she loved him that night. And how grateful she'd been. So grateful, she would have done anything in return. Instead, she felt she'd been the one receiving.

"I love you," he'd said. And did not waken her when he left.

Sitting up in the narrow little bed of their love, careful not to bump her head on the steep slope of the ceiling, she saw that he had left her breakfast. That, after having taken his share of a siege loaf to face the day.

She dressed for the first time in a month. The garments hung on her, even with the corset laced to its tightest. She wondered how Paul could have said he loved such a boney body. She tried a new hair style in the cracked mirror used by housemaids before her. She waited the rest of the morning, then grew restless with empty hands. That showed how well she was.

Around midday, ravenously hungry again, she decided to take the stairs all the way to the first floor. Paul had proven that their rather unorthodox marriage meant more to him than just a stick in the government's eye on a wild night in the Hôtel de Ville. Now that she was well again, she should begin her duties to her in-laws, at least.

Happy. Gratitude. Would everyone she met be able to see the glow of her new love? Or should she just cherish it quietly in her room until Paul came again? Such thoughts made her pause until she heard someone come in the front door far down the stairwell below her, felt her hunger again, and knew she had to move.

Monsieur and Madame Eugène Toussaint, her brother- and sister-in-law and technically her hosts all this long month, lived in the building's best apartment, the full first floor. She made it down all the flights, took time to catch her breath, then lifted the fine bass knocker and rapped.

"Yes?"

"Good morning, dear sister . . ."

Had she been thinking clearly, Nathalie would have realized that a woman like her sister-in-law would never answer her own door. The maid set her straight without cracking a smile. The woman's back, with its loop of white apron strings over black muslined hips, also set Nathalie straight. Her sister-in-law would never wear an apron or such a mob cap. Nathalie followed those strings—looking as if a relationship with Nathalie would even be distasteful to them—as the maid showed her to a cold and gloomily lit parlor to wait "while I see if Madame is at home."

The maid returned. "Madame is indisposed."

This was the first time Nathalie had learned that her sister-in-law might have a delicate constitution. Of course, living on siege rations, anyone who didn't have to go stand in food lines for the better part of the day might well take the luxury of lying in a warm bed. Nathalie found it odd, however, that Paul, in all the long conversations they'd had up in her sickroom garret, had never once mentioned that his brother's wife was not lively, not the perfect hostess when he went to visit. If anything, a little too flirtatious to him. Nothing to suggest—the horror of it—that Nathalie might have passed her fever on to the household. He'd kept her so closely sequestered.

Perhaps Paul had been covering for the woman in whose house and good graces he had deposited his new bride. In truth, Madame Eugène Toussaint had never made the climb up to the sixth floor to visit. All sustaining broths and gruels were brought up by the maid, if not by Paul himself. Hence this present air of resentment under her mob cap? Nathalie realized her sister-in-law—when all Paris should be pulling together—had been shunning her.

"Madame says you may eat in the kitchen with the cook." The maid led her there. Which was a good thing, because Nathalie had no money and didn't know if she was strong enough yet to stand in a food line for who knew-what-skimpy-reward at the end?

The kitchen was warm, the food good and plentiful. Nathalie knew the cook, Mademoiselle Joséphine, by the works of her hands if not by sight. Mademoiselle knew just what sauces were needed to make roast cat surrounded by rats, like little sausages, palatable, as if she'd been born to such appalling scarcity.

"Ah, there you are, *chérie*," Mademoiselle Joséphine greeted Nathalie as warmly as her stove was popping—on rich man's fuel. The woman was just as Nathalie had imagined her from her dishes: tending to roundness—under different culinary circumstances—and motherly. "I wondered if I would ever get to meet the patient who, I heard, was so appreciative of my efforts. And Monsieur Paul seems to be very enamored of you, which goes a long way in my book."

"I'm sure I wouldn't have survived these last weeks without him. And without your excellent cooking. I'm so lucky to be his wife."

Nathalie was quite unprepared for the reaction these words evoked. "His wife? His wife! Why, Madame, that's wonderful. All these years—I began work as a scullery maid under his lady mother—we despaired that he would never find the right woman. Always too busy with his causes, head in the clouds. And no one was good enough for him. Then his brother—Eugène is the younger, you know—married first. We assumed he would have the first children. Oh, I am thrilled."

Nathalie was a little less than thrilled. So they'd considered her Paul's concubine all these weeks? They still considered her thus? No wonder her sister-in-law had been indisposed.

Mademoiselle Joséphine beamed as she set two steaming bowls of vegetable soup enriched with horse meat on the bright oilcloth of the kitchen table between them. "Bon appétit. Of course, go ahead and eat, Madame, while I just finish up here."

With her first spoonful, Nathalie could tell it was better than what she'd had at La 'Tite Chope. Juniper berries were an inspiration. The crumbly siege bread that accompanied it, which Mademoiselle Joséphine baked herself in these hard times, was tolerable when dunked in the rich broth. The oil cloth reminded Natalie of the treated calico of the balloons she should be working on.

"No, they didn't tell me you were married. Congratulations." The cook approached to give Nathalie a hug against her ample, aproned bosom, then stopped herself. "But excuse me, Madame. That of course means you are now la Comtesse. Would you prefer more formal address?"

Nathalie dropped her spoon in surprise. "I . . . I had completely . . . I hadn't realized."

"You know of course that Paul is le Comte d'Ermenville."

"Yes, but we always . . . I mean, we just sort of used it to tease him." Then Nathalie remembered the correct facts. "France has outlawed the peerage. For many years now."

"Of course. Citoyen Paul." Mademoiselle Joséphine shook her head fondly. "He would rather be rid of the title. Of all titles for all Frenchmen. In the interest of égalité."

"I know. I share his political beliefs." Nathalie was beginning to wonder if the champagne and red-tape rosettes in the Hôtel de Ville had all been foolery. Did Paul see it only as such? Then why would he have cared for her so carefully since the night of Toussaint? He had spoken out in favor of "free love," in favor of giving the wives, widows, and unwed mistresses of soldiers the same benefits. Did she share that belief? She'd always thought so.

"Which is no doubt why he chose you over those debutantes in their fluffy tulle. Much more practical for what we've been enduring, *je vous assure*."

"Please, Madame. I'm sure since Paul prefers that you address him by the familiar *tu*, for me—*on peut se tutoyer*—as well."

"As you wish. I mustn't let Madame," she gave a nod in the direction, "overhear such familiarity, however."

This exchange had brought a smile of memory to the Cook's face. "Once when Monsieur Paul was still in short pants, I remember him sitting just there on this very kitchen table; Monsieur Eugène had it brought from the family's country home along with many finer pieces you'll see in the parlor." She ran her hand over the embedded butcher's block where no doubt she'd wielded many a knife.

At the moment, Nathalie was wondering if she'd ever be invited into the parlor.

"His mother had him dressed in those velvet knickers with a lot of lace. They might have been dressed to go to Versailles fifty years before, before the Revolution." The Cook shook her head, then continued. "What a picture he made, looking like that, contrasting so sharply with the words coming out of his mouth. Like currents with a rich venison. I remember he was eating a cream puff. I made them especially for him."

Nathalie took another spoonful of soup, briefly wishing for something other than what she had before her.

"'The Revolution,' he had just learned and parroted then, 'did away with the aristocracy, all comtes and ducs and princes either gone to the guillotine or fled to England.' He had a child's fascination with the details of this history. 'So I had to ask my tutor, "How is it that *maman* and *papa*—?"' It seems that Napoleon, picking up the pieces of Revolution, made an all-new aristocracy from his favorites, with all-new lands and privileges, and the first Comte and Comtesse d'Ermenville."

"But forgive me this gossip." The cook stopped herself by settling down before her own bowl of soup. "I'm sure there couldn't be a better couple in all of Paris, of any class, than the pair of you."

"You mean Madame Eugène Toussaint didn't say anything to you about our marriage?"

The cook shook her head as she took her own first bite. "Good. The salt's just right. The temptation, in times of shortage or less-than-fine foods is to over-salt, which never helps."

"Perhaps it just slipped her mind," Nathalie suggested, having taken the advice about salt to heart for future housewifely duties. Being in the presence of a cook made her wonder if her new status meant she would always eat food made by other hands. She decided that was too impersonal for the relationship she wanted to share with Paul Toussaint.

"Impossible." Mademoiselle Joséphine crumbled bread across her soup. "I think, Madame Paul, you—"

"Please call me Nathalie."

"Madame Nathalie, you should know that Madame Eugène is very jealous of her position."

Nathalie remembered the conversation she'd heard between Paul and his brother while she was so ill. Yes, Paul had announced they were married.

"You're married." A grimness to Eugène's tone. Then, "I won't tell anyone, Brother, if you won't," he had said, as if it were a joke.

Maybe her brother-in-law, despite the dismissive chuckle, had been as true as his word and hadn't even told his wife.

Or was it—? No wonder Madame Eugène Toussaint wouldn't see her, if she thought Nathalie was only her brother-in-law's fancy woman, as any comte had a birthright to.

Nathalie was trying to decide what she should do about this as she filled her mouth with spoon after spoon of soup. Or should she do anything without consulting Paul, who knew these people far better than she did?

Before she reached any conclusions, Mademoiselle laid down her own spoon and exclaimed, "But you poor thing. To be but newly wed and your husband gone off to war as he is."

"Gone off to—?"

"Indeed. They all are. A great last-ditch effort to break through the Prussian lines and meet up with the forces of free France on the outside. Maybe. We should all pray it be so."

Mademoiselle Joséphine, Nathalie saw, was a religious woman. A crucifix hung over her sink and, when she didn't have soup to eat or potatoes to peel, she prayed her rosary.

"No. I . . . I didn't know," Nathalie said weakly.

"He didn't tell you? Didn't say good-bye?"

"I suppose he did." Nathalie felt tears stinging her eyes. "In a way."

"Didn't want you worried, no doubt. Thought it might bring on a relapse."

Nathalie left her soup and got to her feet, pacing the two steps from one end of the kitchen to the other. "But how can I not be worried? Frantic?"

"Indeed, poor thing."

"After last night . . ." Natalie remembered Paul's description of what the morning would bring better than she'd heard it as he spoke it.

"Last night, many a young man—the inexperienced, the long-time married man, the grandfathers, too—thought on the day to come. He hoped to leave a little bit of himself behind in the future in case fate decreed he should have none."

Nathalie wished the cook hadn't put it like that.

"But sit down and finish your soup," the other woman continued. "Sometimes I am not so sad I have no one. No one but our good Lord in whom I trust."

"Has Monsieur Eugène gone to fight as well?" Nathalie thought that might explain her sister-in-law's behavior today. Nathalie herself thought crawling back up to bed might be just the thing to do.

"Monsieur Eugène? Oh, no, not he. He's probably off at the *bourse* trying to save his investments."

"Men are dealing at the *bourse* when the city is under attack?"

"When the Prussians enter Paris and murder us in our beds, I'm sure not all Monsieur Eugène's material possessions will do him a bit of good."

A dull thud rattled the kitchen windowpane, and Nathalie sat back in her chair, hard.

"Hear that?" Mademoiselle Joséphine asked and crossed herself.

All of Paris had grown used to distant artillery over the past few months, first from this side of town, then that, a smattering of it most days. But this was closer, continuous, from the southeast only and, with the cook's news of the all-out onslaught, heart stopping.

Mademoiselle went to the window and opened it, letting in cold air and a wet dampening to the burning wood and good food smells of the kitchen. More cannon-fire rolled across the distance. A whiff of gunpowder made its way into Rue Férou.

"Ah, there's old Michel." Mademoiselle Joséphine had spied someone in the street. "Monsieur Michel—Michel," she called out the window, "what news?"

The man said two words Nathalie couldn't catch and hobbled on.

"Nothing," the cook reported. "Nothing yet."

As the day progressed, Nathalie was grateful for Mademoiselle Joséphine's company, her warm fire, and as much food as Nathalie's nervous stomach would let her digest. At one point, they went up to the *chambre de bonne* under the eaves. From there, they sometimes got a view of smoke clouds rising over rooftops to go with the booms, but it was impossible to tell which side belonged to which noise or how the battle was progressing. And, up on the sixth floor, it was impossible to call to the people passing in the street to question as to what they might have heard or seen.

XVIII
LA BELLE ÉPOQUE

Madame Toussaint tried looking at Paris through a black-net veil as she bade farewell to Jeanne-Marie at the stage door of the Moulin Rouge, opened only the slimmest crack to let the girl out.

While the three of them—Madame Toussaint, the young housemaid, and Coco—had still been at the *bouillon* window watching Monsieur Hervé the construction foreman leave, yet another man in a smock, this time in tawny red, and beret had entered the frame. He, too, was familiar, carrying a portable easel and artist's case with canvases under his arm.

"Why, it's Monsieur Mahler, across the hall from me on Rue Férou," Coco exclaimed.

"Ah, Mesdames." Jeanne-Marie clapped her hands to her cheeks made rosy by two drinks of her own. "I forgot to tell you, listening so intently to Monsieur Hervé's tale. I met Monsieur Mahler up on the butte. He, like others, did not want to spend the day under that roof on Rue Férou where the unspeakable happened. And since his model had left him and the day was so fine, he thought he'd 'knock off a canvas or two'—his words—for the tourist trade.

"And Madame," she said, the blush growing deeper. "It is as you said. He asked if I would pose for him."

"Hmm," Coco and Madame Toussaint said together, exchanging a glance.

"Mesdames, I am willing to do it. He said I should meet him at the café *Chez Maman*—you know, next street over from the Rue Férou—to discuss it. He'll buy me dinner if I meet him there. I sort of said I would. I don't have to go home with him afterwards."

"No, you don't," both older women said, again together.

"But it would be a perfect way to get to know him . . . to learn if he has any useful information about the murder . . ." Madame Toussaint mused.

"Yes, I never could get close to him," Coco said with a sigh. A further revenue source that had dried up for the dancer/mistress/madam.

"And you are in the trade." Madame Toussaint acknowledged professionalism. "I am just the lowly concierge."

"I am too old." Coco's offense was still raw. "He told me so, point blank."

"Coco, you must be ten years his junior."

"Exactly. By which I mean to say, once they hit twenty-five, he stops seeing women. Stops giving them the time of day. They certainly can't pose for him."

"That leaves only me." Jeanne-Marie broke into the dialogue, repeating her offer.

"He is a German." Coco and Madame Toussaint turned together to warn Jeanne-Marie, as if that explained everything.

Madame Toussaint's mind flashed back to the horrors of the Prussian siege, when Paris had tried so hard to keep any man with Mahler's accent out of their streets. Twenty-five years ago, had anybody asked her who in the building was most likely to have murdered a fine, upstanding French citizen, she would have immediately fingered the artist on the fifth floor. And he would have raped every woman in the building on his way out.

In the new gilded world that had become normalcy, however, she told herself she should move with more deliberation towards her conclusions of who was evil and who innocent. Even Jeanne-Marie. Was she so very innocent, with her flushed eagerness to become an artist's model? The girl had been Monsieur d'Ermenville's *bonne*, after all.

Jeanne-Marie clapped her hands, excited and nervous at once. "Then you'll let me do it?"

"I never said that—" Madame Toussaint protested.

But Coco, who had a different perspective on the power women could hold over men even when such women seemed most powerless, leaned a different way.

The list of reasons against the plan turned into a list of warnings, then cautions, followed by questions it would be good to learn Mahler's answers to. In this manner, they left the *bouillon* and returned directly to the Moulin Rouge.

Once back at the Moulin Rouge, they let Coco rejoin her dance troupe.

"I will try to be there on Rue Férou to extract you later, *chérie*," Madame Toussaint promised as concierge and housemaid prepared to part.

While thirty pairs of high heels tapped in rehearsal on the floorboards overhead, Jeanne-Marie embraced Madame Toussaint. They wished each other luck, and Jeanne-Marie pressed through the narrowly opened stage door and reentered the street.

Watching through a peep hole the performers had installed for the many occasions when they had to discern whether their own exits were clear of unwanted attention, Madame Toussaint watched the police tail perk up, observe, then try to make up his mind. Should he follow one half of the pair that had been practically inseparable throughout his whole assignment?

Madame Toussaint watched as he made his choice: The young housemaid was innocent. She was not the one who would lead them to the vagrant murderer. The gendarme settled back into his watchful pose. Jeanne-Marie was not worth leaving his post by the door to follow. He would not call for backup to split the pursuit. Jeanne-Marie was not going to lead the flics to Paul.

The policeman in the worker's smock had been replaced by the one in the top hat and evening tails who returned for the late afternoon shift. Both of them seemed to imagine that women, those strange creatures, could simply do the feats of cabaret just by virtue of having female parts and splitting their legs, no constant rehearsal required. The regimen Coco and her colleagues followed impressed even Madame Toussaint, who had had some inkling of it before. But the flics' incomprehension worked in the women's favor.

From the stage upstairs and to a hammering piano sounded the call, "Step-ball-change, step-ball-change, and turn-two-three. Mignonette, head up. Smile. It won't kill you. Or do sultry. Yes, sultry's good. And turn-two-three."

The women had decided to make their trackers think tonight was going to be a repeat of last night: Madame Toussaint taking shelter in the Moulin Rouge's dressing room again. Boredom would make the flics unobservant. And the long black net veil studded with tiny black beaded butterflies would do the same.

Madame Toussaint—with a wary glance at Cleopatra's boa constrictor who seemed to be either asleep or dead in his terrarium now—fitted herself into the slender black dress Coco had been wearing all day. The corset, pulled tight with the help of the dancer who was still nursing her twisted ankle, made the feat possible. Coco was taller, about ten centimeters. The borrowed clothes would stand the chance of dragging in the mud, but Madame Toussaint hoped the gendarme wouldn't notice.

She redid her hair to match the way Coco did hers for the street. The hat, the longer black veil with butterflies from the costume wardrobe, went on. Madame Toussaint took a deep breath and was ready to go.

"Swish those feathers on your ass," rang out from upstairs.

If she found the *flic* following her, she would just turn around and try something else. This had to work, or she'd be sleeping with the snake again. If not in jail.

The *flic* hardly glanced at her. He stayed behind, and now Madame Toussaint stood alone and—she hoped—unnoticed, on the left bank of the Seine. Carefully, she observed all through Coco's veil: the Quai des Augustins, the Pont Neuf and, to her right, the Pont St. Michel. Farther on, the great old lady, Notre Dame. Now, that was what a church should be. Time-heavy. Respectable. And not under construction, as Sacré Coeur was, to cover up the griefs of people still living. Telling them to count their losses as nothing. Worse, as a deserved evil.

With all the recent rain, the Seine was running high, a yellow flood with tree branches floating in it. And the sky, which had been so clear and fine all day, threatened to restart its downpour at any minute.

Notre Dame and, as far as Madame Toussaint could tell, no police trail. This would be the test. If Madame Toussaint walked up to this clochard and all hell broke loose, she'd know she'd miscalculated. Another night in jail would be the least of her worries.

"Hello, Jacques," she said.

Jacques lived in the open air under the final arch on the Pont Neuf. He seemed very happy there. He had his pile of blankets, a feather coverlet for winter. When they became dated, newspapers, which had gained such cachet during the siege as material for poor men's shirts, served this present man as a mattress.

Such would be Paul's bed. If he were lucky.

Jacques had been in the war, too, where he had lost his left hand. He had a chair he'd found on the curb, which he had re-caned himself with one hand and a stump. He always had a bottle, of course, and if he liked your company, he'd offer you a swig. And he had his books. Sometimes, when he'd finished a tome, he'd try to sell it. An ever-changing array of them on every subject stood displayed on a broken music stand. He was a great friend of the *bouquinistes* who had their stalls along the *quai*. They'd lend him interesting titles and then argue with him over the contents. In summer, he tended a pot of geraniums on the south side of the arch. This was prime real estate for the clochards, within sound of the grande dame of all distribution bells, in a heavily touristed area.

The *quai* did not suddenly explode into police whistles and flying, red-lined capes when she made this address. So far, so good. No flics in that alcove, at least.

Jacques recognized her at once, even in the disguise. "Hello, Madame Toussaint. Can't say that I'm too surprised to see you. I do read the papers. Every morning. In the café. Over coffee."

Madame Toussaint put a finger to the black net covering her lips. Jacques grew instantly wary, although he did offer her the chair. "Let's go someplace less public," she suggested. "Let me buy you a little something to crunch, Monsieur."

He took her up on it; she had Coco's reticule with Coco's money in it. They made themselves comfortable at a corner table in the bistro where Jacques' daily papers hung on the wall on bamboo poles. Students from the nearby Latin Quarter frequented the place; food could be ordered all day. The establishment specialized in a grilled sandwich made with day-old bread, the butt-ends of sausages and hams, cheese from next to the rind, all glorified by a rich, buttery béchamel.

The man behind the pewter bar knew Jacques by name, and probably knew Paul as well. Wasn't that just Paris, where socializing went from one café to the next, and there was a different establishment for each occasion, for each character?

Madame Toussaint said, "I need to find Paul."

"I know what kind of trouble you've got him into." Now that the sandwiches were on the grill, Jacques could be less cautious of his feelings. "I read the papers," he repeated. He also slept on them. "I won't let you get him into more."

"I?"

He rubbed the stump of his arm, pinned within his shirt with a rusty pin fallen from some cab-horse blanket. Then he added, "He would not abandon me when I was wounded. I won't abandon him. And all I can say is, if he did murder that reactionary fat cat, the man deserved it."

"It's his greedy, selfish, overweening brother who's got himself killed—and it was a long time coming—me arrested, me and my friends followed and harassed—" Madame Toussaint had to stop herself. The tension she'd felt all this time and kept bottled up until now suddenly threatened to overwhelm her.

Jacques spoke, not without sympathy. "You see why I can't tell you where he is."

Madame Toussaint found herself speechless with exhaustion and fury until the dishes were set before them. "I just want to warn him. They're after him."

"He knows they're after him. He's known that for twenty-five years."

Yes. For as long as he'd lived on the street. As long as she'd known him, truth be told. "And I want to ask him questions that might help me discern who the real murderer is. Jacques, he is my husband."

"A lot of us are on the streets because we want no contact with our former family lives."

That stung like acid. "That's not Paul and me!" she almost screamed so the man behind the bar looked up, nervous. After all he must have seen and heard in his day with a clientele of rowdy students—

Jacques shrugged. After that, the silence between them stretched into Jacques' last bite. Satisfaction altered his demeanor a little. Since he wasn't paying, he got up immediately.

"That's it?" Madame Toussaint demanded. She herself was finding the meal hard to get down, leftover everything. For two days now, she'd been victimized and accused by those in power of things she hadn't done. Now she was being blamed again, this time from the bottom up, when all these years she had covered for her husband, fed and clothed him, loved him . . .

She hoped she would have had the same impatience, the same strength of righteous indignation if a policeman had been the one countering her just now. It wasn't because Jacques the clochard was less powerful even than she, at the bottom of the pecking order like among the chickens at home in Normandy. Was it?

"Wait here," Jacques seemed to relent at last. "I'll see what I can do." Turning up his collar, he vanished into the thick rain drops that had begun to fall.

He was gone for a very long time. Madame Toussaint began to think he was never returning, that she'd been played the fool by someone they tell you not to encourage with handouts when they were panhandling. The man wiping down the pewter of his counter over and over was giving her dirty looks between coming to ask her if she wouldn't have something more.

Just as she was getting to her feet, afraid this next time she said, "No, thank you," she would be shown the door in no uncertain terms, Jacques returned, dripping wet. Under the stub of his arm and within his coat, he cradled a small, battered bandbox papered over with a pattern of full-blown roses.

"Here." He thrust it at her.

"What is it?" She reached for the box and attempted to open the lid to see.

"Careful." Jacques slammed the lid back down, nearly taking off her fingertips. "You want to let him loose?"

"Him? What's in there?"

Prewarned, she moved more slowly. She heard small scrabbling claws and opened the box a crack.

Her heart fluttered. "A pigeon?"

"You can get a message to Citoyen Paul that way. He knows where the cote is. The flics do not."

Her message could go that way, but she knew Paul had sent her a message coming this way first. The bird had a brown head and a missing toe. And a tough, cunning personality. Malin. Or Malin's great-great grandson, in pigeon lives. Echoes of the balloon workshop in the Gare d'Orléans.

Memories threatened to immobilize her with tears, but she could not let them.

❦ ❦ ❦

The flower shop on the main floor of the building was just closing for the day when Madame Toussaint reached Rue Férou. She lifted the veil on Coco's borrowed bonnet for the first time since Montmartre. Malin *fils* scrabbled in the bandbox under her arm.

The selection of cut flowers was very limited by this time of day and by the season as well. Just a few forced tulips in dull, faded colors on curved, wilted stems, come perhaps with their more vibrant brethren on barges upriver from Holland. And a lot of hardy ivy. In some seasons, after the owner had just returned from a purchasing trip at the *marché* on the Île de la Cité, the shop would explode with color, reel with fragrance. Now there was a vague undertone of vegetal rot, moss, wet soil.

Madame Toussaint's heart leapt into her throat as a dark figure moved out of the shadows answering her shove through the door that set the bell jangling on its loopy spring.

"Ah, bonsoir, Madame."

The girl recognized her at once. Madame Toussaint did come by for the rent on a regular basis, only now was not the time. That was the wariness in the girl's greeting. Also, she could not be ignorant of what had happened to the building's owner and builder just over her head two days ago.

Often, Madame Toussaint and the girl would both be sweeping out onto the pavement at the same time and exchange a greeting, a comment on the weather. Preparing for this encounter, Madame Toussaint had wondered why she never saw the girl in the building lobby, passing through the rear door of the establishment with an armful of spent stems and ferns for the trash in the courtyard, or crockery broken on the solid tile floor that could be hosed down.

The concierge blinked as she came in from the street already in darkness to the lighting that could make the blood red of a dozen roses pop. But her interest remained focused on the door at the back of the shop. She strode past the confused girl through the cramped aisle where skirts could take the pollen off forced pussy willows on either side. Past the counter where pastel ribbon was being formed into rosettes . . . the rosettes of the Hôtel de Ville's red tape on her wedding night . . .

Enough!

"May I help you, Madame?" The shop girl had a definite African accent—exotic—making the shop like a jungle, even at the end of the day. Might there be man-eating leopards to tear out a man's insides?

Madame Toussaint observed that no one took trash out that door into the yard because boxes were stacked in front of it. Boxes of spare vase stock. Boxes of doilies and tissue paper. Boxes of ribbon. She touched the corner of one, and the black glove she'd borrowed from Coco with the rest of the outfit came away dusty. Even if a criminal had had the key to the shop's front door—or broken in—he had not moved these boxes to get to the rest of building. Not any time recently.

And Madame Toussaint saw that she was not going to be able to sneak into the building—*her* building—that way, as she had hoped.

"Madame?"

"It's nothing, Mademoiselle. I think we are all a little jumpy since the death of poor Monsieur d'Ermenville."

The girl took a relaxing breath. "Indeed."

In a way, Madame Toussaint was glad the shop's owner wasn't here. That woman, Madame Auguste, took a lot of oxygen out of any space with her figure and personality like a full-blown peony. The girl was much quieter, observant.

"The boxes in front of that door—they are always there?"

"Yes, Madame."

"The proprietress never has you move them?"

"No?" The upward lilt of the girl's voice indicated a question. Was that the right answer?

"I must speak as a concierge," Madame Toussaint said. As if she still had the job, of which she was not at all certain. "The pompiers can't be too happy to have escape doors blocked. I mean, in case of fire." She struggled to extinguish the image that exploded in her mind. Of the Commune. Firebombs at the front of stores. Stores without exits.

"I cannot move them without Madame Auguste's permission," the girl said with an anxious glance towards the door. "But I will mention it to her in the morning."

Madame Toussaint saw there really was no other place to put anything in the crowded, narrow space. She was certain that if she was ever in a position to oversee such matters again, she wouldn't be responsible to enforce that law too stringently.

"Do you have any information the police might have missed that would help them capture the culprit?" Madame Toussaint asked instead.

"Not at all, Madame. The gendarmes were already here when I

opened the shop door yesterday. Madame Auguste and I were both as horrified as anyone. We cannot explain such a horrible deed." The girl's tone was meant to indicate that others might suspect the building's concierge, but *she* never had. Bouquets could often be wrapped in yesterday's newsprint; the shop girl had read the headlines at least—or Madame Auguste had read them to her if she was illiterate.

"No strange customers? No one lurking around?"

"No, Madame."

Perhaps that was all Madame Toussaint needed to ask. Let the girl get home as quickly as possible through the dark streets . . .

No. One more question. Madame Toussaint turned back to the girl from the door. "Do you have many customers from among the tenants of this building?"

"Of course, Madame. We are so conveniently located."

"Of course."

"Can you give me specifics?"

"Well, that German artist—what's his name?"

"Mahler."

"Yes, Monsieur Mahler." She gave a little chuckle. "He often comes at the end of the day to rescue something from our trash for his paintings. He once asked me to pose for him." The girl's cheeks warmed.

Madame Toussaint thought of Jeanne-Marie and hoped the housemaid's sortie with that man was going all right. "I hope you didn't."

"No. I have a good job here I wouldn't want compromised."

"Other tenants?"

"Mademoiselle Sylvie shops for la Comtesse. Usually ghostly pastels. Roses for—for his breakfast tray."

Madame Toussaint remembered the rose among the shards of that tray Jeanne-Marie had dropped in her horror.

"They have put in a big order for the funeral tomorrow," the young woman added in such a way that Nathalie suspected her native country had taboos against mentioning the dead.

"Of course."

"Second floor, the military family?" The shop attendant moved on quickly, gratefully. "They're not flower fanciers much. The only ones I remember for them were some marguerites when one of the daughters had her first communion. A simple wreath to fix the veil, some to carry.

"The musician often orders two dozen red roses for his wife, so romantic, like the piano music that wafts out of their window on a summer's day. And Monsieur Pépin, camelias when he comes to visit Madame on the fifth floor, if we have them."

Madame Toussaint wondered if that was a little joke between Coco and her fancy man, based on the popular novel about a kept woman, *La Dame aux Camélias* by Dumas *fils*. Junior, like the name of the pigeon in the box under her arm.

So many women's names were those of flowers.

"Otherwise, lilies. Although, thinking of this client, Madame Auguste has bought a lot of camelias and lilies recently and no one has come for them." The girl confirmed what Coco had told Madame Toussaint of her tenuous current living situation—that Monsieur Pépin, who rented the apartment for her, had suffered a stroke at Christmas and might not ever return.

The girl went on: "The widow Flôte—"

"The medium with her séances on the third floor."

"Yes. She'll buy a purple orchid if she has an important occasion coming up. Madame Auguste special orders them. I have to say, they give me the creeps."

"And Monsieur Arnaud?"

The girl didn't seem to recognize the name.

"I'm sure you'd recognize Monsieur Arnaud, by sight, in any case. The dandy? Monsieur Arnaud and his—"

"His boutonnieres," they said together.

"Yes, every day, on his way out," the girl continued. "He stops in to see what we have and makes a selection. Something different every day. He likes variety."

"He likes boys," Madame Toussaint remembered Coco divulging.

"What was it today, for example?" Madame Toussaint asked.

The girl reached for a small round Chinese vase on the counter. "These." Spring's first jonquils—tiny, fragrant, and spotlight yellow.

"And the day before?"

"I can't remember."

"Was it narcissus?"

"Yes. That's right. And sometimes, too, although always later in the day, he buys something—an African violet, perhaps. 'For a friend,' he says."

"*'Une amie?'*" Madame Toussaint repeated. "A female friend? That's what he says?"

"Yes, Madame. Always feminine."

"Thank you, Mademoiselle. You've been a great help." Madame Toussaint turned to the door to let the girl get home.

"Madame, here." The girl took the jonquils out of the vase and held them out to Madame Toussaint.

"Thank you, Mademoiselle, but I'm afraid I haven't the money for flowers tonight."

"No, take them. Free. You see they're a little limp and brown around the edges. I'd only have to toss them out, and they might brighten up your loge for a day or two."

The brilliant yellow in the black hands was like day and night all in one image. If Monsieur Mahler had any artistic sense, that's what he'd paint, and stop with these pale demoiselles.

"Thank you, Mademoiselle." Madame Toussaint struggled to take the flowers along with her reticule and the bandbox. With the girl's help, she managed. "And what's your name?"

The girl grinned as she opened the door and the bell jangled again. "Jonquille," she said.

· XIX ·
THE TERRIBLE YEAR

—

Aᴏᴛᴇʀ ᴀ ʀᴇsᴛʟᴇss night broken over and over again by bombardment, Nathalie decided she would have to leave the building on Rue Férou for the day to see what she could find out about how the French sortie against the Prussians was faring.

And Paul? Where was Paul? Fighting on the front lines? Was he well? Was he even alive? She and Mademoiselle Joséphine the cook had still heard nothing.

Nathalie went first to the Gare d'Orléans. The balloon works were dispirited and echoed hollowly. All the men—from sailors to old blind Henri the basket weaver, and even a few of the women—had gone to the battle. And well before the sortie, cholera had hit the ranks hard.

"Our friend Bernadette is sick, very sick," women at the half-empty trestles greeted her. "You shouldn't go see her, only just recovered as you are."

"And Louise?"

"Ah. Our lively Louise—dead. With one final '*Enfin*.'"

Only Coco could speak and welcomed the chance, although her needle moved in a most desultory fashion. Perhaps there would never be another balloon launch. What was the point?

Coco had not seen Paul. "But you two certainly made yourselves scarce this past month."

"Yes. Sorry. I was sick."

"So he told us. And then ran off to see you again." Coco made no attempt to conceal the resentment in her voice.

Was the dithering of the balloon project to be laid at Paul's feet? At Nathalie's, because she distracted him? Paul Toussaint did not really belong to her, but to all France.

Nathalie decided not to say anything about their marriage.

"No. No one has seen him since he led a troop of men out the Gare door, as if they'd follow him to hell and back."

I'd do the same, Nathalie told herself.

But which way was hell? It seemed all around her. And when would the coming back happen?

"Vive la France," the young women said to each other as they embraced and then parted.

Perhaps, Nathalie thought, she should just go back to Rue Férou and wait for Paul to find her. No. She would go stark raving mad sitting and doing nothing like her sister-in-law while everyone else was making such sacrifices.

Nathalie didn't dare go any closer to the continuing sounds of battle. She feared not knowing worse than knowing, but she also feared she'd get in the way.

As Nathalie reentered the streets of Paris, she noticed that planks painted with red crosses had appeared on the faces of many buildings. Under each one, a field hospital had sprung up where ambulance after ambulance dropped off the horribly wounded and those who'd died on the way. Every bourgeoise woman, it seemed, found it fashionable to nurse the casualties even if her skills might be no more than cooking soup and tearing sheets for bandages.

Natalie tried to stop one or two of the men entering these establishments groaning and screaming on blood-soaked stretchers between the hands of their grim-faced comrades.

"Not able to talk, Madame. Can't you see the wound in his neck?" The next one couldn't speak either.

She tried the ambulance drivers. "No. No Colonel Toussaint."

"No Citoyen Paul."

"Get out of the way. A careless jerk could kill him."

Other women bombarded the drivers, too, clamoring with cherished names of their own. Sometimes it seemed like another assault against which the poor men had no defense.

Nathalie wondered if Madame Eugène Toussaint would consider opening her house up as a hospital. "It is all the fashion," she could hear herself give the one possible tack that might sway her sister-in-law.

Or, "As they heal, some might speak."

The idea made Nathalie laugh out loud, there in the middle of the street. Paul's death was exactly what her sister-in-law was hoping for, praying for. If Paul the elder son died, the title—if the peerage were ever restored—would devolve upon the younger and his wife. Nathalie wouldn't even bother to ask.

By the end of that day and of her still-invalid strength, she decided that working in such a place run by other, more charitable people, difficult as it might be, would be the way to proceed. On the Friday, she visited a number of these field hospitals closest to Rue Férou. Paul, if he returned, would surely come there, looking for her. If he could.

"A hospital with a real doctor in charge would be best," she explained to one nurse she met dumping waste in the street. "More good seems to be happening there than in those with just a well-meaning housewife doing her best." The nurse grunted with exhaustion. "Too many failures would be more than I could bear, each drop of blood possibly my husband's."

"You've come to the wrong place then," the woman said, wearily more than mournfully. "Hospitals with trained doctors are larger."

"Yes. So the chances of meeting someone from the front who knows Paul are better."

But the nurse let her in anyway, to see if she could manage the work. The wounds Nathalie saw were so horrific they made her head reel. The men's copious spilled blood had frozen in the cold. The limbs often needed amputation. When that was the case, the bourgeoise women were obliged to send the casualties to the larger, more skilled establishments. Places that had brute strength at hand, because that's what it took to part a man from an arm or a leg.

That's what it took to hold screaming men soused only with wine. That's what it took to saw through meat and bone as cleanly as possible. In the yard of the second establishment she visited, she almost stepped over what she took to be a pile of mud, only to find it to be splattered, ripped limbs. Natalie had to look away or lose the precious food in her stomach—or run back to her garment room to die.

A weeping and bone-weary French surgeon came from one such operation at a third care facility to talk to her, wiping his hands and cheeks on a much-used cloth. "For all my skill, I haven't saved a single man," he admitted; he had just lost the most recent one to come across his table. "I've never seen wounds like these before—what modern warfare does."

"What do you mean, modern?" Nathalie was almost afraid to ask.

"This is war on an industrial scale. The thrust of locomotives brings troops and supplies to the battlefield. Generals can issue orders by telegraph, hundreds of miles from danger. Like the revolution happening in our factories, individuals taking profits without individual risk. Women sit long hours in what used to be theatres on the Boulevard de Montparnasse, folding paper around black powder and these new bullets. Each bullet contains dangerous substances. Each, the ruined life of a man."

Nathalie thought of her own trestle tables sewing balloons at the Gare d'Orléans. "Of his wife and children too."

The doctor hardly seemed to be listening. "The Minié ball, invented here by a Frenchman (a pox on him) but perfected in America by their recent civil war, concluded only six years ago now. The Prussians were not slow to pick up such weaponry, often from our men when they capture them, so everything we hoped to give us advantage they use against us. The lead of this ball fits to the rifling inside the gun barrel, setting a spin on the bullet. You can shoot five times farther, ten times more accurately. You can fire lying down, protected by a boulder or hillock. And this bullet you can load so much faster in the breech rather than ramrodding into the muzzle—"

The man stopped to wipe his face again on the cloth stiff with another man's blood, then continued. "Lead is a soft metal. With the heat of firing behind it, it forms itself to the shape of the barrel. Still hot, when it crashes into a man, it flattens. And what it does to meat and bone. A lady should not see such things. A man should not—not and live to be a man again afterwards. And these new percussion artillery shells . . ."

The doctor sat wearily on a pile of bandages and shook his head. "We've just lost this one too. My aides are mostly older, men who honed their skills in butchers' abattoirs. That's what my operating room looks like. A slaughter house. My men are used to the fact that anything they touch is already dead." He said that word "man" so often, it was as if he were clinging to it, as if the creature were about to vanish from the world given over to industrialization.

Nothing he said made Nathalie want to join in this effort. Only clinging to the hope that she might still pick the man, Paul Toussaint, out of these horrors forced her to swallow bile and say, "I would like to help."

"In the Palace of Luxembourg, the Americans seem to have more success," the doctor told her, as if dreaming of a far-distant heaven rather than a place in the same arrondissement. "A Dr. Swinburne on a retirement tour has been pressed into service."

A nurse passing with a candle revealed that, to the elbows, the doctor's sleeves and all the front of his smock were dark with blood; he had nothing else to change into. Behind him, men were groaning, screaming, dying before her eyes, infection setting in.

Where, oh where, was Paul in all of this?

"I desperately need help—I can't lie to you. But maybe you can learn something with the American and come back?" The uplift in the end of his sentence indicated he hardly thought she would do that.

Nathalie took the suggestion only a little too hastily. And the American took her help gratefully.

"Cleanliness and ventilation," were his great secrets. "Yes, I'm afraid I honed my skills on that most horrific of training fields, our Civil War," he continued. He met her in the Salle des Conférences, dizzyingly decorated with paintings of Renaissance allegories in a network of solid gold. A row of bundled wounded on the cold marble floor down each side and a third down the middle. The inside of a gilt jewelry case contrasted with the ventilation. "Now it's your turn."

Natalie thanked him for all her nation. "But this isn't a civil war. The Prussians are invaders."

"Not yet, it isn't," the American said in his loose-slung accent. "But it's coming. Mark my words. You followed our Revolution with your own. Your turn for civil war is right around the corner. Brother fighting brother. It isn't pretty." The brothers foremost in her mind at the moment were Paul and Eugène Toussaint, but she tried to focus on what the doctor was saying.

"And I'm afraid in France, you may not have as easy a time of it.

France is not as big as our country, where there's still space enough out in the Wild West to allow men to vote with their feet. The good Lord forbid it, but it could be even worse here than our horrible times."

Despite the American's words of doom, Nathalie decided to work with him, minimal success and sheer numbers of wounded being the deciding factors.

They repeated the drill ten, fifteen times a day: the alcohol—lots of it, which Paris fortunately didn't seem to be in danger of running out of. Strong stuff into the man, weaker stuff on the wound. Tie the man down. Saw. Brute force. Blinding screams. Every scream she endured, for Paul. Cauterizing iron. The choking stench of burning flesh. Bandages. Then—wait and see. She wished she had Mademoiselle Joséphine's ability to pray.

Nathalie returned to the building on Rue Férou whenever she needed a rest, to see if they had any word of Paul from the fields of battle where, they learned more each day, were a total defeat. Heaps of bodies grew ever higher as the world moved inexorably into December.

"I keep praying for him," Mademoiselle Joséphine promised Nathalie. "And for you. For all the men. But I have to tell you, the lady of the house does not. You know, if Monsieur Paul dies without a child, she becomes a Comtesse."

That was the crux of it, wasn't it?

. . .

Sometimes, as she walked through the well-lit streets of La Belle Époque, Madame Toussaint heard the echo of her footsteps. All the panic of trying to find Paul during the Terrible Year came back to her from the faceless walls, one lonely panic conflated with the other. And now finding him could be worse than not, if she led the *flic* to him.

But she had thought the same in those dark days of 1870, desperate to find him yet at the same time hoping against hope that she would not, because of what she might find.

And then she remembered how, at the hospital, an ambulance brought in a young wounded aspiring officer named Herlement.

XX
LA BELLE ÉPOQUE

Past the curl of gas pipe and shut-off valve, a sign for firemen read "gas on all floors". Two steps beyond the florist's door stood the door to the residential portions of the building: heavy oak, a definite air of dignity, of permanence. Black crêpe announced the death inside, but not a word of the grisly cause. If the weather hadn't been so bad, the dead man's family might also have set a black-bound book and a pen and ink on a rostrum on the sidewalk so passersby could set down their condolences without bothering a family smothered in grief.

Madame Toussaint had never spent much time standing on this side of the front door. But they had taken her key from her. She would have liked to read that book of condolences, in any case. What clues to the murder might it contain?

She wondered what would happen if she pulled the chain and rang the bell now. Who would answer, since she wasn't in her loge? The notion that it might be Mademoiselle Sylvie occurred to her. Come down all the way from the first floor? Just for the sake of busybody control?

Madame Toussaint even reached out a hand—the one carrying the jonquils—to catch the chain, just to see if she was right. In the end, she resisted. Instead, she walked around the block, past the seminary for the Christian education of young ladies and a fountain inaugurated by Napoleon I, to the door of one of the three buildings fit together like a cabinetmaker's dovetailing. These shared her inner courtyard.

The rain renewed its efforts.

❧ ❧ ❧

"Yes, Madame? May I help you?" Madame Toussaint realized that Madame Bernard, the short, plump concierge of number 77, did not recognize her in Coco's somber dress and veiled hat. Madame Toussaint managed to step into the foyer and out of the rain before lifting the black netting. The space was so warm, cozy and sweet . . .

Now, in the flickering gaslight, Madame Bernard made the identification. "You? What are you doing here? Do you mean to kill every landlord in the sixth arrondissement? Coming disguised as a respectable woman of fashion." (If she only knew!) "I'm calling for the police."

She made a lunge for the door and filled her lungs. Madame Toussaint, however, was able to counter the move physically and verbally with a "Please, Madame," and then finally by presenting the woman with the bunch of tiny, trumpeted jonquils.

Madame Bernard was not easily dissuaded. She did not take the flowers. But at least she did not step out into the street to call for the police. It would not be young, sympathetic Théophile alone on the beat at this hour. It would be two of them. Maybe young Clémence with his hand still bandaged from trying to climb the wall. He would be in no mood to hear things out. And with his partner? Two flics were always worse than one, as each tried to outman the other.

"Madame, please." Madame Toussaint wished she knew the other woman's given name. You'd think women who poured their mop buckets down the same drain would have a camaraderie that would allow such familiarity. But perhaps, doing tasks that nobody else had a regard for, they used the "Madame" not as a distancing tool, but as one of mutual respect.

"You cannot believe such evil of a fellow concierge," Madame Toussaint continued her plea.

"Can I not?" Madame Bernard hadn't lost any of her hesitation. "They say you were in the Commune, that you were a *petroleuse*. Who can trust such a person?"

Madame Toussaint felt her heart sink to her feet. So that was floating around the rumor pond now. *Petroleuse.* They thought of her not just as today's murderer of her benefactor, but someone who, twenty-five years ago, with sagging breasts and wild eyes, had flung firebombs at innocents. Such was the political cartoonists' witch-hunting view; Madame Toussaint herself could only remember feeling so very young and alive.

The memories evoked by the blocked doorway in the florist's shop lay very near the surface. The hand holding the jonquils sagged. Madame Toussaint almost stepped out into the rainy night of her own free will and to a nonexistent future.

Then Madame Bernard closed her work-worn hands around the bouquet, so bright and foreign in her lobby with the gas burning frugally low. Her eyes, as dull as the grey wallpaper, seemed to catch light from that gold as if from the rags sputtering out of a weaponized wine bottle.

"Thanks," she said. "How thoughtful. I was also in the Commune."

Relief swept off Madame Toussaint's shoulders like a heavy cloak at this confession, never shared in all those years of side-by-side, wall-separated mopping. But had guesses not been made—day in, day out?

"Who of us here on the ground floors of Paris was not? Come in," Madame Bernard added. "I'll make us some tea."

"I don't mean to bother you."

"No bother at all. I was just going to make some for myself." Once in her loge, Madame Bernard nestled the jonquils in a chipped blue bowl and set it lovingly in the middle of her small, round table.

"I can't stay long." Madame Toussaint continued to suffer scruples, feeling the pigeon scratch in the bandbox under her arm. He no doubt enjoyed the indoor warmth as much as his new mistress, but that probably stifled him in his close quarters all the more.

"Nonsense," said Madame Bernard. "I've just finished another batch of *marrons glacés*, and I shouldn't eat them all by myself. I love to cook and bake but rarely have anyone to share with."

That was the lovely, tantalizing hot-sugar and earthy chestnut smell filling the lobby. For a moment, Madame Toussaint resolved to fill her own building with such smells on a regular basis. Then she dismissed the idea. *Marrons glacés* took two or three days. And who could say that she would ever have a kitchen, even her cramped little one on Rue Férou, again? She could just share in Madame Bernard's obvious, if guilty, pleasure.

Madame Bernard's loge was bigger than Madame Toussaint's and included a little sitting room beside the kitchen where the *marrons* came from. Two armchairs faced one another. The cat considered one of them his own and gave up only sulkily for Madame Toussaint. In Coco's black skirt, she sat on a nest of white fur.

So they drank tea and ate *marrons glacés*, and didn't say another word about the Commune. The jonquils began to exude their fragrance from the middle of the table. The cat rubbed Madame Bernard's leg as if annoyed. Which made Madame Toussaint, as she sat, think of her own cat who hadn't had any care for two days. More scrabbling in the bandbox made her set down her cup and saucer.

"I'm sorry. I really must be going. With everyone suspecting me as they do—suspecting a man I believe to be innocent—I must get back to my own building to try to discover who may in fact have done the horrible deed."

"Of course. And for how long can a building survive without its concierge? There's hardly ever time for her to run out for a bit of liver for her dinner in the regular course of a day."

Madame Toussaint rose, her hostess rose. The cat instantly reclaimed the chair. When Madame Bernard began to lead the way to the front door, Madame Toussaint stopped her. "Excuse me, Madame. Would it be possible to go out this other door?"

"To the rain-slick courtyard? Whatever for?"

"I would like to take the chance to dismiss the idea that the murderer entered my building from the courtyard."

"The police think such a thing possible?"

"They did a sloppy job of investigating the matter." Madame Toussaint told about the young Clémence's hand cut from the broken glass along the top of the wall. "In my opinion. As if I'd let a *flic* mop my foyer. Or scrutinize the people I let into my building. You can imagine the job they'd do of it."

Madame Bernard understood completely, put that way. "But are you suggesting that either I or Madame Lenoir next door let in a vicious intruder, who then climbed over our mutual wall?"

No more than I did, Madame Toussaint thought, with a brush of worry about Paul.

Aloud, she said, "Of course not, Madame. It is the police who are so suspicious."

Madame Bernard nodded at that assessment of *les flics*. "We concierges have to trust each other, *n'est-ce pas?*" We *communardes*, went unsaid.

Madame Bernard found them an extra wrap each, lit a lantern, found a step stool. Then, together, they began a thorough search of the deep well of the yard, cut in three by high, defensive walls, encircled by seven-story buildings. Even at the height of summer, the space never got sunlight lower than the second-floor windows. It smelled of moss, mold, and garbage bins, no matter how diligent the concierges tried to be. A very female smell, some men might say.

Besides looking at the obvious, close surfaces, Madame Toussaint stole glances at the looming face of her own building. Over the courtyard wall, she could see all but the lowest two floors. Every apartment had at least one window that overlooked the yard and the facing buildings. It interested her to see who had lights on, who did not. The top floor was completely dark; the *bonnes* and governess still had their tasks. The painter Monsieur Mahler must still be out; no lights there either. How was Jeanne-Marie faring?

No lights illuminated the fourth or third floors either: Monsieur Hervé's workmen had gone home and Madame Flôte had either retired early or was holding a séance in the dark. Monsieur and Madame Cailloux—their window boxes full of herbs, even at this season—must be at another concert. And Monsieur Arnaud—where was Monsieur Arnaud? Madame Toussaint hoped he was not at the window looking out at the suspicious sweeping of lantern light in the yard below him as he had looked down two nights ago and seen Paul slip into the lobby.

Was Monseiur Arnaud keeping the newly widowed Madame d'Ermenville company? Or was he with a boy? Madame Toussaint imagined he kept his perversions at Montmartre, the Mount of Martyrs. On her watch, she herself had never seen him with a potential victim. But now she was beginning to doubt just how watchful she had ever been, to let such a murder happen above her.

Only the second floor blazed, every lamp lit. Adults prepared for dinner. Children chased each other with pillows in the nursery. At one window, a child—boy or girl, Madame Toussaint couldn't tell—pressed its face against the window, saw the light, turned back to the room behind to regale its occupants with an unheard report. Before Madame Toussaint could suggest to her companion that she mask the lantern for a moment and hide with her in the shadows, she saw that the child got no takers to show equal interest.

"If someone did climb the wall," Madame Bernard was saying, "he would have had to know about the broken glass and then bring something along to cover it with. A thick blanket, a jacket. I cannot imagine scraps would not still be sticking to the shards. Nor can I imagine that dead leaves would not be pulled off more in one spot than another."

They kept their voices down as they brought the step stool into play to take a look.

It was still spitting rain. Concierges did not clean the tops of glass-studded three-meter-high walls very often, although they both realized now that most of their tenants could look out and complain of untidiness.

"Nothing," they agreed, climbing down.

"Here's an odd spot on your wall." Madame Toussaint pointed to what looked like a smear at just below eye level.

Madame Bernard raised the lantern high, and together they examined the spot. Because she'd just met with the clochard Jacques, and he had given her the pigeon, Madame Toussaint imagined that the stub of an arm might have rested there. While he climbed with one hand over the glass-studded wall? It hardly seemed possible, certainly not without a step stool, which Madame Bernard would have noticed had it been moved from her cleaning closet.

"Ah!" Sudden realization dawned in Madame Bernard's eyes lit by the lantern and made her laugh. "That's where I prop the mop end when I pour the bucket down the drain."

Of course. That made perfect sense. A matching spot probably existed on Madame Toussaint's side of the wall. And once again, the possibility that the murderer had been someone, a stranger from outside, diminished.

"The rain's picking up." Madame Bernard shrugged deeper into her shawl. "Come on in. Maybe another cup of tea? Then I'll send you on your way."

"Just one more thing." Madame Toussaint, who had left bird and reticule in a corner of the lobby, bent over, letting rain run down her neck into her hair, and shivered.

"The grate?" Madame Bernard asked. "What interest can you have in the grate that lets excess water flow between our yards?" Plenty was flowing now, with the rain.

"It's one more way someone could have entered my yard."

Madame Bernard bent, too, although not making the effort to do so steeply. "Impossible."

"It would have to be a small person, I agree."

"Not me." Madame Bernard patted her *marron*-thickened sides. "Few men are so small. And it seems only a man would have the strength, the fury, to commit the act the papers have described."

"Do you have a screwdriver?"

Under attack from the tool, the head of the bolt broke off. No one had removed this grate for decades. "I'll have to get a man in tomorrow to see to that," Madame Bernard said without real complaint. She wasn't paying for the work, but would get docked if it wasn't done.

"Do you use the Kampe Brothers?" Madame Toussaint asked between gritted teeth. "Flemish iron workers? In the Rue Cherche-Midi?"

While they discussed the various merits of different metalworkers, Madame Bernard held the sputtering lantern and Madame Toussaint twisted and chipped at the bolts on the grate. The other three fasteners came off whole, if lighter, having lost a few scales of rust. Madame Toussaint moved the grate aside, got on her knees and peered onto the wet flagstones of her own yard on the other side of the wall.

"With the bustle off, I think I can do this," she declared, and began to pull off Coco's skirt.

"Why in heaven would you want to?"

"It seems to me, if I'm home without everyone knowing it for a while, my investigation might go better. Also, they took the front door key from me, and I'm not at all sure they'll let me in if I ring. Not a few of them think I'm guilty, even though the police have released me."

And if they tell the police, I'll be shadowed again, she thought.

"What about your things? In your loge?" Madame Bernard asked, as if the loss of material goods must be the deepest tragedy. "They won't let you have your things?"

"I don't have any place to take them if they did throw me out. Except perhaps to leave them with Jacques under the Pont Neuf. The quieter I am about this, the longer I can put off crossing that bridge, so to speak."

"You can always come over here," Madame Bernard said.

"Why, thank you. That's a very kind offer." In fact, it almost made Madame Toussaint cry. She had the rain to hide her emotion behind and the last of the skirt to wriggle out of. She decided to keep the bodice and corset on, although this feat was probably going to ruin them, and she and her needle would owe Coco new ones. The way they compressed her torso would help.

"Bring your things. We could be cozy. You on my sofa. For a little while. Until something else comes your way." What that might be could not enter Madame Toussaint's imagination. Without a reference beyond police suspicion?

There was nothing for it. She would have to go through with her assault on the drain. Still, she stood another moment or two as if preparing to take a dive that had a good chance of killing her.

Madame Bernard seemed to have the same feeling. "My name's Berthe, by the way."

"Nathalie," Madame Toussaint said, taking as deep a breath as Coco's narrow corset allowed.

She sat on the ground. Rainwater instantly wet and chilled her to the bone, but it seemed to help her edge her way forward. As soon as her torso was against the wall, she had to lie down, scooting with her heels. She raised her arms above her head to narrow herself further.

She tried not to think of mice or rats, of the times the drain had backed up. Of the moss she slid on so easily. Of how absolutely no other person could have taken this same path. She would have noticed the scrapes. She was wet all over now. Stone grazed her legs, her knees, her back, her breasts, even under the corset boning. He face. Stone scrunched her chemise up immodestly.

Never mind. She was through. Madame Bernard—Berthe—handed clothes, hat, bandbox and reticule through the gap after her. Madame Toussaint whispered her thanks and good night to the blank wall as the lantern light blinked out.

Madame Toussaint let herself into her loge with the key she kept under the pot of dead geraniums. When she opened the door, her snarling cat shot out into the yard. "You'll have to catch a mouse tonight," she called after him.

As soon as she closed the door behind her, Madame Toussaint released the bird from his bandbox. The cat couldn't come in again until—until something happened to send Malin *fils* on his way elsewhere.

Madame Toussaint was home. She stood in soaking clothes, the bodice torn. Her chemise was filthy from crawling through the hole, sticking to her backside. The other undergarment she owned seemed to have been taken by the police as evidence along with her sheet. Scrapes and bruises stung everywhere.

The loge smelled bad. Mildew and—the cat had let her know what he thought of her absence by relieving himself on the unmade bed. Her bed she had last slept in with Paul. The unwashed dishes had attracted a colony of roaches. Malin *fils* swooped to perch on the edge of the cassoulet and cleaned that problem right up.

And now, here was the pigeon, relishing his freedom, flown to the top of the bend in the stove pipe. He would not have stayed there long had the fire in the box not been dead for two days. Madame Toussaint shivered at the thought of having to relight that fire.

The pigeon preened, getting ready for his night's roost—and putting more droppings on the pots and pans. Madame Toussaint wanted to wring his thick neck. Home was now worse than any concierge could allow and maintain self-respect. But the bird was a vital link to Paul.

She'd made it to her loge. No one—she hoped—had seen her arrive. And, the unusual angle at which she'd arrived into her courtyard had reminded her of yet another door she would have to investigate, that leading to the cellars. She only cleaned there once a month unless an emergency required otherwise. And only by daylight. But each tenant had his own padlocked cave down there in the levels of previous Parisian lives. There they kept wine, bicycles, broken chairs. Or . . . ?

Wait until it was light, pigeons could fly, and the cave wouldn't be so terrifying. In the meantime, she was home. The investigation could truly begin now.

XXI
LA BELLE ÉPOQUE

Madame Toussaint decided her first plan of action should be to get to Coco's apartment on the fifth floor and borrow a clean chemise. She couldn't think straight in what she had on, dripping wet and filthy.

Fortunately, she did still have her spare sheet, clean and folded neatly in the cupboard. She threw that on over herself so she didn't feel completely naked. As many coins as Coco had given her in the reticule, she had not given Madame Toussaint the key to her apartment. In case something happened to the concierge, Coco might have to let herself in later. Madame Toussaint took the one dangling on the building keyboard instead.

Then Madame Toussaint opened the loge door a crack to listen at the stairs.

She pulled it almost shut again and listened to Monsieur and Madame Cailloux, she in dress heels, on the stair preparing to go to a chamber concert—Haydn, by the discussion. Madame waited while Monsieur went out and hailed the cab.

While Madame Toussaint bided her time, she remembered to reach into her empty tea tin on the upper shelf and was relieved to find her own stash of coins still there. She grabbed it and slipped it into the reticule, too. That way, she didn't risk it being stolen. And she felt much better able to face what might come, knowing she could buy her way out of perhaps not everything, like her late brother-in-law had been able to, but many of the common things on a concierge level.

Then the lobby was clear.

Madame Toussaint listened up the entire stairwell for another moment or two; even if someone was to enter the stairway on the sixth floor, she would hear them. Then she could proceed.

Something on the floor of her lobby stopped her, or rather, something that was not there. Monsieur Arnaud's ash and narcissus petals no longer decorated the tile. It had been two days, but still. Who in the building would have bothered to do her job, to clean them up in her absence?

It was a puzzle she couldn't solve at the moment. Instead, she began her climb, sheet trailing.

First floor, the d'Ermenvilles. You would expect silence, the household swathed in horror and grief. For a moment, Madame Toussaint thought she heard a laugh. A man's laugh. Monsieur d'Ermenville's ghost? She shuddered and told herself it was just the cold. She heard nothing more and pressed on.

The usual hullaballoo of a flat full of children—their parent's military career never quite able to contain them—greeted her on the second floor. And suddenly, the apartment door flung open.

Madame Toussaint quickly squatted down on the stair, gripping the balusters for balance. What would the lieutenant-colonel think to discover the concierge of his respectable building in the sixth arrondissement running about in a bed sheet?

Madame Toussaint found her gaze just at the level of a child—the two-year-old with a mop of curly blond hair, fresh from his bath, not a stitch on. His little boy parts bounced joyfully at their freedom, but his escape skittered to a halt when he saw her.

A flood of protectiveness washed over her. This little boy lived in the same building as a murderer. He lived in the same building as Monsieur Arnaud with his peculiar tastes.

And she remembered that in many buildings, it was the concierge's job to carry up water whenever anybody wanted an evening bath. She had to be grateful that this building had plumbing.

Madame Toussaint laid a finger to her lips for the boy's silence. His eyes widened. Good. And it kept him from attempting the stairs on his own, which might not go well on those pudgy knees.

His had probably been the face at the window, looking onto the dark courtyard while she and Madame Bernard scouted out the wall and drain.

Very well. Tonight was the night he learned life was not about all the regimentals his family had on offer. Not always the warm, bright, protected place his family wanted to present when keeping him from any knowledge of the crime committed two nights before on the floor below.

The nanny was there in a moment, her skirt soaking with soapy water. She didn't even see Madame Toussaint in her crouch on the stairs before scooping up her little charge and sweeping him off to the nursery.

The third floor, dark and quiet. The Cailloux, Madame Toussaint already knew, were out for the evening.

Monsieur Arnaud—? Hmm. Well, she couldn't very well knock on his door tonight, dressed as she was. Otherwise, she might have done so, using as her innocent excuse a query about whether or not he had received his important delivery from the haberdasher and apologizing that she had not been able to see it carefully delivered to him herself as was her custom.

Like the third floor, the fourth—because the added steps made the rental value descend—was divided into two apartments. Left was where Monsieur Hervé and his crew were working during the day. Refinishing the parquet, she remembered. The smell of paint and wet plaster reached her through the closed and silent door.

And the right—?

A strange red glow like fire seeped out of the apartment and onto the floorboards in the hall where she stood with bare feet. A heavy moaning followed, like a soul in torment. Madame Toussaint tried the door handle and found it open. She burst in, expecting to wrap the widow Flôte, having spilled burning oil on herself while cooking, in the damp bedsheet.

There was no out-of-control fire. Eight or nine people sat holding hands around Madame Flôte's table in the center of her sitting room. A lamp with its glass chimney painted red stood in the circle's center, casting strange shadows on the heavily curtained walls with its otherworldly glow. Madame Flôte sat at the head of the table, her hair swathed in an exotic turban fixed with a brooch of cut glass.

Madame Toussaint's ghostly appearance caused loud exclamations among the party, although they had been trying to be quiet and focused. One of the women fainted dead away, her face flat on the table.

"Do not break the circle!" Madame Flôte's voice was shrill with excitement, with disbelief, toward those who might go to the fainted woman's aid. "At last. At last. The spirits have favored us with an apparition above and beyond the usual voices and rappings. Do not force her to return to the other side until we have answers to our questions."

"I recognize her," said one of the men. "I remember seeing her standing on the top of the barricade, lobbing firebombs."

"Indeed, I remember too," said another.

Madame Toussaint remembered it as well, the smooth neck of the petrol-filled cognac bottle, the poor man's grenade, in her hand, fuse sputtering . . .

"It's Citoyenne Nathalie. Comrade Paul's wife."

"I had no idea she had gone to the world beyond," said Madame Flôte. "They must have killed her by torture in La Santé Prison."

The fainting woman groaned.

"And yet, who has had word of her in fifteen, twenty years?"

Madame Toussaint found it interesting that they could recognize her wrapped in a bedsheet. They hadn't when in concierge's invisible guise she'd let them in the building's front door for many a previous séance. But perhaps they hadn't acknowledged her under those circumstances for everyone's safety.

She could not put a name to all their faces, although some seemed vaguely familiar under a crust of twenty-five years. The men especially. Interesting that they all wore greying beards now. What better cover for faces once aglow with youthful idealism?

She should have disabused them of their delusion: She was not a conjured spirit. She didn't even believe in such things. But then she would have to explain why she was wandering around this building with little more on than what would pass as a shroud.

What would be the best way to get these people to divulge any secrets they might know of this world or the world beyond? Going along with their belief.

Madame Toussaint drifted as ghost-like as she could to an empty chair against the wall, facing Madame Flôte. A seated posture seemed less likely to threaten with death and destruction than one many might recognize from a barricade summit.

"Please, Nathalie, have you any news of my brother?" one woman begged. "Guillaume duBois, defending the Rue de Rivoli barricade at the start of the terrible bloody week?"

"My father and I fled to Brussels," said one man. "I was twelve, but I had thrown stones. We sought shelter with Victor Hugo, who opened his home to all refugees from the conflict he felt he had in part ignited. But the French army was there before us. My father and I were separated. I haven't seen him since."

My son? My father? My mother? My husband? My lover? The terrible week? The terrible year? Even the fainting woman revived to press her unanswerable questions on the apparition, one on top of the other. So many loved. So many missing. So many dead and gone forever in unmarked mass graves. No wonder mediums who could conjure spirits were popular. There had even been a man in the Montmartre quartier who took photographs of mourners in which their shadowy loved ones appeared just behind them, but he had been discovered to be a charlatan and was put in jail.

Madame Toussaint groaned with helplessness. The woman threatened to faint again. "Friends, I understand your desire for answers, for conclusions to your long, heartbreaking searches," Madame Toussaint said. "And I held Madame Flôte's aged mother in my arms as she died from malnutrition. She had given all her food to younger mouths."

"The spirit speaks true." Madame Flôte's voice was choked with tears. The two women had worked this connection out when the medium had first moved into the building, and they had shared recognition.

"She is now in a place where she knows no hunger." Madame Toussaint didn't believe in the spirits she was enacting; she didn't believe in life beyond. But she did think that what she said was accurate: Whether in oblivion or paradise, she was willing to wager the dead felt no hunger. Whatever people need to believe to get them through what we've been through, she told herself.

Monsieur d'Ermenville, too, could no longer feel hunger, she thought. He could not feel guilt, either.

Madame Flôte gave a great sigh of relief—clearly, not at the state of Monsieur's recently departed soul.

Madame Toussaint shifted the focus of the psychic dialogue. "The reason I have answered your summons tonight is not because of those who are resting peacefully but because of one who died under this very roof not forty-eight hours ago. I think you are all aware of the man I mean, and that he cannot possibly rest in peace until his murderer is called to earthly justice."

Murmurs among the party indicated that they knew what she said was truth. But they were also very reticent to tell what they knew of Monsieur d'Ermenville.

Madame Toussaint thought she would have to sweeten the pot if she were to get any useful information out of this chance, but very lucky, visitation. "You cannot expect people long dead and at peace to come to you and bring you that same peace if you will not help one haunting these walls due to a most recent but violent escape from this mortal coil."

"It was, in fact, attempting to conjure Monsieur le Comte that we gathered here tonight," Madame Flôte admitted.

One of the women seemed to explode. "We want to give him a piece of our minds." The gesture she wanted to give jangled the bracelet on her wrist and would have broken the circle had not the gentleman seated next to her held her hand fast.

"He doesn't get off that easy," the gentleman assured the lady.

An image of Monsieur d'Ermenville's gutted carcass passed before Madame Toussaint's eyes: No, it had not been easy . . . but then there were all the other carcasses marching behind, also uneasy. . .

A silence among the séance attendees seemed to apologize for that disruption to the spirit who had come: Madame Toussaint, the apparition from the barricade, in her bedsheet.

Then slowly, slowly—still clenching each other's hands tight in a circle—the group began to conjure the dead man.

· XXII ·
THE TERRIBLE YEAR

—

On the third day of the sortie slaughter, fog continued to roll off the Marne until it filled the whole Île-de-France basin. The fog was as thick as pea soup—the hungry always made comparisons like that—but cold, bone chillingly cold. Ice crystals in the marrow.

That day, into the well-ventilated Luxembourg Palace hospital, the wounded brought the name of Champigny on their lips, blue with cold if not with impending death. Champigny had once evoked images of *guingettes*: of drinking parties riverside on summer Sunday evenings in the open air. Of boating hats, ribbons fluttering, and lively music to dance to. Of love under chestnut trees.

During the sortie against the Prussians, starving soldiers had attacked those trees to open the spikey fruit and eat it raw; the trees' brittle limbs went for their skimpy campfires. And there the soldiers died as the enemy came through those groves, bayonets at the ready.

The fog rising into the city from that place of death was still so thick by midmorning that Nathalie was tending to the less-injured men by the light of the last stubs of candles from the night before. Many of the patients were in too much pain—screaming, delirious or unconscious—to speak. Few could even give their names. But one, whom a paper pinned to his thread-bare blanket labeled "Herlemont," had a broken leg and a wound from a bullet that had passed clean through his shoulder. Setting the clean break and dressing the shoulder had been hastened by the surgeons' need to see to more serious cases.

Nathalie helped the man to use the chamber pot and to sit up to drink some weak tea. She spoke to him as she always tried to do for her patients, about matters unrelated to the battlefront. Trying to sense the state of their minds, she waited until she was certain she could bring the subject around to what preyed on her most: "You haven't perhaps heard of a Colonel Toussaint? Paul Toussaint?"

Many she had spoken to had replied, "Yes. Of course. Who does not know Citoyen Paul? He is one of us, a true hero."

But Subaltern Herlemont was the first with more current information and able to share it. The wounded man blinked rapidly, an expression she came to understand as characteristic—and beloved, even, after what he said next. "Citoyen Paul was with us. Right in the thick of things, of course. He wouldn't ask anything of us he wasn't prepared to do first, to lead the way."

Nathalie's heart raced with hope conflicted with fear. "He was all right when you saw him?"

"Yes. But not for want of trying to run head-first into a Prussian bullet." Herlemont winced and cradled his shoulder. He personally must have had enough of Prussian bullets for that day.

"When? Where?" Nathalie had to know.

"When? This morning, just after I was wounded. He had some of his men help him bring those of us who were out of commission to a roadside where the ambulances would be sure to find us. He gave me his coat to replace mine that was torn to shreds in the shoulder. He used his scarf to wrap the wound. All this before leading those still upright back to where the fighting was thickest."

That dear scarf, blood-soaked, it had probably gone to the brazier upon Herlemont's arrival.

"Where?" she demanded. "Where was this?"

"Now that . . . I'm not so sure. You know, they give you orders to march, then they ride up ahead on a big white horse. You march, no more concerned about what's around you, just struggling with the mud caking each boot step. Until that horse gets shot from under them. Then you cut a steak or two off the beast with your bayonet as you pass, eat it raw while you scramble for cover, and start shooting in the direction of the bullet that gave you breakfast.

"You know," Herlemont continued. "The fiasco with the emperor at

Sedan? They only gave our leaders maps of Germany, expecting us to be in Berlin before we lost our way. No maps of France. They never imagined us to be wandering like chickens with our heads cut off in our own country. But—so we were."

"And Colonel Toussaint?"

"Not Citoyen Paul, of course. He seemed to know the place like the back of his hand. I'd follow him anywhere."

"Anything? Can you remember anything of where you were?"

"The river. Not the Seine. The Marne, they called it. Where the pontoons the generals had ordered set got washed away. The waters were high. Because of all the rain." Herlemont shuddered at the memory of what must have been very cold and rushing water, sweeping away men and supplies.

"Anything else you can remember? The name of a village? Anything?"

"Champignons? Champigny? Something like that."

Nathalie dismissed the thought of food and latched onto Champigny. Other incoming patients had said the same name.

Herlemont's mind was still there, wherever it was. "We were holed up in the sort of pit peasants use to store potatoes. No potatoes left, you may be sure—the Prussians had been there. And scavengers from Paris. We discovered the body of one—clearly Parisian—half standing against a post like a scarecrow in a cabbage field. Even the stalks had gone for soup. The potato pit, its walls running with water and sloughing off mud until your boots were over their tops—"

"And that's where you last saw Paul Toussaint?"

Herlemont had diarrhea from raw horsemeat, from raw chestnuts, and Nathalie had to deal with that. When she returned to the Salle des Conférences, turned hospital ward, patients were being crowded together so more could be lined up on the floor beside them. More crowded ambulances had just returned from the front.

"How is it?" Herlemont asked the new arrivals. "At the front?"

As answer, a very young driver reeled away from the burden of his stretcher and collapsed back against the elegant doorframe he'd just passed through. "I won't go again," he declared, not just to Herlemont but to the room at large. "The fog is a curse from God. You can't see anything—Frenchman, Prussian—until you're already upon them, and then it's too late. It's too late—for anything. Even to pick up the pieces. Everyone's already dead out there. Either that or, like this poor fellow," he nodded to the body he'd just placed on the floor, "as good as. Not worth the fodder for the beasts to carry us there and back."

Nathalie took a hurried look at each of the new patients. None of them was Paul. She rushed out of the palace. Cold snapped at her ears and nose, but her senses were blessed by the sudden stillness of no screams, no groans of pain, no stench of gangrene and bodily fluids. She took the marble stairway down which fine ladies in ballgowns must once have swept.

On the gravel drive below stood a rank of ambulances, lanterns casting tangible beams through the soupy fog. Their horses' heads hung with exhaustion, blowing with defeat.

"Isn't anyone going back out to the Marne again today?" she demanded. "To Champigny?"

The drivers looked at one another.

Her heart sank. "It's too dangerous?"

"Not so much that, Madame," said one.

"I am not afraid," she insisted. "I'm willing to take any risk you will."

"Then you're a fool." Another put in his sou's worth, none too kindly.

"The Prussians have marched off further east. To mop up Ducrot's men who tried to rendezvous with ours."

"Truly, there's nothing left to entice them to that Champigny sector."

"It's a land of the dead, a no man's land."

"Then take me, a woman, there."

All the men laughed bitterly.

"It'll give you nightmares," warned another one, spitting tobacco he'd rolled in a dried maize leaf.

"Haunted."

Only one wiry old wight spoke up more gently. "I'd go if one of these cowards would come with me to carry the other end of the stretcher. If Philippe there would lend me his off-side gelding. My Bisou's gone and thrown another shoe and won't be any good until he's been to the smithy. Or the knacker's. If—"

"I'll go with you." Nathalie cut his ifs short. "I'll carry the other end."

More ifs followed, most of them variations on, "If only you were a man."

"I've been working here at the hospital," she argued. Only two days, she did not add. "I can offer some care to the soldiers we find as we travel. I will not be squeamish." She suspected that last was a lie.

"My husband is out there," did not seem to curry any more favor. How many more women could say that?

"You will not want to see him when we find him," the old driver cautioned.

"But he will want to see me."

The driver raised a brow but said nothing at her assumption that Paul would be able to see.

The driver didn't begin to comply until Nathalie proved her competence with horses, learned as a girl on the family farm. She went to where the reluctant driver had already let his horses out of the shafts to graze upon the palace lawn. It was clear which horse was Bisou; he limped on his unshod foot. She took the other one, a mare, and led her to the right side of the ambulance. The driver named Philippe seemed shamed to the deed and brought his off-side gelding to the other shaft.

Soon Nathalie was on the ambulance box riding out into the fog.

. . .

The route was easy enough to find once beyond the edge of Paris, straight-lined across mostly flat, featureless farmland. Fog muffled it like a crêpe on a mourner's door. Corpses pointed the way, sometimes literally. More than a few seemed to have died with one arm in the air, pointing or waving for aid. These specters materialized out of the fog as if out of tumbled-down crypts. Or perhaps the arms had been outstretched as the men had fallen prone across the ground. And when some earlier ambulance crew had come by, turning the body over for signs of life, the limbs had already been frozen like that. The would-be rescuers had hurriedly stepped away from the horror of a face blown beyond recognition or a famine-whittled chest spilled into the moistness of a beet field. She found only two beets, protected by the corpse, cavernous and pithy. She knotted them into her apron.

At first, she felt the need to stop the driver to allow her to jump down from the box and repeat the exercise at every seemingly slumbering figure, and then follow the trail of carnage to the edge of fog-limited sight. Soon she learned to discern the strangled croaks of crows, the black wings that might flap out of nowhere at her with their prior claims to the harvest of war. Also the dogs in starved packs; their sentries snarled and lunged at her. It was best then to stay safe on the box and indicate the man beside her to drive on. None of the bodies she investigated was Paul, even the faceless ones. She could tell. They gave her that comfort.

Nathalie and the driver made it almost as far as the sortie had—which seemed a pathetically short way. Perhaps the most soul-crushing thing to discover was the cone-shaped shelters the Prussians had had time and ingenuity to dig into French soil: the men could sleep in one of these shelters, feet towards the fire built in the center, heads radiating out like spokes on a wheel. All the while, native Frenchmen had died of exposure at their guard posts. The Prussian pits were deserted now, the enemy after more lively game.

The war-battered ruins of Champigny—its sign having been used for target practice from both sides—seemed like the best place to turn around and head back to the hospital. It was growing dark, hastened by the fog.

"We don't need to go back with an empty van," the driver's grandfatherly voice was sympathetic beside her. "We can do service to a few corpses. Spare them, at least, from an anonymous burial in some mass grave. Let their wives and mothers know . . ."

Where Champigny's banks and blown-out bridges met the Marne, a place where once patrons of *guingettes* had frolicked, half-submerged corpses of men and horses showed where the pontoons had failed under the pressure of fast-moving, mud-laden water. These seemed to be the only citizens of the once-flourishing market town..

Nathalie helped the driver to fill the back of the van with corpses. It didn't matter who, just the first to hand. She straightened, holding the poles of the last stretcher-load, the "one more" the driver thought they could carry, the dead requiring less space for comfort and breath than the living.

The building they were near had had half its façade blown away by a cannonball. What sort of building was it? More solid, more workaday than a *guingette*. A wash house, perhaps, where laundresses brought the baskets of linen, where they could scrub it, themselves, and their children. Sheltered in inclement weather, they could still reach the river water for their toil.

Something made Nathalie want to give the place a second look. The telltale sound of a gun hammer cocking stopped her short. It seemed to echo from inside the ruins. She looked to the driver for confirmation. He'd heard it too and didn't want to speak. He only nodded and backed away.

"It's a revolver. He is one of ours," she whispered. "The Prussians will have already seen that none of their officers is left behind."

She dropped her end of the stretcher; the dead man on it tumbled to the ground again.

The driver caught her arm. "It may just as easily be one of them who has taken the weapon off the corpse of one of ours. Madame, don't go."

"I must see." She shook herself free.

On a ledge under half a blown-away arch he crouched, motionless as a gargoyle, and in the same pose—only with an officer's sword at his side and, in a rather limp right hand, an officer's personal handgun.

Surely, he couldn't have died that way?

The blue jacket, dark with blood from a torn shoulder that matched the wound she'd treated in Subaltern Herlemont. No, the eyes. They were the same as when they had first met on the steep slope of Montmartre. Only staring. Purpose gone from them.

"Paul!"

He gave no sign of having heard. Perhaps explosions had ruined his ears.

"Paul," she tried again, and began running towards him.

Still no response, no sign that he was alive.

She clambered over rubble. A movement. She almost screamed with relief—and then stumbled to a halt. He had lifted the barrel to sight, directly at her.

"Paul. It's me. Nathalie."

Still, it seemed he hadn't heard, but slowly and deliberately he rotated the muzzle of the gun towards the blue cap on his own head.

Nathalie lunged. She grabbed his ankle. She used it to pull herself up and grab the right elbow.

The percussion exploded in the closed space

He stared at her, unseeing. Had an explosion stolen his eyesight as well?

The ambulance driver must have scurried into the building. She heard the scrabble of boots on rubble behind her, but she did not take her gaze from Paul's empty eyes.

"I was not brave enough," he murmured. "Why else did I not manage to die with all my men?"

"That's not what Subaltern Herlemont said," she told him. "He had nothing but praise for your courage and leadership. Subaltern Herlemont? Do you remember? He, by the way, did not die of his wounds but is almost ready to be discharged from the hospital. Herlemont, whose life you saved. Among many others, I have no doubt."

Paul didn't seem to hear her.

"Paul, Paul. You didn't die because you needed to come home to me. Me—Nathalie."

He couldn't comprehend just what a miracle it was.

"Paul—" She swallowed and whispered, "Vive la France."

Perhaps she only imagined a re-glimmer of purpose.

The ambulance driver came and helped her lead her husband down from the ledge.

"We should put him in the back," the driver suggested. "He's not well. You could keep him company if we pulled out a corpse or two."

Sitting enclosed with a pile of corpses did not seem to be something that would be good for her husband's health at this point. Probably not for her own, either.

Under a tumbled slab of stone where a woman might kneel to beat her wash, Nathalie found a kerchief full of snails. The meal she could make from these might be just the nourishment Paul needed. If she could find some bread to feed the little creatures until they cleaned out what might be toxic herbs they'd eaten beforehand. Then, if she had some butter—and garlic and parsley . . .

All three people pressed together on the ambulance box. Nathalie sat in the middle. On the right-hand side, Paul kept calling for a halt to do the same thing she had done on the outbound route: fight off crows and dogs, search for a sign of life.

"Paul, my dear, our van is full. We cannot bring in any more dead," fell on deaf ears.

The driver began to refuse to stop on the dark, empty road. It would be a hell of a place for anyone to die. And to rest for all eternity? Still, Paul would think he saw some sign of life and jump down without waiting for the ambulance to stop. After that, they put him in the middle of the box. Nathalie wrapped her arms around him and held him tight while he wept.

And night fell. The lanterns on either side of the vehicle did their best to stab over the horses' heads until they reached an advancing wall of fog.

...

Nathalie spent a lot of time over the next few months cradling him like that, like a baby.

"Why do you do this for me?" he would ask.

"Why did you sit with me all those evenings when I was sick?" she'd retort. "You enjoyed my company, sick as I was? Let me say the same."

"Enjoy my company? I let the balloon factory go to hell."

"You didn't. They just ran out of supplies."

"The hospitals are full of men in worse shape than I am. You should go to them."

"I do go to them. Many hours every day. When you seem like you can be left alone."

"You should divide your time more equally, more communally."

"What? How? With a stopwatch? I should time myself, two minutes for each man?" She didn't add that even then, she doubted she could comfort each casualty. And what was two minutes spread so thin when they all needed hours and hours?

She did go back to the Salle des Conférences in the Luxembourg Palace and did try to seek out Subaltern Herlemont in particular, to thank him.

"Oh, his fiancée came and got him a while ago," they told her. "She thought she could give him much better care at home and clear up space for another."

Nathalie had no doubt that both were true.

And now, in 1895, Herlemont's military career had elevated him to lieutenant-colonel. He was filling the second floor of the building on Rue Férou with happy if somewhat regimented children alongside that fiancée-now-wife of his who had chosen to give her all to one man.

XXIII
LA BELLE ÉPOQUE

"Le Comte d'Ermenville." The people around Madame Flôte's table picked up the subject and ran with it, all the while clinging to one another's hands like people on the top of a barricade, still defiant though they have lost their last weapons.

"He liked to call himself a comte."

"Eugène Toussaint, the younger son."

"Yes, I remember him."

"He made great profits off people's need during the siege and by trading with the Prussians."

"I was a young carpenter. I had to pawn my tools to feed my family during the siege. He refused to give my tools back, even when the Commune ordered them returned."

"He wanted us bakers to work all night long so he could have fresh baguettes in the morning while the rest of us ate ground bones."

"I was a young housemaid at my first job," said the woman who had fainted. "One night, while his wife was out, he raped me. I had to keep serving him to keep my job."

Madame Toussaint couldn't help but think of Jeanne-Marie. It was the same story—only in her case, Eugène was even older. But perhaps the man's age had spared Jeanne-Marie the result of the fainting woman's fate.

"And then, when I became pregnant, I was shamed and let go without a reference. I worked as a washerwoman on a barge floating on the Seine.

Truly, I don't know how my young son and I survived until he grew old enough to help me out—what with le Comte owning bakeries and conspiring with friends in all the great houses and workshops so I could never work there."

The man next around the circle took his turn: "I put all my hard-earned savings into a scheme the old bastard made sound so good. For my retirement. Little did I know he and the bankers were making deals in smoke-filled rooms behind closed doors. Deals that put all the money into their own pockets."

"He was among the bourgeoisie watching the fall of the Commune through his opera glasses like some sort of stage comedy, cheering on the murderers."

"Would you fight if the Commune happened again today?" One man took his turn to ask a question rather than to give the litany of his misfortunes. Silence was the only answer to that.

And then a man and a woman who seemed to be his wife, a crown of greying braid perched regally on her head, contributed a long, rambling story, finishing each other's sentences.

"We both grew up not far from here."

"We were poor but happy enough."

"The whole neighborhood was a slum, now that you think about it."

"But we didn't care. We had each other."

"A community."

"Everyone looking out for the next one."

"We'd tend each other's children."

"Our parents could live right next door so we could look in on the old folks."

"If someone was sick, we'd take soup in to them or all pitch in to pay their rent."

"Or overlook the rent, for we owned many of the houses, worn-down as they were."

"And then—"

"Then he comes around. He comes around with that 'Baron' Haussmann."

"Investors." The word was foreign on the man's tongue, set off with scorn.

"Holding their noses in perfumed handkerchiefs."

"Investors look at an old, tight-knit community like ours as a ripe walnut. They crack it open and take the meat, leaving us—"

"They promised us new, modern buildings."

"Running water."

"Sewers."

"They bought up our houses for next to nothing."

"What they told us they were worth—"

"Empty, without life or history."

"Well, you know, if you didn't like their price, if you held out, they'd get their friends in l'Hôtel de Ville to order it condemned."

"Then you'd get no money at all. No community. Nothing."

"Who'd have thought you can turn the beating heart of a community into cash?"

"A human being. Into cash."

"The same thing happened to us in the tenth arrondissement." One of the other women put in her sou's worth at this point, clinging to her neighbors in the circle of hands.

"And to us in the eighth," a man said. "Where the Champs-Élysées runs through."

"A classical Elysium for some. Not for us," said a man in pince-nez, of a Grecian bent.

"I'm not certain it was Eugène Toussaint behind the renovation of our neighborhood. But I'm certain it was one of his cronies, that they formed their plans together, one learning from the other."

"That is why I've always come here to Madame Flôte," one woman declared. "Not that we always successfully raised the other side, but that I wanted to raise the conscience of that man. And now he's dead without a brush with guilt or repentance." Several agreed with her.

The woman of the first couple picked up her personal thread again. "Oh, it was he in our sixth arrondissement. I'll never forget his face as he watched his men throw my grandmother's belongings into the street. None too gently, I may say. Dishes were broken. Then it rained on her featherbed. All she wanted was to die in the same house where she was born. Instead, she died a beggar. I remember his face as he watched—all too well. So smug. So self-righteous. I could have murdered him right then myself. I should have. The only thing that stopped me was the fact that

I knew the law would be on his side. Another with the same smugness would have stepped into his place the very next day."

"When I tried to get a job clearing space for the boulevard," her husband picked up the tale, "there was no job for me because I'd joined the Commune."

"I couldn't get my tools back."

"They sent me to the colony in Guyana."

"Me to the *bagne*—the galley."

"Stole my health away," the two last men said together.

"The tropics and its diseases."

"Harder to regain, even, than pawned tools—that health."

"When a man has nothing but his body with which to toil."

"I learned that the running water, broad tree-lined streets, and clean new buildings were not for us—not for those who'd lived on the same spot for generations before."

Madame Toussaint felt the very walls of the building around her—as she had so often before—crying out their remorse, their injustice. They literally ran with blood.

"Now we can only afford to live far from where the work is."

"Before it was just in the atelier on the first floor."

"Or in the shop just around the corner."

"Close to where my children were so I could run home in an emergency."

"Getting to work comes out of your pocket."

"And then he pays for the military to enforce the laws that exploit us. The Commune . . . the Commune was not like that."

"The Commune rose up in place of our lost community."

"Yet, how could we win? How could we win against such a system with roots sunk so deep into every aspect of life?"

All the séance attendees had joined the litany now, not in argument, but speaking over one another in their anxiety to be heard. This was how Monsieur d'Ermenville was conjured upon his death, Madame Toussaint thought. Any of these people seemed capable of that murder. As did any of the relatives of the thirty-thousand dead of the Commune. Of the rigidifying of the classes since.

And yet none of them had acted. In twenty-five years, that was the wonder. Why was that? Because no matter how idealistic they'd started out in life, they'd all come to realize there were the haves and the have-nots, and they were destined to be on the losing side? If so, then the murderer would have to be someone who did not accept the way things were.

The conclusion was simpler than that, of course. For one of these spiritualists to have done the deed, he or she would have had to be in the building two nights ago. Madame Toussaint was the concierge. She knew everyone who came and went in her building. Just to be certain, however, she asked Madame Flôte, "You did not hold a séance on the night of the murder, did you, Madame?"

"No, I kept to my usual quiet, contemplative ways." The turban nodded. As if such a thing allowed a head to keep down and out of sight.

Now Madame Toussaint was certain none of these people could have committed the crime, even though they all had motive. Only Madame Flôte had been in the building that fateful night; only she could possibly have had opportunity.

Madame Toussaint's question allowed one of the men suddenly to remember her presence. "But Madame." They all turned from their red-lamped circle to her for revelation again. "Surely you suffered as much as anyone, and personally," the questioner continued. "Your husband lost his title to that man, his brother."

Madame Toussaint gave a little laugh, very un-spirit-like. "Paul didn't lose anything he didn't want to give away. A hereditary title handed out by a king or a despotic emperor? What is the justice in that? Where is the community? The Commune?

"The unfortunate thing, the thing he didn't realize," she went on, "is that when you try to shed such things from your own account of guilty power, there is always somebody right behind, ready to scoop it up because he can wield it better than you. Better meaning, in his book, with less compunction." The circle all nodded solemnly at her words, as if this were something you'd have to come from the great beyond to understand. In truth, it was all too simple, all too common.

She took her opportunity to continue. "In order to help the proper spirits rest in peace, is there anything any of you can tell me about the residents of this building that might help?"

The assembly hemmed and hawed, but it appeared that none of them could, beyond, "Were it not for Monsieur le Comte, my brother/son/father/sister would be alive today."

"Oh, and Madame Flôte too, of course." Eyes turned to the figure at the head of the table. The gem on her turban winked in acknowledgement.

No one said it in so many words. The widow on the fourth floor might not truly be able to raise the dead, but she had been raising spirits in people who had lost so much and knew no other way to regain hope than this one.

And when the séance attendees figured out Madame Toussaint wasn't dead at all? Was just the concierge wrapped in a bed sheet? Well, perhaps it would never happen. None of them had noticed her before, when she'd opened the building's front door to them over the years.

"It is very curious, Madame Toussaint," Madame Flôte pronounced just when everything that needed to be said between this world and the next seemed to have been said. "I am getting the distinct impression that there is a spirit from beyond who wants to speak to you."

Madame Toussaint's blood ran cold, and it was no more playacting.

Through her trance, Madame Flôte continued, her voice thin and reedy. "I see a child. An infant almost. Can it be? A son? Your son, Madame Toussaint? Yes. Your son has a message for you, Madame."

"No. Impossible."

Madame Toussaint rose, hitched up her bedsheet and drifted out of the room as ghostlike as she could manage—all the while feeling that she was the one pursued by a voice from beyond.

· XXIV ·
THE TERRIBLE YEAR
—

Nathalie held a trembling Paul through a full month of the Prussian bombardment, never knowing if the next moment the mansard roof over their heads might be blown right off.

At last, under terms rumored to be crushing, the Prussians entered Paris unopposed. They gave their field canteen supplies to the bourgeoisie; the starving poor attacked vegetable carts at the gates. Letters began to trickle in from the outside. News. Fuel.

Prussian horses leapt over the barricades at the end of the Champs-Élysées; soldiers in pickle helmets lined up in perfect, mindless discipline in the Place d'Étoile.

A few reports of unruly behavior circulated, but these might have been what people expected to happen, not what really did. The statues on the Place de la Concorde were draped in black crêpe, especially the stern-eyed lady representing the Alsatian city of Strasbourg. A few barbarian officers were given a tour of the Louvre, otherwise no one spoke to them. The one café that offered drinks to the conquerors was later trashed.

Nathalie and Paul in the garret on Rue Férou saw none of it.

Two days later, the Prussians were gone. The greatest indignity happened then: King Wilhelm of Prussia was proclaimed Kaiser, Emperor, of all the Germanies, in Versailles, the palace of the king guillotined three quarters of a century before. And then the victor seemed to be more the Hessians' problem, the Alsatians', the Bavarians'. What happened to the rapes and pillages Paris had so feared? The deaths in your own bed, the cannonade taking off your rooftop while you slept?

Braving what seemed like such atrocities still hanging over her head, Nathalie joined a group of women—including her friend Coco, whose idea it was—on a trip to la Place d'Étoile. The walk turned into a march, each woman armed with a bucket. Nathalie found it a welcome escape from all the things weighing on her mind back in the sixth arrondissement.

A row of gendarmes—Frenchmen—met them at the edge of the square, poised to turn them back. Women in the front ranks explained their purpose. The gendarmes looked at each other, then stepped aside. From then on, they stood guard so that no man with Prussian or French imperial tendencies would stop the women.

Coco and other women had brought packets of purple potash crystals, which they sprinkled, a portion into each bucket. Then the women filled their buckets at a public pump until the whole was dissolved into a caustic mix.

They marched out to different quadrants of the square and got down on hands and knees. Hands already chapped by winter weather and no salves then set to work, though the water stung.

"That's right, girls," the leaders urged. "Scrub every last scuff of Prussian boots from Parisian flagstones."

Some men in handsome business suits heckled them. "Why don't you set about some really useful work instead of symbolic nonsense? Don't your husbands need their lunches? Aren't your children naked?"

"Yes, and whose fault is that?" muttered the woman next to Nathalie, who sloshed her bucket so, had there not been a cordon of police between them, someone's fancy spats might have become soiled.

"Those of us whose men haven't been killed by your emperor's idiotic war," said another, grown hard and determined.

"Pah!" exploded one man who tossed his cigar butt to land a little too close to Nathalie's damp skirt, on the square of limestone she'd just cleaned. "We should have given you all over to Bismarck's men for their pleasure. You'd never see my respectable wife out here doing such a pointless thing."

"Nor your *poufiasse*—doxy—either, I'd lay odds," Coco called back.

"I wish it were so easy to scrub Paris of greedy bastards like that," grumbled the woman on Nathalie's other side.

"Of the whole empire debacle, which he no doubt still supports."

"Wasn't it the emperor who brought us into the war?"

"And marched us off on that failed adventure to Rome before that."

"Some men just can't keep it in their trousers."

"Any man who had a vote in what was a very bad government of our own. I'd like to see him brought to account."

"And, now that the Prussians are gone, France will revert to such men."

"I don't expect I'll be getting off my knees any time soon. And I don't mean praying."

"This is more useful than prayer," the other woman said. "And they call it vain symbolism."

Back at the pump, Nathalie's knuckles bled into the water in her pail. Coco kicked at a mound of dirt just behind the jet of water. Stone edging circled the spot where bare clods lay.

"What's that?" Nathalie asked.

"More vain symbolism, I suppose," Coco said.

"What?"

"Before the siege, a tree grew here. Not any tree. A tree they planted during the Revolution of 1789."

"A liberty tree?"

"Yes. People would come here to celebrate on Bastille Day, other holidays. There'd be music, dancing, food, and drink. France's liberty, roots sunk deep."

"We had such a tree in the village where I grew up," Nathalie mused. "I think it had been there since the time of the druids."

"Our ancestors of the Revolution took the emblem from the French peasant, no doubt, and adapted it to the life of the republic in the city."

"We'd hang it with ribbons. And dance and sing." For the first time since moving to Paris, even throughout the siege, Nathalie felt a bit of nostalgia for her childhood.

"Right. Well, during the Revolution, they'd hang it with heads, fresh from the guillotine. Or whole bodies, too, if they wanted to save a trip on the tumbrel cart. If the tree—it must have been small then—could hold them all. It had grown bigger by the time I saw it, but always some stalwart youth would climb up and put a red Phrygian cap on the top branch, like the revolutionary Marianne, liberated breast and all."

"Do you suppose they'll make a revolutionary emblem of us as well? Ragged clothes concealing the famine shrunken bosom? Bucket? Chapped hands?"

Coco threw back her head and laughed at the absurdity of it. "But they should." Yes, she'd be great on a mural.

"What happened to the tree?" Nathalie asked.

"Cut down during the siege, of course. For firewood. Maybe under cover of darkness, but down it went like all the others." Coco kicked at the soft dirt again.

"Cut down a liberty tree?"

"And dug up the roots. Don't tell me you wouldn't have gladly done the same, one of those cold nights we've just been through."

"We should replant the tree." Instead of undertaking this mere symbolic scouring?

"And who could say that such trees don't now represent the status quo, the Party of Order, meaning the party that wants to keep you and me in our place and uses 'liberty' as bait to keep us docile?"

Nathalie stroked her belly. Keep her in her place. Should she tell Coco? Not yet.

And definitely not yet, as men had started bringing wood to the Place d'Étoile and passing it through the cordon of watching gendarmes. The men themselves wouldn't light the fires, but they encouraged the women before slinking off again, afraid to be seen by any stray Prussians. Or by their own government who'd sold them out to the enemy.

"The refiner's fire. More cleansing even than potash."

They blackened the stones with raked fires.

Nathalie felt it was not the end but the beginning of something. She smoothed her skirt again.

"Come with us to the club." Coco and a line of women she linked arms with, swinging empty buckets, urged Nathalie. It seemed as if potash and fire had restored the lightness and frivolity of earlier days, if not to the square, at least to her friends' faces.

Nathalie had heard people speak of the clubs before but had never been. How did they differ from a regular nightclub, equally ubiquitous?

"I'm sorry. I can't. My husband—"

Paul hardly left their room on the sixth floor in Rue Férou. She hated to leave him alone for very long. Besides, who could justify frivolity after the somber if cathartic task they'd been at all afternoon? Or perhaps it was the cleansing that had enlivened their spirits so much. It had not had such a complete effect on her, although it had felt good to be doing something.

"There are clubs in every quarter," they assured her. "You needn't be too far from your home."

They told her that even Saint-Sulpice hosted a club. Intrigued, she got off the omnibus a stop early on Boulevard St. Michel and walked home by way of that square. The massive pile of stone, only slightly smaller than Notre Dame, although built much later, stood just at the bottom of Rue Férou.

Golden light streamed out of the tall, arched windows and onto wet cobbles as if it were Easter midnight mass. People in laughing, chattering groups came and went through the pillared portico. They drew her towards them. She longed to be part of their unaccountable joy.

But she remembered her defeated, surrendered city. How could these people be so merry?

She remembered Paul and hurried on. Another day. Perhaps.

When Nathalie reached the building on Rue Férou and prepared, weary but happy, to climb the stairs, she was surprised to find her sister-in-law, Madame Eugène Toussaint, waiting for her on the first-floor landing. Usually, the woman kept to her apartment, not interested in cultivating the relationship.

"Paul's gone out," she announced.

"Oh." Nathalie felt a sinking in her heart. She knew she shouldn't. Paul's willingness to go out, even just with friends, helped her believe he would soon be back to normal. If anything could ever be normal again in their Paris that had suffered so much.

But she had the uneasy feeling he might have been driven out, and by this woman.

"Thank you." Nathalie tried to accept the news graciously. "I'll wait for him upstairs."

"Do you really think exposure to potash is good for an unborn child?"

Nathalie froze on the second step.

Evening papers might have announced the potash, with engraved illustrations. It was the other news that bothered her, her sister-in-law knowing—the child.

Nathalie had known, of course. But she was barely three months along. She had told Paul and, once he'd stopped being nervous about what kind of father he could make, he, too, had rejoiced. Could she actually be showing, the bump more obvious on her starved body? Few women in Paris had been able to conceive at all during the siege—including, it would seem, Madame Eugène Toussaint herself, although her rations had not been stinted as much as many others'.

Or perhaps Paul had told his sister-in-law.

Nathalie's hands went protectively to her belly.

Madame Eugène Toussaint had not finished what she had to say. "If you think that bastard you're carrying will ever be le Comte d'Ermenville, you've got another think coming."

Nathalie had to take two deep breaths before she could turn and face the attack. By then, her sister-in-law had closed the door to the apartment behind her. And Nathalie had to run all the way up to shut her own door on tears of terror.

She got into bed, trying to regain the warmth she'd discovered walking by the church and lost to her sister-in-law on the first floor. But she was still awake, teeth chattering, when Paul returned, much later and smelling of cheap wine.

She sat up, her head against the sloping ceiling of the room. "Paul? How are you?"

He didn't answer, but tumbled onto the bed face first. She managed to remove his filthy boots and get the duvet over him, but she slept that night trying in vain to get warmth from the body in the damp overcoat next to her.

It tore at her heart—how lonely it was for a man to be drinking alone.

· XXV ·
THE TERRIBLE YEAR
—

*E*ARLY THE NEXT morning, Nathalie awoke to a light tapping on the door. Beside her, Paul groaned but didn't wake. Nathalie crawled over him, hitting her head on the low ceiling, and was able to open the door, still kneeling on the bed and rubbing her head with her other hand.

Madame Joséphine, Eugène Toussaint's cook, rolled her round face in at the door. She had stopped on her way down the corridor to the stairs from her own garret room. Nathalie threw a shawl over her shoulders and stepped out into the hall to join the older woman, closing the door softly behind her.

"Is everything alright with you two?" Madame Joséphine asked.

"Yes, of course. Paul is just—" Nathalie could think of no way to explain how not right things were.

Madame Joséphine nodded her mob cap with complete understanding, then let a broad smile spread across her round face. "Madame tells me you're expecting."

Nathalie frowned, remembering Madame Eugène Toussaint's confrontation with her the previous evening.

"But *chérie*, that's wonderful."

And Nathalie found herself in a large-bosomed embrace. "Certainly good news in these dark days," Madame Joséphine added. "I know just the recipe to strengthen the mother. My mother swore by it and she had twelve of us. Let's see, raspberry leaves and ginger in a thick gruel. If only

I can get the ingredients now that the siege is finally relieved." Then she thought to add, "Vive la France."

"Vive la France," Nathalie echoed.

"Monsieur Eugène has also heard the news."

And displayed the same hostility his wife had to this threat to their inheritance?

"He asked me to stop by and see if you wouldn't come down sometime this morning and visit with him."

Now Nathalie felt truly nervous. "Surely he meant Paul should come—"

"No, no. Poor Monsieur Paul." Madame Joséphine acknowledged the man Nathalie knew to be in a drunken sleep behind the garret door. "Monsieur Eugène wants to speak to *you*, Madame."

"Very well. Please tell him I will be down shortly." Hesitation weighed on her shoulders and in her throat as she got the words out.

"But now I must run. Monsieur Eugène likes his breakfast promptly at eight-thirty by the bells of Saint-Sulpice every morning." Another quick embrace. "I'm so happy for you. For Monsieur Paul. Cheer him up. Happy for all of us. It would be so good to have new life in this building."

Nathalie dressed slowly while Paul slept on, snoring softly. Usually the sound, even when it woke her, was comforting. Paul was there beside her, not—not in a mass grave, where he very well could have been.

Then she went down to be shown into her brother-in-law's rooms; he was just finishing a breakfast of a croissant and a bowl of coffee. He received her not in the sitting room, but in a small private office, its dark green walls hung with black and white etchings of famous Parisian landmarks. He did not rise, paying Nathalie no more respect than that due to a servant. He did, however, offer to have Madame Joséphine bring her something as well.

Although she was hungry, hungry enough for two, Nathalie declined the offer. She thought she was past the time when she couldn't keep anything down in the morning. Still, she was too wary to be that cozy with the husband of the woman who had been so hostile to her and her child the night before.

Eugène had the maid depart and close the door against the rest of the house. "I understand that congratulations are in order," he began.

Nathalie dropped her gaze and stammered, "I'm sorry if it annoys—"

"Annoys me?" the man boomed. "Not at all."

Nathalie glanced at the closed door.

"Ah, yes. My wife. She is annoyed, but then she is annoyed at everything. And being a comtesse was important to her."

"Not to you, Monsieur?"

He didn't suggest that she not call him Monsieur. "Titles are becoming passé," he said. "I try to tell her—the wife—which would you rather have? The diamonds and pearls money can buy you? Or the title?"

He took a final sip of coffee and looked at her. "Oh, don't get me wrong. A title would be all fine and good. But people pay much less attention to you when you don't have a title. I find, in a bank or on the floor of the bourse, people are much more likely not to notice you if you are just a plain 'Monsieur'. It's always best that people don't get their guard up. When you're making a deal, if you know what I mean."

Nathalie didn't know, but she didn't say so. "Are you making deals then?" was all she could think of to ask.

"The war's over, the armistice signed, thank God," he said. "Not that the war didn't offer many opportunities—all those cheap surplus American Civil War guns—but finance, development, real estate, that's where a man can really be a man in this modern age. Now that the Prussians have agreed to move off and forget the emperor's ineptitude. The war was just an inconvenient hiatus to get the gears of commerce greased again."

A hiatus? Nathalie remembered her ride out to the no-man's-land of Champigny. She remembered Paul sleeping off a drunk in his overcoat upstairs.

"I always thought that's where Haussmann went wrong—applying to become a baron, like Rothschild, no less. And insisting on using the title even before it was granted, which it never was. No one would have complained about his creative financing until the benefits of his development were visible to all if he hadn't. He'd still be in office. Well, we must muddle on without him now, but in the grand city plan that he laid out. Time to go, as a railway magnate might say, 'full steam ahead.' Which is where, my dear, you come in."

"Me?"

"Of course. You and your child. You have a child to think about. You know you will always have a place, as my brother's wife, under our roof.

With a child on the way, we might think about giving you a larger apartment. One of those on the fifth floor, perhaps."

Some might think an apartment on the fifth floor—for a comte and his family—would be demeaning. Nathalie did think of the climb—all those stairs—with a baby! But after sleeping for months, two on a narrow cot under a sloping roof in a single room, the fifth floor sounded like the lap of luxury to her. She could move and raise her family there.

Eugène Toussaint wasn't finished yet. "You also need to think about supporting yourself and your child. Poor Paul doesn't seem to be able these days. It is that way with many who saw action, not just those who lost limbs. Pity."

Nathalie knew her brother-in-law spoke the truth. She had it in her mind that counts and maybe even high officers didn't need to work for a living. But what did she know? A simple seamstress, she'd always assumed she would work all her life, no matter whom she married. That was the "normal" that would return if the war was over. Even when children came and she could no longer work in a tailor's back room, she had always assumed she would help support the family by taking in jobs from neighbors and friends along with fashioning clothing for the children, herself, and her husband—at least his linen. How much more so would that assumption be valued, now that she would have not only a child, but a husband who was in many ways as helpless as a child.

Eugène continued, unaware of her internal struggles. "There has just come into my possession"—the description of the process seemed purposely vague, almost as if such thing floated down from heaven into one's hands—"a certain property. Over near Notre Dame des Champs, near where Raspail and Montparnasse intersect. Perhaps you know it?"

"By the railway station? I know there are some old houses there."

"Exactly the spot I mean."

Old, ruinous houses? Why would this elegant man be interested in such property? A mystery beyond her. Nathalie continued to listen.

"In one of the buildings, on the ground floor, there is a shop."

"A butcher's, I think."

"Exactly."

"I think it's been vacant for several years, even before the siege."

"That's right. It will need work. It comes complete with a counter that folds down onto the street to show wares and a green-painted metal rail that is, well, pretty rusty now. Above, there are hooks on which to display the rabbits, the chickens, the braces of quail, the strings of sausage, the ham quarters."

No more horses, Nathalie hoped. She nodded.

"That's where I plan to put you. In that shop. Free to you. No rent. And there are two rooms and a kitchen next to the flagstone yard in back and a storage loft above."

Nathalie considered. At home on the farm she had killed, plucked, and cleaned chickens; pulled the pelts off long, skinny rabbits; and helped with the autumn pig slaughter, holding the bowl to catch the tumble of steaming entrails. She could just specialize in fowl, *volaille*. That was a more female job, the smaller animals. She might even work something out with her brother and old neighbors near Giverny. Meat could come daily on ice into St. Lazare station, although, given the shop's location, Montparnasse station would be better.

But she? A woman-butcher? Did French even make the word feminine?

"Shops are a good place for mothers," Eugène was saying. "They can have their babies with them, sleeping in a cot in the back room, riding on their hip as they wait on customers. Many women will come in just to see the baby."

While she wielded a cleaver with the other hand? "But a butcher shop?"

Eugène laughed. "It doesn't have to be a butcher shop. What would a woman like? A torte shop? Maybe not today, but soon. Soon Paris will be ready to indulge like that again. A candy shop? Flowers? Or a second-hand shop? Just buy up items at the local *brocantes*. In hard times like these, people are willing to put their grandmothers out on the curb for a franc or two." Eugène had a darker chuckle for this image. "But who would buy her? Another mouth to feed?

"In point of fact," Eugène went on, "you don't have to sell anything."

"I don't have to—?"

"Of course not."

"But how will I get money?"

"I told you. I will give it to you. Rent free. And perhaps a little for the groceries as well. *Donnant, donnant.*"

He used that peculiar phrase about giving and giving, which—on the tongue of what Paul would call, embittered, "a capitalist"—didn't make much sense at all.

"Just sit in the shop, have it open a few hours a day. Put out your own pots and pans as window dressing, and then tell people they're not for sale after all when they inquire. Sit in the shop with your baby and live happily ever after."

Nathalie couldn't wrap her head around the full picture, but in the end, she agreed to meet Eugène—who continued to seem so helpful and congenial—at the building in question that afternoon.

"I would take you there myself directly." He got up from his desk and reached for his smart frock coat with the wide lapels. "But I have a number of very important meetings for much of the day. The peace treaty is signed and suddenly everybody is in a scramble to make up for lost weeks and months of trading."

By the time she reached the top floor, Nathalie had a plan.

Then she opened the garret door to a flood of early spring sunshine—only to find Paul sitting on the edge of the bed, still in the overcoat she'd patched so often, head in his hands in despair. And she had to wonder if her taking charge, of going along with Paul's younger brother, was a way to help her husband le Comte recover after all.

· XXVI ·
THE TERRIBLE YEAR
—

$\mathcal{E}$VEN AFER A month of bombardment, there really wasn't a lot of damage showing in Paris that day, warm for mid-January, with gusting clouds. It was almost as if the Prussians had merely aimed and fired to terrify the citizens but to leave everything intact. For themselves. Or for someone else?

Their French collaborators? Dreadful imagination.

Perhaps, Nathalie thought, it was just men's souls that bore the scars.

Saint-Sulpice, in particular—where she had, almost without thinking, led Paul after forcing him out of hangover and garret into the bright day—had not a scratch. Like the night before, happy groups of people were going in and out. Some, it seemed, treated it like their home. And who but a monk thought a church his home?

"Shall we go in, Paul?" she asked, almost without hope. "To see what a Red Club is like?"

To her astonishment—and cheer—he said, "Let's."

The ecclesiastical skeleton was there: Blocky rococo columns soared up to the vaults. Plaster papal tiaras over the apse gave no doubt whose power had made this, unlike gothic interiors that suggested perhaps some forest deity had also been present in disguise at the building's inception. Gold leaf adorned a towering pulpit. Again, do not doubt who's in charge here.

And yet Saint-Sulpice was like no church Nathalie had ever been in in her life. Rich marble and carved saints of intimidating beauty and mien on the walls were covered by draped *tricolours*. The national blue, white, and red—yes, but they were also interspersed with swathes of plain red. If blue symbolized the aristocracy, white the church, then red was the people whose blood was always spilled upon the line.

Placards with various slogans were also in evidence. Nathalie didn't read them, partly because many of them seemed very long, pleading verbosity to shore up logic, but also because something else spoke much more eloquently, and that was the people themselves. The place, this church become a Red Club, was packed at midday, not just when it might stand in for a nightclub. Natalie had never seen a church so full, not even at a midnight mass at Christmas.

The famous Cavaillé-Coll organ throbbed in the massive space, not with "*Adeste Fideles*" or "*Minuit, Chrétiens*," but with tunes it took a moment to pick out in these surroundings: patriotic anthems. Indeed, the "Marseillaise" started up the moment Paul stepped under the high open space, as if on cue, as if they'd seen him coming.

Allons, enfants de la patrie,
Le jour de gloire est arrivé…
Aux armes, citoyens!
Formez vos bataillons!

"Form your battalions!" Nathalie had a sudden wrenching memory of the day she had marched arm in arm, singing with her friends Louise and Bernadette towards the Gare d'Orléans on what they thought was a great patriotic adventure. Her friends were both dead in less than half a year.

The effect of the music on Paul was something else again, a bolt of lightning. The first notes, all stops open, brought most of the crowd in the church to their feet, singing at the top of their lungs. Paul froze where he stood.

At the end, when whatever patriot was in the loft over their heads—pounding the keyboard as if stamping out munitions—cut the final chord, the echoes died. And the musician launched into something else, something with a dancing lilt, also foreign on a church organ, one of the grandest in the world.

Paul startled Nathalie by snatching her up and twirling her once or twice around to the music.

"What—?" she exclaimed, trying to catch her breath.

Up close, Nathalie saw the tears running down Paul's face and into the beard he'd let grow unkempt since Champigny. He spun her out so that she staggered to a stop when she saw Saint-Sulpice's priest sitting on a wicker chair at the door, an almost-empty collection basket at his elbow. This was the corner he'd been shoved to; he didn't look happy. He looked like a solitary vulture, waiting, watching. Which was more of an anathema to him? Paul's tears or the dancing?

The spell over her husband broke after a few bars of the dance during which time those who didn't continue whirling in couples around the baptismal font settled themselves like a startled flock of birds returning to their roost.

"My love—!" was the only way Nathalie knew to express her surprised emotions.

Paul caught her arm and pulled her out of her hesitation in the face of the priest. "Didn't the ancestors of all these people, our neighbors, sacrifice enough when this place was built? Finally, they're getting some use of it instead of a few old ladies in their widow's weeds rattling around once or twice a week in this hollow. Those blackbirds—" Paul meant the priest. He, too, had seen a carrion bird in the figure. "—Charge you to be born, to wed, to die. Coming and going. Opiate of the people. Don't give that fellow a sou."

They hadn't gone two steps beyond the priest, unable to do a thing about what was happening in his church, when someone recognized Paul. Time seemed to run backwards again to the square in front of l'Hôtel de Ville that night at the end of October when they wrote their names in the log as married without benefit of clergy. A time before the siege and surrender, before death and destruction.

Paul came to life in response to the shouts of, "It's Citoyen Paul. Hooray, Communard! How we need you. How France has missed you."

And it seemed as if Paul's men from Sedan and Champigny rose from their muddy, bloody beet fields to greet him. They regrew limbs. The blind could see. The insane relearned the civilized ways of Frenchmen. Backs were slapped, arms embraced, kisses even exchanged. Nathalie had to step aside.

One man demanded gruffly, "So where've you been these last weeks, Communard?" Sarcasm filled the title one didn't inherit but had to prove.

"While we've been starving, shivering? Living the high life of a comte, I understand. In the home of your bourgeois brother, isn't it?"

Nathalie tried to push her way between her war hero and his attacker, but Paul motioned them all aside. He would fight this one on his own. He would prove the man wrong, here and now. So Nathalie backed away. She couldn't bear to hear how her wounded veteran might fall again. Unless he asked for her, she would make her own assessment of this Red Club.

Around the church, braziers blackened marble with soot and did what they could to take the chill off the air inside Saint-Sulpice, lacking its usual wafts of incense. The closeness of bodies did the rest until Nathalie felt resurrection in her hands and feet. She could feel the flush on her cheeks. At first determined to stay within calling distance of Paul's side, receiving the crumbs of his accolades for a while. But then the crowd drew him towards the foot of the pulpit.

"No, no, friends." Paul resisted those in the throng who wanted to drag him up to the pulpit directly. "Let me listen for a while, to see how the cause has grown and evolved with the will of the people."

The pulpit was kept full, people—mostly men—lining up with their sheaves of paper for their turn to express their plans for France's future. Their voices competed with the organ and the chatter of those not attending or those arguing the point just made among themselves, but the more popular voices called for silence. Those clustered at the foot of the gold-encrusted podium were mostly men, but women were definitely allowed, even encouraged to attend. "Mark my words," more than one man shouted. "We will give you the vote. These rascals would not be in power if women had the vote."

Indeed, one tall, lanky, mannish woman even climbed up to the lectern to speak her mind. Nathalie learned her name: Louise Michel. The Red Virgin, they called her. Nathalie felt as if her friend Louise had been resurrected. *Enfin.*

Leaving Paul in his suddenly rediscovered element, where any woman beside him who might be seen as a minder would be detrimental, Nathalie found more interest in the rest of the club's crowds. Women controlled other sectors. This wasn't just a political rally.

It didn't take her more than a moment to understand: A widow with children and no fuel since the siege could bring them here for warmth at no cost. There was more: food in what had been a chapel to the patron of charity, St. Vincent de Paul. Red-draped now, the benevolent statue of a priest holding two adoring children oversaw the usual dole of the bells for the clochards, now for the whole neighborhood. For children with flesh-and-blood cheeks. And their human parents.

Two men carried in a kettle of cassoulet which women spooned out into cracked bowls brought from home until they scraped the bottom. Then in came a kettle of rich barley soup to receive the same treatment, all from the donations of green grocers and butchers. Nathalie spelled a woman whose arms had grown weary at the task.

Every once in a while, phrases fell from the pulpit over the whole: "There is a duel to the death, a war with no rest or mercy. If society does not annihilate socialism, socialism will annihilate society. Look around you. Who is feeding your children? Bourgeois society? Or proletariat socialism?"

A wine merchant rolled in casks of wine. Nathalie worried that with free drink available, Paul would repeat last night's adventure. But when she looked across the nave at him through strings of laundry drying out of the weather, she saw him with coffee instead.

An elderly gentleman was helped up to the pulpit where he, instead of the usual harangue, recited a poem of Baudelaire dedicated to Victor Hugo, something about a swan in a butcher shop in Paris. Nathalie was glad to discover there were two more hours before she had to meet with her brother-in-law about a butcher's shop when the gentleman came to the final verse:

Paris changes . . . but in sadness like mine
nothing stirs. New buildings, old
neighborhoods turn to allegory
and memories weigh more than stone.

In the chapel just to the right of the entrance to Saint-Sulpice hung a painting of Jacob wrestling with the angel. Delacroix was the same man whose patriotism painted the famous picture of bare-chested Marianne leading the Revolution. Between that painting and the one it faced—also by Delacroix: *Heliodorus Driven from the Temple* in the Book of the

Maccabees—a pair of barbers gave free haircuts and shaves in the slants of sunlight from the south-facing windows. The marble floor here was carpeted with hair trimmings, and parents combed out the lice from their children's scalps. The barbers also helped with famine-diseased teeth, mostly pulling them from scurvied gums.

Another man in the pulpit—a fiery redhead—railed against "the inquisition and monkish terrorism" which made the priest at the door slink away. "You are against barricades since the Prussian threat is past?" the man went on, raising a great deal of shouting both pro and con in response. "What else does Thiers' government want to do but raise the barricades of order? But what has order ever done for you, people of France, but to keep you in your place? The barricades of religion, the barricades of family and finance. Mark my words, they are planning a St. Bartholomew's Day night for socialists, just like in days of yore when Catherine de Medici made the Seine float with the bodies of Protestant men, women, and children. You are opposed to more barricades? I say we must strengthen the barricades against the bourgeoisie, now more than ever."

Shouts drowned the rest of his speech.

Nathalie moved on to the middle of the nave, the side opposite the pulpit. Here women had laid out blankets like at a summer picnic, mostly concealing a curious line of lead embedded in the floor that ran down from an obelisk. This marked the solstices by the sun coming in through a southern window as well as helping with the determination of the date of Easter.

The women sat, skirts spread out. They nursed the little ones quite openly while the older ones ran about, playing hide-and-seek around old sarcophagi. When Nathalie joined the group, she instantly got a needle passed to her hand. She wished she'd brought her grandmother's thimble, and promised to do so the next time. Yes, there would be a next time.

It might be the child she was carrying, but the sight of a community of women brought her tears of joy.

Armed with a tin of beautiful spare buttons, a whole basket of rags and kilometers of thread of all colors, the women took in siege-worn mending. When a grownup's clothes were beyond another patching and turning, they were cut down for smaller and smaller children until the scraps went into the rag basket and made patched quilts or hooked rugs.

Nathalie had been doing some mending for her sister-in-law, sitting in the kitchen beside Madame Joséphine, but this felt so much more immediate and worthwhile.

"Here, let's use that bolt end of calico to make a shirt for this communard who wore shirts he formed of old newspapers throughout the siege," one woman offered. The wound festering on her leg was like that of a lot of others; starving people don't heal well. Another woman was busy tending her with what smelled like a combination of comfrey and wood sage, but the wounded woman still commanded plenty of attention.

"I can do that," Nathalie offered. Without her thimble, she was already hurting from pushing a needle through the thick wool of trousers. "I worked in a tailor's shop. Before. I'll get the measurements and pieces cut, anyway," she added, remembering that she did have an appointment that evening. "Perhaps some other can finish what I cannot."

"Best to keep this work in our own, the Commune's hands," said the woman with the bad leg, "not in a shop owned by a man who does none of the work. Much less in a factory doing such work *en masse*, one-size fits all, where the owner who hoards the profits doesn't even show his face on the floor among the sewing machines. Just a manager hired for his brutality."

The women had no measure marked with centimeters, just a string they marked with chalk. But that worked well enough, once you remembered which mark was which. Nathalie decided to give a little extra space in the garment, hoping that barley soup would soon put more meat on the communard's bones starting through his thin flesh like repoussé.

As she measured, her thoughts went briefly to the shop Eugène said he'd put her in. She should be thinking more of that, so she would have a whole business plan to present to her brother-in-law when she saw him. But then she looked up to see Paul enjoying himself so much, and the bourgeoisie's bottom-line went right out of her head, signifying nothing.

She returned to the active conversation among her new friends as she laid out the fabric over the lead line running to the obelisk, laid the chalk-marked string over that—a more human scale—and began to cut.

· XXVII ·
THE TERRIBLE YEAR
—

As she set about sewing the communard's shirt, a speck on the floor of the towering Saint-Sulpice, Nathalie listened to the discussions of the women around her.

"The Red Virgin is encouraging us to form a Women's Union." This was an older woman, given one of the few available stray prie-dieux left from more pious times in Saint-Sulpice to squat upon, clenching a tobacco-less pipe between her teeth.

"Louise Michel. What a great woman!" exclaimed several in the group.

"Even though she does spend a lot of time with the men."

This reminded Nathalie to look after her own man. From her place squatting beside a pillar, she caught sight of him. Someone had given him a red revolutionary Phrygian cap to wear. Once she realized that, he was very easy to follow across the open space of the church, always in the center of things. He looked great, not a trace of his recent melancholy. He looked handsome, even, and Nathalie felt a rush of gratitude to whatever gods there might be in a rococo church in Paris's sixth arrondissement for the quirk that had married them. Although she wanted to, she knew that to go to him now would be selfish.

"But that's what we need."

Nathalie's attention returned to the discussion among the women.

"We want someone to harangue them with our needs for once."

"We must do it for ourselves."

"We must organize."

"Louise Michel reminds us that votes for women were among our demands in forty-eight. That's over twenty years and no movement on the matter."

"This Commune will be different."

A chorus of voices said, "Vive la Commune."

"Food for my children first," insisted one woman with breasts so shrunken, it was hard to understand how she managed to breastfeed. "I'll worry about votes later."

Another was nursing a friend's child in place of her own who had died during the siege. "So vote for the man who feeds your children, Communarde. That is what we must all do."

Nathalie took the opportunity to smooth the front of her gown as she gathered up the four simple pieces of a smock she'd cut plus scraps for the bands at cuffs and collar. Surreptitiously, she studied nursing technique, for her own future use.

Then she thought of the three buttons she'd seen in the tin that would go so well with this calico—carved wood. She also remembered the little girl of four or five who was being given her first lessons of the power of a needle by sorting through the jumbled tin and sewing the similar buttons together in bunches. Nathalie remembered having been given the same task by her grandmother at about the same age, although with a much smaller button tin.

The organist changed, from the men who like the "Marseillaise" and other martial tunes to someone whose fingers were more used to the tinkling of a brothel piano. More couples danced, but then there was a call for quiet, and a woman named Augustine Kaiser—probably Jewish with that name and that origin, Alsatian—claimed the pulpit. Several of the women around Nathalie knew this women's reputation:

"She used to sing evenings in the Eldorado on the Boulevard de Strasbourg."

"Just. She hails from Alsace."

"She is one of the theatre's stars."

"I read one of the reviews that called her 'rude, that's the best one can say.'"

"'Name, allure, height, diction—all of this is bad *chez elle*.' That's what I read."

"I read 'war songs full of "victory" and "glory," but bloody, but heroic, but murderous.'"

"I guess that's what we need here in the Red Club." After that, reviews ceased, and people could form their own opinions. Augustine Kaiser sang:

I am a daughter of the people.
O my people, how noble is your name.
You'll never see me hide my face
Under powder and carmine.

The delivery might be "rude," yes, but that's what the people wanted. And when Augustine Kaiser's song ended with,

We cry, to arms!
Aux armes! Marchons, citoyens!

the very words of the anthem, she received three encores.

Nathalie got the shoulder seams in, then her thoughts were drawn outside herself again. The discussion around the pulpit turned to burials. Nathalie heard what she thought were several very good ideas.

"All these corpses we've seen over the past few months."

"The fees the Church charges to bury a Christian—"

"If you've lost five or six in your family, you can't afford it."

"Not that and feed the mouths that are left alive."

"That's the point. That's what the Commune proposes. Free burial with the dignity of your fellow communards marching behind your bier. If you're interested, please see Citoyen Jean-Marc, the redhead over there by the Chapel of Saint-Paul. We'll contact you when we need support. And see you don't die in the gutter."

Nathalie inserted the smock's sleeves with neat little gathers for fullness.

"Communardes, now is the time to put this Women's Union into action." A woman who had taken the patches she had to sew over to the foot of the pulpit hurried back to the women's encampment. "There's a man haranguing now that every woman who slept with a Prussian should have her head shaved and marched through the streets bearing a placard declaring her shame. They want to brand them."

This man didn't have much of a voice. Or perhaps he was pitching it so it didn't carry in the church's vast space. On purpose.

"Sounds like what they did to Jeanne d'Arc. So medieval."

"Who of us has not slept with a man for food or safety?"

"And who of us knew that the Prussian victory wouldn't descend into complete pillage? Better not to get hurt in the process."

The women stuck their needles in their work and got to their feet.

"I can't say that I want the communal good to go to raising a Prussian bastard," one woman grumbled.

"They are traitors."

"More than the men who sold the Prussians arms? Who sold them our city?"

"Fine. You can stay behind with your man-centered feelings," the rest told those who wanted to keep silent, then shouted, "Protect the Union of the Women of France!" as they got to their feet and marched to the other side of the nave.

"They've already undertaken this punishment in the streets around Montmartre," the little man in the pulpit grumbled back, and was then drowned out.

Nathalie had a sinking feeling: Montmartre was where her friend Coco lived. She'd seen her friend at the scrubbing of la Place d'Étoile and had noticed no signs that she might be at risk of such a hazing. Nonetheless . . .

When the man had been shouted out of his gold-plated aerie by the Union of Women, her throat hoarse from the same activity, Nathalie felt an arm around her waist. She turned and fell into Paul's embrace as their circuits of the club brought them briefly together.

"Aren't you happy?" he asked her.

"I am," she replied. "Very content." It surprised her to renewed tears just how true the words were.

"Me too. Better than in months."

Nathalie had to agree, just by looking in his face, at the strength in his arms, that this was true. Her own spirits soared. And just at that moment, the sun must have come out from behind a cloud. Light burst through the stained glass in the hollow of the Chapel of the Souls in Purgatory and fell right on them, warming, almost like fireworks.

"That—that is for us," Paul said.

"Yes," Nathalie sighed and hugged him closer.

"Yes, yes." Paul's attention had already wandered to the next group of men he thought he should meet with. "This is exactly what I was fighting for when I joined the army instead of sitting around as a comte. When I fought at Sedan and Champigny, this is the France I was fighting for. It was not in vain. I can still do good." And he was gone.

Somebody else with another proposal full of hope had mounted the pulpit.

"But how are you going to pay for it?" a gruff voice challenged him from the floor of the church. When had anyone ever challenged a sermon from that site before?

"How are we going to pay for anything? Contributions from the people."

"The people who've been starving for months?"

"Where do you draw the line between contributions and taxes?"

The man in the pulpit's gaze wandered to the church's apse, to the altar that stood right where the two arms of the building's cruciform met. "It has occurred to me, sitting here, that there's an awful lot of glitter in this building. This building that belongs to the people. Why, if someone were to melt down just the pyx and the gem-studded dove sitting on that table under our red flags there—"

"Monsieur *le curé* might object."

All eyes turned to the spot where the unhappy man in black had been sitting with his nearly empty alms basket at least as long as Nathalie had been in the building. The place was empty, but the presence lingered as an unquiet memory.

"There is such a thing as citizen's arrest. With cause."

Many a citizen's head nodded at that.

When that discussion disrupted into such confusion that she could no longer follow from her distance, Nathalie bunched up her needlework and decided to tour another part of the cathedral for a change of scenery. Behind the altar, centered on the Chapel of the Virgin, hanging lamps cast the shadow of a statue of Mother and Child standing precariously on the orb of the earth. Here women who preferred not to cook, clean, or sew had cordoned off the area for children. They taught them games, songs, and tended their woes so their mothers could get other tasks done.

Nathalie exchanged words with the woman who had taken charge of this arc of the cathedral, a cheerful motherly sort who had managed to maintain something of her bosom through the siege.

"We are through with the Church being in charge of French education so that when a child comes out, all he can do is recite the catechism. 'I believe in the one true and Catholic Church'? What rubbish. Isn't it better that a child memorizes the Declaration of the Rights of Man? 'Men'—and women, I may add—'are born and remain free and equal in rights.'

"Of course."

"If the Church can't do it, we must. Take education on ourselves."

Nathalie agreed. She had her own child to think of, after all.

Before she knew it, Nathalie found herself with a sweet little poppet in her lap, a girl with her head shaved against the lice, but with a brand-new white cap tied under her chin. "A cap with ruffles," the child was proud to announce. With a bit of chalk and a piece of slate from the mansard fallen from bombarded building, they began to learn the alphabet.

"*A. A* is for *une abeille*—a bee." Nathalie's bee looked rather crude, but the girl had been stung. She would not forget that shape.

"*B* is for *un bateau*—a boat."

"My brother made a little boat. He used to sail it on the fountain in the Luxembourg Gardens. Before he got hungry and died."

"Why don't you draw it?"

With earnest concentration, to the memory of her brother, she did—a half-moon and a triangle on a stick floating on waves surely larger than any that had ever been seen on a water feature in a Parisian park. The effort was at least as good as Nathalie herself would have done.

"And *C*—" When she'd been a child, Nathalie had learned "*C* is for *un couchon*—pig." Now she said, "*C* is for la Commune."

"Vive la Commune," the little one chirped.

"*Bien sûr, chérie.*" Nathalie gave the girl a hug, hugging her own child to her between them. "Vive la Commune. Vive la France."

Overhead, the church bells began to ring. Five o'clock. A timekeeper for citizens who couldn't afford a watch, also provided by the church.

Nathalie passed the little girl to another woman—promising they'd come to other letters tomorrow—and hurried away. She was supposed to be meeting her brother-in-law at Montparnasse. She was late. She didn't even stop to tell Paul where she was going. She would be back to the club for supper. Having seen him as engaged as he was with activities of the Commune, she knew he certainly wouldn't be ready to leave before then.

Nathalie had had a flash of inspiration as she'd picked up a needle again. She needn't work in the back room of a man's tailor shop if she had her own. She was pregnant. Children's clothes were what she had in mind: little caps and pinafores laid out on the drop-down counter. Those were the easiest, the quickest to turn out, and mothers always needed new ones.

She could go on to pretty frocks, to little boys' short pants and jackets. Sailor suits that were so popular. She would tell Eugène all of this—if she pulled away from the warmth of the Commune in good time.

But being in the cathedral all afternoon had opened up other dreams in her mind on which to nurture the child she carried. It would be very lonely to sit in a shop all day. Why couldn't she ply her needle with the other women, as she had today?

And a school. Soon enough, her child would need a school, and the one under the precariously balanced Madonna would be such a nice one. She could teach, and then never leave sight of her child from morning to night.

Was the little shop Eugène promised her the best choice?

In any case, Nathalie had learned the name and address of the quartier's midwife. She'd even met the woman—briefly, because the caregiver had been undertaking her immediate duties in the small Chapel of Sainte-Geneviève. From the chapel blocked off from the rest of the church by hanging red flags came the groans of a laboring woman.

The midwife had assured Nathalie all was well after palpating her still-flat belly, feeling her pulse, and asking a few questions. "We'll hear your groans here soon enough," the midwife had assured her. "And give you the strength to face it."

"Thank you," Nathalie had replied.

• • •

"Sorry I'm late," Nathalie apologized to her brother-in-law.

As she stepped into the darkened shop, setting the little bell ringing merrily to almost-empty space, she carried in her mind the stretches of empty land she'd passed on her way. Blocks of limestone from ancient workings in the catacombs had been dumped here when "here" had been outside the city of Paris. More recently, rubble from Baron Haussmann's renewals added to the heap, Montparnasse, named for the mountain in ancient Greece where the muses had gathered. The name was something of a joke. Artists so poor they were forced to live in the neighborhood were beloved of the muses? What new, bizarre mythology was that?

"No problem," Eugène Toussaint assured her with a slim smile. "I told you it just needs to be seen to become a shop. No rigor about the hours. And I welcome the chance to get a better look at my new property. I only glanced at it briefly before."

There wasn't all that much to see. It was pretty much as Eugène had described it earlier that day in his office: a ground-floor former butcher shop in need of a lot of work, two rooms, a loft, and a cold, wet courtyard behind. It smelled of mold, decay, and mice droppings. There were no lights, no gas, and night was drawing close this January evening.

Nathalie had begun to express her gratitude to her—their—benefactor. In her mind, the little frilly caps and pinafores were already laid out. She knew just where she would put her infant's cot, the bed she and Paul would share . . .

When Paul burst in through the butcher shop door, snapping the bell off its spring.

"Hello, Paul," Eugène said.

"Paul, dear, your brother was just showing me the space he was offering us—"

Paul panted for breath. He'd been running. "I know very well what my brother's up to."

Nathalie turned to point out the features of the place. "Yes, there is no running water, and the privy we share with ten other households in the court—well, it's pretty vile, but—"

"This place is freezing," Paul announced. "If you think I'll let my wife and child live here to catch tuberculosis—"

"Paul, there is a stove." She pointed it out to him in the corner of the central room. It would have to do for the whole establishment.

Eugène, for some reason, seemed to have stepped back from the fray.

"Yes?" Paul snapped. "Did he show you how well it draws? Probably fills the whole place with smoke any time you light it."

Not only was there a stove, there was, for some unknown reason, kindling and twigs beside it. Paul knelt, turning his back purposely on his brother, and opened the stove. He began to lay the fire.

"Of course, he didn't think to warm the place for his potential tenant."

"It's no problem, Paul, really," Natalie said. "We can see to all that later."

"Never lit your own fire, have you, Brother?"

Eugène's silence said that Paul was right. That he actually took his lifelong lack of dirty hands as a point of pride.

"Nathalie," Paul said from his position on his knees, but with no less force because of it. "All the rents and fines that were in abeyance during the siege have come active again. Surely you met people at the club who are already suffering from this. They can't get paid yet, but they can be tossed out of their homes. They can be denied food on their overrun tabs.

"My brother is offering us this space for two reasons. First, because he—or perhaps more specifically, my sister-in-law—wants us out from under their roof. In particular, our child. She hates it already, this little future comte of ours."

Again, Eugène said nothing to counter the charge.

"But that's all right, Paul," Nathalie said. "I don't want to stay where I'm not wanted. And I mean, if you consider all those stairs, even if we're only on the fifth floor—I get exhausted just thinking of them."

"And the second reason, Paul?" Eugène spoke quietly. Dangerously.

"Why do you think, Nathalie, that he wants us here keeping shop? A shop—he doesn't care if it makes any money or even if there are any wares in it. Why?"

"Because your brother is a good man?" Nathalie knew even as she said it that this was not the answer her husband wanted.

"Because if my brother can show to the authorities that a building that really should be condemned and abandoned actually has a functioning store in it, the government will pay him twice the price to tear it down and build his elite apartment blocks upon it. Of course, when I say 'government,' I mean the taxpayer. Not his friends, of course, who have their tax shelters, but all those people you spent this afternoon with at the Club."

Nathalie opened her mouth, then shut it again, considering the truth of her husband's words.

"He'll think nothing of throwing us out the instant he gets the price he's looking for. Or tear the roof—which probably leaks—down over our heads. No, Eugène Toussaint gives no free lunches. Our new friends will pay for it, mark my words, while they lose the roofs over their own heads.

"But that's not the worst of it, is it, Eugène? What I just learned today, among our friends. What the government has agreed to pay to the Prussians to get them to leave so quietly. What the taxpayers, at the same time that they are lining my brother's pockets for his schemes, must pay, and pay in one month's time. Five milliard gold francs. That's five billion. Who can imagine such a number? How are we to pay such a crushing sum? Be sure, my brother won't pay a sou of it. People who have just come through a siege, given their all for their country, are now asked to give more while their leaders feed at the trough and enjoy the fruits of victory as if they, too, wore pickle helmets. Our child must be born under such a debt, his future in hock."

Eugène didn't deny a word, but his grin spread. "Paul, you always were the clever one—"

Paul leapt to his feet and threw his brother against the door frame so hard that dust and straw sifted down from the loft—covering everything, clinging to Nathalie's hair and to the beard Paul had just had trimmed under the painting of Jacob wrestling with the angel. In fact, the two brothers held very much the pose of the antagonists from Delacroix's brush. How many times had the men held this pose in their lifetime, for there was a lifetime of hate in that narrow space. Might that not be Jacob wrestling with another implacable enemy, his brother Esau?

Nathalie gave a little cry of protest, of horror, of disbelief at the hidden violent nature of the man she'd married.

"I could kill you, right here and now. Gut you like a pig. String the entrails like sausages across the hooks of this fine shop you own. Do France a favor," Paul said between gritted teeth.

Eugène laughed in Paul's face. "And leave your child an orphan?"

Paul, strong and fit from battle, gave the door post another hard hammer with his brother's flabby body. More debris sifted down.

Eugène laughed again. "*Mon Dieu*, you are such a communist. You always were. Always thinking you can share everything when you can't. No, Paul. Jesus Christ couldn't. And you can't, either."

As if communist were the worst thing you could call another man. Worse than effeminate, worse than a coward.

Behind the struggling pair, the pile so carefully laid in the stove suddenly burst to brief life, etching them with chiaroscuro. Unfed, though, it died.

"Paul, don't," Nathalie finally found voice to say.

Another two heartbeats—it seemed forever—and Paul dropped Eugène like no more than a sack of potatoes, although a sack of potatoes was still a rare treasure in Paris.

"Will we take this little shop, Paul?" Nathalie asked.

"No, dear wife. That we will not," was the reply.

Nathalie felt that like a punch in her gut—right where the baby was.

Paul brushed himself off as if from filth more than what had come down from the loft. "Nor will we ever live under this man's roof on the Rue Férou, not in the garret, not on the fifth floor. Never again."

Paul put his arm around Nathalie's waist and gently but firmly led her out into the gathering night. "We know where our friends are, in the Red Club at Saint-Sulpice. That's where we will live. Vive la Commune."

And Nathalie kept quiet about that other thing she had seen in her brother-in-law's eyes before Paul arrived. He was ready to kill if he didn't get what he wanted. Kill her and her inconvenient heir of a child. She knew the war wasn't over. It was only just beginning.

· XXVIII ·
THE TERRIBLE YEAR
—

On the evening of March 17, word came to the citizens camped out at Saint-Sulpice.

Nathalie, for one, had been trying not to make it seem like camping. She was trying to make their little alcove behind a cold stone altar rail in the Delacroix Jacob-Wrestling-Angel chapel, complete with red flags for drapes, at least as comfortable as she would have made Eugène Toussaint's decrepit butcher shop. And at least she didn't have to cook.

"Thiers' men have been ordered to take the cannons from Montmartre tomorrow at dawn," a fresh-faced youth flush with his first responsibility told the huddle of men squatting on the church floor, most of them smoking and dropping their ash.

"We have a spy among them," he added modestly.

The reaction was immediate and furious. "Those cannons? Montmartre is such a key position. It commands all of Paris, you know. The people of Paris own those two hundred cannons. They donated their all to forge them during the siege. Their ladles, their cooking pots, their mother's rings. They donated it all."

"Well, we, the Commune of Paris, will not let Thiers have them." Paul's decisive voice cut through all debate.

There was no time to lose. Men were already stubbing out their smokes, pulling on their jackets, and running down into the crypt where a cache of Chassepot rifles has been stashed since Monsieur le Curé came under citizen-arrest. Nathalie was among the women throwing on shawls and putting on hats.

"Stay here," Paul told her.

"I won't." She adjusted his red Phrygian cap. With the blue, white, and red of the circling ribbons of its cockade—like what they wore to their wedding—it made such a target. "Not this time."

"Nathalie, the child."

"I am doing this for the child."

And he didn't say another word as they walked hand-in-hand into the night to reach Montmartre by dawn, the flood of their footsteps gathering more followers with every Commune Club they passed.

. . .

The last time she'd seen a gun in Paul's hand, he'd been aiming it at himself. Her heart skipped a beat as he took another weapon handed to him when they reached the top of the hill. The east had begun to lighten.

She joined the women who doled out hot buns donated by local bakers and bowls of coffee.

And then, shouted orders to troops clashed with the birdsong on the early morning air. From between the shadowed houses at the foot of Montmartre, French soldiers in their bright blue began to form their ranks, row upon row.

Paul was there on the crest, giving orders to turn the cannons, showing his ragtag bunch how to load. They didn't have much ammunition, maybe enough for two firings per gun. After that—

In good order, Thiers' army ascended, bayonets fixed. They would get even closer. At such range, and with the communards so crowded together, they wouldn't miss.

And then, there was Louise Michel—tall, lanky—the fiery woman Nathalie liked to think had come to replace her friend Louise, who had died in the siege. "Women of France," Louise Michel called. "Leave your cooking pots. Paris needs you here more than at your ovens now. Let us stand, as we are, soup ladles in our hands, between our men and the traitors. Let us see what French soldier will fire upon his mother, his sisters."

So they stood, shoulder-to-shoulder, forming their own ranks.

Nathalie looked out and decided she wouldn't mind dying on a morning like this, with all Paris stretched out before her and the first light glinting off the Seine. With her sisters.

It was a black-and-white morning, still, but on this day in March you could smell the soil. Buds would be seen to dot the trees and shrubbery once the sun rose higher in a clear sky. Every revolution should begin with the new hope of spring.

"Nathalie," she heard Paul's anguished voice. "The baby."

Nathalie pulled back her jacket, pulled her skirt tight. Let the men who had their sights on her know they shot at a woman with child—they slaughtered the future of France.

"Look, Sisters," sang out Louise Michel. "They have no horses with them. Generals ordered them to reclaim the cannons, but leaders lower down the chain of command forgot to order horses. Have no fear."

And Nathalie felt no fear.

Nathalie and her companions could hear the generals shouting from the cover of the fences and trees that formed the base of the butte. "Company. Forward, march."

Soldiers' boots marched, hobnails on stone.

Louise Michel shouted, "Women of France. Three steps forward to meet them."

They took three.

"Ready."

And then six more.

"Aim."

They could see the pimples on the young men's faces.

"Fire."

Birdsong alone filled the ray-streaked sky.

As one man, to no order, the soldiers swung their rifles to their shoulders, butts in the air, barrels pointed harmlessly to the ground: the common symbol that the military was now siding with the people. The men in blue came up to receive buns and coffee at the hands of the women and to take a look at the cannons, offering advice. Better loading next time.

That afternoon, two generals were shot by their men in the Street of the Rosebushes for the crime of ordering fire upon Frenchwomen armed with only soup spoons.

After that came seventy-two days of the Commune's reign. For seventy-two days, the life of the Clubs spilled out of the naves and throughout the whole city. Seventy-two days not exactly of peace, for hot discussions spilled out of the churches and l'Hôtel de Ville into the cafes and onto every street corner of the whole city. It was chaotic—but with the joyful chaos of a wild party. The difference was that every man knew his voice was being heard. The farrier could shoe horses the way he knew was best. The same with the baker, the cooper, the furniture maker. Artists formed a self-help federation believing that every person had the right to live in a pleasing environment. Power and sewer workers sent these services into the slums.

All immigrants were guaranteed equal workingmen's rights. Every woman, too, saw her voice heard. "Food, clothing and education for our children. Something they can use. Not the catechism handed down from on high."

"And girls equal to boys."

Women sat on the councils, where they voted.

Many landlords fled to their lands outside Paris. Paul warned his brother that if he did, the Commune would claim all his property. He promised his brother he would protect him and his wife in the building in Rue Férou if he gave up the other buildings. Eugène agreed.

On the bright morning of the tenth of April, Nathalie joined a group of mostly women. They marched on the Place Voltaire in front of the Prison de la Roquette in the eleventh arrondissement and burned down the guillotine. Once the symbol of freeing the people of the aristocracy's yoke, the dreaded machine had begun to dispatch too many men who spoke with the voice of the Commune. Thiers and his followers, holed up in Versailles like some kingly heir and his retainers, periodically sent forays into Paris and jailed communard leaders. At least now the dropping blade could not be used against these new prisoners.

The communardes' fire left only five marks on the pavement that a person could trip over and never know what had once stood there.

On May 16, the artist Gustave Courbet, called "the most infamous man in France," committed yet another scandal. Used to outraging everyone with his paintings of real-life prostitutes showing their underthings and of female genitalia with the title "The Origin of the World," he turned his attention to the Place de Paix. In the Square's center stood the monument Napoleon forged of the captured cannons of all Europe, which offended Monsieur Courbet's artistic sensibilities. He led the destruction of the Column of Vendôme in the name of freedom.

Nathalie attended that, too, her condition newly visible in lighter spring clothes made by Commune needles.

• • •

Seventy-two days. That was how long it took Thiers in Versailles to buy up a new army from the provinces, and for this army to be armed by the Prussians. On the sixty-ninth day, Paul told Nathalie: "We should have stopped the banks and the *bourse*, the stock exchange. In the name of freedom, we let them continue. Now we see they've been lending money to Thiers right under our noses."

The evening of that seventy-second day, Saturday, there was a concert in the Tuileries Garden, free to every citizen. In the candlelight, Paul murmured in her ear, "So much better than the balls I attended here under the now-disgraced emperor. Let the people define their art, not have it filtered to them from the top down."

After that, everything became a red-tinged blur. By the evening of the next day, a quarter of the city had fallen to the army from Versailles. This was the quarter of the city where most of the bourgeoisie lived, cordoning themselves off from the people who made their clothes and drove their carriages. Eugène d'Ermenville regained most of his property. Nathalie and Paul couldn't even dream of living in the building on the Rue Férou anymore.

"We will never live under that man's roof," Paul had said. "Never again."

The Bloody Week had begun. The Commune fought fiercely for their lives but retreated from barricade to barricade across the city. Centimeter by centimeter, cobblestone by cobblestone.

The last time she looked up to find the Paul she knew, his right hand was swathed in a dirty cloth through which blood was soaking. He tipped his cap to her. But the Versaillaises had burst into the door of a nearby building, shoved the occupants out of the way—or killed them—until they reached the top floor. They began to fight among the chimney pots on the rooftop, firing down on the backs of the communards. In the smoke, she lost sight of him.

Paris was burning. The Versaillaises set fire to the slums, as you do to a nest of rats, shooting the families as they fled for their lives.

"Sisters," declared Louise Michel, "Communardes. They do this to make turning out the poor for their grand projects easier. Tit for tat. We need to burn them out in return."

So Nathalie, who couldn't find Paul and assumed he was dead, took the cognac bottle she was handed and let it be filled with petrol.

L'Hôtel de Ville burned—and the fire that burned the Tuileries and the lavish wealth of the empire for forty-eight hours spread to one corner of the Louvre.

But Nathalie wasn't there. After throwing her bottle—where, she wasn't exactly sure—she was arrested and spent several nights in a cell in La Santé prison with ten other women.

On the first of June, Eugène d'Ermenville bailed her out. "I've pleaded your belly," he told her, referring to the old law that made things easier for female prisoners who were pregnant.

Nathalie clung to the bars and said, "I would rather stay with the communardes, my friends, and have our baby here."

"Don't be a fool," Eugène hissed in her ear. "Half of these women will be taken out and shot in the yard before sunset. Besides, I've put in a good word for Paul too."

"Paul? Paul is here in La Santé? Paul is alive?"

That was all the word she needed. And, indeed, it was while she was waiting for Eugène to sign some paperwork swearing to her good behavior that she saw Paul being led in chains through a distant hall in the prison. She ran to him until the muscles holding up the baby strained. "Paul! Paul!"

He turned at the sound of his name. "Go, Nathalie," he ordered sharply. His mouth was swollen and missing teeth.

Eugène said, "Give me the title, Paul, and I'll do more to get you released."

Nathalie hated her brother-in-law enough in that moment to kill him with her bare hands, but it was he who held her.

Paul laughed bitterly. "You think I want to be released to such a world as you'd create?" His ruined mouth was painful to see. "Monarchist titles mean nothing in a truly modern France."

Nathalie screamed as the guard gave Paul another whack. She tried to go to him. Eugène held her back.

"People who believe as you do, Brother—"

Eugène growled the words to Paul, but they were closer to Nathalie's ear. The baby in her twinged. "You have lost this mad bid to change the world. The old law of the market, of kill or be killed, will return to bring stability to French life. To the world."

Paul's reply was shouted as two guards dragged him off between them. All she heard was "Take care of them, Eugène. You're a bastard, not an heir, but I charge you by anything you hold holy to take care of them. My time is up, Nathalie. Go and live."

Nathalie sank to her knees. She had never felt less stability. She wouldn't let it be. She threw herself and the baby against the guard who had begun to beat her husband with the butt of his gun.

The man—whose face she never would forget—turned the butt on her until she crumpled to the ground and Eugène pulled her away.

"Come, Sister," he told her. "We can put you in the concierge's loge. Our old Madame Sale disappeared three days ago. We hear she lies in the square in front of Saint-Sulpice, food for the dogs and rats. Women of fashion are taking tours to the various mounds of corpses, poking at the bodies delicately with the tips of their parasols and laughing at the state of the dead's underthings."

Nathalie gave birth to the son she named Paul in the concierge's loge, and for six weeks she did not leave the little room nor the duties she had begun to take on—until she heard that Paul, still alive, had been tried and sentenced to deportation to Devil's Island.

The baby died.

. . .

Nine years later, the last ship from New Caledonia brought back prisoners who had received amnesty. Paul was among them, her fearless Paul, a changed man who couldn't bear a roof over his head or to sleep in the dark.

And twenty-five years later, she still suffered hallucinations of silk-screened coffins she couldn't step on to approach the mountain top of the martyrs where she and the citizens of Paris had saved the cannons, which in the end had served little purpose.

And now, finally, Eugène d'Ermenville was dead.

⁂ XXIX ⁂
LA BELLE ÉPOQUE

In the haven of Coco's apartment, fifth-floor-left, Madame Toussaint washed, warmed, and cooked an egg with herbs and the tail end of a wheel of brie she found there. She would have loved a baguette to complete her meal, but that would have to wait 'til morning.

Madame Toussaint remembered when once the murdered man had suggested she might have this suite of rooms for her own. If only . . .

Well, she could pretend now, for one evening.

There was no cat. Coco had told Madame Toussaint that Monsieur Pépin was sensitive to cats and wouldn't have one, "Not even for company. He won't have birds, either. His daughters at home have a whole window cage full of them. When he comes to me, he says he just wants peace and quiet. No nagging, no daughters' dramatics, no birds." Although she had spoken in the present tense, Coco's sigh had indicated that she didn't think Monsieur's return likely. Coco's rooms did feel lonely. Too tidy. Too quiet, five floors up from the nighttime street.

In the bedroom, thrown casually over the arm of a pink-flowered armchair, lay a white-lace peignoir, suitable for greeting a lover. Madame Toussaint tried it on and, even though it was full enough not to leave gaps in the front, she felt ridiculous. The mirror told her it was ridiculous, that full-length mirror that seemed to greet her every way she turned.

Madame Toussaint had lived without mirrors—nothing but the occasional shop window—for twenty-five years. What did a woman with her history—or her future—need of mirrors?

It was far too late, and she was far too exhausted by the events of the day to attempt even the widest of her friend's corsets, although Coco had given her free rein to try on anything she chose. Madame Toussaint decided to doff the lace and just crawl straight away under the duvet.

In the midst of the struggle with the bow turned to a Gordian knot—amazing how these thinner, finer fabrics resisted you getting out of them—she heard noises on the fifth-floor landing just outside the apartment door. Lively chatter. Laughter? She kept the peignoir on and crept to the door to investigate.

Arm in arm on the landing, the gas burning low, stood Jeanne-Marie and the painter Mahler, holding each other up, both a little worse for the drink.

"Ah, Madame la concierge," Mahler said in his thick accent.

Madame Toussaint hadn't disappeared back into Coco's room fast enough. Her state of dishabille didn't even cause him to raise an eyebrow. Was that but an indication of how far off his scale of interest she was? Once discovered, she couldn't very well pretend she didn't exist now.

"*La petite* here," he continued, "has just been telling me about you."

So Jeanne-Marie had managed to sneak her way back into the building as well. Nonetheless, Madame Toussaint flinched. She had hoped it wouldn't be this way—the girl on the arm of yet another exploiting male.

Before Madame Toussaint could say anything, noises echoed up the stairwell at them. She peered down and saw activity on the main floor, a swirl of red-lined blue capes in the lobby.

"What's that?" Jeanne-Marie asked.

"Hush," Madame Toussaint warned her in a whisper, pulling back. "The police. They see that I've shaken them off. They've come to search the loge." She didn't call it *her* loge. She never did, but was even less inclined to now. She distanced herself, hiding the connection. She was glad that she'd thought to leave the door as she'd found it: unlocked from police inspection. They would have no reason to suspect she'd been there, or to make their search very intense.

"In here." Fumbling, Monsieur Mahler had finally found his key and inserted it.

If the *flics* looked up, would they recognize her in the aberrant lace? Probably not, but she couldn't risk it. Finding the loge empty, did they have cause to start a floor-to-floor search of the building looking for her?

Or would they imagine she must still be out somewhere on the streets of Paris?

The police would think twice before disturbing households in this neighborhood, especially households in mourning, at this hour. On the other hand, being alone in Coco's apartment when they broke down the door did not offer much protection. It seemed better to have the bear-like Mahler answering the door than herself in peignoir, cowering in an apartment not her own. Madame Toussaint decided to accept the man's invitation. On silent feet, the three of them pressed inside his domicile.

Just before she left the hallway, Madame Toussaint heard another layer of sound from the stairwell, millefeuilled somewhere between the police activity on the ground floor and their aerie on the fifth. The voices of a man and woman exchanged companionably, as if they'd done so for most of a lifetime. Monsieur and Madame Cailloux returning from their concert?

Madame Toussaint stepped to the rail for a better listen, only to be driven back to the artist's door by another flurry of police capes that seemed to have decided to limit their search to the ground floor. She dove back to the beckoning open door.

The artist closed the door behind them with two hands, for silence. It was only in that silent darkness that Madame Toussaint realized that the reason she hadn't understood what the couple had been saying to each other was neither the wild echoing within the stairwell nor the police commotion overriding it. The couple had been speaking a foreign language.

Did the musicians on the third floor speak a different language together? Yes. Italian sometimes, on their return from l'Opéra as they recounted the libretto of the arias to one another. The program that night, Madame Toussaint remembered, had been Hayden however, not Rossini. German, perhaps, when they'd heard Schubert lieder.

Did she only think German because of Monsieur Mahler's presence?

"Was that German being spoken below, Monsieur?" she asked.

He shrugged and shook his head. More concerned with getting them out of the stairwell and into his apartment, he hadn't been listening. But surely if it had been German, he would have understood it immediately. Because she couldn't wrap her head around the inconsistency, she let it flee back to what seemed the more pressing problem: the gendarmes in her loge.

The three of them stood together in the dark in an overpowering smell of pine trees and licorice.

"I don't think they found the pigeon, asleep, roosting on the stovepipe." Madame Toussaint heard herself muttering under her breath before she could stop her tongue. "They're looking for a woman-sized occupant after all." She muffled the indiscretion at once, telling herself—inaudibly this time—that she hoped the police wouldn't be able to tell that she'd been in the building. Cat feces on the bed would lend support to that belief.

Monsieur Mahler found the gaslight in the dark from long use. "What's this? Pigeons? Stovepipes?" He spoke as if he didn't understand the French words.

"Nothing." Madame Toussaint choked, feeling she'd already said too much in front of a man she didn't trust, who might be a murderer. For all that he had lived in the building for twenty years, she knew very little about him beyond the fact that he called himself an artist. And preyed on young models. Oh, yes, and was a German, which made him least trustworthy of all.

But "Welcome, Mesdames," this barbarian said. "Make yourselves at home."

"You did manage to lose the *flics*, didn't you, Madame?" Jeanne-Marie, who had been giggling drunkenly as if at a game of hide-and-seek, seemed surprisingly sober with these questions. "And get here undetected? And, Madame—your husband?"

"Hush," Madame Toussaint repeated, avoiding Mahler's eyes. "The whole world doesn't have to know my business."

All the reasons she had found before not to let the girl undertake this dangerous liaison came flooding back to her. Now the concierge added even more to the tally. Instead of discovering secrets, which had been the justification, it seemed Jeanne-Marie had been divulging them. And that was the one thing Madame Toussaint did not want: her closely guarded secrets divulged.

"*Entrez. Entrez, mesdames, je vous en prie.*" The painter begged them both to expand out of their huddle in the space near the door and into his room. He seemed in no hurry, to Madame Toussaint's surprise, to get Jeanne-Marie on her own.

The gaslight slowly came up, revealing chez Mahler. It was hard to call the place a home. It was an atelier, a workroom, a studio—nothing more, nothing less. No cooking happened here, not unless pots and pans crusty with burnt soup had been shoved among the old tin cans with a rainbow of paint colors dribbling down their sides. If there had been soup, once, the smell of art in the making had scoured the fragrance away.

A dull zinc wash basin and stale painter's smocks on pegs appeared through a copse of easels with occupants. Where the man slept looked like a jumble of drop cloths shoved between canvases. Turpentine and pigment smoldered on rags only one degree shy of spontaneous combustion. On her daily moppings of the stairs and landings, Madame Toussaint had caught whiffs of this creativity. Perhaps she had thought the renovations of the fourth floor were partly to blame and would be over soon. Only now she realized there might be danger to the inhabitants of the building, and not just the young ladies. This was the bower Madame Toussaint had stepped forward to save the young housemaid from. Was the whole building in need of saving from fire or toxic fumes?

First things first. "When the police have gone, *ma petite*," Madame Toussaint said, "we can share Mademoiselle Coco's bed across the hall tonight. It's a large one, with many fluffy feather pillows."

"*Mais non.*" Mahler resisted the suggestion—but she hadn't made it to him—his accent as thick as ever. "Will you deny me—not only me, the future of all artistic expression—the raptures of how I shall capture your image tonight, Madame?"

Vraiement? The Germans spoke such ludicrous words in clumsy seduction? No wonder the race could never be successful artists. Madame Toussaint tugged at the peignoir to assure the front had not sprung open. He seemed to be talking to her, not the young housemaid he'd spent the evening plying so carefully with drink before inviting her up to see his etchings.

"Surely you don't mean me?" Madame Toussaint was almost indignant as she corrected the absinthe-soaked error. "You mean Mademoiselle."

"Ah, Mademoiselle," the man said, turning his artist's gaze with longing—but briefly—upon Jeanne-Marie. "Mademoiselle, yes, she is a gem. But a gem cut so that it shines best by daylight, and outside. You must know, Madame, that I came to France to study not just art. Modern art, art that has broken out of the staid constraints of the Salon, where artists chose classical, allegorical subjects, posing everything in the studio." Mahler, clearly, was borrowing his phrases word for word from other, French artists he had heard hold forth.

"Mademoiselle should be set outdoors," he went on, "captured with quick, broken brush strokes, one color laid next to the other, not fading into one another, not blended. Like leaves on a tree, each one capturing light and shadow differently. The light on the surface being the focus, not the dross form below. Photographers give us that these days, the grim black-and-white. I would show you an example, side by side, but that I refuse to contaminate my studio with such."

His gaze went back to Jeanne-Marie. "Yes, Mademoiselle. Dancing to a band at the Moulin des Galettes. Warm galettes are like her, those rough, buckwheat pancakes stuffed with a hearty cheese."

Jeanne-Marie giggled.

"Cheap food, street food," Mahler went on. "In the arms of some fresh-faced swain in a straw boater hat." Monsieur Mahler himself wore a bristling black beard, unkempt, which he unconsciously tried to groom with his fingers as he described the image in his mind.

Jeanne-Marie flushed at the attention as the imagined delights filled her senses, which made the painter shift his tack. "Or perhaps it should be something so particularly Breton, to match her origins. A pardon, when after prayers and processions, pilgrims eat their peasant fare in the grass, in the open air." For a German, he knew a lot about the traditions of the native peasantry.

He began to thumb through canvases stacked ten deep against every wall, the easels, the chairs, any vertical fixture. More to himself as he did so, he said, "Monet's *Luncheon on the Grass* was bluntly refused admission to the Salon in 1863."

Having rifled through a stack of canvases, the artist produced the painting he described. "What honor! What notoriety! For posing a nude woman between two fully clothed men. What I could do with this girl and the quaint Breton tradition of the pardon pilgrimage!

"Or, if I pose her, should it be against the misty grey cliffs of her native Bretagne captured with little twists of the brush as did Monsieur Manet? *Impression, Sunrise.*

"Here. I do have that as well."

"You have a Manet as well as a Monet?" Madame Toussaint couldn't help but ask.

"Of course." Mahler stopped himself and his hunt with a laugh. "Not by Manet, Monet. No. Of course not. These are what I myself have painted when I set up my easel in front of the master. To learn."

"I see."

"Here."

The hunt turned suddenly successful. A triumphant Mahler thrust the canvas at her. A boat appeared on a river with tricks of white light, the red streak of rising sun. Madame Toussaint would not have been able to tell this one from the master's.

"You see?" the artist went on. "Light is the important thing. Not the trounce of lonely, physical mortality weighing each of us down."

Madame Toussaint found herself warming to the man. He wasn't exactly what she'd call charming, brought up in a culture where every impulse towards that virtue must be crushed by mechanical practicality; at least Madame Toussaint had always thought it so. But he did recognize the lack in his life, the French fizz of light, and tried to capture it in a very mechanical way on his canvases.

She regretted having to say, "Excuse me" and going to the door. She stepped out onto the landing where the carpeting ended for the final rise up to the servants' quarters under the roof—the floor she had stayed on all that first year of her marriage. She listened down through the heart of the building.

"I think the flics have gone," she announced, slipping back into the studio. "Had they found anything disturbing to them, they would be knocking on doors right now. I think, perhaps, it is time for the mademoiselle and me to be finding a bed across the hall."

If Malin *fils* had attracted attention, or worse, had flown out of his nighttime roosting to escape, they would be hearing about it.

"But Madame," Jeanne-Marie protested. Ah, when the night and its occupants were young. "We haven't learned anything from Georg yet. About, you know—"

Georg, was it?

The girl had taken off her bonnet, the new one of which she was so proud, and twirled it by the ribbons in her left hand. She twirled it in the direction of the door to the landing Madame Toussaint had just closed behind her. In all this time, it seemed, Jeanne-Marie had not asked one question concerning the murder, which had been the whole reason Madame Toussaint had thought it permissible for her to spend time with such a man. The girl had become this drunk without thinking once about the crime. What had they discussed? Monsieur Mahler did seem able to talk forever about his art, but apparently not actual issues of life and death.

"Now I am intrigued," said Monsieur Mahler. "What is it you think you can learn from me?"

"It can wait until tomorrow," Madame Toussaint said apologetically.

"No, it can't," Jeanne-Marie insisted. "Madame, how can you sleep if you don't learn what you can?"

Madame Toussaint agreed she would find sleeping difficult, but doubted she could discover anything if she approached it so blatantly.

Monsieur Mahler cleared a rickety chair and a tuffet of the wreckage of his creativity for them. "Please, mesdames. Sit. We can cover this in comfort and in a leisurely fashion tonight."

He jangled through a shelf of bottles. Madame Toussaint hoped he read labels carefully so as not to retrieve linseed oil or wood alcohol by mistake. He poured drinks into jam jars that might also hold badger-hair brushes.

"I wish you'd been with us, Madame," Jeanne-Marie said after the clink of glasses died and she'd taken a sip of the fiery liquid—cognac again. As it turned out, it did not help her focus on investigating the crime. "After *Chez Maman*, Georg took me to places on the Boulevard Montparnasse. Restaurants where painters—giving proof by showing the stains on their hands—can get a sausage, frites, and a glass of wine for one franc. Or heftier fare if the maître d' likes the picture they bring him rolled up under their arms. The famous painters he introduced me to, crowding around the little tables—only now I can't remember any of their names."

"I'm certain they have remembered your name, however, my innocent," the artist said. "And that you will have all the modeling jobs I had hoped to keep you for my own." The man sighed. "Ah, well, I do always manage to undermine my own career in the interest of furthering it."

And this admission won Madame Toussaint over completely, even though she was still dressed for the boudoir. She settled back with a creak of the chair, patient for what she might learn and no longer wary for the young Jeanne-Marie, nor even for herself.

XXX
LA BELLE ÉPOQUE

In Monsieur Mahler's studio, Madame Toussaint reached over and righted Jeanne-Marie's glass that threatened to spill. "Perhaps, *chérie*, you should just let Monsieur Mahler pose you how he likes and sit still for a while."

"Ah, but Madame," the painter interjected. "As I was trying to explain. I need daylight for *la petite*. It is you I would like to draw by gaslight."

"Me?"

"Yes. As you are dressed now."

"In this peignoir? It isn't mine."

"Of course not. I never thought it was. It is the contrast, I think. Your sad, sort of Madonna face. And the froth. It seems to be a type of Paris in this age. So if you would please lie back a bit—"

"Tonight?"

"Why not? I often work through the night. Sometimes that is when I discover my best work."

Madame Toussaint looked over at Jeanne-Marie for help against this drift of things. The girl had spilled her drink after all, and was sound asleep, her head on her arms crossed dangerously close to a palette full of paint. Madame Toussaint watched as the artist, in a rather fatherly way, removed the palette and set it aside.

"It won't take long," Mahler continued to urge. "Just a beginning sketch. Just while the idea is so fresh in my mind."

No more than the prospect of seeing herself in a mirror did Madame

Toussaint like the idea of having her picture sketched. What would this foreigner use it for? It wouldn't get into the papers, would it? Monsieur le Comte's murder was on the front page. Her image had already appeared there. When done by a good artist, even more people would recognize her in the street, even if she did manage to clear her name. People would never see her but that they would remember something distasteful about her, even if they couldn't quite place it.

Still, she hated to try to move the girl now and realized that she couldn't sleep herself until this interview was over. She wouldn't call it an interrogation. Perhaps if his hands were busy, the artist's tongue might wander less guarded. It might wander where she wanted it to go.

She posed.

"Head a little more to the left and up. Defiant. You are in borrowed weeds, yet defiant. Guarded. Good."

The scratch of charcoal on rough paper, then the rub of a kneaded eraser became the only sounds for several long minutes.

Madame Toussaint was surprised how quickly her body began to ache from being still. And she had been thinking she had been still in her life for so long, she should be used to it. She pulled her mind away from the discomfort by recalling she had questions to ask.

"Did you know Monsieur le Comte well?"

"Not at all, poor man. Just to nod to in the hall."

"You know of the murder, of course."

"Yes, and the police have questioned me. I could tell them nothing." There was a flurry of erasure, a smearing with the finger. "Madame, you have shifted your left shoulder. If you could— Yes, fine. And the eyes again. As they were."

Madame Toussaint couldn't remember how her eyes had been, but surely talking about the crime must put her in a different frame of mind that must reach deep into her gaze. She tried this expression and that until the artist said, "Yes. Exactly. Thank you."

When the pain returned, Madame Toussaint had to open her mouth again. "Where were you on the evening of the murder?"

"Here in my room."

"Can anyone verify that?"

Mahler didn't answer.

"So you were in a position that you could have entered Monsieur d'Ermenville's apartment without being seen. At least from the street."

"Nor by you and the homeless stranger you had as your guest."

Madame Toussaint flinched. The news had circulated, then.

"Madame, the eyes."

Madame Toussaint begged to stretch, was allowed to. They spent five minutes getting the pose right again.

"Can you imagine any reason why someone would want to do such a thing to the man?"

Monsieur Mahler sketched in silence for a while.

"You can imagine?"

Silence.

Madame Toussaint had the uneasy feeling that his silence covered a desire to accuse her or Paul. The way he seemed to snatch at her image and not complain about what definitely must be changes in her expression, if not in her whole carriage.

She hated her reflex to let the best defense be an offense, as an army general might phrase it. It didn't make the offense good, just an offence. "Monsieur, I heard you and a woman having an argument on the stairs the evening of the murder. She left in tears."

"She is—was—my model. Having an argument with your model is not going into a man's apartment and murdering him."

"True, but she might be able to testify to your state of mind or activities that evening."

"If you must know, I painted a very dark picture that night. You see that I like to work late."

"Indeed, I do see. Would you show me the painting?" The very dark notion that crossed Madame Toussaint's mind was that he might have used the victim's blood in his project. Or at least used the experience to spur creativity. She had heard that Manet used execution victims as models for his paintings recounting events of the Commune. With a modern artist, since they had stopped celebrating joint public spirit in huge canvases full of solid forms and allegory, who could tell?

"Unfortunately, I cannot," the painter replied.

"And why is that?"

"Because I slashed it with a knife and burned it."

That was convenient. That was also an image of what had happened to Monsieur le Comte. Was that the way this man might solve any of his problems?

"Why did your model leave you?" she asked him.

"It cannot be easy posing for me. For any artist, as you yourself are now experiencing. Especially when funds run dry. Especially—" Mahler considered how to say this next sentence, stroking the charcoal furiously as he did so. "—especially when, as they say, you only know your picture is done when you want to sleep with your subject."

Madame Toussaint darted her gaze protectively to the sleeping Jeanne-Marie. And what about herself? That didn't feel comfortable. She gave up the pose altogether and pulled the peignoir closer. Mahler seemed to be drawing completely from memory now, quickly, furiously.

"You have lived in this building on Rue Férou a long time, haven't you, Monsieur?"

He seemed to relax with the change of topic. "Over twenty years."

"I remember when you came here. Where did you live before your arrival?"

"Frankfurt am Main." His face was blank; what he might feel about his home after so many years did not escape it.

"So you came to Paris very close to the time when our two countries had been at war."

"Yes, and after the horrors of the Commune. The glittering Paris I had heard of was a ruin."

"So I must ask. Why did you come? And why did you stay, finding it as you did?"

"The truth, Madame?"

"I hope you would tell me that."

"After you've been so guarded yourself in the pose."

Had she? Maybe she knew no other way to be. Certainly not when anyone brought up the Commune.

Mahler laid down charcoal and eraser, folded his hands in front of him, and spoke. "My elder brother Karl-Heinz was conscripted by Bismarck for that war between our nations. I adored him, didn't know what to do with myself when he marched off. Definitely didn't know what to do with myself when he didn't return."

"He didn't return?"

Mahler shook his shaggy head. "After a while, I decided I must come to France. Perhaps I could find his grave. Learn news of how he had died. But, in truth, I was more interested in finding his killer. If I found his killer, I would kill that man in revenge."

Was that the roundabout confession of a murderer? "Monsieur le Comte was not that man," she had to tell him.

"Or perhaps, the man who had ordered the guns fired."

"Monsieur le Comte never raised a gun in the defense of our nation." But Paul had.

"Yes," the painter agreed, his mind clearly not churning like hers was. "I soon realized my quest was impossible. Most likely my brother's killer had also died the next moment."

"So why didn't you return to Frankfurt?"

"For a while, on dark nights, I thought about killing any Frenchman, all Frenchmen, and avenging in that way."

So part of the visceral reaction Madame Toussaint had always felt in the man's presence was true. She a Frenchwoman, he a German; he was her ancient enemy.

"But you didn't do that either," she stated for confirmation.

"I picked up a paint brush. I came to know the artists here. To understand that they were using their art to overcome their own losses that were equal to mine. How can you hate a Renoir?"

"Some people find it all too easy. The Impressionist: a man of the people, instead of catering to the self-flattering tastes of the upper classes."

The artist nodded his bearlike head. "During the Commune, Renoir had set up his easel and was escaping into his painting along the banks of the Seine. Such a bourgeoise thing to do. Have you heard the story?"

Madame Toussaint had not.

"Members of the Commune came up to Renoir, accusing him of using his canvases as a blind in his work as a spy. They planned to hogtie him and throw him in the river. They would have done so, too, had the communard leader Raoul Rigault not come by just then and remembered the artist having saved him from an attack of the Versaillaises earlier. So was one of the world's great artists saved to delight all humanity."

"The story is true?"

"I heard it from Renoir's own lips. I will never be a Renoir. I know that. But I am a Parisian now. A Parisian, and in my own clumsy way, an artist. To the memory of my brother. But also to the memory of the Frenchmen he may have killed."

"Your drawing is finished, Monsieur?"

"Just a sketch. But perhaps you will come again some time, and we can continue."

"You don't want to sleep with me, then?"

A little smile burst in the midst of Mahler's beard, but he gave no other answer.

"May I see it?" she asked.

The artist shrugged. Madame Toussaint got up—so glad to be able to move her legs out of the last remnant of the pose—and walked around to the other side of the easel.

It was just a sketch, black-and-white. But Madame Toussaint remembered her discomfort in Coco's room at all the full-length mirrors.

"Am I really like that?" she asked.

Her limbs were barely lines, the peignoir thick charcoal, removed by the eraser in lacy swirls.

"I mean, the eyes," she articulated. "What am I hiding?"

"That, Madame, the artist cannot tell."

"Can everyone see it as you do?"

"I would doubt it. I am a foreigner, and foreigners can often pick up on things the everyday local does not."

For a while, she had forgotten to hear his accent. She heard it again now, but instead of finding it threatening, a reminder of those days during the siege when she expected to be raped by the invaders at any moment, she now found it curiously comforting.

Monsieur Mahler went on, not considering his accent. "And yet, I would say this look—it is something all the best French artists are capturing these days. Just by painting the light in dabs of color instead of the heavy forms below, they tell us this in a sort of code. Paris is gay, as ever. But it is gay as illusion. No one painted the ruins I saw when I first came. Nothing is what it seems in Impressionism. It rose not from happy boating parties but from the bombed-out hulls of the Commune de Paris. In the dabs of paint, nothing is what it seems. The artists who rebelled against the Salon de Paris paint the survivors and how they try to numb themselves. Well, there is a corner of the burned out Hôtel de Ville in one painting, but I can't remember which. Mostly the paintings are happy young people dancing on boulevards and in places recognizable, but recognizable as places where the worst of the fighting occurred, the most blood spilled. The bourgeoisie trying with gaiety to expunge the Commune and what was done to their fellow citizens from their memory. Look. Look closely at the faces. Manet's *A Bar at the Folies-Bergère*. Do you know it?"

Mahler got quickly to his feet and crossed the room. Had he copied that painting, too? Of course he had. He produced it from its stack and held it up to the gaslight, studying it in silence for a long time before he turned to show her.

"Degas gets something of the same look in the *Little Dancer Aged Fourteen*. The dancer herself is cast in bronze. Only her clothing and hair ribbon are the softness of fabric. Even at fourteen, that little one has learned to put on the face. To hide her thoughts with a tough aloofness." He brought the canvas over to where Madame Toussaint stood. They studied it together.

"You see?" the painter said. "Here is a woman serving at the bar. We even know her name. The artist told us. Suzon. She has tried to perk up her looks with a bunch of bright flowers in her bodice, in a vase on the bar in front of her. But she wears mourning in the midst of the dazzle of impressionistic light reflected over and over in the mirror and serried ranks of liquor bottles. The matte of her bodice lets no light escape. Nothing touches her heart.

"We can even see the man she is serving—but only as a reflection in the mirror. In Impressionist terms, that's hardly an existence at all. She stares directly at him; he talks and talks. And she doesn't hear him. Look at those eyes, Madame. They are far away on some horror they have seen. In the streets of Paris."

Monsieur Mahler turned his gaze from the master's painting to her. "Madame la Concierge, your eyes are the same. I don't know if I captured them as well as the master did. But yes, the same. My God, it's a wonder any man gets his correct order at the bar in times like these. Absinthe? A cocktail? *Une bière à la pression*? She doesn't hear them, anything. Nothing but gunfire and screams."

This assessment of herself, given in such a way, cut to the quick. But the painter was right. Her thoughts, too, were wherever Suzon's were until finally Mahler reached across that far distance. But she knew he wouldn't turn her image in to sell newspapers.

And she knew he was not the killer.

"Madame, do you think you and I together can carry Jeanne-Marie to Madame Pépin's across the way? Truly, she would sleep much better in that bed than here."

Madame Toussaint nodded, and the deed was soon accomplished, the burly German taking her shoulders and Madame Toussaint her feet. The young innocent gave a little groan at being disturbed, no more than if she rested in her Breton mother's arms.

Only, crossing along the rail of the stairwell did true horror grip Madame Toussaint again. But it always did, looking down from that height.

She heard the sounds of a couple rising up from several floors below, a couple in evening dress coming home late from a Hayden concert. The woman's hand ran along the rail in an elegant glove, which Madame Toussaint recognized. She had accepted the pair from the glover's boy—the little spray of pearls at each wrist—and carried them up to Madame Cailloux just at the beginning of the season. The couple must have enjoyed the concert very much, and the late dinner with friends afterwards.

"Monsieur," she asked. "Is there anyone in the building to whom you can speak your native language?"

"Not at all, Madame. I haven't spoken German in years. I write letters home to my sister maybe twice a year and find I can't remember the simplest words these days."

Monsieur Mahler and she shifted the weight of Jeanne-Marie between them and went on to Coco's apartment.

Madame Toussaint felt that she had made it, here at the top of the building. In the morning, all that remained was to work her way back down and to discover—what? She had yet to reach the depths of this Paris where everyone held the distracted grief of Manet's bartender close to their flower-covered, black-and-white striped bosoms.

Somewhere between where she was meant to sleep next to innocent Jeanne-Marie and the escape of the front door, a murderer lay. Could he sleep with his crime?

And then, without turning on the light in Coco's bedroom, Madame Toussaint glanced out into the Rue Férou and saw the gendarme standing under the streetlamp, also lying in wait.

XXXI
LA BELLE ÉPOQUE

Saint-Sulpice's bells—now once again firmly in the grip of a flock of black-cassocked *curés*—woke Madame Toussaint while dark still blanketed the Rue Férou.

After her mounting of the stairs as a ghost, then posing for the artist in peignoir the night before, she dressed quickly in something she could find of Coco's that barely fit. She had to find a paper of pins to take up the hem, and all this without turning on the gaslight to awaken Jeanne-Marie.

But at least skirt and bodice were a respectable black. A black suitable for a brother-in-law's funeral. For today would be the day they laid le Comte Eugène Toussaint d'Ermenville to rest in the Montparnasse Cemetery.

Leaving Jeanne-Marie still asleep in Coco's bed—perhaps the girl would start posing for the artist today, in the sunlight—Madame Toussaint left the apartment. Once in the stairwell, when she didn't feel the need to be so quiet, she lifted up her skirt with its pinned hem and began to run down the stairs. She had to make sure the pigeon, Malin *fils*, was all right. And then, if he was sound and fit to fly, she had to send him immediately with the message to Paul: "Stay away. They think you killed your brother." Would she add, "I don't believe them"? She wasn't sure yet.

As she reached the third floor in her descent, she skidded to a halt on the landing. The sound of the key turning in Monsieur Arnaud's door stopped her. She had yet to question the man, to take him off her suspects list.

She had hoped to wait for this interview until after the bird had flown, but since that turning lock indicated that the tenant of third-floor-right would very shortly step into her view—might leave for the day straight away and not be back until late evening—she decided to do her best with the exchange now.

"Good morning, Monsieur Arnaud," she said the moment the cane and bright white spats stepped out.

Monsieur Arnaud stopped dead in his tracks as if he were an acolyte of Madame Flôte, whose apartment was directly over his, and had just seen a ghost. As if he had hoped never to see the concierge alive again.

"Madame la Concierge."

"Excuse me, Monsieur. I hope I didn't startle you."

"In fact, Madame, you did. I must confess, I thought you— I'm . . . I'm not used to meeting people on the stair this early in the morning."

"And I expect we are all a little jumpy. On account of Monsieur d'Ermenville, may he rest in peace."

"Indeed." A sour expression crossed Monsieur Arnaud's face. "But did you actually mean to see me? The rent is not due until the end of the month, I think, and I am all paid up."

He acted so guilty. Why? He was all paid up.

Madame Toussaint hurried to reassure him. "Of course, Monsieur. It's just that there were a few months back there—near the end of summer—when I was afraid you would be forced to leave us. You were behind several months and could give me no sign as to when you could bring the accounts up to date."

A door opened somewhere in the stairwell, and there were busy morning footsteps. Madame Toussaint was surprised at how difficult it was to tell, from this place in the very heart of the building, where the sounds came from. In her loge, everything came from above, and she prided herself on being able to tell the step of every tenant. These steps, from this angle, she did not recognize.

But perhaps Monsieur Arnaud did, for he grew even paler than he was at discovering her unexpected presence on his third floor. "Madame, would you care to step into my apartment so we can discuss this further?"

Madame Toussaint had not expected such an invitation; the sleuth as opposed to the concierge in her had hardly dared to hope. She usually did not step inside the tenants' rooms. Usually, she was beneath them in every sense of the word. They sent servants down for her. They spoke to her through their doors when she came up. Or, if they did come down to her, they left messages as they passed through the lobby.

But nothing could define a man as well as a glimpse of his apartment. She couldn't resist. "I don't know that it's necessary, Monsieur. But thank you."

The first thing Madame Toussaint noticed in the apartment after the thick smell of his cigars was through a window to a still-dark street. In the lamplight spilling over the sidewalk to the cobbles, her police tail still stood, waited, and watched. The man in the red-lined gendarme cape turned so his face caught the gaslight. It was Théophile, the young recruit, taking his turn on duty.

As she watched, Madame Toussaint saw Jonquille, the girl from the flower shop, come to open up early for funerary trade, cross the street, and present the young man a bowl of something warm to drink. Steam wreathed his grateful face. They stood chatting for a moment in youthful camaraderie. Madame Toussaint wished she could escape to a world like that; her days of carefree youth had been overshadowed by siege and revolution.

She followed Monsieur Arnaud's upright back and wondered what boutonniere the man might order today. Then, with his empty buttonhole, he invited Madame Toussaint into his salon. "Madame, please. Have a seat."

"I don't mean to take your time. I just wanted to make sure you got your delivery from the haberdashers."

"The haberdashers?"

"Yes. The last time we spoke, Sunday evening, you asked me to be sure to bring the delivery to you the moment it came, which would have been some time on Monday. As you must know, I was unavailable to receive it on Monday."

"You were in prison. Not a good character reference." That seemed more important to him than whatever new hat box might have arrived. If he had ordered a hat and not used a fictitious delivery as an excuse to linger longer in the lobby when she had been letting in Paul.

"Yes, but I'm out now."

"But not restored to your duties."

"I rather hope that I am—and must know that your delivery arrived in good condition for you. I did not see a new hat on the hat tree in your entryway."

"I returned it." Just a beat too slow. "The color in daylight turned out to be too mauve."

"I see. What a disappointment that must have been for you."

Still no word as to who might have received the package in Madame Toussaint's place.

So now this single man of forty had fulfilled the prospect of the historian Hippolyte Taine, who wrote that once the man of mode had thought about "his toilet, his furnishings, his little image of himself, he has come to the end of his ideas."

"Can I get you some tea?" Monsieur Arnaud asked.

Which was a surprise, since Madame Toussaint herself didn't think the conversation had got off to a good start at all. "Thank you."

While the kettle boiled under her host's gaze in the kitchen, Madame Toussaint took in the bookshelves, ample as in any apartment whose tenant aspired to culture. Among the titles were many she couldn't read. She thought the language was English, like she suddenly expected the tea to be.

Monsieur Arnaud's reputed predilection for boys, as Coco had declared with such authority, was nowhere in evidence. Except perhaps in the bronze copy of a Hellenistic statue of a naked boy pulling a thorn out of his foot on a fluted, white-plaster plinth beside the fireplace. Potted ivy climbed up the plinth from a brass cachepot at its foot, very close to the chair Monsieur Arnaud had indicated as hers. But any cultured home might choose to display similar art replicas. To recall the boyhood days of a beloved son, perhaps. Except not, if she understood correctly, an English home under the reign of the stern Victoria.

Madame Toussaint just had time to shift her eyes from the statue to the blank wall behind it before Monsieur Arnaud reentered the room. She didn't want to appear too suspicious, reading too much into a man's aesthetic choices.

"Ah, yes," he said. "That wallpaper. Hideous, isn't it? I've really come to loathe it. One of us is going to have to go, the sooner the better."

Mostly, she had been interested not in the paper but in a woman's portrait hung in a heavy gilt frame. The woman seemed to be French, an aristocrat from the time of Marie Antoinette, the same powdered pile of hair. Not a lot of French people flaunted such relatives—if they had them. But something about the eyes was the same as Monsieur Arnaud's. An ancestor?

Madame Toussaint strained and squinted. From this distance, it almost seemed as if the title in an elegant hand below read, "Comtesse d'Ermenville." She was about to get to her feet to step closer.

Monsieur Arnaud brought tea in on a lovely, doily-covered tray. The wealthy knew how to host. The tea, as she had guessed, was English, not the Mariage Frères most socially aspiring Frenchmen might choose. The cup not a French bowl, but with a saucer and a fragile, handled, porcelain tulip shape. And a waft of bitter almonds rose on the steam, barely concealed by the ambient smell of the room: stale cigar.

"I hope that doesn't mean you're going to leave us any time soon, Monsieur, your quarrel with the wallpaper." Madame Toussaint took the teacup offered her—with lemon, just imagine—no sugar, no cream.

"No. I mean to get the decorators in next week. I guess as concierge, you should be warned of that situation."

Wallpaper paste on the stair carpet now. "Thank you for the warning. I hope it may console you for the returned hat." She bent her head to take a sip of tea, but it was too hot. The smell of almonds was strong indeed. Was this a peculiarly English addition to the beverage?

"It is good to hear, Monsieur, that your finances have amended themselves so well that you can consider renovations. After—how long have you lived in the building?" Madame Toussaint knew exactly how long Monsieur Arnaud had lived in the building. She was the concierge; she could say the same of every tenant.

It was the fall of 1878, nearing the end of l'Exposition Universelle, supposed to celebrate France's recovery from the Terrible Year. Coco had lured her to take an afternoon off to visit the grand fair, constructed on the Left Bank on the Champs de Mars, military fields given over to a celebration of world unity and progress. The friends had marveled at an inventor from America's "telephone," which they had dismissed as a passing fad, for who would want a substitute for meeting with friends over coffee in a café? The huge head of a statue of a crowned Liberty made in France but destined for the United States presided over the sister countries' pavilions. While they were studying some large—just over life-size—female statues representing the continents of the world, Coco had announced that she might at last have found a *régulier*: a married man willing to take her out of the brothel and the cabaret and give her a home of her own as his mistress.

"Is that apartment on the third floor you told me about in your building still available?" Coco had asked. "It is so elegant in the sixth arrondissement there near the Luxembourg Gardens."

And Madame Toussaint had had to tell her, "Sadly, no." It had just been let to Monsieur Arnaud. "But there might be one coming open on the fifth."

"That would be cheaper than the third."

"Right. The commandant with the young growing family there has just received the advancement he needed to look for a bigger home for his brood. And the second floor is available."

Monsieur Arnaud's "Fifteen years or more," was less precise than Madame Toussaint's recollection.

"You were curious, Madame, about my recent and sudden inability to pay a while back," he continued, "and now my returned sufficiency."

Madame Toussaint had actually forgotten that she had been making conversation about these details only moments before. The well-to-do had mysterious ways with money; the rest of the world who knew that two plus two equals four were not initiated. She just took the rents when they were due, counted them out, marked them in the book, and took the money to her brother-in-law. Or to Mademoiselle Sylvie if "le Comte" were not at home. "Le Comte" had rarely asked for an accounting, because if there were any problems, Madame Toussaint was expected to have dealt with them.

But Monsieur Arnaud seemed determined to justify himself somehow, so she lifted her not-quite-scalding-now teacup and let him talk, this time avoiding even the steam.

"My father passed away in late June."

"Ah, Monsieur, I am sorry for your loss."

Monsieur Arnaud acknowledged the sympathy with a mere nod. Madame Toussaint registered in her mind that she had never seen the signs of mourning about the tenant from the third floor; no black armband, no letters with black edging that she was asked to see to the post. No trips away to—wherever Monsieur Arnaud the elder might lie in state. No day without a boutonniere. The same dearth with the present loss.

"Felicitations are due since then, however. The will has been read, and you are now flush." Madame Toussaint stated rather than asked it.

A light went on in Monsieur Arnaud's eyes as if this were a new wrinkle to the story he liked very well. Rather than outright confirming, however, he said, "Something along those lines." And as if he realized after the fact that that might have been so vague as to be suspicious, he added, "I now have a kind patroness who does so much."

"That's very nice." Madame Toussaint bent for another sip of tea, but pretended it was still too hot. Her eyes focused for a moment at the space behind her host's head. Two doors stood open to the apartment's two bedchambers. More careful housekeepers would have closed them from public view, but Monsieur Arnaud had clearly not been expecting a guest this morning. Although he had spoken in detail of wallpaper, pride of home was not foremost on his mind.

Two bedchambers, not one bedroom and a gentleman's library or smoking room.

One of the rooms—the one on the west side—was already lighter than its companion: larger, more elegantly furnished. Its shutters opened onto the courtyard through which the first grey of morning made the white and gold of chair legs and headboard glow. On a dresser with vine-like handles lay a woman's brush and comb set, a frilly print robe over the chair. It was such a room one might expect Coco to inhabit—if her *régulier* didn't somber her rooms to his taste.

And the bed Madame Toussaint seemed to remember perfectly well being in her sister-in-law's chamber many years ago, before she got ill.

The companion chamber was mostly still in darkness: heavy furniture, not much of it and not very elegant. Another piece of sculpture, this the alabaster bust of a curly-haired boy, stood sentinel over the bed. A washbasin under a heavy oak-framed mirror, beside it a mug, shaving brush, and razor. These were the only things that caught the light. The razor in particular, cleaned but not yet snapped back into its case, seemed grim and ominous. If Madame Toussaint didn't know better, she would have guessed that a married couple occupied the apartment, he making his conjugal visits to the brighter room through a door or a joint bathroom.

Madame Toussaint had heard that some men like Monsieur Arnaud— like he was rumored to be—relished dressing in women's clothes in private.

Did this man shift from room to room as his fantasies carried him? She would have to ask Coco about this.

In the meantime, Monsieur Arnaud was being the perfect host, asking tasteful questions. "Will you attend the funeral today, Madame?"

"Yes, I have that duty. But this reminds me that it is an even bigger duty of mine to answer the door as mourners arrive to pay their respects. I should steal no more of your time, Monsieur."

"Please. Do not insult me by not finishing your tea."

So Madame Toussaint plodded on, the good guest. "It is a sorrow to lose a man like Monsieur d'Ermenville. And in such a horrible way."

"And your brother-in-law. That must be particularly difficult."

Now, how did Monsieur Arnaud know that about the connection? She thought the relationship was a secret—at le Comte's request, many, many years ago. Most everybody knew him only by the d'Ermenville name, the name connected with the title. Nobody had ever asked how she got the job of concierge, why she stayed on. The relationship was a secret because that was what Eugène Toussaint had wanted. Because he hadn't wanted anyone to know his connection to a communarde. He hadn't wanted anyone to question his right to the title.

Yet Monsieur Arnaud knew at least some part of the whole. Who else did? Madame d'Ermenville, surely. But as an invalid, was she ever able to divulge this information?

"And you, Monsieur Arnaud? Are you planning to pay your respects?"

"That's just where I was going when you stopped by so unexpectedly. I need to buy a boutonniere—something suitably somber. Then I mean to go right away to console the family. I mean Madame la Comtesse. Sit with them before the hearse comes."

"Very kind of you, Monsieur."

"Not at all. My duty."

"Do you have any idea who can have done such a horrible deed, Monsieur Arnaud?" Madame Toussaint came right out and asked it.

"None. It is unimaginable. He was—he was like a father to me."

But still no black armband.

And the bitter almond smell in her teacup. Why would that have been added to her beverage—except to keep her from continuing her testimony that Paul had been with her. Because Monsieur Arnaud himself had reported on them. Or was covering for the person who had.

"Anyone in this building you suspect of the murder?" she asked.

"A fine building such as this in such a fine neighborhood— It seems unbelievable."

"So you suspect someone from the outside?" Why was he hesitating to mention seeing Paul that night? When he'd been so anxious to tell the police? She would force the issue. "Didn't you see a stranger come into the building two nights ago? Everyone says you did."

For a moment she thought he'd deny it. He lurched to his feet and began to pace. "Yes, yes, I saw him. A filthy madman of a clochard. And you, Madame. You let him in." He put his accusing finger only inches from her face. "Betraying all the trust the tenants of this building put in you. Putting all of us at risk of our lives. He was the killer. I will swear to it before a court of law."

"And I will swear he was with me all night."

She wasn't perfectly sure this was the case, she reminded herself. But to save Paul, she'd swear to anything. And that ivy under the *Boy with Thorn* statue looked very dry.

She set down her empty teacup. "Excuse me, Monsieur. A concierge has many duties, particularly when there is a funeral in the building."

He took up the cup as if it had been his own, not as if he meant to do the washing up himself. He sank back into his chair. As if he wondered how he'd drunk it so fast.

He looked up and their eyes met. The contact was like a physical slap.

She rose to her full height. In Coco's clothes, it even felt like Coco's height and Coco's resoluteness. Madame Toussaint fingered the tea tray's doily, almost decided to pinch it to wave at Théophile the gendarme as she passed the window on the way to the stairs, then resisted. The slight mend in one corner was too inexpert a repair.

In a very ungentlemanly fashion, Monsieur Arnaud remained seated. She saw herself out.

"No one believes a concierge, after all," were his parting words, reassuring himself rather than her.

She hoped English ivy didn't suffer too much from the strychnine in apricot pits poured at its roots.

XXXII
LA BELLE ÉPOQUE

It took only two of Madame Toussaint's rapid heartbeats for her to descend from the third floor to the second, instinctively avoiding the loose wood at the side of the fourth step. She really had to get a man in to fix that. Perhaps Monsieur Hervé, whose men's heavy work boots probably caused it, because it wasn't there before. But later. Much later. First, she had to get the pigeon to Paul. Immediately. He must not come to wrangle with the unnatural anger of Monsieur Arnaud or his teacups. Let alone the police.

When she reached the second-floor landing, however, she heard Monsieur Arnaud's door reopen in some haste directly over her head. Monsieur Arnaud who'd just tried to poison her with strychnine in a cup of English tea. He wouldn't let her get away. He was coming after her with his sharpened cane. With the same butcher-knife he'd used on Monsieur le Comte. With the brace of pistols he'd pulled from the top drawer of the sideboard.

At the same moment the door to Lieutenant-colonel Herlemont's apartment assailed the lower landing. The lieutenant-colonel himself advanced upon the hall. What a piece of luck!

Madame Toussaint couldn't let the military intimidate her for a second, she who had stood on a barricade during the Commune. She set her hands on the lieutenant-colonel's chest, knocking the brass buttons, tangling in the braid and the red sash, and setting the medals jangling on their ribbons. The ceremonial sword clanged against the door jamb. Although such men, commanders of the French army, were part of her continuing nightmares, she gave a sharp push.

Herlemont, taken by ambush, stumbled back into his apartment, into the rank-and-file phalanx of his sons following on his heels.

"*Pardonnez-moi*, Madame," exclaimed the startled military man, although it was she who should apologize.

But she kept pushing. She pushed until the father was well inside the apartment and the lads in their military school uniforms had pushed ahead and out into the hall. A classic example of the penetration of the center maneuver.

There the boys stood at attention and saluted their father. "Have a good day, Sir," in unison before clicking heels and marching toward the stairs. This martial parade took the descending Monsieur Arnaud by surprise, so much so that he failed to see Madame Toussaint, who had slipped behind Herlemont's commanding form.

Before Monsieur Arnaud had regathered his wits, which seemed particularly jarred by the sight of men—even men under fifteen—in uniform, Madame Toussaint had pushed the apartment door shut on the hallway. To the lieutenant-colonel, she hissed, "For the memory of Champigny, Sir, help me."

Under his massive, heavily waxed moustache and stylish goatee, Herlemont appeared more startled than a military man ought to look even under enemy fire. The whispered name of Champigny, however, worked its dark magic. A flood of pain and terror and the self-sacrifice of the heroic Colonel Paul Toussaint must have come back to the man. The mere memory set one of his medals, the commendation for wounds sustained, trembling.

"Madame la Concierge," he stammered. Then, "Champigny. Yes, of course."

He began to lead the way into the salon, but found it full of petticoats: his daughters with assorted nannies and governesses. Truly, most families of means of such a size would have a sprawling country estate where the women and children would stay while the men did battle in the city. Madame Toussaint knew the wife's family had such an estate, because that was where Subaltern Herlemont had gone to recover from the wounds sustained during the failed sortie two and a half decades before.

But the lieutenant-colonel wanted only the best military school for his sons. And, Madame Toussaint surmised, he wanted to keep making more little Herlemonts. The best counterintelligence of the Statistics Section did not tell him, however, how to deal with members of the female persuasion, so foreign, when he created them.

He made a click-heeled about-face out of the salon instead—and almost impaled his two-year-old with the blunt of his sheath. The curly-haired little boy had escaped again, this time with the infirmary-issue wrapping of a diaper still threatening to drop about his ankles.

"Soldier!" the lieutenant-colonel barked in his best parade-ground voice. "Go tell Sergeant *Nou-nou* to put your uniform on."

The boy was impressed and stared wide-eyed: his father, the full-dress uniform. He must have missed the parade, still a captive in the nursery. But more, the ghost woman he'd seen the night before on the stairs, now in new attire. All in one gaze.

As serious as could be, the lad stood to attention, clicked his dimpled heels and saluted. "Yes, Sir," he lisped, first words. "Papa, Sir." Then he turned and marched on bare feet back into the barrack of chambers and his *nou-nou*'s arms.

"This way," Herlemont ordered the concierge.

She almost saluted him herself.

"'Our family is a young tree that never stops growing,'" the lieutenant-colonel quoted the old saw as perhaps an excuse. What he said next seemed to have more truth behind it: "This Dreyfus business has us all up in arms."

He led her past the kitchen to a door on the north side of the building. Familiar with the layout of apartments in general, Madame Toussaint had forgotten how there could be space between the hallway and the stone of the outside wall for a room behind that door.

There wasn't much of a room. The lieutenant-colonel turned a key switch; gas hissed on and caught in the flame he fed it from a match. She found herself with him in what she would call, from the smell of flour and root vegetables and the dark shapes of preserve jars and wheels of cheese, a pantry. A crate of oranges on the bottom shelf wafted a fragrance like Christmas.

Vents to the outside of the building between shelves in the windowless space could be opened or closed according to the weather to keep the room a good temperature for storage. But more than half the space was also taken up by a stuffed *bergère* armchair of more-than-kitchen comfort.

"My war room," Herlemont said with less-than-disciplined wryness.

Indeed, it looked like a war room. Not the windowless bunker Madame Toussaint imagined where maps spread under cigar smoke and long sticks were used to tactically shift wooden divisions and battalions. Such sticks wouldn't fit in this space. Instead, it was a room where death and destruction had occurred: loops of sausage and a still-feathered pheasant hung from hooks in the ceiling to ripen. The bird swinging into Madame Toussaint's shoulder and its dead, glazed beads of eyes nearly made her jump out of her skin to become a carcass herself.

Shifting helmet and sword out of the way and conscious of the difference of social rank between them, Herlemont settled himself in the chair. The act was not completely one of privilege. He did want to give her as much air and space as possible.

The lieutenant-colonel attempted to explain the strategy of his incongruous surroundings. "I sometimes come here for a smoke and a bit of peace and quiet." Yes, tobacco was one of the fragrances present and accounted for, but a gentler form than in Monsieur Arnaud's rooms. And Madame Toussaint had just been feeling her usual pang that she would never have the family she had dreamed of, except vicariously through her tenants.

"Naturally I prefer my office in the War Ministry in l'Hôtel de Brienne, but I can't always make it there when I need a little break from the family, and this is the place for it. If the cook needs something, she knows she just has to keep stirring the roux until I'm done.

"So, Madame. What can I do for you?"

"You are aware, I'm sure," Madame Toussaint said, "of the recent death of Monsieur le Comte d'Ermenville, the owner of our building."

"A great tragedy, yes. I wear my uniform today in honor of him. I will be part of the funeral procession."

Only with the man's gesture towards his left sleeve did Madame Toussaint notice, among all the decorations, the black velvet band on his left arm. The band itself jangled with dependent ribbons and many metal hearts as was the custom when the dead man was particularly honored.

"Colonel Toussaint saved my life." Was this grown man, a lieutenant-colonel, going to cry? "During the Prussian siege, at Champigny."

"Excuse me, no, Monsieur. The dead man, 'le Comte', may God have mercy on his soul, he was Monsieur Eugène Toussaint. The man who saved you at Champigny was my husband, the older son, Paul Toussaint."

The lieutenant-colonel blinked in surprise.

"I know this, Monsieur, because I was at the hospital that had been set up in the Palais de Luxembourg that winter's day when they brought you in from the front. Broken leg and a bullet wound to the shoulder."

With a nurse's granted intimacy, she touched the place at the same time he did, the place on his shoulder now protected by solid epaulettes and a meter of gold braid.

"I don't remember," he apologized.

"It's all right. I'm sure you saw many doctors and nurses. You were in a lot of pain."

"But you must have seen many patients and many in much more serious condition than I."

"It is true, Monsieur. But you were different because, despite your pain, you gave me word of my husband so I could ride out to Champigny and save him in his turn."

Herlemont blinked again. She remembered the expression from his bed on the palace floor.

"But I was certain I recognized the face when I first met him—or thought I remet him—on the Rue Férou," he said.

"The men are—were—brothers. They do—did—resemble one another in many ways." In fact, truth be told, at his death Monsieur le Comte had probably resembled the handsome, pre-Commune man she had married more closely than the present's thin, haggard, untended man who lived in the streets. Who had been, it must be recalled, le Comte d'Ermenville at the time, even if he had preferred the title Communard.

"But I think you must have remarked," she added, "not in character."

Herlemont nodded. "I told myself, war can certainly change a man."

"True." Madame Toussaint's heart ached with just how true it was.

"I did wonder why le Comte did not seem to remember Champigny as I did. Usually, a man with whom you've shared such an experience will be the first to invite you out for a drink, no matter the difference in rank. Monsieur—Eugène—is it?"

"Yes."

"Monsieur Eugène was never like that."

"No, he was not. They were very different men."

"In fact, when I first approached him about the room on the fifth floor—when it was just me and my wife, and our eldest was an infant, with number two on the way, when we really couldn't live with my wife's family anymore—he at first declined my request to rent the place."

"You did not approach me, the concierge."

"No, forgive me, Madame. But I knew him; I did not remember you, for all your service. His wife, he told me, did not like children. And we, as you know, were destined to be blessed with so many."

"In fact, Monsieur, it was I, as the concierge, who recognized you when you stood on the doorstep asking after the vacancy. I recognized you as the man who had helped me save my husband. I put in a good word—I may even say a forceful word—with Monsieur d'Ermenville my brother-in-law. I would not have done that for others. Otherwise, yes, he would not have been inclined to allow children in to pound up and down the stairs over his head—his wife's head—all day."

"But then, when the family grew, when my salary likewise grew with my advancement, Monsieur le Comte asked us first if we wouldn't like to move into this larger space—right above his head."

A tender spark for her brother-in-law blossomed in Madame Toussaint's core. "I think by then— Well, let me be discreet as a concierge must be. By then his wife had flung in his face the fact that she blamed him for their childlessness, for the fact that no one would be Comte d'Ermenville after him. That was her main, perhaps only, interest in children: to carry on the line. And . . . and something else."

"Yes, Madame?"

"Under duress from her lady's maid, I believe, Madame d'Ermenville confessed to him. Confessed as a taunt more than anything, the reason why Paul and I will also die childless."

Herlemont blinked. "Madame, I— Forgive me. I will not pry."

Madame Toussaint nodded her thanks for his gallantry, leaving him no doubt to think the cause a war wound of some kind. If only he knew what she suspected—more today than ever before—he'd wink at war wounds. Because such things happened to others, never to him.

After a suitable pause of respect for threatened family life, Herlemont blinked again. His train of thought had been diverted by something that made him chuckle. "Forgive me, Madame. I have to think of poor Madame la Comtesse, condemned to have this family over her head for all eternity."

As if under marching orders, just at that moment, sounds from out in the hall gave clear expression to his meaning. The two-year-old, no doubt uniformed at last, could be heard riding a stick pony and shouting "Monsieur Papa. Yes, Sir, Monsieur Papa," up and down the hall.

"Sometimes I would apologize to Monsieur le Comte for the racket when I'd meet him on the stairs or in the lobby after what even I knew was a loud row up here.

"'Nothing to forgive, Monsieur,' he would tell me. 'Nothing to forgive. I, personally, enjoy the patter of little feet on the parquet.'"

Madame Toussaint and her host exchanged careful smiles.

"But Madame, forgive me. You are the widow of Colonel Paul Toussaint?" Herlemont got to his feet.

"Not his widow, Monsieur. His wife. I am Madame Nathalie Toussaint."

This did take the lieutenant-colonel by surprise. "Forgive me. I guess I never learned your name."

That was the way of it. Concierges were like keys, like door handles, like garbage bins. Tools to get people the access to the high-class buildings they wanted without having to learn to say more than "Bonjour, Madame la Concierge."

Herlemont blinked and wrinkled his brow in a bit of confusion. "But then I must meet him. He doesn't live with you? But I must—I must take him for a drink."

"That would be very nice, Monsieur. But I must tell you that my husband—he is not well."

"I am grieved to hear that."

"Hasn't been since—"

"Since Champigny? He saved my life but not his own?"

"Since after, actually. Since—"

Madame Toussaint saw the blink, the flinch, when the words "La Commune" passed through Herlemont's brain. Both of them knew better than to say the words aloud.

Herlemont shook his head. "A terrible business. A terrible year. I regret that I was out of commission for that time, recuperating at my wife's family home in the country once the siege broke."

"Do you, Monsieur? Do you regret it?"

Men dressed in uniforms such as yours fired upon us, French citizens, in the streets of Paris. If you had been healed of your wounds at the time, would you have done the same? Would you have beaten Paul senseless, saying it was orders? Would you, yourself, have given the orders to fire? Would you have fired upon us as if we were no better than animals? Madame Toussaint thought these questions and tried to wring the answers from the man's bewhiskered face—without success.

"Please, Madame, you must take the chair for the duration of our conversation."

"I do not need to take much more of your time, Monsieur."

If only she could get him to accompany her down to her loge so she could get the pigeon off to Paul. If she couldn't think of a way to do that, she'd have to proceed with caution on her own and hope that Monsieur Arnaud and his bloody intentions had left the stairwell for a time, seeking her elsewhere.

They jostled each other in the close quarters.

"No, I insist. I have much more to tell you, Madame."

And his tone demanded a salute and full attention.

XXXIII
LA BELLE ÉPOQUE

Madame Toussaint wanted to warn Paul. She wanted to tell the police what she knew, hoping they wouldn't think her mad. And that would help Paul, to turn the investigation elsewhere. But she also felt very safe huddling with the lieutenant-colonel in full martial dress in his war room.

Monsieur Arnaud had come bolting down the stairs in pursuit after having tried to poison her. He hadn't found her, nor taken his butcher knife to her, not yet. Where was he, still no doubt thirsting for blood? Had he imagined she'd fled the building and followed her into the street? Perhaps to enlist the police in his search? Was he lying in wait for her in her loge? Had he climbed to the top of the building to make a floor-by floor search? Would she bring danger upon her host and his family by continuing to shelter with them?

She had no answers. To try to find the answers would be dangerous. More dangerous than she had the courage to face at the moment. So Madame Toussaint sat on the lieutenant-colonel's *bergère* in his war room cum pantry, and the lieutenant-colonel jostled for rank with the pheasant until feathers drifted down onto her, onto Coco's skirt, from the fray.

"You are most kind, Monsieur le Lieutenant-Colonel."

"Not at all. I would go through hell for Colonel Toussaint. Or his wife."

Madame Toussaint shifted with the discomfort of what she might in fact lead him through. She also had to say something before they proceeded any further. Discomfort caused her to get flour on the skirt from pressing against the bin. But finally, she said it. "You must know, Monsieur le Lieutenant-Colonel, that the police suspect my husband of his brother's murder."

"Do they? Impossible. I did understand there was some stranger, a clochard. The police, when they questioned—"

"My husband."

"*Hélas*, Madame." Concern furrowed the man's brow.

Madame Toussaint didn't want to waste too much time on sympathy. "It's in all the papers. Although perhaps they don't give him a name, either. Just 'a clochard.'"

"I confess I haven't been reading the papers. It's this bloody Dreyfus affair. The lies they print! All lies—that he sold us out to the enemy, just because the man's a Jew. Against a worthy soldier of France, Madame. All lies, coming, I am ashamed to say, from my department. It wreaks havoc on the morale of the men. In some respects, your husband is lucky not to be part of this."

"*Vraiment*. I need to be getting a message to Paul to take care not to be arrested."

Then the lieutenant-colonel did a strange thing. He reached over Madame Toussaint's head and closed the vents to the outside that were keeping the pantry as chill as an icebox. She shivered now, only after the fact.

"Rest assured, Madame, I would testify to Paul Toussaint's good character and his love of France even if—even if I saw him wield the knife myself—which I assure you I did not. The farthest thing from it." His words so touched her after the past days' events that she had to pull out Coco's handkerchief to wipe away tears.

To give her the privacy of her grief, Herlemont mused a little on what other events rested at the top of his mind. "Captain Dreyfus is a good man, a good officer. He's been framed, as I assume Colonel Toussaint has been. But I can't prove either of them, and now Dreyfus is going to Devil's Island—leaving his family and France—for life."

The lieutenant-colonel had, Madame Toussaint noticed, also dropped his voice. She shivered again, even though she knew the place in the colonies of everlasting imprisonment was unbearably hot and humid. "Paul was banished to Devil's Island."

"Madame, again, I am so sorry."

When she could, she said, "You closed the vents, Monsieur."

"Yes."

"I assume it wasn't just in the interest of keeping me warm."

"I did notice you were shivering, and I do try never to upset the cook's produce when I'm here alone, no matter how cold. But the fact of the matter is, when they're open, it's much easier to hear what's going on in le Comte's apartment below."

"I do not believe you could complain about more noise coming from down below than Madame d'Ermenville could have for that coming down from above." Madame Toussaint tried to put a teasing lilt in her voice. Perhaps it was time to conclude this dialogue and get on to other important things.

"No, but I did hear what I take to be the first mourners arriving below. If I can hear them, they can hear us."

"Oh. I hadn't noticed. I suppose I thought it must just be more activity of your children."

But now that he mentioned it, she did suppose she had heard hushed voices, the rustling of silks, perhaps even a "My sincere condolences, Madame la Comtesse," or two.

Madame Toussaint jumped to her feet. "But this is a reason I must get going. A concierge should be there opening the street door and ushering the mourners to the first floor."

Not to mention contacting Paul. And searching the visitors for clues.

Herlemont set a hand on her shoulder. "First hear me out, Madame. I may have useful information. Sitting in that very chair, I may have overheard something that may exonerate your husband."

As pressure from the man's gloved hand eased, Madame Toussaint sank back into the chair. "Tell me. Did you—did you hear the murder, Monsieur?"

"I did not. Not from this room which is at the other end of the building from the bedrooms."

Madame Toussaint worked out the floorplan in her mind and saw that it was true. The first floor echoed the second quite closely. "But the murder happened at night," she said, "when I assume you all would have been in bed."

"True, we were. And it is also true, now that I've put two and two together, that our daughter Valentine—"

"Yes, I know her. Quite a lovely lady she's becoming. What is she now? About twelve?"

"Eleven, and tall for her age."

"She takes after you, Monsieur."

"And after her mother in looks. In one thing she does not take after Madame Herlemont, however. Madame Herlemont and I could sleep through bugle call, but Valentine is a very light sleeper. And that night—Sunday night, the night of the murder—she woke us all with a nightmare. She and her sisters sleep in the room right over Monsieur le Comte's room. Madame and I have given the larger rooms to the children because they need to sleep in one room, in one room the girls, in the next—"

"Which would be Madame d'Ermenville's."

"The Comtesse's, yes. And the two youngest in the nursery with their nanny. Anyway, Valentine, poor child, woke us, governess, nanny, everyone."

"Perhaps you exaggerate, Monsieur. I did not hear you all, down another floor in the concierge's loge."

"For that we must be grateful," the lieutenant-colonel said.

"Could Mademoiselle Valentine describe what she heard?"

"No. We convinced her it was just another bad dream."

But perhaps if I could interview the young lady. Believing her, I might jog something loose, Madame Toussaint thought. One glance at the lieutenant-colonel told her it was very unlikely he would allow such a thing, fearing more trauma to his child. Perhaps if she met her alone on the stairs . . . No. The Herlemont daughters never went out alone . . .

The lieutenant-colonel mused. "No, my wonder is that, if she did miss the murder, which must have been done quite silently, how did she manage to sleep . . . ?"

"But you just said Valentine had a nightmare."

"She—I don't mean my daughter; I mean she, Madame la Comtesse. How did she sleep through all our calming of Valentine—the hot milk, the hugs all 'round, the songs—?"

"Monsieur, I take your point. Madame 'la Comtesse', sleeping right next door, must have awakened in time to hear the murderer leave or clean off the knife and return it to the kitchen or— It did appear to me that he spent quite a lot of time with the corpse." She shuddered at the memory of the sight of the man gutted with such fury. "Fifteen minutes at least. And did not leave a footprint for the police to find. Unless someone—a very good housecleaner—cleaned it up."

"Madame la Comtesse was always the first to complain, to send her maid up in the middle of the night when our little Rémy had the colic. Every night!"

"Yes, I see. I see. Why didn't she awaken that night? Discover her husband? Call for her maid? Call the police long before I discovered the body?"

"Why, indeed?"

Madame Toussaint got to her feet again. "Monsieur, thank you for this information. For your concern and support. Your kind words about my husband. But I really must go now."

Again, his white-gloved hand kept her in the chair. "But I haven't told you what else I heard. Before."

"Before the murder, Monsieur?"

"The day, the afternoon, before."

Madame Toussaint sat on the upholstered edge of the *bergère*. "Please, Monsieur. Continue."

"It was Sunday and raining hard, as you may recall. The children couldn't be sent out to play in the park in such weather, and I—coward—I withdrew to this room to smoke a pipe in peace and quiet. Once Cook had finished with Sunday dinner, of course."

"Of course."

"So I was sitting quietly, right where you are, vents open so the smoke wouldn't bother my wife and the children too much. That was when I heard two men enter the space below.

"Now, this was very odd."

"It had never happened before?" Madame Toussaint queried.

"Never. Usually, I would not stoop to eavesdropping. A military man is not a gossip."

Except for some of those surrounding the case of Captain Dreyfus, Madame Toussaint thought.

"But it was so strange," the lieutenant-colonel continued. "Why did Monsieur le Comte bring a guest to this part of the house, the kitchen part of the house?"

"Unless he didn't want his wife—his bedridden wife—to overhear."

"Exactly."

"And the cook, their cook who has a cot in the kitchen for when her poor old legs can't carry her up to her *chambre* on the sixth floor. She is really quite deaf."

"Now, I didn't know that, but all the more reason, *n'est pas?*"

"Indeed. Please, Monsieur, continue. So you overheard Monsieur d'Ermenville talking?" Madame Toussaint wouldn't call her brother-in-law a comte. Never. "To whom?"

"Now, I can't say with certainty."

"A man?"

"Yes. And, as I said, I wouldn't have eavesdropped. People live on top of one another in a building. They are entitled to their privacy. Except that it was so strange to hear anything but teakettles and the cook's chopping at this end of the house."

"Go on, Monsieur."

"It really caught my attention when I heard Monsieur le Comte say he would go to any lengths to cancel the other man's lease. He meant to throw him out on the street. 'Don't think I haven't done it many times before to many others, from many a building, for much less cause.'"

"Eugène's exact words?"

"Yes. So he advised the man to move himself of his own free will as quickly as possible. 'If you can find anyone who will take you.' It must have been someone—some man—from our building."

"Monsieur d'Ermenville has—had—many buildings in many parts of the city." Madame Toussaint struggled to find another explanation for the one she feared. "The other man could have been any tenant, come cap in hand to be allowed to make up the rent one more month."

"Do you think so?"

"No one in this building is behind in their rent. I know this; I collect them. I am the concierge."

"That may be so, but—"

"Please, Monsieur. You haven't finished your account. Please, go on."

"Well, the other man pleaded his case, over and over. 'The skipped payments were only because my father died. Haven't I since made them up?'

"Then Monsieur le Comte dropped a bombshell. 'I would desire, then, that you not make up the difference from funds my wife la Comtesse gives you.'"

Madame Toussaint froze. "Madame la Comtesse? Funding him since his father died? Of course." It wasn't an absolute given that Monsieur Arnaud had acted alone, or even that he was the main perpetrator. His goal in hurrying on the stairs may not have been merely in pursuit of her, but to find allies. Madame Toussaint was very glad now that the vents were closed.

The lieutenant-colonel continued to relate what he had overheard. "'Even if the money had not come out of my own pocket, gone through her to come right back to my pocket again,' le Comte said. 'Even if that were the case, even if you were her gigolo—which I sincerely doubt—I wouldn't mind half so much as that there have been complaints against you from other occupants.'

"'Complaints? About what? I am a model tenant. No children, no loud parties, no drunken behavior. I'm clean—'

"'I don't know what you call it, if not drunken behavior, for surely no sober man would behave thus.'

"'I protest, I do not know.'

"'I think you do, Monsieur. You and I both know very well what I'm talking about, what you have been accused of by respectable people.'"

Madame Toussaint considered that her brother-in-law, who took advantage of his female staff as his birthright, from Jeanne-Marie to who knew how far back, had a nerve accusing people of being unrespectable. But the lieutenant-colonel was of the same belief system, so it made no sense to say anything about his daughters being under threat.

"Then the other man launched into such abuse of Monsieur le Comte as I dare not report to a lady. 'You are just as bad as my father, condemning me for what I am, for what I cannot change, for what years in prison cannot change.' Words to that effect."

Herlemont blinked, then added, "Which made me guess at the man's identity right away. I am an army man, what can I say? Men are men in the army. Because I, Madame, was the one who complained to Monsieur le Comte just on Saturday that I didn't like raising a family in an apartment where a pederast— 'A pederast, Monsieur le Comte, passes by the door where my young sons rest on a daily basis.'"

Madame Toussaint had a very clear picture of the two-year-old cherub on that stair fresh from the bath just the night before. "I'm quite certain the other man in that conversation was—"

They said it together. "Monsieur Arnaud."

Madame Toussaint was on her feet, and this time all the brass in the army wasn't going to stop her. "He tried to kill me. Just now," was the most complete explanation she had time for.

She pushed out into the hallway—surprising the two-year-old with unregimental behavior yet again.

She had to get the pigeon sent and then tell the police. She only hoped she wasn't too late.

XXXIV
LA BELLE ÉPOQUE

As Madame Toussaint reached the lobby at a run, the building's front door rang. She flew to open it before considering whether or not she should. She admitted mourners, two gentlemen and a lady in somber black. She admitted them, keeping carefully behind the door panels so as not to be seen by young Théophile on his beat, watching for her, watching for Paul. Who had admitted the earlier callers? Well, she'd find out. Sooner than she liked in any case.

"Good morning," and "a very sorrowful time," everyone agreed. The men removed their hats. One of them carried a wreath of white carnations wrapped with black ribbon.

Madame Toussaint closed the door firmly and told the visitors, "On the first floor. They'll take your wraps there." She followed them as far as the door to her loge, far enough to see a skirt at the top of the stairs she recognized as Mademoiselle Sylvie's best. Mademoiselle was surprised to see the guests already admitted.

Then Mademoiselle Sylvie caught a glimpse of Madame Toussaint, who tried to swing quickly around the banister to prevent it. Her haste revealed something the lady's maid was trying to keep hidden in the pleats of her skirt: the razor from Monsieur Arnaud's dresser.

"*Chienne.*" Madame Toussaint heard the lady's maid swear, which shocked the visitors into falling back on one another on the stair.

There followed a confusion of apologies, lame explanations, and reattempts at gracious greetings. Concealed by the commotion, Madame

Toussaint managed to get her loge door open and slip in, which wasn't easy because Malin *fils*, the pigeon, was ready to fly the coop. She flapped her own wings and made hissing sounds to keep him back until she could lock the door behind her.

As fast as she could, Madame Toussaint scribbled out the note she'd been phrasing in her head all the previous evening. She applied the blotter, then decided to add the name of the person she was now certain had committed the murder of Paul's brother.

The bird fortunately gave way to a certain docility, having cleaned out the cassoulet pot. With nothing left to eat, he was willing to come with only a little coaxing to the human who found a three-day's old baguette end under an over-turned bowl on the dresser.

The furious pounding on the door would certainly have sent Malin *fils* out of reach onto the stovepipe in terror if Madame Toussaint hadn't had a grip on him that grew tighter at the sound. The bird's heart pounded quicker than hers as she rolled the note with practiced fingers around the little twig-wide leg and wrapped it securely with a piece of thread. The high-pitched squeal of a police whistle outside must have pierced the little bird brain like a needle.

Beyond the door, whoever was thumping thumped some more. A voice she recognized as Mademoiselle Sylvie's urged, "Harder. I know she's in there. I saw her with my own eyes. You'll have to break down the door. She's a wily one, although I don't think even she can fit through the window that's only wide enough for a cat."

The door splintered at its locks, first the lower half and then the upper, just as Madame Toussaint opened the tiny window, let the pigeon out and the angry cat in. Even as strong hands grabbed her, her gaze soared upward to where Malin *fils* disappeared out of sight around the top floors of the buildings that surrounded the courtyard like the walls of a well.

• • •

"*Et bien*, Madame." The young gendarme Théophile closed both halves of the shattered door behind him for some privacy and so as not to disturb the mourners who would continue to jangle the building's front door. "What have you done?"

Madame Toussaint thought he meant the pigeon. Fusiliers might be right outside, waiting to shoot poor Malin *fils* out of the drab January sky. The thought made her slow to reply.

The young man pressed her gently into the loge's single chair. He couldn't sit on the cat-ruined bed, and so he couldn't help but loom over her. She could see it made him uncomfortable to be so threatening. To her surprise, that didn't seem to be his purpose.

Such was not the case with police commissaire Monsieur Roule-Armagnac. Drawn no doubt by his subordinate's whistle, the large man threw open the ruined door and pulled Théophile out of the way.

Madame Toussaint's pulse raced. Reminders of the bloody events of twenty-five years ago had assailed her for the past two days, from the sight of her brother-in-law's brutalized corpse to confinement in La Santé prison, to the flight of the pigeon. Her patience and reason seemed stretched to the breaking point.

There really wasn't space for the two of them in the loge, Madame Toussaint and the corpulent commissaire. But displacing all the necessary oxygen seemed to be one means of torture the man used to get his suspects to confess. He had other means, too, of course. The half-light of the loge smeared the commissaire's features as if Monsieur Mahler had sketched the present respectable face and then smudged the charcoal to the lean, mean features of a quarter of a century ago.

Madame Toussaint's memories sprang vividly to mind: the swing of the young officer's rifle butt towards Paul's head, her husband holding up manacled hands, then slumping as the blow broke through all his defenses. She screamed—in her memory only, her present voice strangled—and the rifle butt swung towards her and her unborn child.

The commissaire sputtered and fumed from the effects of his exertions to answer the whistle, which impinged even more on the available air. "You gave us the slip, Madame. *J'accuse.*"

"The slip, Monsieur?" Like a drowning woman, she struggled for air.

"Surely you knew you were being tailed by Paris's finest."

"Was I? I had no idea."

He studied her. Girlish innocence? More like girlish terror, but he did not seem to see through the invisible cloak she pulled over herself with twenty-five years of practice. "Of course you didn't. Our men are most adept at their skills."

"Why would you want to follow a poor concierge like me?"

"You know why, Madame. Your husband is accused of killing his brother on Sunday night."

"He didn't do it."

"No one else is as convinced as you are. And you vanishing for the past twelve hours must cast suspicion on you covering for him, Madame."

"I don't think I should be held accountable if you and your men cannot follow a simple woman across Paris."

The commissaire harrumphed. "But where did you sleep? You were not in the loge at a very late hour. We checked."

She decided not to mention the fact that she knew this, that she had witnessed the raid from the fifth floor looking down. "Do I look like I slept on the streets, Monsieur?" In Coco's pinned up skirt and bodice, Madame Toussaint knew she did not. She looked more respectable than usual in a kept lady's clothes. "Your man posted at the front door, he did not see me enter. So it must have been early, right? Before you found that I had shaken your tail, and you thought you should take that precaution. Hardly time to contact any nefarious person in town, if that had been my purpose. I do have some skills at detection, Monsieur. They are part of a concierge's job requirements, to keep her building safe when the gendarmerie seems unable to do it."

A jangle on the loge bell indicated more visitors come to pay their respects. Like an automaton from one of Jules Verne's fanciful stories, Madame Toussaint moved to answer it as she had done every day for more than twenty years.

The commissaire shifted his monocle uneasily, as if he thought that would help him see better. "Officer Théophile will let the mourners in."

"It cannot be comforting to people in grief to see you or your subordinate at a funeral. I should, the invisible concierge—"

Commissaire Roule-Armagnac was not ready to let her pass. "But where were you last night?"

"A woman, Monsieur, a concierge cannot keep her job if she is not discrete."

The commissaire let his gaze wander up through the seven floors of the building, trying to parse out the discretion. He knew well enough not to press further. The exercise made the monocle drop from his eye and dangle by its ribbon on his well-fed form.

"Monsieur le Commissaire, if I did not sleep in my loge last night, nor in the streets among the clochards, you cannot expect me to say more." And your investigations of the tenants must indeed be lacking if I can say this, she thought. I hope you are also thinking along the same lines and will be discrete about the high-class residents of this neighborhood. At a funeral, no less.

But an aspect of the man's jowly, hairy face without its monocle brought the same face hairless and with better eyesight to her memory. Twenty-five years ago, that face had seemed befuddled because he had been young and angry and full of life and self-righteous evil, untamed by too many good meals.

Now would be the time to tell what she had deduced, what she knew, about the murderer's identity and who might have assisted that person. But the past kept infringing on her mind. She had a hard time trusting the police, and especially this man. Even after all the passage of time, Madame Toussaint found it difficult to confront that face. She struggled, but her heartbeat spiked.

So she did as she always did when she was uncomfortable. Since she couldn't sew, she stood—the commissaire's bulk less intimidating from this pose, even if her head only reached to his shoulder—and set about cleaning. The cat mess would have to be first if she hoped to sleep in that bed that night. She gathered up the soiled sheet and carried it to the window. There was more space, more air in the kitchen alcove. The cat himself shot out again at his first chance, not liking the loge crowded with humans and no food yet. Madame Toussaint shook out the worst of the sheet and stuffed it into the kettle with the other sheet soaking these two days with le Comte's blood.

The Commissaire had at least enough respect for the persons in the city who cleaned up the messes left by him and others that he watched her in silence for a moment. Then, perhaps with a nudge from behind, he burst out. "Madame, if you cannot give a decent account of yourself and your vagrant husband here, I will have to take you in again—"

She stood to her full height, wiping her hands, cold from the stagnant water, on a still-dry corner of sheet. She spoke quietly, but no less fiercely. "Monsieur le Commissaire, if you can live with yourself and your lofty position earned by beating a helpless, shackled Frenchman senseless with the butt of your bayonetted rifle—a fellow Frenchman, a veteran of the Prussian War and the siege, beloved by his troops. A fellow Frenchman and a comte, as if such archaic titles mean anything in a free republic. If you can live with yourself, having pushed away and beaten that Frenchman's wife who tried to stop you. She, heavy with child, a child the future of a splintered France. You beat her until she went into premature labor and was only saved by the begrudging goodness of the man lying murdered in his coffin upstairs. If you can live with yourself and the stolen life you have had since, then go ahead. I dare you. Arrest me again." She hoped her voice didn't carry too far, just far enough. Perhaps it could go farther later. Soon.

The pallor that overtook Commissaire Roule-Armagnac's usually flushed face was good enough evidence of at least his present state of mind. This indicated some recognition, some shame.

"Arrest me again. Now. Vive la Commune."

The flush came back in anger—at her? Or at his former self and how that had paved his way to his present position. But Madame Toussaint didn't stop. "You don't know how long I've wanted to say that again. To you. Arrest me and do not listen while I tell you who the real murderer is, because I have ferreted it out. But please, close the door."

The commissaire resettled his monocle onto his assumed adulthood. He moved to close the loge door, still open to the lobby and whoever crowded behind his large bulk. He would not be comfortable in the narrow space without that air, and he would no doubt claim the single chair for himself. But for all her brave words, Madame Toussaint felt her confidence slipping under the high tide of the past.

"Surely you are going to re-arrest this woman, Monsieur le Commissaire?" This was the voice of big-boned Mademoiselle Sylvie. Come to answer the front door? Certainly, she had shoved Théophile out of the way.

"I have no cause to do so just yet," he replied. "I will first hear some new piece of evidence she is willing to divulge."

Over the commissaire's big bulk, Madame Toussaint saw the lady's maid's face grow soft—with effort, but it was welcome. The face was in such contrast to the remembered brutality of the commissaire that Madame Toussaint moved towards it.

For nearly twenty-five years, Paris had pretended the events of 1871 had never happened. The citizens all pretended there had never been a brave, foolhardy attempt to make ladies' maids a thing of the past. The deaths of thirty-thousand Parisians, their imprisonment, their deportation, their torture—it was not in good taste to remember such things. Madame Toussaint moved towards the formality of that smothering good taste. How many times had she imagined herself teetering with her infant on the lip of a mass grave, the rifles of fellow Frenchmen pointed at her heart. No matter how he'd died, her brother-in-law's death was not the horror of a mass grave.

Madame Toussaint stepped back from that brink to the safety of the world she had hidden in away from the past.

Mademoiselle Sylvie offered the escape. "In that case, Madame la Comtesse asks if she couldn't have the concierge upstairs to help with the lying-in-state of her honored husband le Comte. He was a very popular man, God lend him grace. All these guests. We have just lost our house-maid." That possessive "our" was curious. "There's food and drink for the after-funeral reception to prepare and the crippled cook is worthless. Just for the morning. You may question her later, as soon as we're done with her."

"Please, Monsieur," Madame la Toussaint might have said. "In memory of the child I carried all those years ago. Let me tell you my suspicions first, then I will be happy to lend my services." She might have said it, but she did not.

Cowed by the forms of convention that covered the past, the commissaire shuffled out of the way. Madame Toussaint regretted having called him to task for his brutality all those years ago. Because now he was overly conscious of his dignity; he would not rough up a woman today. He would follow the forms. Théophile stood by in the lobby, mutely awaiting orders—that never came.

Outside, as the door closed against the cold, Madame Toussaint caught a glimpse of the hearse just reining to a halt. Black ostrich feathers whipped damp in the wind. Crêpe looping over the open rear sagged with new-falling moisture. Because of the weather, the *pompes funèbres* firm must be short-handed today. One of the horses wasn't a pure black and was skittish, unused to pulling somberly in the traces and balking at the yoke.

Pulled away from that brief view of normalcy, Madame Toussaint found herself being shuffled up the stairs with Mademoiselle Sylvie at her back on the step below and the jet-beaded skirts of a pair of regally moving high-society ladies above.

When they found a pauper's grave for Madame Toussaint, one who had fought and lived on the barricades, there would be no such elegant rig waiting for her outside.

~ XXXV ~
LA BELLE ÉPOQUE

Bunches of flowers and wreaths with black ribbons and the names of the donors worked in gold were piling high on the closed coffin. "To our landlord, who will be sorely missed." "To our business partner," and so on. The weight of the smell of all those somber blooms mingled with the hot beeswax of the candles made the head reel.

It was all as it should be, *comme il faut*. No sign of the past.

Elegant brass fittings caught the light of those candles and little else in the salon, whose street-facing windows were heavily draped. The oak panels enriched by this brass sat on what must be the extended dining table. Meters of black crêpe shrouded it. A brass vase at the foot of the table held boxwood twigs. Each mourner took a twig as he or she entered, dipped it in a similar vase of holy water and sprinkled a sign of the cross, keeping the piled wreaths fresh.

After that, the mourners shuffled on to take the Comtesse's hand—that must be she in the chair in the far shadows—and murmur their solemn words. At her side sat Mademoiselle Sylvie and at the maid's stolid side, Madame Toussaint saw Madame Flôte. The medium was no doubt telling the new widow that she, who had been in that state longer, knew of a certainty that souls lived on and could communicate with those left behind.

And Madame and Monsieur Cailloux were just leaving.

"You're needed in the kitchen." Mademoiselle Sylvie seemed determined to keep Madame Toussaint from participating in the somber forms of her brother-in-law's memorials, but the musical couple, from the third-floor-left, passed so close they had to be greeted.

"Such a deep loss."

"The building will never be the same." The couple spoke together and to the same effect.

Madame Toussaint said, "I hope you enjoyed your concert last night. Wagner, was it?"

"Oh, no," replied Madame Cailloux. "Hayden, wasn't it, dear? The violinist was particularly good, a man we know well—"

Madame Toussaint knew her interruption was rude, but the viewing was so normal that she had begun to think of sleuthing again. "So it wasn't you speaking German—or perhaps English—in the stairway last night?"

"Not at all. We found—"

The next rudeness was forced not by Madame Toussaint but by Mademoiselle Sylvie's reaction—could it be?—to the mention of English. The lady's maid pushed the concierge away from the somber, ceremonial company and said, "The kitchen." Always the kitchen. That was how normal a normal funeral was in the Belle Époque.

So many from the Commune had not had such obsequies; only a mass grave. Nor would Madame Toussaint enjoy such. "I should be allowed to show my respects to my brother- and sister-in-law." That's what Madame Toussaint wanted to say to her captor when she saw that she was not going to be allowed to take her place with the rest of the mourners and their boxwood. She did not.

The passage through the hall was so common, so every-day, that Madame Toussaint could take notice of the carelessly mended old lace of a doily on a table in the hall. Once again, she wondered that a lady's maid should have such bad sewing skills . . .

And then, to Madame Toussaint's surprise, Monsieur Arnaud came out of the kitchen instead of out of the candlelit salon where she had expected him to be lingering in the shadows.

And Madame Toussaint realized that escaping the horror of her memories into the forms of the present had been a mistake. The last time she'd seen Monsieur Arnaud, he'd been chasing her down the stairs. Her heart pounded in her ears. The way the two were looking at her, lady's maid and dandy— Very similar eyes, she noticed. A family resemblance, nudging her backwards. Before the dual gaze, she only wanted to use a concierge's usual ploy and fade into the woodwork. Divert attention to anyone else.

"Is Mademoiselle Joséphine the cook all right?" she asked instead. "I'm here to help—"

That diversion didn't work. Madame Toussaint did what she had done neither in all the Terrible Year nor in all the years since. It had never seemed necessary before as horrors happened to her. Now she screamed, but found the pantry door slammed on her.

What would the mourners think, if her noise found its way to their muffled salon? Only that the help were expressing their grief in a very indecorous way, which is why they were the help and not the upper class. She screamed again, a word—*Help!*—but knew it couldn't go beyond the now-locked door. Only through the pantry's outside vents.

"There she will stay," she heard Mademoiselle Sylvie say outside the door, "until you, Brother, become man enough to take her someplace to dispense with her. I did the last one for you. You will do it, once the people have gone to the funeral."

Madame Toussaint could hear the nervous pacing creaks of new leather shoes, shoes no doubt topped by spotless spats. She imagined her own blood on them. Their wearer probably did, too. It heightened the nervousness. Madame Toussaint pounded on the pantry door.

Mademoiselle Sylvie and Monsieur Arnaud switched to speaking something the trapped concierge thought at first must just be blurred by the heavy door. Then she realized it was a different language. Of course. The language Madame Toussaint had heard in the stairwell the night before. English.

Were the lady's maid's foreign words something along the lines of, "See? Alive and well and every bit as dangerous. You can't even serve tea laced with strychnine properly. Even such an effeminate means of murder"? Madame Toussaint also thought she heard the name Arnie said in a tone a governess might use to express disappointment in a troublesome child. Madame Toussaint knew Arnie to be an English name, a corruption of the French Arnaud.

Monsieur Arnaud dithered in that strange language. Did Mademoiselle also repeat, "I took care of the last one, the Count. Your turn now"? Madame Toussaint had no way of knowing if that confession was part of the foreign dialogue.

It wasn't going to be the kitchen knife this time. Madame Joséphine stood guard over her cutlery now. Madame Toussaint imagined, however, Monsieur Arnaud with the razor she had seen in his room earlier, in the lady's maid's hand at the top of the stair. The thought made her knees weak.

Then the two left, to divert any attention away from their captive's prison and back to grief for Monsieur d'Ermenville.

This pantry had no stuffed chair to sit in. So rather than making her drop, the image of that blade sharpened Madame Toussaint's blunted wits. She pounded again until her fists hurt. She gave another cry she hoped someone could hear. The cook, of course, could not hear, and the sound failed to reach the bourgeoisie in the salon. Or if it did, it was dismissed as just the lower classes being irrational again.

Madame Toussaint flung herself at the door. That only bruised her shoulder joint. She tried again. This time, disoriented in the dark, she propelled herself into a canvas sack of dried peas that burst and spilled like marbles on the floor. She slipped on them as she staggered backwards. She landed hard on her already-bruised wrist against the shelves at the back. She gave another, louder, futile scream.

Very well. How long would it take Monsieur Arnaud to decide to prove himself a man? That's how long she had before his razor hit her throat.

First of all, Madame Toussaint got to her feet, pulling herself up with her right arm through the shelves stuffed with provisions. The peas on the floor continued to make her feet unsteady, although she brushed them to the corners as best she could with her toe.

Next, she felt for a gaslight such as Lieutenant-colonel Herlemont had in his war room. She couldn't find it, and even if she did, she decided she wouldn't want to light it, filling the pantry with explosive gas if she didn't trust herself with a match in the dark.

Mademoiselle Joséphine must know her way around her supplies in the dark, as she knew her way around her kitchen in the silence of her deafness. And she didn't take up pantry room with a comfortable armchair. Her comfortable chair was in the kitchen by the fire.

Certain now that Mademoiselle Sylvie and the coward Monsieur Arnaud must be out of hearing, Madame Toussaint attempted a shout. If the sound couldn't go through the door, it would have to go through the vents. "Lieutenant-colonel? Monsieur?"

But the military man, his wife, and who knew how many of their children must already be out in the street, waiting by the hearse to form part of the procession as soon as the men from the *pompes funèbres* brought down the coffin hoisted upon their burly shoulders. The Herlemonts would claim a position of honor near the front just behind Madame la Comtesse's hired black carriage, first on the march to Saint-Sulpice and then on to the cemetery.

Not the Père Lachaise Cemetery on the other bank where the communards had died in their thousands and laid buried in mass graves. Eugène Toussaint, the so-called Comte d'Ermenville, would lie in Montparnasse, in an elaborate stone tomb complete with stained glass and a prie-dieu before a narrow altar, the words "Famille d'Ermenville" chiseled in an arch over the doorway. The family tomb crammed next to other similar tombs, row upon row upon row.

Not Toussaint. Her name was Toussaint, but they would never let her be there when this day and her life were over.

Saint-Sulpice first. Madame Toussaint was trying to time how long the pomp would last, but in truth her sense of minutes and hours was more slippery than the dried peas. Minutes, hours, years, going back into the distant past. Saint-Sulpice. She hadn't been in the church, any church, since it had been so full of the Commune, so full of hope, Paul at her side and their child in her belly.

And now her hope was confined to the space of a dark pantry, its vents open to the spit of frigid rain outside. Madame Toussaint closed the vents. The warmer air would cause the cheese to ripen too quickly. But would any of it be edible once spattered with her heart's blood? She tried the door handle again, then sank to the floor, weak with terror.

After what seemed to be a very long time, noises dropped on her from the war room over her head. Plop. Plop roll. Careful of her left hand—which throbbing was almost her whole consciousness—she rose again to her feet. She reopened the vents to a blast of cold air. Another plop. A baby's prattle. The Herlemont two-year-old must have discovered the crate of oranges in their pantry, dropping them and rolling them across the floor.

"Soldier!"

The plop of oranges stopped. The little voice piped something with a query at the end of it.

"Go tell Sergeant *Nou-nou* to come here. Double time. It's a matter of life and death."

The silence of two-year-old consideration.

"You, Soldier, must save France."

"*Oui, maître*," he lisped, probably accompanied by a smart salute. Little feet pattered off.

Two minutes later, a female step, her voice. "Oh, la, la. Mon petit, what a mess. What have you done to the oranges?"

"Mademoiselle, please," Madame Toussaint yelled. "Listen to me—"

But the nanny was gone again, carting off a two-year-old in the middle of a tantrum at not being able to get his point across and save France. The nanny's shouts to their own cook and the infant screams in her ear made her as deaf as Mademoiselle Joséphine here on the first floor.

Then, as soon as her head cleared, Madame Toussaint heard the handle of her own pantry move.

XXXVI
LA BELLE ÉPOQUE

"*Sacré bleu!*" exclaimed Mademoiselle Joséphine as her hunt for, discovery, and finally use of her pantry key revealed huddling Madame Toussaint to her. "Madame la Comtesse. What are you doing here?"

The fact that the old cook still called her Comtesse after all these years fairly made Madame Toussaint weep. But there was too much else to worry about at this time. And it wouldn't be any good to give Mademoiselle Joséphine more knowledge than she needed about what had happened. Indeed, it might endanger her.

"Mademoiselle Sylvie told me you might need some help for when the family comes back from the cemetery," Madame Toussaint decided to say. "And I foolishly got myself locked in the pantry."

That seemed to make sense to the cook, and she nodded. "Thank you. Much appreciated."

Madame Toussaint escaped to the air and light of the apartment hallway. "And sorry about the split peas. I'll clean them up first of all."

"But, *chérie*. What have you done to your wrist?"

In the light, Madame Toussaint's wrist really did look bad, blooming with bruises. Weakness swept over Madame Toussaint at the sight, but she managed to stay on her feet by grasping onto the cook's plump arm with her good hand.

"You're no help to me with a hand like that."

"Yes, I am," Madame Toussaint insisted. Better to stick close to the cook and company than to find herself alone with the lady's maid again.

Until she could reach young Théophile or another gendarme she trusted more than the commissaire. "I can fetch and carry for you with my good right hand. My good legs covering for your bad ones. If you could only find me something to wrap this bad hand with."

"Of course. But come and sit here first while I go find some sheeting. Between you and me, there's plenty Mademoiselle Sylvie hasn't gotten around to mending yet."

Madame Toussaint had hoped to be set down out of sight in the kitchen. Instead, she got set in one of the elaborate Louis Quinze *fauteuils* in the hall. "Would Madame la Comtesse approve of setting the concierge here?" Madame Toussaint asked.

"Never you mind," Madame Joséphine insisted, then gave a merry wink. "The faux comtesse will be in her carriage at the cemetery for a long while yet." She went at her slow pace to rummage in a closet in the spare bedroom.

Not trusting her feet under her yet, Madame Toussaint decided to stay where she had been planted. A wicker chair in the kitchen would have been more comfortable than this slick satin. While she waited, Madame Toussaint gained enough presence of mind to take in the apartment surrounding her. She'd been in it many times before, of course, but always about some business, as a petitioner, a poor relation. The discoverer of a murder victim.

She had never really stopped to see just how plush the furnishings were. Furnishings, she remembered Mademoiselle Joséphine telling her, had come from the family country estate and really should have been split between the brothers. Even the chair in which she sat was calculated to intimidate the likes of her, to indicate clearly who had won the Franco-Prussian war, despite all capitulation treaties signed at Versailles. Yes, who had won the Civil War of the Commune that had followed. That was very plain.

Facing her across the hall hung a mirror, elaborately framed in gold rich with carved flowers, ribbons, and cherubim. She couldn't see herself in the glass. It was hung in such a way that it reflected back a corner of the third bedroom into which Mademoiselle Joséphine had disappeared, searching for bandages. The corner Madame Toussaint saw was empty, just the lines of polished parquet catching dull light from an unshuttered courtyard window.

But that corner hadn't always been empty. The memory flooded back so acutely that Madame Toussaint gasped with the pain of it. Once, a cheap wicker bassinet had stood on that parquet.

· XXXVII ·
THE TERRIBLE YEAR
—

THE BASSINET BORE the body of her infant son. Just there, on that square of parquet. She rushed in, her heart thudding with dread, to find him. Blue in the face. Dead.

"It is the way with infants." Her sister-in-law's disembodied voice echoed in the room. "They are so fragile. So many die. For no reason."

But maybe Nathalie was so disoriented by the horror of the sweet little body grown light and cooling and stiff that what she had always remembered as her sister-in-law clumsily offering comfort had been another voice entirely.

Nathalie couldn't prove it. But she would never been able to shake the disquiet.

. . .

She felt that disquiet from the first moment she climbed the stairs to her sister-in-law's apartment that day in desperation, carrying her son and his wicker bassinet. The concierge's loge was already hers, hers and her son's, since the haven of Saint-Sulpice had gone back to priestly hands at the Commune's bloody fall. Eugène had insisted and she had complied to keep a roof over their heads. For as long as they had to be alone.

Alone, she had given her infant all the aristocratic names she and Paul had discussed: Paul d'Ermenville Thomas Jean Luc. Even Eugène was in there, more names than a little mite should be burdened with. But

Nathalie had only ever called him Paul. This was encouraged by the fact that Paul in prison and the infant Paul had never been in the same room at once since the birth.

"Please, Sister. Care for your nephew for a while."

"I'm very busy here, can't you see?"

But Mademoiselle Sylvie was there, too, wasn't she? Tall, big boned, commanding. Mademoiselle Sylvie had bent to her mistress's ear and whispered.

A change came over Madame Eugène Toussaint's features. Nathalie thought it was at the sight of the helpless little face looking up at her so trustingly. Who could refuse that?

"How long?" the sister-in-law asked.

"I can't say. They have told me they are moving Paul from the prison to the galley that will carry him to Devil's Island. Devil's Island, Sister. How can he bear it? How can I? I must do what I can to keep him in France."

"Why don't you take the child with you?" The coldness in Madame Eugène's voice blew an arctic blast into the salon on that hot summer day.

"It could be very dangerous: touchy soldiers, gendarmes—"

"It may be the last time Paul will ever see his son."

"It won't be." Nathalie tried to convince herself more than her sister-in-law.

And how could she know it could be more dangerous for her son in his bassinet on the first floor of the building where they had shelter on the Rue Férou? More dangerous, even, than the final days of the Commune.

"He's been sleeping such a long time," Madame Eugène said when Nathalie returned—defeated, exhausted—eight or nine hours later.

Nathalie had pushed past the woman. Just the thought had made her milk let down, relieving the pressure but drenching the front of her bodice. And the next thing she heard was her own scream as she threw herself on the floor beside the bassinet, her dead son in her arms.

That she had first given the perfect little creature life after all the Commune's death had seemed such a miracle. It seemed less likely that she couldn't rouse him now, a brief six weeks later. He was still warm; such a tiny body cannot have had much time to lose heat at all. The sweet infant smell of him . . .

Nathalie's grief had been so intense at the time that she hadn't bothered to try to parse the feelings—or callous lack of them—displayed by her sister-in-law. And, come to think of it, the sort of rigid stance of Mademoiselle Sylvie at the same time. A stance of power, like the statue of a general lording it over the town square, impervious to the misfortunes of others, many of which he himself had ordered. Superior. As if, were she, Mademoiselle Sylvie, to have a child, her child would certainly know better than to die.

Madame Eugène Toussaint's stoney reaction had been blood-curdling but not unexpected. The woman had everything to gain by the death of this infant nephew of hers. With Paul bound to die in a distant land for his seditious actions, and his title removed besides, her path to being a comtesse was clear, the title of count for the children she still hoped to have.

Madame Eugène Toussaint had even said it aloud in Nathalie's hearing. When the newspaper—Eugène's reactionary, not to say monarchist, paper *Le Soleil*, of course—had reported on the "collateral" deaths of the children of communards, she had said what the paper had in part suggested: "Kill the nit before it becomes the louse."

But Mademoiselle Sylvie? What to make of her solid, commanding stance as she looked on little Paul's death, offering no help, no comfort?

XXXVIII
LA BELLE ÉPOQUE

It wasn't until she sat on the Louis Quinze chair in the hallway of the first-floor apartment, rocking her wounded wrist, that Madame Toussaint had an inkling of what might have happened. From that position, gazing at the mirror hung just so, she could see the empty spot where little Paul's bassinet had been, where she had knelt on the floor, inconsolable with grief, his lifeless body in her arms.

Madame Eugène Toussaint had been hovering with her haughty impatience. She had helped herself to what suited her refined tastes. Now she waited with growing irritation for the messy trash to remove itself from her gracious home. As if she herself never made waste at all.

Madame Paul Toussaint's job ever since: to haul the dust bins of all the building, every other day for twenty-five years, from the courtyard to the street for the trash collectors. And when the trash had been herself and the corpse of her six-week-old son . . .

She could still feel the pain of it, as if it had happened only an hour ago. She could feel the deep wound, but at least now she could understand. Mademoiselle Sylvie was the one Madame Paul Toussaint never really understood. Until now. But if Mademoiselle Sylvie had been sitting—or even standing, waiting to be called to duty—just in the spot where Madame Paul Toussaint was now, she would have been able to watch not only the concierge's grief but also what had happened just before.

Because Madame Toussaint was certain she remembered correctly, the bit of warmth still lingering in little Paul's tightly wrapped corpse. And a body that small would cool very fast.

But what if—? Madame Paul Toussaint could almost hear the voices in that long past hall. Madame Eugène Toussaint: "Mademoiselle, keep an eye out into the Rue Férou. If you see this brat's mother, the concierge, hurrying home through the twilight from her fool's errand, let me know at once."

Her lady's maid: "*Oui, bien sûr,* Madame." And once Nathalie's arrival was announced, the lady's maid kept watching.

Or perhaps the maid had lifted the cushion herself. Either way, blackmail—

"*Et voilà.*" Mademoiselle Joséphine hurried back into the hall.

The cook would have been busy in the kitchen with supper preparations on that day so long ago. Now she brought liniment from the kitchen, fragrant with thyme and comfrey, almost like that with which one might baste a pigeon.

"Tell me, Mademoiselle." Madame Toussaint turned her gaze again to the spot where the empty bassinet had stood, jarred by her own grief-stricken movements. "Do you remember that day—?" She couldn't form the words right away.

The cook looked in the direction her patient was staring and knew immediately what event in the past she was remembering. "Ah, *chèrie*. That was a terrible day in a terrible year. I know how new deaths make us remember old losses—Monsieur le Comte's funeral being today and all. But if I could put any salve on your heart like this sovereign liniment, my mother's old recipe—"

She stopped herself from saying more and began to wrap Madame Toussaint's wrist tightly with strips of clean linen. As the white cloth was wrapped expertly, Madame Toussaint noticed again the clumsy stitching of a mend that could only have been made by Mademoiselle Sylvie's inexpert needle, after which the sheeting was only good for bandages.

And Madame Toussaint knew that she had written the wrong name on her pigeon message to Paul. But that hardly mattered when there was so little chance the message could get through. Or that anything could be done if it did. Just like during the siege.

Madame Toussaint pressed on, as she knew she had to do. "No, I want you please to think back to Mademoiselle Sylvie on that day. It seems to me that her sudden control over Madame la Comtesse dates back precisely to that day. Correct me if your impression is different, but up until that point, she had been your average, powerless, 'yes, Madame, no Madame,' sort of servant. Coming from a foreign country—"

"Is Mademoiselle Sylvie a foreigner?"

"English, I think."

"You wouldn't guess. What makes you think—?"

"Don't ask me how I know. She is very good, but what helps the illusion is the absolute power she has over Madame la Comtesse. Suddenly, on that day, she knows she belongs here. Why? It happened on that day. I'm sure of it."

"Yes. Yes, I think you're right, Madame. Now that you mention it. Before, I had more standing in the household as an old servant of the family, my family serving yours for generations.

"After the Commune, so many of the working-class dead, whether for actual—just—rebellion, or simply for the working-class clothes we were wearing. It's as if the whole class, coming to understand what injustices we faced, was suddenly wiped out with that memory. So new blood had to be brought in—from the countryside, from foreign parts. From the colonies in Africa, like Jonquille the flower girl. From the Caribbean, like Théophile the nice young gendarme. From Brittany, like Jeanne-Marie."

"From England," Madame Toussaint said.

"I suppose, yes."

"The city intimidated the new blood who didn't know its history. It would be at least a generation—until our time—before their children started wondering about their own dignity as humans. Hearing the phrase, '*liberté, égalité, fraternité.*' Thinking it might refer to them. Then shouting it."

"I think you're right, Madame."

As a sling, Mademoiselle Joséphine pinned a large triangle of the same poorly mended sheeting across Madame Toussaint's front to stabilize the arm. It might have served as a diaper . . .

"I think that's exactly what happened," the cook went on. "I mean, we all were so grief-stricken about the baby, God rest him. And the horrors of the put-down of the Commune. And the thought that Monsieur Paul—the kindest, most thoughtful of the brothers—had somehow got caught up in it and was being shipped off to Devil's Island. And there was nothing any of us could do about it. We were really *bouleversé* for weeks and weeks. But when we got back to life again . . . yes, it seemed like something had happened between the lady and her lady's maid. It was Mademoiselle Sylvie who got Madame le Comtesse to fire that housemaid. What was her name?"

"I don't remember." Yes, Madame Toussaint didn't remember much of those times.

"No, I don't either. But it didn't seem right. The housemaid had been with us longer and had never given any reason for complaint. To be let go like that. Without notice, without a reference."

Perhaps she knew. Or guessed too much.

"Although they continued to be their former selves, it was almost as if they were both playacting. Madame Eugène Toussaint . . . yes, it seems her inclination to keep at home and then to her bed started at this time. Melancholia, perhaps? Coming to realize God would never bless her with children? My mother had a tisane for that as well, but Madame would never take it when I offered.

"Or perhaps . . ." The cook added an afterthought. "Perhaps it would be more accurate to say, Mademoiselle Sylvie would not let her be dosed by anyone but herself.

"There." The cook surveyed her healing handiwork. "That should keep you fit as rain while you lend me a hand. Yes, your one good hand will do just fine. Madame Eugène Toussaint doesn't usually like her servants to appear injured or sick, nothing to draw attention to the fact that we are actually human. Me with my bad legs—I should stick to the kitchen. But today, on top of everyone's grief, she's just going to have to put up with it."

"Could we see if there's a policeman still outside first?" Madame Paul Toussaint interrupted the flow, now that she was no longer trapped as a patient.

"Certainly. Come to the kitchen window. It has the best view of the street."

It did. The gendarme on duty was still the delightful Théophile. Monsieur le Commissaire, the compromised commissaire, offered no sign that he was back from claiming his place of honor in the *pomps funèbres*.

"I'd like to talk to the gendarme first, if I may." Enough time had been wasted while Madame Toussaint played patient and aggrieved mother. Time she couldn't safely spare. "Before I lend you this single helping hand."

Madame Toussaint didn't say that she hoped the world would have changed to include some justice before then, some justice besides the slogan *"liberté, égalité"* and that other word that didn't seem to include women. Before Monsieur Arnaud and Mademoiselle Sylvie returned from the cemetery, at least.

"Of course."

Mademoiselle Joséphine pushed open her window and waved a white dish towel out at the young man. He signaled that he'd come up right away but that a well-dressed couple walking a poodle had stopped to ask him for directions. Who turned off the boulevard and onto Rue Férou if they didn't know where they were going?

"I should set the paté out on this dish, the best china." The cook puttered maddeningly. "Fetch me the silver paté-knife please, *chèrie*. In that drawer—yes."

Madame Toussaint found the knife and handed it to the busy, plump hand, but she maneuvered so she could keep an anxious eye out in the street. Who took this long to get directions? The trio had completely vanished from the frame of the window.

The bell of the main door downstairs rang. "That'll be him." Madame Toussaint pushed herself past the stout cook in the narrow kitchen and made for the hallway.

"You don't have to play concierge now, *chèrie*," the cook said. "I've got that dear little Jeanne-Marie—her losing her job without a reference was just not right. Like what's her name I can't remember, just after your sweet son's death. Anyone would know Jeanne-Marie couldn't possibly have had anything to do with the death of Monsieur le Comte. I saw her this morning, while you had yourself locked in the pantry, I suppose. I thought she could see to the door on this busy day."

Not a bad idea. Keeping the girl in the public eye would keep her safe.

"The poor girl did seem to be suffering a little *bonne gueule* this morning. A little too much to drink? Who would have thought? I gave the child a swig of my mother's remedy . . ."

But Madame Toussaint had to see Théophile. Her arm in its sling felt like the weight of a baby, but she hurried to the apartment door to admit the gendarme.

Only to run face to face into Mademoiselle Sylvie, her cheeks a feverish pink from the cold of the funereal walk. And with fury. And with murder.

XXXIX
LA BELLE ÉPOQUE

"I HOPED MADAME Toussaint would help me in the kitchen," Mademoiselle Joséphine protested. As she had said, despite her seniority on the staff, the days the cook could have her way about running the household were years gone.

"I just need the concierge to come down to the cave with me," Mademoiselle Sylvie said, her gritted teeth very close to Madame Toussaint's ear. "To fetch up the wine we'll need to serve the guests on their return from the cemetery."

"But her arm—" the cook suggested futilely.

"With this basket, she can manage." Mademoiselle Sylvie scooped up the cook's shopping basket from its place of pride on a table in the hallway near the kitchen door.

Heart pounding, Madame Toussaint went where Mademoiselle Sylvie wanted her to go. The lady's maid let her know she had the razor again. And was even more inclined to use it. And that it pressed hard against her ribs so that one false move—

Jeanne-Marie's usual wide-eyed innocent wonder was a little squinty the morning-after as lady's maid and concierge came down the stairs and met her in the lobby. The girl nonetheless made an attempt at bubbling cheerfulness. Inappropriate as it might be in a house of mourning, it was the attitude of someone who knows she spent the previous evening in good company and can even remember who that company might have been.

The details, however, eluded her; a little hesitation implied she hoped the company had been as good as her memory.

"Ah, Madame. How good to see that you are well. But what have you done to your arm?"

"Remember, child," Madame Toussaint replied, "this is a somber occasion. You must keep that mood when you answer the door."

Jeanne-Marie collected herself. "Of course, Madame."

"Don't worry about me, child." Madame Toussaint tried desperately to know what else she might say to keep the girl out of this, to keep her safe, to warn her away. "Take care of the visitors. Take care of yourself. Take—" Mademoiselle Sylvie gave a painful yank on a corner of Madame Toussaint's sling, which Jeanne-Marie might have seen and tried to do more about, but fortunately the front doorbell rang again just then.

Jeanne-Marie scurried to open it, to prove herself worthy of the responsibility.

As Mademoiselle pushed her towards the rear of the lobby and the courtyard door, Madame Toussaint had a view of the Rue Férou over the black hats of the arriving mourners. Madame la Comtesse's hired carriage had just pulled up in front, the crêpe bunting and black ostrich feathers limp with rain. But between the horses' rumps and the coachman's step, Madame Toussaint saw two figures that made her heart stop still. What she saw made her abandon all hope over to her captor's will and Mademoiselle Sylvie's razor's edge.

The young gendarme Théophile had suddenly reappeared in front of the building. He had the filthy sleeve of a clochard in his grasp. The two were in heated conversation. The clochard was Paul Toussaint. Damn that pigeon, all pigeons. Those that hadn't been able to get the messages through to save Paris under siege.

And those that did get through with messages that drew loved ones into danger.

Madame Toussaint heard someone scream in the street, "There's a dead woman in the equipage!"

And someone else, "It's Madame la Comtesse."

Mademoiselle Sylvie didn't seem to be in a position to see what Madame Toussaint had seen, or even to hear it.

But Paul saw into the building. Madame Toussaint heard him call her name. "Nathalie."

The gendarme held him fast, even tighter now that the new death had been announced. How did Paul, with his usual belligerence, resist taking a swing at the young man and getting himself arrested on the spot?

Mademoiselle Sylvie focused on getting her prisoner out into the back courtyard, into the rain, around the dustbins, and to the door to the caves.

"You do not need to worry about anyone out there coming to your rescue." Mademoiselle Sylvie had enough control now that she didn't have to hiss in Madame Toussaint's ear. She could say what she wanted, and no one else could hear. "What they find when they open the carriage door will keep them plenty distracted for the next few hours."

"Madame la Comtesse?"

"The poor grieving widow, yes."

"Dead." Madame Toussaint didn't have to ask. She knew it must be true.

But keeping the woman—always so taciturn, so English—keeping her talking, bragging, would be one way to keep that razor away from Madame Toussaint's throat.

"Your brother?"

"Finally, he managed to do a deed worthy of a man. La Comtesse invited him into her carriage out of the rain in the cemetery, heedless of what the gossips might think. She herself didn't need to make an appearance at the tomb. Everyone knew her delicate condition. Something she said to him there must have made him snap."

"Something like, 'Now we are free to marry'?"

The stairs to the caves, cut into the living rock at Paris's feet, began right below the open doorway. Without the safety measure of a landing, they plunged straight into the darkness at the heart of the earth. Madame Toussaint had always hated this prospect, and if she had to see it, always came well prepared with an oil lamp or candle in its holder.

Mademoiselle Sylvie had not thought her plan out quite so well, but she suddenly heard what Madame Toussaint had said: all the way back to "brother," perhaps. Certainly "marry." Things the average person shouldn't know, the concierge knew. The lady's maid gave the concierge a shove so she staggered down the steps into the darkness and only barely managed to keep from falling the rest of the way onto the hard stone floor invisible at the bottom.

"I keep a candle and matches in the niche at the top of the stairs." Madame Toussaint hated the tone of almost begging she heard in her own voice. She hated the dark of the caves more than anything.

"What do you know about my brother?" Mademoiselle Sylvie demanded.

Madame Toussaint found she could take a breath as candlelight flared. "Your younger brother, I think. You the protective older sister. Arnold, the diminutive Arnie. I have heard you call him that when you speak English together. When you think nobody is listening."

Madame Toussaint paused to let her captor correct her if she would, but she did not. Madame Toussaint also had to center her attention on taking the treacherous steps slowly because Mademoiselle Sylvie's taper bounced anywhere but at her feet. A shove now and then, a whisper of the razor across some exposed flesh kept her moving down and down, however, reaching into the dark void with the toe of her shoe until she found solid ground.

"So when you crossed the Channel, came to France, and required a pseudonym—" Silence was like the clammy darkness all around her, so Madame Toussaint did what she could to combat it. "—the very common French name *Arnaud* came naturally. And you were the English *Sylvia*, I think, before becoming the French *Sylvie*."

They had reached the bottom. Madame Toussaint's foot found only rough-hewn stone floor stretching out before her. Mademoiselle Sylvie still said nothing, which her captive took as confirmation of all she said. If Madame Toussaint had said one syllable wrong, she was certain the lady's maid would have taken great glee in correcting her with verbal, if not physical, abuse.

But Mademoiselle Sylvie had also reached the cellar floor now, so the candle grew tamer, revealing stone walls running with the recent rain there in the bowels of Paris. An image of her brother-in-law disemboweled came back to Madame Toussaint. That would be her fate now—only here, in the dank and unpleasant place, on the edge of Monsieur Arnaud's razor at his sister's hand. Madame Toussaint fought the image as hard as she could.

"During our childhood," Mademoiselle Sylvie had fallen into a musing mood now, "I always had to protect my brother against our father. Our father who was hard on him, always wanting him to 'be a man.'"

Much as she hoped to keep her captor in this mood—she seemed less dangerous this way—Madame Toussaint felt a need-to-know that she couldn't suppress. "I think you were telling your brother the same thing these past days. You insisted he kill the Comte. I heard you tell him that when you locked me in the pantry. The strychnine in the tea before that."

"He couldn't even manage such a feminine weapon as poison." Mademoiselle Sylvie snorted.

"And finally, the Comtesse."

"It was I who had to kill the Comte. Just to show him how it was done."

Mademoiselle gave the concierge a fierce shove. Madame Toussaint cried out in the pain to her wrist as she landed hard against a damp wall. She would have preferred it if the sound she made were closer to one of discovery. "Ah ha. I suspected as much." But she had also given Paul the name of Monsieur Arnaud, which was going to lead exactly no one to proper conclusions in time to save her own skin.

The caves under any haussmannian building provided storage for the tenants, each apartment having a locked closet of sorts. Eight doors, all shut, faced the two women who had intruded upon them. Wine, of course, was the best thing to store here, the coolness being as perfect for the precious bottles as their native cellars in the countryside vineyards were.

But all sorts of things could also be stored here. The Herlemonts, in particular, had spilled their abundant household even out of the space under lock and key they were allotted. This wicker baby carriage could only belong to them, its front wheel having had an accident that bent it out of shape and lost its spokes. The little two-year-old would have to trust to his own legs from now on, to the dismay of his caregivers. These bicycles in gradated sizes; this rocking horse, paint chipped and one rocker in splinters. Chairs with broken rungs in want of fresh caning. They slumbered here in cozy retirement, always with the dream that they might one day be resurrected.

Madame Toussaint could not share such optimism about herself.

What the other households kept tidier behind closed doors, even as concierge she would never know. But she did know some things, and she again filled the silence with them. "You are of an aristocratic family."

This struck a nerve with Mademoiselle Sylvie as nothing before had. Her tone was sharp. "How can you know that?"

"Your needlework, Mademoiselle. Someone may have taught you to embroider screens or edge pillowcases in your youth. Mending, however, you only began when you became a lady's maid out of necessity, when that skill was of course required of you. No guiding hand made you take the stitches out when they clumped and knotted. I have noted your handiwork everywhere in the d'Ermenville apartment, here on this sling of mine and on the tea tray of Monsieur Arnaud, as well. He tried to poison me with strychnine this morning. No doubt at your behest, because I can testify that Monsieur Paul Toussaint is not the one who killed his brother, much as you would like to throw suspicion that way. To deflect it from yourself, Mademoiselle."

"You're mad," Mademoiselle Sylvie said. And Madame Toussaint kept silent because sometimes she suspected the same thing herself.

"I hate sewing." After a moment, Mademoiselle Sylvie fairly spat the words. "I hate the whole degrading lady's maid business—I, who should have had a lady's maid or two of my own. I particularly hate sewing."

Madame Toussaint nodded sympathetically. Innocent fibers should not be put through such torture. "It shows."

Mademoiselle Sylvie's candle revealed a dangerous temper rising red in her cheeks. She stabbed at the lock on the first floor's cave and threw open the door. It was clear what le Comte had used his cave for. Not bicycles and broken chairs. Candlelight caught the curves of floor-to-ceiling wine bottles lying properly on their sides, worth a fortune.

Mademoiselle Sylvie shoved a bottle of cognac in Madame Toussaint's hands, le Comte's favorite label, and began to fill the basket with a variety of wines. The memory of le Comte's murdered and dismembered body burned on the back of Madame Toussaint's eyes as the bottle neck formed the shape of her hand. But there was more to the recalled heat of anger burning through her, a feeling of dangerous power. Her hand remembered carrying just such a bottle, the dregs of fiery alcohol in it, as Paris burned.

"The treacherous Versaillaises are burning our homes, our children." The one-time words flared in her mind. "Communards, we must retaliate. Burn their fine buildings that weigh like the law on us. The elegant buildings where they make their homes and let us in only to mop their floors." This was after Paul had already been arrested. Her life and that of their unborn child hadn't seemed to matter at the time. Nathalie had held the bottle neck with a firm grip as gasoline spigotted into the vessel to fill what was missing of cognac. The wadding, the wick. The dented, warm tinder box she carried across the arrondissement to the one building she wanted to see burn on the rubble heap of Montparnasse, the butcher's shop.

"Now, Monsieur le Faux Comte," she remembered yelling, not knowing where Paul was or if he was even alive, but feeling the child kick inside her. "Let us see you gouge the citizens of France their tax money to pay you more than that place is worth." She lit the fuse. "I will never live there for you."

Idealism and love had made her a liar.

Now, in the caves under Rue Férou, Madame Toussaint lifted the bottle once again, like a club over her head, and swung it at the white lady's maid's cap in front of her.

XL

LA BELLE ÉPOQUE

Madame Toussaint's swing with the cognac bottle was too slow. In candlelight, Mademoiselle Sylvie must have seen the rising shadow. She turned, hefting the laden basket in defense. The cognac bottle crashed against the far wall. Bottles in the basket crashed against one another and spilled like blood down both women's skirts. Mingled alcohol fumes filled the confined space, biting the nose, stinging the eyes.

Mademoiselle Sylvie's greater weight pinned Madame Toussaint to the damp wall. The rough surface clawed through her concierge's cap, even through the boning in Coco's corset. Gingerly, the lady's maid worked her hand up Madame Toussaint's pinned arm and removed the bottle neck she still grasped, disarming her of the jagged edges.

"So *you* murdered him, didn't you?" Again, the concierge regretted what she had written on the message she'd tied to the pigeon's leg. With incomplete information, she'd blamed the man who'd just tried to poison her. But she'd been wrong. "Not your baby brother."

"I was glad to do it. The way 'Monsieur le Comte' abused me when I first arrived."

Of course. The fury in the disembowelment. An abused woman of her station could nurse that sort of fury for years. If she didn't just shrink, as most of them did, into thinking, "This is my fault. I am cheap and common, worth only a few sous in wages. I deserve this."

Madame Toussaint's own fury surfaced. "Yet you wouldn't protect the wave after wave of other *bonnes* he would hire over the years. Our present Jeanne-Marie for example?"

"Silly geese. They deserved it. I never did."

"You, a duke's daughter."

"Marquess, please. The Marquess of Margate."

"And the granddaughter, perhaps, of a French comtesse who fled the Revolution across the Channel."

The candlelight caught the quirk of brow Mademoiselle Sylvie couldn't suppress. Madame Toussaint explained. "The portrait Monsieur Arnaud has hung on his wall. The wallpaper is going, but not the portrait."

"The true Comtesse d'Ermenville."

"Only 'true' aristocracy has been outlawed in France for almost fifty years."

"What a very foolish people."

"So I ask myself, why would the son and daughter of a noble house come here? Looking for a title?"

"Besides that, it is ours. From our grandmother."

"And I have to think that your brother, who would have been the heir, the Marquess, as you say, must have found himself in trouble. Disinherited in favor of—"

"Our younger brother, William. Yes. I only wish he was in reach of my blade." The razor glinted in the light of the flame centimeters from Madame Toussaint's nose.

"So, knowing Monsieur Arnaud—as a concierge gets to know all of her tenants—I think perhaps as a young man he went to prison for sodomy. Your Victoria, cornerstone of your antiquated peerage, does dislike any perversion."

"What a public mortification of a trial Arnie endured, after which our father took the title from him forever. And even after Arnie served his term, Father would give him no more than a certain skimpy stipend—and only if he would never darken Margate again."

"An interesting quandary you found yourself in. You, yourself, Mademoiselle."

"Yes, I was the eldest, but I was the girl, wasn't I? With Arnie in prison, Father decided the family had endured enough scandal. And I, at twenty-two, was taking too long to marry, rejecting suitors willy-nilly. In preference to staying a spinster with my brother, you see."

"I see," Madame Toussaint agreed, and thought she could see even more than that.

"So, taking a lady's maid as a companion to visit an old maiden aunt, I ditched the maid,"—Madame Toussaint thought the poor English girl was lucky to escape with her life—"skipped the visit, and came here, understanding that so many tens of thousands of your working class had died in the foolhardy Commune. The bourgeoisie who gained the day were desperate for workers. I could quickly find work as a lady's maid, knowing something of the station."

"From the other side. And not how to mend, which should have had you sacked in normal times."

"I found the job and have held it ever since, gaining the apartment for my brother and his stipend when, seven years later, he was freed from jail."

"Which, again, I do not quite understand—" In fact, having stared into the mirror in the first-floor apartment that morning, Madame Toussaint thought she did now, finally understand. But she wanted to hear it spoken aloud. By someone, not herself. So she pressed on, "—why you were not sacked. You got the Comte to stop forcing himself on you by turning his attentions to the string of housemaids you had power to hire. You got your brother in as a tenant, with his shady background. You had la Comtesse wrapped around your little finger all these years, hosting your brother at lively parties—"

"At which he was meant to win the affections of Madame la Comtesse, to marry her—"

"In name only, although she thought she might get an heir out of it, at her age and in her health. To get the title, that was his purpose and yours. The title that had once been your grandmama's. Once Monsieur d'Ermenville was out of the way."

"An excellent plan."

"Yours, I have no doubt. Your brother could rest content as long as his special needs were met."

"A good plan. And it was working. All we had to do was wait. But then our father died."

"And younger brother William, now Marquess, decided to make economies and cut off the stipend. So, after a few months of unpaid rent and, I have no doubt, unpaid brothel bills—"

"Arnie finally got Madame la Comtesse to start paying the bills out of her pin money."

"And yet, I wouldn't be surprised if you, twisting Madame's arm, were in greater part responsible. What is this strange hold you have on her? Have had, for over twenty years?"

"My French is very good. An aristocratic accent."

Madame Toussaint almost laughed aloud. "Which I'm sure Grandmama made certain you learned. Which any daughter of a Marquess would be required to learn. Always the best governesses, with the finest accents."

"We always spoke French around the dinner table. When we were *en famille*."

"Of course. But the hold was stronger than that." Madame Toussaint lost patience, and suddenly, her words came in a rush of anger. "Let me tell you what it was. That warm day in July, when I left my young son in my sister-in-law's care, you were set to watch for me at the window open for air. Watching for me returning from trying to rescue my imprisoned husband."

"Filthy communard."

Madame Toussaint spoke over the other woman's words, refusing to hear them. "You—and she—must have suspected I wouldn't return either. That the net for communards had been spread wide, and any were at risk. If I didn't return, she would keep the child, pretend it was hers. Well, the brothers looked enough alike. She meant to raise my little Paul as her own, to continue the title she found herself unable to continue on her own.

"She failed to count on several things," Madame Toussaint went on. "First of all, that her husband Eugène would come home, find the child, and learn where I had gone in such haste and why. He came—the second time, I owed him that—and saved me and Paul. Paul for the colonies and Devil's Island, yes, but at least alive.

"Which was more than could be said of our child." Madame Toussaint had to take a gasp over tears before continuing.

"When you announced at the window that you saw me hurrying down Rue Férou—breast milk soaking the front of my bodice—Madame d'Ermenville had to go with her second plan. Telling you to stay out of the room, she killed our son.

"You stayed out of the room, but you stood where you could see the bassinet reflected in the mirror. Today I stood in the same spot and saw how it must have happened. You saw her put the cushion over his little face and smother him. He was still warm when I held him." Madame Toussaint gasped again. "You can tell me even what color the cushion was. But you didn't stop her."

Mademoiselle Sylvie took over the tale, as if to hasten things along, no doubt tired of her captive getting any triumph out of what was going to happen, down here in the caves. "Yes, yes, I saw her. The cushion was her favorite blue. She had me burn it after. But that was the last thing I ever did for her that I didn't want to do."

"Because, with this knowledge, you basically became lady of the house, and she a helpless invalid. If you told what you knew, she'd go to the guillotine, like all good aristocrats."

Her basket refilled with wine and another bottle of cognac, Mademoiselle Sylvie locked the first-floor cave behind them. Was she really going take Madame Toussaint back up into the blessed daylight again?

No. Of course not. Not with what they both now knew she knew.

The door to the cave for the fourth-floor-left apartment stood slightly ajar against the street-side wall of the cellar. The old tenants had cleared out, and the new ones had not yet moved in while the renovations continued. Mademoiselle Sylvie pushed Madame Toussaint toward this door.

The small room, as she had suspected, was empty. And yet, not quite. For some reason that could only make Madame Toussaint weak with horror, a manacle dangled from the wall beside the door, just like in a dungeon. Her good arm was trapped in it before she even registered its existence. She had to wonder if Mademoiselle Sylvie or her brother was responsible for the feature.

Now Madame Toussaint would hold still for her own disembowelment.

Also in the cave, across from the door, was something no one would give much notice to: the point where a gas pipe entered the building from the street. Mademoiselle Sylvie set the candlestick on a ledge chipped into the stone just beyond the curve of pipe, so it appeared in dark silhouette. Better placement would help the butchery go cleaner. Should the concierge offer that bizarre suggestion?

But except for the pain, which she thought would hardly be more difficult to bear than that she'd lived with daily, Madame Toussaint was ready for her life to be over. Her last words were already said, about the death of her son. The little nit, smothered in his bassinet.

Mademoiselle Sylvie, too, was a silhouette, a shadow leaping with action. In her right hand, Madame Toussaint saw the sharp edges of the cognac bottle. The attack was going to begin with glass to the eyes? Madame Toussaint closed her eyes tight and tried to scream. It came out a gurgle. But the gurgle was only one spit, which she shot towards her attacker. The spit any good communarde had for aristocracy.

Mademoiselle Sylvie laughed hysterically. "Here, hold this." She wrenched Madame Toussaint's carefully bandaged hand and shoved the glass into it. Not shard first. Mademoiselle Sylvie wrapped her victim's fingers around the smooth cold neck. The same feel as when Madame Toussaint had firebombed the abandoned butcher's shop in Montparnasse.

Then Mademoiselle Sylvie said, "When they find you, if they find you as more than a pile of ash, they will only know that you, charged with the safety of the building all these years, finally destroyed it. Once a *petroleuse*—always a revolting *petroleuse*."

She switched so the razor was in her right hand now. Madame Toussaint prepared to defend herself with the broken glass in her bad left hand as best she could; she knew it could not be much.

But Mademoiselle Sylvie carried the blade to the pipe instead. A lead patch stood out against the iron of the rest of the conduit. Madame Toussaint remembered that the new tenants for fourth-floor-left had asked, among their other requests, if they couldn't have a gaslight fixture added in their cave to help when they had to visit the place.

Madame Toussaint, conferring with Monsieur Hervé, had said the task was doable. He had a man on his crew who was particularly good with gas and would see it done safely. But now she remembered the man had turned off the gas for only one morning, when it would not be needed, and had it back on before anyone could complain of the lack of light. A lady's maid in the first floor might have learned of the situation, told by the workman just for courtesy's sake. The man had been called on to work on the fixtures in the apartment itself since then, leaving this one until last, just a patch over the hole on the pipe. And the gas turned on and flowing.

Mademoiselle Sylvie flicked the lead patch off with the razor, no harder than flicking eyes from a potato. Unseen, silent, gas began to leak into the basement space. The lady's maid was gone in an instant, hurrying up the stairs and out of the fated building.

Madame Toussaint sighed and prepared to die, as she had not done during the siege, as she had not done during the Commune. Then she had had something to live for. And she thought: Of people who spoke of the Commune, if they ever spoke of the Commune and didn't find it in bad taste. Of people who said, "How could anyone ever believe in such a fairy tale? Such a dangerous fairy tale of equality and brotherhood. These people are evil. You see, such beliefs only get tens of thousands of people killed."

And she thought: The other option is the fairytale of Perrault's Cinderella with its glass slippers and pumpkin coaches and Marie Antoinette periwigs. She thought of the portrait hanging in pride of place in Monsieur Arnaud's apartment that he shared with his sister so she didn't have to live in a *chambre de bonne* on the top floor. And that, two women, both servants in the same building, could dream the two different tales: one dreamt that she should lift all those around her—and the other, that she alone was born to be lifted above those she served. That she was the princess—no matter how many got pushed back, got their heels or toes chopped off to bloody the shoe, or died in her quest.

And Madame Toussaint thought: How many will die in this building today? How many of those she had served and heard and helped over the years, watching them come and go—from little Rémy Herlemont, playing below the chandelier lit against the day's gloom with his sisters, to grumpy Monsieur Mahler, to old Madame Flôte.

The gas-pipe entered the building from the sidewalk, next to a sign posted on the exterior wall that warned the *pompiers* there was "*gaz sûr tous les étages.*" The gas would have exploded through every floor before the fire brigade and their pumps arrived to read the warning sign, which would be the first object to explode in a shower of rubble spewing out to the gathered onlookers in the street.

The whole building would be engulfed before brave men in their gleaming casques even reached the lobby. They would never find the shut-off valve on every floor concealed by what was called a "baguette," because it had the shape of the ubiquitous loaves of daily bread and every effort was made to conceal the ungracious fixture. The gas company's meter reader could access the baguette, and the concierge could turn off the valve behind the baguette if there were workers in the building or if the tenants on that floor hadn't paid. Fire would have exploded out of each baguette long before the first white brigade horse had galloped into Rue Férou. This was all through the failing of the concierge, whose first duty was to keep the edifice safe.

Gas-pipe no bigger than her thumb snaked through every wood and plaster wall, to lights at every mantel, through the ceilings with their rosettes and intricate moldings to every chandelier. All of this would come raining down. Glass and brick would fly through the air, slicing like razors even before the obliterating burns. From the blocked rear exit of the flower shop on the ground floor, to the explosion, to the fireball that would happen among the paint-soaked rags on the fifth floor.

Of course, the concierge would be beyond knowledge of these things, having burned to ash in the first wave of explosion, her alcohol-soaked dress—Coco's dress—going up like the wadding in a firebomb. Madame Toussaint tried only twice to blow the candle out. It was too far away, and when it sprang back, it came all that much closer to the billowing gas.

She dropped the bottle neck, and with her bad hand, hitched up Coco's skirt, fumbling for the pins. The hole might take one or two to plug it. Pin in hand, she stretched towards the pipe. Then she didn't dare. A single spark, pin on iron, would set it off. She didn't even dare drop the pin.

Once the pin sat safely back in the fabric of her skirt, Madame Toussaint could lean toward the hole. Stretching the manacle as far as it could reach, she wrapped the pipe with the hand of her injured arm. The pain was so fierce that her hand began to tremble.

And then, closer to the thickness of the wall, she thought she could hear muffled sounds from outside. Madame d'Ermenville's body being removed from the black carriage. Monsieur Arnaud being taken into custody in his blood-soaked garments, all gendarme hands on deck. Were those Mademoiselle Sylvie's shrill tones? Still not safely away from the building? Still trying to save her baby brother?

Madame Toussaint yelled. If she could hear their funereal conversations, could they hear her scream? She tried again, her hand slipping with the effort. Gas escaping. The pain of regrasping the pipe added to her volume. No luck. It was like her screams during the Commune. There had been too much horror for anyone to hear her over the rest.

But then she heard, quite distinctly, very close to the building, a man's voice. "What's that crazy clochard doing? Turning off the gas? He thinks he's a fireman? The man's crazy. Stop him."

"Paul." She screamed again. Were her words even coherent? "Tell them. Get them to believe you. Don't let them turn the gas back on. There's a leak. A candle. Please. Messieurs. Don't turn the gas back on."

And then there were footsteps on the floor overhead, footsteps she recognized. Footsteps in the courtyard. Footsteps running down the cave steps. She knew he couldn't stand enclosed spaces. Deathly afraid of the dark. She heard hesitation. "Paul. It's all right. I'm here, Paul. Please, be brave. Save France. This time, you can do it. Vive la Commune." Finally, at the door to number four, left, after fumbling at two or three more.

Locked.

She couldn't breathe. "Here, Paul." The clochard stumbled into the closet, smelling of the wet wool she had knit. He blew out the candle, plunging them into darkness. Darkness, where all they had to hold onto was each other.

XLI
LA BELLE ÉPOQUE

Monsieur Arnaud, the the Englishman Arnold, sat on the curb in front of the building on Rue Férou. It had only just stopped raining, a brief break in the clouds. His hands in their shackles hung dejectedly between his knees.

Gendarme Théophile kept an eye on him: the prisoner had, after all, admitted to killing Madame la Comtesse d'Ermenville in her own carriage as they buried her husband in the cemetery of Montparnasse. It was the guillotine for him as well as for his sister, but first it was prison. The Englishman had been in prison before, for a different crime, true, but both crimes came of resisting the imposition of other's plans for how his life should be. He'd come through the first incarceration brought on by opposing their overweening, now-dead father with the help of his sister. For all her self-sacrificing care for her misfit brother, in the end, she hardly understood him any better than their father had—and that betrayal, more than the execution blade, was what would kill him.

He hadn't been able to murder his father, who loomed as an apparition in the form of le Comte d'Ermenville, so he left the task to his stronger sister. But he had not balked at covering for her and resisting her plan for him to marry and then murder the woman who could secure them financial and social security, not to mention the title. He would draw that blood—and go to prison, and even die, rather than marry a bedridden woman in name only, under false pretenses.

Monsieur Arnaud seemed too dejected to need young Théophile

to keep an eye on him; hence, most of the law's attention was going to Mademoiselle Sylvie. Besides being of aberrant interest to the public and the press, a lady's maid cum butcher was a shocking enough betrayal of the trust upper-class society wanted to place on the supports to their lifestyle.

Mademoiselle Sylvie was proving to be a more difficult prisoner to wrangle, fiercely cursing all of Paris, particularly her uniformed captors, drawing blood with her nails before they could restrain her hands. After that, she kicked hard at their soft spots with the heavy, serviceable shoes of a lady's maid rather than the delicate slippers she had been born to. She was a large woman, heavy-boned and solid. She caused damage.

"The Commune will only ever be a madman's dream." The voice came from the shackled man in the gutter, near Madame Toussaint's feet. He had, it seemed, chosen the most hurtful words he could for the woman who had foiled his plot and, if that was the case, he had succeeded well.

Madame Toussaint didn't necessarily want to hurt the man in return, but she needed to say something to soothe her own pain. "You are wrong, Monsieur. It's the aristocracy, that title of comte you committed these crimes for, that is no longer and will not rise again. Not here in France, in any case, where we have a motto of *liberté, égalité, fraternité*. As long as we the people are here, so is the Commune."

Yes, that silenced him.

While the growing crowd's attention was focused elsewhere, and finding that Paul had vanished into the city's underbelly once more, Madame Toussaint hitched up Coco's skirt. Calculating that she owed her friend the sewing of a new skirt anyway, Madame Toussaint proceeded to sit down on the curbside, not so close as to intrude if the man wanted to be alone with his thoughts. If those thoughts were too burdensome to carry alone, she was here.

And, as it proved, he was overburdened. "I apologize for poisoning your tea," he said. Well, yes, that was a good place to start. With priests losing their grip on the populace, with the Commune banished, concierges often took over the job of holy confessors in the teeming, anonymous city. She didn't exactly relish the job, especially not in this case.

Had she actually done what he was expecting her to and sipped that tea, they wouldn't be sitting here side by side in the gutter. Anger flashed before her eyes at the betrayal of trust. She had probably taken charge of the strychnine herself in a delivery from the chemist's for third-floor-right.

That's what her commitment to be a concierge covering the indiscretions and foibles of her tenants had brought her.

When she counted her own sins, she wondered if raising the matter of Monsieur Arnaud's unsavory predilection with her brother-in-law at her first inclination of this deviation might have saved several lives—Eugène's, his wife's, and now this English brother and sister's. No. She was still a product of the Commune, live and let live.

The gutter was a truly unpleasant place to be, but at the moment she had no desire for better. The gutter was often Paul's place, and the concierge loge was just a step up from it on the social scale. Silence reigned in the space between her and the shackled man. Madame Toussaint idly ran the toe of one shoe around the edge of a cobble. There had been no street sweepers since the rain had started.

A horse still in the traces of the Comtesse's now-empty carriage let loose a flood of urine that steamed in the cold, wet air and slowly worked its way through the cracks between the cobbles. Madame Toussaint shifted her foot out of its path, but didn't move more than that. She took a sideways glance at her neighbor. He didn't bother to move his feet out of the way of the yellow stream trickling towards his fine shoes, now scuffed, and their usually brilliant white spats, no longer spatter-free. The boutonniere that had been in his lapel for less than two hours was in tatters, as had been the one on the night le Comte was murdered, the petals falling in betrayal.

The pathos of the usually meticulous man in this condition might have elicited Madame Toussaint's sympathy in any other situation. But he had come one sip of tea away from murdering her. Not to mention the boys Coco had introduced her to as his victims up near Montmartre. Through the haze of hate, she realized the man was talking to her. "She made me do it. She bought the poison the day after le Comte said I had to leave the premises and we had nowhere else to go."

"Your sister?"

"Sylvia, yes. Poison, she said, is a weak man's murder weapon. A weak man's, a woman's. She had to show that she was the strong one and could murder with a knife. I could mention the truth, that I saw you let a clochard in the building. I hoped that would be enough for her. But as long as you were around to speak for the stranger, it wasn't. And I was too weak to use even the strychnine, even to keep her safe. Too weak to keep you from breaking a concierge's discretion, from figuring out that it was she who murdered your brother-in-law after what was meant to be our last evening together at the card table."

"Because he wanted you to leave the building, the wonderful little nest you and your sister had built together under this roof. But since your father's death—"

"Yes. And the elevation of my brother to the estate in my place. My brother who cut off our funds. Exactly."

Madame Toussaint found the tension in her neck had loosened it to a nod. She wasn't a priest, not even a believer in the judgment this man was going to beyond the mortal tribunal he would face first. But the feeling that came over her was beneficent. There was no other word for it. Such a feeling had not sat around her—like Coco's corset laced too tight, hardly letting her breathe—ever since the bloody week that had brought down the Commune and every hope she'd ever had.

"I would have done the same," she heard herself saying. "I was preparing to do the same to protect Paul—my husband. I couldn't believe he'd murdered his brother, even though I couldn't swear that was the absolute truth."

Monsieur Arnaud stared at her in horror and astonishment. She had bluffed? Her testimony to the police had some grey areas to it?

"Those few members of our family we can trust to stand by us when others betray us—falsehood to the rest of the world, even a death is a price we are willing to pay. It is worth it to keep these people ours. When you can't trust the government, not the police, not the courts."

Monsieur Arnaud heard her, thought about it. He could not bear to look at his sister off to their left when he could not help her, but Madame Toussaint could tell that he wanted to, the strain in the cords of his neck he had to fight. He began a nod, but was cut off from more as surely as the drop of the guillotine blade a few months later.

"Time to go," the commissaire yelled impatiently.

Madame Toussaint recognized the voice that had ordered Paul off to Devil's Island. The voice she hated, that haunted her dreams.

Théophile and a fellow police officer hoisted Monsieur Arnaud, gone limp, to his feet and then into the waiting black Maria. The horse at the police van and the one at the funeral equipage seemed to have an ancient grudge of snorts and kicks. To keep calm in the streets, neither vehicle could wait long.

Nobody helped the concierge to her feet. She drew the toe of her shoe around the cobble again, and thought of the men who had laid the paving, stone by stone, in these intersecting arcs. Over blood and ruins, men from elsewhere—from the provinces, from different countries—had come to Paris and hammered in a life of their own over the life she had thought would be hers.

But if cobbles could be laid, they could also be pried up. A crowbar and a strong man would dig out the first one, but once that had happened, children could do it and carry the stones to their parents on the barricades. Madame Toussaint had seen it done; she'd done it herself. She could teach others.

The thought that, in time of need it could happen again with more success, gave her the comfort to get to her feet and return to her loge. Once that was clean, perhaps the gawking crowd would have dispersed. She could come out again and wash the sidewalk down.

Four months later, as the papers announced that Captain Dreyfus was on Devil's Island, Monsieur Arnaud and his sister were dead in quick justice.

On a bright May morning, Madame Toussaint helped the carter pass down her newly purchased second-hand dress form from the bed of his vehicle. Then she stood on the sidewalk, next to what she had come to think of as her new best friend, and wondered what to do. Only for another whole franc would the carter carry it up to the fourth floor. When she'd helped load it in the cart, that task had seemed doable. Now, she wasn't so sure.

Fortunately, Jeanne-Marie came out of the front door first, dragging the dustbin to set on the curb. "Help me with the other bin, and together we'll manage, Madame," she said when she saw the dilemma.

Between them—Jeanne-Marie at the knobby place where the head should be, and Madame Toussaint down at the wiry stand and the cage that would support gowns in the place of the woman's thighs—they got the form in the building and on its way up the stairs. Madame Toussaint had helped many a tenant with such climbs up the stairs during her twenty-five years in the loge. Sometimes she'd been asked to carry impossible burdens upstairs alone for minimal tips. She'd make sure Jeanne-Marie got at least the franc she'd refused to give the carter

For, in spite of her youth and inexperience in a job that usually demanded the steadiness and discretion of an older person, the young Bretonne had taken over Madame Toussaint's duties as concierge and her place in the loge—with Madame-Toussaint, of course, close by to advise and assist. The girl might marry, after all, and it proved a step up from both the *chambre de bonne* on the sixth floor when she'd been housemaid and the impermanence of Monsieur Mahler's studio. The painter had, in fact, moved on to a new, younger model after several long sessions with Jeanne-Marie in the early spring light of Paris. Some fresh, new face . . .

For it had come to light that Monsieur le Comte Eugène Toussaint d'Ermenville had made a new will in the week between his confrontation with the tenant Monsieur Arnaud—who was stealing his wife's affections and also degrading the morals of the building—and his death. In fact, Madame Toussaint thought she could remember letting the lawyer in one drizzly day: a frock-coated man like so many others. What she remembered was how she'd been just a piece of furniture upon his entry but when she let him out, he'd tipped his hat to her and called her by name. She remembered the strangeness of that, and the signing of this will was the only explanation.

Monsieur d'Ermenville had left his wife of thirty years the apartment and a comfortable stipend for the rest of her life but not enough to pass on to a lady's maid or a new husband or lover. Most of his other holdings—and they were numerous throughout Paris and France at large—he had turned over to a management firm, these nameless men hiding behind a corporation with whom he'd associated for years.

But this one building on the Rue Férou—this he had left to his brother Paul, "the rightful Comte d'Ermenville, to be held in his interest by my sister-in-law, Nathalie Toussaint."

Two new families, both with children, had rented the empty apartments: the full first floor and the third-floor-right that Monsieur Arnaud had been forced to vacate. Monsieur Hervé was overseeing the renovation work on both of them at Madame Toussaint's suggestion. In fact, Monsieur Hervé himself, moving up in the world with his wife and two sons coming into the business with him, had taken the third-floor-right, for himself. That was another reason the new landlady had thought Jeanne-Marie's youth no hinderance to the concierge job, with three handymen on site to see to any problem immediately.

The new family on the first floor were in search of a cook and were glad to take on Mademoiselle Joséphine. "Our cook was once cook to the nobility," they could brag, as if anybody cared anymore, and had even given her a room in the apartment so she didn't have to climb the stairs to the sixth, and a room and a scullery maid to take over the more onerous tasks.

Coco's *régulier* had died of his stroke around Easter and, rather than lose her friend as a neighbor, Madame Toussaint had allowed her to keep the rooms facing the painter's on the fifth floor, paying a little whenever she could.

"*Vraiement*, you know me," the entertainer said. "I don't need much for my baguette and my cheese."

Coco had filled the window facing the Rue Férou with canaries of every bright color the market on the Île de la Cité offered: red, yellow, orange, green. Their squabbles and songs could be heard in the street while Madame Toussaint had wrangled with the carter: spring intensified.

Intensified spring also wafted out of the florist's on the ground floor. More than the usual blooms loaded their shelves and their metal vases set on the flagstones inside and out, anticipation of the marriage of the young assistant Jonquille to Théophile the gendarme crowded the air with fragrance. Madame Toussaint had promised them first choice of the next apartment to become available.

Madame Toussaint herself had decided she needed no more than the apartment on the fourth- floor-left. The people for whom Monsieur Hervé had been renovating these rooms had decided to stay in the South after all. The building's double murder sensationalized in the papers was harder for them to overcome at a distance than for those who had lived through blood running down the walls preceded by the horrors of the Commune.

While Madame Toussaint and Jeanne-Marie rested their burden on the second-floor landing, the Herlemont's two-year-old burst out the door. Children learn so quickly at this age, and the lad had perfected his technique over the past few months. He left the house with clothes on, having learned that a pile of abandoned clothes at the nursery door was a dead giveaway and hampered adventures quicker than stopping to ask permission.

The safety of the tenants of her building foremost in her mind, Jeanne-Marie didn't think twice before steering the little boy away from the stairs and diverting him with the mysteries of the dressmaker's form—how the hinges flexed: "*la maman*," and then collapsed, "your big sister Valentine." She had the child in stitches in no time, no longer at all interested in making it down to the caves anymore.

Valentine, perhaps drawn by the shrieks of laughter bearing her name, was the caretaker who came out looking for her brother. He took her hand and explained "*maman*" and "you, Valentine," until she, too, laughed out loud.

"The form is mine. I've been letting ladies of fashion know that I'll be setting up shop for made-to-measure gowns out of my apartment on the fourth floor," Madame Toussaint explained.

As the pieces snapped back into the smallest size with almost no bust or hips, Valentine asked, "Could you really make a gown for me?"

"Of course, Mademoiselle."

"*Maman* says I might have my first floor-length gown for the military ball in June in the Tuileries Garden, but Papa says *Maman's* dressmaker will cost too much."

"I would not charge so much as Madame Orly."

Valentine swung her little brother up to her nonexistent hip and followed the two women with the form between them upstairs. "*Vraiement?*"

"I promise. I am just starting out, and people will see you at the ball and ask, 'Who is that lovely young lady and who is her dressmaker?' That will be good for me."

"*Maman* says I must not have it off the shoulder."

Madame Toussaint smiled as she and Jeanne-Marie struggled the form around the turn in stairs. The girl had nothing to hold up a dress with bare shoulders. "We shall most definitely not have it off the shoulder."

After a sigh, Valentine asked, "What color will you make it, Madame?"

"That, of course, is your choice."

"I like lemon yellow. Or peach."

Madame Toussaint smiled again. "I remember, when we were all young seamstresses together and very hungry, we, too, liked the silks named for food." She stopped herself. The girl knew nothing of the terrible things that had happened before she was born. And why should they color her happy anticipation?

Monsieur Cailloux's ten-o'clock student was pounding away at the same scales he'd murdered the week before. Madame Flôte's spirits were at peace, and all was right with the third floor.

"I think tiny silk roses across the bodice," Madame Toussaint said.

"Can it really be silk?"

"Peach, I think, suits your coloring best." The girl flushed to have someone consider her coloring.

And then Madame Toussaint got her apartment door open, and she and Jeanne-Marie, panting, hauled the dress form in. The apartment looked suddenly professional, the second bedroom already set with a three-way mirror, also bought second-hand. Her threads arranged in rainbow order, her pins and needles in their cushion, her grandmother's thimble on a small table beside them. If her clients did not care to make it up the three flights of stairs, she would of course make home visits. "And, in a while, I might afford a machine for the more tedious seams. But your dress, Mademoiselle, will have every stitch by hand."

Valentine saw it, too—the future, the potential. "Let me go right away and ask *Maman* to talk to you, Madame Toussaint. And you, Rémy. The dressmaker's is not a place for little boys."

As she patted the little boy good-bye, Madame Toussaint took the opportunity to check out the seams on the child's little sailor suit. She meant to use the scraps for children's clothes, and knew she had a steady source of income on the second floor.

As soon as the girl and her brother were gone, Jeanne-Marie handed Madame Toussaint two *cartes de visite*. "These came while you were out." Two ladies had called while Madame Toussaint was buying the dress form, hoping to have a consultation. She took the cards to the window to read the names and addresses better. Good names, good addresses. She might have to send notes to them by Jeanne-Marie, while she herself sat back in the concierge loge.

But as she opened the window onto chattering canaries and the fragrance of lilies and roses in the florist's, the figure of a clochard made his heavy-footed way up the Rue Férou.

"Thank you, Jeanne-Marie." She pushed the franc tip into the new concierge's hand. "I will definitely get to these—when I get back." She snatched up a cotton garment lying beside her sewing basket and beat Jeanne-Marie out the door.

The clochard was out of sight by the time Madame Toussaint reached the street, but she headed in the same direction he had been going, knowing the way well. She stopped by the baker's on the way, the one with the fresco on his outdoor wall of happy peasants encircled with sheaves of plump wheat. This baker had his ovens going all day so that baguettes almost too hot to carry in their sheets of newsprint were available at any hour. She bought a second, day-old loaf too. Neither of them mentioned the communard law that had once forbidden bakers from working at night.

It was the same bench in the Luxembourg Gardens, always the same bench. "Hello, Paul."

No answer.

She sat, then shifted closer. She handed him the shirt she'd just finished for him, a workman's smock, and not a day too soon. She noted that she needed to start on a new sweater, and burn this one in its turn. He put the shirt on the bench between them without comment.

Then she handed him the warm baguette and took a torn-off piece herself. The pigeons fluttered down at once. "This one is for them." She insisted he not give pieces of the warm loaf to the birds.

"It's good to see you, Paul."

No answer.

It was good in the park: the sun warm, the flower beds newly planted in their sweeping arcs of color. Children were floating their boats in the fountain. For some reason, Madame Toussaint remembered the little girl she'd held in her lap in Saint-Sulpice while she was still pregnant, while the Commune had been so full of hope. She remembered teaching the girl her letters. "*C* is for Commune. Vive la Commune." She whispered it, and remembered that the girl had told how her brother had died of hunger during the siege, but before that he had sailed a boat in this same fountain.

Madame Toussaint saw Paul rubbing one hand with the other. That was the hand she'd seen bandaged on the barricades, scarred with powder burns. It still bothered him in bad weather. But the weather was good, and she took it and rubbed it herself in the way she knew helped.

Beside her, she felt Paul relax, but a moment later, shift anxiously.

Down among the pigeons was a large cock, brown-headed and white-bodied.

"Malin," she said. "Malin *fils*."

"*Petit-fils*." Paul spoke for the first time.

"Yes, grandson by now. But still a terror to the hens." She took another piece of bread for herself and sat back comfortably on the bench. "Ah, Paris in the springtime. There's nothing like it."

Beside her, the man's voice cracked from disuse. "With you, Nathalie. With you."

THE END

ACKNOWLEDGMENTS

I dedicate this book to Melvin J. Grossgold, who introduced me to the boundless personality of Paris's architecture. Thanks to him, I was staying in a small concierge's chamber when a domestic altercation on the stairs over my head made me wonder—what if? With Mel, I visited the settings in these pages and attended events commemorating the hundred and fiftieth anniversary of the seventy-two days that marked the rise and fall of the 1871 Paris Commune. His gift of a red kerchief hangs on the wall in my study.

My two sons were my patient young companions when we first went to the Museum of the Commune and were fascinated by the rats.

My long-time critique partners, the Rough Drafts and the Wasatch Mountain Fiction Writers, deserve their usual thanks for their patience and encouragement.

My agent Vaughne Hansen was supportive and did her best. Dory Mayo and Colin Rolfe of Epigraph Press have once again performed heroics.

ABOUT THE AUTHOR

As a child, Ann Chamberlin learned to walk along the Rhine River in Strasbourg, France. In recent years, she has split her time between an old farmhouse in Salt Lake City, Utah, and Paris—where one night, as she slept in a concierge's old room, she awoke to a domestic argument on the floor above. It sparked this murder mystery.

Ann is the author of twenty published books, mostly historical novels. Her trilogy set in sixteenth-century Turkey spent over a year on the Turkish bestseller list. Her recent success is an award-winning memoir of her grandmother entitled *Clogs and Shawls: Mormons, Moorlands, and the Search for Zion*.

Milton Keynes UK
Ingram Content Group UK Ltd.
UKHW030908271124
451618UK00013B/365/J